BOTTLED SPIDER

This book is for my oldest and best friend.
We met when we were both aged seven. Seven
years later we lived through the time in which this
novel is set. On and off we have been in touch
ever since, and we have never forgotten.
So this one's for you old friend,
John Hunter

BOTTLED SPIDER

John Gardner

Severn House Large Print
London & New York

This first large print edition published in Great Britain 2003 by
SEVERN HOUSE LARGE PRINT BOOKS LTD of
9-15, High Street, Sutton, Surrey, SM1 1DF.
First world regular print edition published 2002 by
Severn House Publishers, London and New York.
This first large print edition published in the USA 2003 by
SEVERN HOUSE PUBLISHERS INC., of
595 Madison Avenue, New York, NY 10022

British Library Cataloguing in Publication Data

Gardner, John, 1926-
   Bottled spider - Large print ed.
   1.   Women detectives - England - London - Fiction
   2.   Detective and mystery stories
   3.   Large type books
   I.   Title
   823.9'14 [F]

   ISBN 0-7278-7200-1

Printed and bound in Great Britain by
MPG Books Ltd, Bodmin, Cornwall.

MARGARET:
Poor painted queen, vain flourish of my fortune:
Why strew'st thou sugar on that bottled spider,
Whose deadly web ensnareth thee about?

William Shakespeare, *Richard III*

Author's Note

Though I vividly remember the real time covered in this novel – November–December 1940 – I have taken a few liberties. The Reserve Squad did exist at Scotland Yard but certainly never in the size or formidable expertise that I suggest here.

I have also taken huge geographical liberties regarding the position of the almshouses for the Laverstoke and Whitchurch areas in Hampshire. Even worse, I have added a further village between Whitchurch and Andover just within the Hampshire county border. The reasons for these places being where I have put them are simple: I wanted no accidental similarity to real people in these litigious times.

Come to that, I have done something even more brazen. I have invented the Borough of Camford within the Metropolitan area of London. I have also invented many police officers and some seriously dodgy civilians, including the unpleasant, unsavoury and unhinged Golly Goldfinch. But I have not invented the flavour of London, and indeed the whole country, as it was during the Blitz, coming up to, and just after, Christmas 1940.

John Gardner

One

You could see your way by the silvery, shadow-less moonlight across the bit of scrubby grass they called the Common. Less than a hundred yards long by fifty wide, the Common is bordered by two roads: one linking with the main London Road, the other, Church Street, petering off near the church of St Michael and All Angels.

The vet's surgery stood next to Dr Bartholomew's grand seventeenth-century mansion in Henry Lane, the street that ran parallel to Church Street. It was hard to believe this was less than a hundred miles from the centre of London; less than a hundred miles, yet cows grazed on the far side of the church, and sheep littered the next meadow over by the water-cress beds – part of Harricky Farm.

In the sixteenth century Harricky had been Lord of the Manor and even in Victorian times many of the village houses demanded that on purchase you signed fealty to 'Edmund Harricky, his heirs and successors'. But the line had dribbled out and come almost to nothing by 1892. Now, in the fourth decade of the twentieth century the manor house, three miles the other side of the village, was a hospital for officers, though old Miss Harricky still had rooms on the third floor.

They now specialized in eye problems up at the Manor and you could see young men, the upper parts of their faces swathed in bandages, or wearing dark glasses, being led about by pretty nurses.

'Lucky buggers,' the locals would say in the White Hart, 'wouldn't mind being bandaged up by one of them girls.'

'Could bandage me 'til closing time – and after,' said Ted Gristwood, who still had an eye for the ladies though he was going on seventy-two come All Souls Day. 'I'd do it all by feel.'

And the lads laughed with him.

The vet's surgery had whitewashed walls and a crimson door, black in the moonlight, like the Common and the strip of grass in front of the house: most things are black at night. Couldn't see a chink of light once the blackout frames and curtains were in place.

There was plenty of light on the inside behind the crimson door. Light enough to perform a delicate operation in the dead of night.

Inside, 'the Surgeon' chuckled. 'Slice carefully along the dotted line,' he said. It was a little joke he always used at this point in the operation as he drew the scalpel blade along the natural seam of the patient's scrotum. 'The unkindest cut of all, this is.'

He usually operated on animals – 'Surgeon' was more of a nickname for he worked as assistant and nurse to Mr Wright the vet – but this time he was grateful to have a real patient, one who could share his amusement.

The patient felt nothing, the area totally dead from the injection of veterinary anaesthetic, but he knew exactly what was going on: knew the procedure backwards because he had studied it in books before he took the plunge to punish himself and find the right doctor.

Now, far away, as in a dream, he heard the ululating air-raid warning siren.

'They're over again tonight,' he murmured.

'Getting to be a habit, but don't worry. We've had it all the time since September. They fly directly over the village, or near enough. That's why they've got to sound the warning, though we haven't had a bomb anywhere near Overchurch. It'll be London again. They've got a moon for it as well, tonight. "Bomber's moon" I heard one of the lads from the aerodrome call it.'

'The Surgeon' cut through the membrane, tied off the two arteries, then snipped off each testicle, allowing them to drop one at a time into the little kidney dish: a pair of tiny white spheres, like small packed rice balls slimed with blood: the quivers filled with unseen arrows; the engines of desire. It was all done in less than five minutes and now he sluiced the blood from the scrotum, pouring in antiseptic because the only real danger was post-operative sepsis. That and shock.

There was a lot of blood, but this was always the case. The first time he had done it, on a dog, he had become alarmed, thought he had not tied off the arteries correctly, there was so much blood.

He glanced at the patient who had closed his eyes. Some day, 'the Surgeon' thought, some day people might understand, and the operation'll be done legally: properly, in a hospital operating theatre, not a hole and corner job like this one, done in the vet's surgery at night after hours, by an unqualified man.

'You all right?' he asked.

The patient opened his eyes for a moment. 'Tired. Wretchedly tired.' He had what people called a cultured voice, an Oxford accent, though Oxford didn't have much to do with it.

'You *will* be able to get me back to town?' the patient asked.

'Don't worry. I've told you. I get a good ration of petrol. I'll get you right back to your door. Now, you sleep a bit. Okay?'

Far away there were dull thuds as the bombs fell on London and the guns barked. Bloody hell, 'the Surgeon' thought, if the Jerries get here, if they invade, they'll take his balls off for nothing. Wouldn't cost him a penny.

Again he soaked the bloody sac with antiseptic and prayed there wouldn't be any infection.

It was a relatively easy two hundred pounds. Who'd believe that a man would ask to be castrated? Normal people just wouldn't understand. Shit, he thought, it would be Guy Fawkes Night in a few days. They cut everything out when they topped Fawkes: hung, drawn and quartered. They didn't hang him to death; he was drawn and quartered while he still lived. The ground reverberated from the

10

bombs forty–fifty miles away. He could feel the ripples through the soles of his feet as he started to sew up the empty scrotum.

They wouldn't have the traditional Guy Fawkes fireworks this year – couldn't get them anyway – the *Luftwaffe* would provide the display. It would be just like any other night in this autumn of 1940.

As he stitched, 'the Surgeon' hummed, 'Run rabbit, run rabbit, run, run, run. Don't give the farmer his fun, fun, fun...'

Isn't it strange, the skein of coincidence? How could it be that this illegal operation would be unknowingly linked to Falcon Cottage, right up at the top end of the village where Henry Lane turns into the Keepsake – as they call it – across from the War Memorial. In Falcon Cottage that night they were sad because the husband and father was off to the war the next day.

But here, in the vet's surgery ghosts of his deviations loitered through the patient's mind. It's best this way, the patient thought. It'll save the suffering and shame of others, and it'll be my just desserts. It's what I need.

Much earlier that year, and many miles away, before a single bomber had ever sought out London, a man walked across a field near Stratford-upon-Avon, and brought horror with him.

11

Two

From the lane he could see right across the field. The house was on the edge of the village and he clearly saw the bus pull up quite close to it. Then he watched the girl get off and walk to the house: she turned and waved to the conductor, and by the end of that week this same conductor was quoted as saying that he knew her and had been at her wedding a month before. Later, it said in the *Stratford-upon-Avon Herald* that the bus conductor was a well-known character. On Shakespeare's birthday he always wore a red rose on his uniform and sang songs from the plays as he went about his work. His favourite was 'Where the bee sucks there suck I'. It wasn't Shakespeare's birthday today but the conductor still sang – 'When icicles hang by the wall, and Dick the shepherd blows his nail,' but the papers didn't say that. Neither did they say he wore plimsolls because of a foot problem that kept him out of HM Forces; nor did they mention that, for a time, the police suspected the bus conductor and interrogated him with a certain amount of hostility.

The man had got off the bus earlier and had watched as it turned left and was hidden by the hedge and a line of trees. Then it came into sight again, before stopping to let the girl off, finally driving away, disappearing as the road swallowed it up.

Round Soho in London they called the man Golly, or Two-Faced Golly because of his dreadful affliction. He'd seen the girl on the bus. Three days ago the woman had whispered in his ear while he slept, and told him to kill a girl at Stratford, where Shakespeare was born.

This was near enough: a few miles from Stratford. The girl, young woman, had been standing in the bus queue in Bridge Street and he couldn't resist her. It was as though the voice was saying this is the one. The one he had to kill. Kill with the wire. He didn't know her from Eve, but later the papers said her name was Patricia Cooke.

He climbed over the gate and walked across the field. It was a clear, warm day and he had too many clothes on: his dark coat, the collar turned up, the muffler over his cotton mask, and his hat with the brim pulled down. He felt a rivulet of sweat run down his ribs from his armpit.

He was quite hot when he got to the house. Saw nobody else. Heard nobody. The wire was in his right-hand pocket, all ready with the insulating tape wound tightly round each end, making thick handles. The knife was in his other pocket. He listened at the front door and heard nothing. Then he put his ear to the back door. His gloves were on and he opened the door, stepped in and killed her.

She was standing in the kitchen by the sink, and she did half the work for him by turning to run away with a little squeal. When the mask came down and his hat fell on the floor she screamed loudly. Then when she glimpsed his face she screamed with terror. A blood-chilling fearful sound that reached into his body, clawing at his nerves. He could almost touch her awful foreboding, and he came up fast behind her, looping the wire over her head, dropping it around her neck, crossing his wrists and pulling.

She made a terrible noise, her fear seemed to rush into his bloodstream, then her feet went from under her, kicking, so he held her up and pulled and pulled, and pulled, talking to her all the time, soothing her until the wire bit through her skin, drawing blood. He heard the gurgle and her windpipe crush, like cracking a walnut at Christmas time. It was very quick.

When she was dead he propped her up against the wall and filled a big pan with water, putting it on the range in the front room. It would soon get hot. The cottage was nice, freshly painted and done up for the newlyweds, though Golly only guessed at the girl just having got married. She was lovely, let him do whatever he wanted. Stripped her. How pretty. Did it. 'Oh my dinky darling, oh.'

Then he went through the house. Upstairs, downstairs and in my lady's chamber, singing quietly to himself, 'When icicles hang by the wall, and Dick the shepherd blows his nail.' He sang it over and over because he didn't know any more of the words. He turned out some of the drawers; saw her private things, like he did when his cousin Lavender was away, then he went downstairs again, laughing. He felt full of energy. Free.

Rummaging through the kitchen, he found a pair of meat skewers, so he did the eyes, and remembered another bit of the song the conductor had been singing – 'When blood is nipped and ways be foul, then nightly sings the staring owl', and 'When greasy Joan doth keel the pot'. He turned the heat down under the pan and left by the kitchen door. It was nothing to him. If he had not done this he would have been in terrible trouble. 'When blood is nipped and ways be foul.' Oh Golly, you've done it again.

He walked all the way back to Stratford, then he took a bus to Leamington and caught the train to London. He kept out of sight. Sat in the lavatory nearly all the way. He heard a man say that in all these years the timetable between London, Leamington Spa and Stratford-upon-Avon had not changed. The times were still the same as they had been in the 1890s. The journey still took exactly the same length of time now as it had done then. 'I don't call that progress,' the man said.

It was May 9th 1940. The next day the Germans went mob-handed into Belgium and the Low Countries. German paratroops and gliderborne soldiers secured bridgeheads for the tanks, with the *Stuka* dive-bombers leap-frogging them. The German code word for the operation was *'Sichelschnitt'* – 'Sicklestroke' – and it finally drove the British Expeditionary Force and the French First Army Group into the sea and 'Operation Dynamo' lifted over three hundred thousand soldiers from the beaches of Dunkirk and brought them back over the Channel to England.

Just after that, another girl was killed with the wire, in a village outside Cambridge. He had never been to Cambridge before, but he liked it. All the colleges and that. He wrote to his mum and told her how lovely it was – all the colleges: old and beautiful – sent her a postcard with his spidery, lopsided scrawl spelling out: 'OLD COLLEDGES LOVLY. VERI BUTIFUL.'

Before they knew it, summer was over and the bombs came: the Blitz. And in the middle of the Blitz Suzie Mountford was promoted and moved towards her destiny.

It was all very well for Mr Churchill to growl, 'Britain can take it,' WPC Mountford thought. The problem was that she couldn't be sure if *she* could take it much longer. She was very down that morning. Low. What was more she was late for work, and Woman Police Constable Suzie Mountford was never late for work. She put it down to last night's raid, but knew that wasn't really to blame because she'd stayed in her flat instead of going down to the basement – the building's designated air-raid shelter.

She had given up going to the shelter in the cellars below the building because it somehow felt wrong: people just sat there looking at each

16

other in an embarrassing silence. She was also slightly claustrophobic, but didn't own to it. Once, about five weeks ago, she had been caught in the Underground and swore she'd never ever get caught again. It stank down there in the station, and people sometimes behaved badly. Some of the older ones organized sing-songs but that couldn't disguise the stench of bodily waste and the acid reek of urine cloying around the back of your throat.

So, very soon after the Blitz began, Suzie had started to train herself to act normally: go about her usual jobs as though nothing had altered. It was better to be occupied in her flat, getting an evening meal, or washing her 'smalls' and stockings, then lying on the bed, fully dressed of course, reading a book and drifting off to sleep. Her body had adjusted and she was only aware of the bombs if one came really close and she knew that on warmer evenings some people would stroll out in their gardens. She had heard that some society hostess had apologized to her guests for the noise.

Last night she had dropped into a deep sleep but was wakened suddenly by a noise nearby. She knew it must have been a bomb, but what she heard through the filter of her dreams was a noise she instantly recognized: she had only been sixteen years old and was in the garden, bringing in the metal numbers from the clock golf set on the lawn when she heard the terrible crash, the grinding of metal and smash of glass, preceded by the scream of rubber on

17

the macadam.

In her head she'd seen mediaeval knights coming together in a joust, but she also knew what had happened and who was involved. She ran and was the first to get to the car and van, butted and entwined together on a bend, and her father covered in blood, and dead. It was a memory that returned often in nightmares and flashbacks. The horror of it never really went away: it did get easier, except for when it all flooded back less than two years later – when their mother married again.

Now in the early hours of this day in the autumn of 1940 she had been dragged back by war to that sad, awful time and so, next morning, on her way to work she felt low and depressed.

The walk from her flat, off Upper St Martin's Lane, to New Scotland Yard usually took twenty-five minutes – give or take a minute. Today it took one minute less than three-quarters of an hour door to door.

Her shift at the Criminal Records Office began at eight o'clock, so her morning routine was carefully crafted to get her to the Yard on time. You could set your watch by her. She was like that, and a note in her annual report said, 'Pays great attention to detail.'

Her Woolworths alarm clock, brass-coloured, strident, with two bells, faultlessly accurate, had gone off on time, but uncharacteristically she had sauntered back into a light sleep, then wakened in a panic. Even after the late start she had been vain enough to linger at the long

18

mirror just inside the door as she straightened the high-crowned, wide-brimmed uniform hat. She looked at herself straight on, face to reflected face, turning to left, then right. She had done this for as long as she could remember, certainly as a schoolgirl in blazer and pleated skirt at St Helen's.

Her elder sister, Charlotte, just under a year older, said Suzie had done the mirror business when she was at kindergarten – long before the not-so-gallant Galloping Major appeared and unaccountably ensnared their mother's heart and, possibly, her body also though they didn't like to think about that. There is a time for all children to believe they were conceived by some arcane method unknown to the medical profession.

In the shadowlands of her mind, Suzie had thought that the face and figure she presented in the mirror were both quite fetching. She was tall, slender, got her looks and golden brown hair from her mother, and the huge, steady green eyes from her father. Also she looked good in the police uniform, collar and tie, the long military jacket with silver buttons and the calf-length skirt. Suzie reckoned she would make a good jailer for some nice man's heart one day, only he would have to hurry up and come along soon otherwise the bloom would be off her.

Outside, the detritus of the raid lay across the road and on the pavements, making walking a bit of a hazard, even in her no nonsense regulation shoes. As she'd walked down to Charing

Cross Station the air itself felt as though it was singed.

But there was a suspected UXB – unexploded bomb – in the station forecourt, close to the cross itself, now swathed in sandbags. Now, this morning, even the great railway station was closed. This meant a diversion, back up the Strand through a sidestreet, picking her way down to the Embankment, the water sparkling in the autumn sunshine as she crunched through the gravel of glass. Above her the silver barrage balloons swayed and swam in the blue sea of sky, beautiful things with their snub noses and stubby tails, protecting the city just by being there.

At one point she had to step around where a flight of incendiaries had dropped and been extinguished right there in the road. The asphalt was scarred with pools of black and white scorch marks, where the ARP people had used their stirrup pumps to smother the things; so Suzie played a kind of hopscotch, dodging between the little tail fins and what was left of the melted tubular casings and the burned-out thermite.

Even though the sun shone it was a chilly morning, so, already tired from the bomb-creased night, she pulled her raincoat around her, hitched the strap of her gas mask and tin hat, which were bouncing heavily against her hip, high on her shoulder, and tried to increase her stride.

The soundtrack in her head played 'A Nightingale Sang in Berkeley Square'. In her mind starlight speckled the streets, and the angels dining at the Ritz sipped *Potage St-Germain*. The last time she was home her mother had a copy of the sheet music on the piano and she had been a shade bewildered because in brackets after the words Berkeley Square, they had the pronunciation as Bar-klee Square. Someone, she thought, would have to be pretty dense not to know how to say Berkeley Square.

The people she passed in the street all looked tired and some had the worm of fear in their eyes. It wasn't fun being bombed night after night: knowing the people you saw in the morning, young and alive, could be dead by midnight. She could be dead by midnight.

It was the last week in November, she thought; it wasn't going to feel a bit like Christmas, even though some of the West End shops said they would decorate their windows with holly and paper chains.

Before the Blitz, the scent of London was one of soot and burning coal. Now you woke to new smells: cordite, gun cotton or whatever explosives the *Luftwaffe* used, mixed with smoke and a different kind of grimy dust from the fragments of bricks and mortar floating in the air. As she passed through the gates of New Scotland Yard she glanced up at the red and white ornate brick building as though she expected it to have been blown away, and was surprised to see it still stood intact, just as the architect, Norman Shaw, had designed it in its Victorian Gothic glory.

'You're late, Mountford!' Sergeant Fulbright, the CRO Sergeant, ramrod-backed with a short, bristling moustache that made Suzie think of walruses.

'The raid, Sarge,' she grinned, taking off her raincoat and hat, letting her hair spring out as she hung gas mask and tin hat on the peg over her coat.

'Sarge nothing, Miss Mountford. Raid nothing as well. Enemy action's no excuse for being late unless you was killed; and you weren't killed, was you?' His voice rose to a small screech at the end of the sentence, demanding an answer.

'No, Sarge.'

'Don't call me "Sarge". I was in the raid as well, young lady. Am I late?' He squeaked again: more like a seal now. He'll have a heart attack, or maybe start playing 'God Save the King' on a row of motor horns.

'No, Sergeant.'

'Right. Learn from that. You are to report to the A4 superintendent immediately. Understand?'

'Yes, Sarge ... Sergeant. What for, Sergeant?'

'I am not privy to the A4 super's intimate thoughts or whims. Nor do I know what you've been up to, Miss Mountford. Make sure your conscience is clear.'

Lawks! she thought, wondering if she had broken some sacred rule.

You didn't hang around when the A4 office called on you, so she all but ran to the lift – running was not tolerated inside the building –

and up the corridor to the superintendent's anteroom. Her hand came up automatically to tidy an imagined unruly strand of hair.

'Sit down, WPC Mountford.' A4 Branch was the Women's Police Branch and the superintendent was an angular lady, sharp-featured with a neat eye that flicked between Suzie and an open file on her desk. On the wall behind her, King George VI and Queen Elizabeth stared benignly into the office.

The superintendent coughed, moving her hand across the file. Suzie saw she wore no rings and that the hand was brown and leathery – like a kipper, she considered – reflecting the outdoor life which the super was reported to lead. 'You've been in CRO for about a year, yes?' She had an amazing drawl, throttling vowels and spitting them out like invisible chewing tobacco.

'Yes, ma'am.'

'About a year, yes?' she repeated, pushing the file away and raising her head to look at Suzie, the eyes without warmth, full of reserve and suspicion. She gave a second little cough. 'You have good office skills and use your common sense, yes?'

'Ma'am.' That simply meant that WPC Mountford got on with her work and didn't have to be told to file A under the As and B under the Bs.

'Well you seem to be the right type.' The Women's Branch was under instructions to recruit 'the right type', meaning lower middle-class, reasonably educated girls, not vinegary

23

spinsterish women.

'Your last report from CRO says that you need a challenge. Mmm? Need stretchin', what?' Down went another G. She lost Gs like some people lose silver threepenny bits.

Never explain, never complain, never volunteer.

'You'd enjoy a challenge, Mountford? Enjoy bein' stretched?' She did not wait for an answer. 'We're in need of young women to take the place of men bein' called to the armed forces. Our more experienced officers're classified in reserved occupations, but we're losin' younger men to the services. We particularly need people to work in CID. You think you could do that, yes?'

'I know I can do it, ma'am, yes.' The Criminal Investigation Department would be the apogee. For a brief moment she saw herself at the sharp end – catching the villains, snooping around the scenes of serious crimes, interrogating suspects until late into the night; feeling the collars of murderers, jewel thieves, bank robbers, all mad, bad and dangerous, they ought to be locked up, given a taste of the cat, which, like hanging, was still an option.

'Should really send you to Regency Street to do the detective course, but time is of the essence and we're short on the ground. You'll be made up to actin' temporary Woman Detective Sergeant and report to Detective Chief Inspector Harvey at Camford Hill Police Station.' She kept her eyes buttoned on to Suzie's face as she explained the fine print. In her spare time she would have to study for the Sergeant's Exam. She'd be assessed in six months and eligible to sit the exam next year.

'You'll learn a great deal from DCI Harvey, so you should sail through the detective course as well. Everything clear? No questions?'

'Yes, ma'am. No ma'am.' Then, in her head, Three bags full, ma'am.

'Right, Sergeant Mountford. Get yourself organized, report to DCI Harvey by two o'clock this afternoon. Good luck. Don't let us down.'

It was like an end of term interview with the headmistress. The worst thing you could do was let down your colleagues and friends.

Camford Hill was in West London, almost out in the sticks. Way beyond Knightsbridge and Kensington, it was ten or eleven square miles of London policed from Camford Hill Police Station, which was really in Camford High Street and well known for its tradition of solid reliability. If she had to be posted out of the centre, out of the West End and Westminster, this would be the best place to go.

I'm putting all my eggs in one basket, she sang in her head as she went down the main staircase at the Yard, and considered logistics – I'm betting everything I've got on you.

Camford Hill was a good three-quarters of an hour by tube from Leicester Square, so she'd have to be up earlier than ever in the mornings. And she'd probably be home later as well. In CID you worked excessively long hours.

Collecting her coat, hat and gas mask, she told Sergeant Rex Fulbright about her promotion – 'Don't get too big for your boots, mind, young lady' – then went home and put a trunk call through to her mother to give her the news: thank heaven she was on more friendly terms with her mother now. Not as it had been when she told them, twenty months after the accident.

She was going to be Mrs Gordon Lowe, her mother had said. Going to be wife to Major Ross Gordon Lowe (who made it sound like a double-barrelled name by putting a non-existent Ross before the Gordon). He had the DSO and Bar, a retired Great War officer, now agent for the local Conservative Party Member of Parliament. To them, the marriage was almost a greater shock than their father's accident.

It was the first time they could recall being really at odds with their mother. They were numbed by it, hurt deeply like a blow to the head, mainly because they hadn't finished grieving for their father. In particular, Suzie remembered a furious, terrible, stand-up scene with her mother, when they were told that their young brother James had agreed to give his mother away. The girls flatly refused to be part of it, and on the day itself, Charlotte went around quoting bits of *Hamlet*, loudly and within earshot: the part about the funeral baked meats providing the wedding breakfast.

Now, in the flat as she changed into her grey twin set and the heather mixture skirt she dragged her mind from the past unpleasantness; checked her stocking seams, then her hair and face in the mirror and went out: walking up to Coventry Street and the Lyons Corner House where she got two poached eggs on toast and a pot of tea.

'You're lucky today,' the 'nippy' told her. 'Didn't have any eggs yesterday. These came fresh up from the country this morning. We'll be sold out by one o'clock.'

After lunch, Suzie took the Tube from Leicester Square out to Camford, and realized that her timing was well out. She had one change and it took her almost an hour and a half, including the walk from Camford Hill Underground station to the nick. There would be more trains during the rush hour, but the journey was still going to take at least an hour, even on a good day.

She had bought a copy of the *Evening News* and she flicked through it on the train, wishing they would make newspapers smaller. She always had difficulty managing the big double pages – especially in public. It was all war news apart from a story on page four, headed MISSING GIRL FOUND STRANGLED. A fourteen-year-old girl – Barbara 'Bubbles' Bachelor – had been missing from her home in Acton for twenty-four hours. Now she had been found, back in her home again, strangled with piano wire. 'Some of her clothing is missing,' the report stated with sinister connotations. Suzie shivered.

Camford Hill nick – the police station in

Camford High Street – was a block-like square concrete building (c. 1920) recessed between three shops and Camford Post Office.

Inside, at the front counter, she had the impression that officers seemed to be moving about with purpose, and a duty sergeant greeted her with a courteous, 'Yes, madam, and what can we do for you?'

She was expected, but the Chief Superintendent was away, attending a meeting at the Yard, so a shy, sandy-haired, smiling uniformed superintendent welcomed her to Camford Hill, enquired about where she was living, sucked his teeth on hearing the length of her daily journey, then took her down to the Criminal Investigation Department's office – a large, long, narrow room in the basement, not unlike the CRO at the Yard. A heavy upright Underwood typewriter sat on a desk near the door; next to it was a pile of blank paper, one sheet already positioned in the rollers, like a museum exhibit of an Edwardian office.

There were two telephones that she could see, with a third just visible in a partitioned office at the far end; a bright glare of strong electric bulbs was reflected off the green washed walls. There was no natural light. A map of London took up most of one wall, the various Metropolitan Police Divisions marked out in a wheel of colours, each with its designated letter of the alphabet. Camford Hill was O Division, and next to the London map there was a large-scale street map of the Camford Hill area.

Near the door, coat hooks were screwed to a wooden batten: just like school, only as well as the hats and coats – no man would be seen without a hat – there were the gas-mask cases and tin helmets. The smell was also a memory of school: a touch of boiled cabbage from the canteen up the corridor, damp serge, and a hint of chalk. A blackboard was pushed into a corner, presumably for briefings, and at the far end of the room a glass partition separated the DCI's office from the peasants. The DCI wasn't home.

Three men worked at the desks, while another, ginger-haired and improbably young, talked guardedly into the telephone. He finally put down the instrument and called to a fifth person, a young woman, who was gathering papers together in the far office.

'Shirley!' he called. 'Super's here with a young lady.'

'Hardly a young lady,' the shy superintendent said with a hint of a smile. Bashful, Suzie thought. Bashful in *Snow White*. 'Your new sergeant. Sergeant Mountford.' Then, realizing what he had said, the super made a hopeless gesture, rolled his eyes and muttered something about of course the sergeant was a young lady. 'Let you get on with it, then.' He did an exaggerated shrug, mumbled that he should be going, made an indecipherable gesture using both arms and awkwardly left. Bashful and Dopey, she decided; both, she thought. Snow White and the Five Dwarfs. Nice, but...

The girl who came out of the office obviously

29

modelled herself on the film star Hedy Lamar – the sultry look; a dangerous figure and hair that shone black smooth, short and silky. She wore a knitted dress, pale blue, tight enough to show in relief where her suspenders lay on her thighs. 'We knew you were coming, Skipper, but we didn't know you were a lady, if you see what I mean.'

'According to the super, I'm no lady.'

Their chuckles were unconvincing, and the ginger-haired young man took a pace towards her holding out his hand. 'DC Catermole,' he introduced himself. 'Dougie Catermole. "Ginger" Catermole. Socializing isn't old Sanders of the River's strong point.'

'Sanders of—?'

'Superintendent Sanders, Skip. Assistant Station Commander. Not very good with people. He's better moving bumf around.'

The other detectives drifted over and introduced themselves. Mortimer; Pinchbeck; Richards. All friendly enough but with a sense of holding back, as if their new sergeant was not yet really one of them.

'So, you're Shirley,' Suzie said when finally left alone with the WDC.

'Yes,' she nodded. 'Shirley Cox. You can imagine how Big Toe plays around with that.'

'Big Toe?' Suzie queried, ignoring the crudity that embarrassed her.

'DCI Harvey. Tony Harvey. Big Toe. The Guv'nor.'

'Ah.' The senior officer was always 'the Guv'nor' and the sergeant was 'Skipper'.

'And he's where?' she asked.

'With DC Magnus and DC Thomas, Skip. Coming to grips with a nasty bit of GBH.'

'Domestic GBH?'

Shirley Cox shook her head. 'Not domestic. Very serious. A couple of bits of brass from down the Cut got themselves done over.'

'You're going to have to explain the geography to me, Shirley. The Cut?'

'Not for me to do that, Skipper. The Guv'nor likes to take new arrivals on a conducted tour.'

And you're afraid of him, Shirl, Suzie decided, detecting the tiny hint of apprehension. She wondered if they were all a shade leery of the Guv'nor. 'Okay, so can you fill me in on the state of crime in this Division, or is that out of bounds as well?' Her tone was harsher than she intended.

Jimmy Mortimer was following up on a couple of white collar problems. Someone had knocked off a lorry load of tinned goods last week. Probably organized in Camford. Also there was a cherry picker on the loose: knickers and bras disappearing from clothes lines like conjuror's props.

'Really tough crime.' WDC Cox raised an eyebrow and canted her head to the right. Pete Pinchbeck was looking into what you might call a sneak thief, she told Suzie. 'Crimes of opportunity: doors or windows left open, that kind of thing.'

'And what's-'is-name? Richards?'

Sammy Richards, local expert on motor crime: car thefts, petrol, petrol coupons, spares. These kind of offences were heavy around Camford where they had a high percentage of people still allowed to use their cars.

'A hive of criminal activity, then?' Suzie grinned, though she knew the war was rapidly bringing new kinds of crime on to the streets: looting blitzed buildings was high on the list – it wasn't all singalongs and togetherness down the shelters as the newsreels would have you believe. Then there was the theft of petrol coupons, a roaring trade in forged ration books, illegal black market deals and a steady business in food, drink and cigarettes.

'And the girls – the GBH – they're street girls from here, or do they come from up the West End?'

'Oh, here. We have our red light district. In fact I think we're getting clients who won't go into Soho because of the air raids.'

'You don't get the raids here?' Sarcasm wasn't really her best thing.

'Exactly the same as the rest of London, Skip, only we haven't had any bombs landing on our patch yet.'

It'll come. Suzie thought. 'So the girls're local?'

'Home-grown, and we've got our own particular brand of villains. You'll soon hear the Guv'nor on them, Sarge: the Balvaks. The Balvak brothers; a very nasty kind of crook. After the Devil made this pair he broke the moulds.'

Suzie waited for a moment, expecting more,

but it didn't come. 'And you, Shirl?' she eventually asked. 'How do you spend your days?'

'Like any other policewoman. I do the typing, make the tea. If I'm very good and they have a female witness, I look after her, hold her hand. Then there's helping old ladies and kids across the road.' She grinned.

'You live locally?'

'I'm lucky. A bed-sitter five minutes from the nick.'

'Plenty to do off-duty?'

'What off-duty, Sarge?' A quick smile. 'Until the Blitz, yes. Nice *palais de dance*, two cinemas – one's a fleapit – the pubs're good and people're friendly: around here, of course, not over in the Cut.'

'The Cut? You said that's where the girls got duffed up. What is that exactly?'

'Our version of the badlands, where the vagabonds live. It's the place where they invented crime around here. The GWR Goods Marshalling and Shunting Yard and its environs. That's what they call the Cut. It's the reason for Camford Hill existing at all.' Shirley raised her head, catching sight of something over Suzie's shoulder. Then, almost in a whisper, 'Here comes the Guv'nor looking bright as a searchlight, God help us.'

The doors into CID clattered open and Detective Chief Inspector Anthony Harvey appeared: Big Toe himself, making an entrance – long, dark overcoat flapping around his calves, trilby at an angle on his head, eyes hard as granite, mouth set grim in his face, all angles and shadows. Behind him the two DCs strode to keep up looking all the world like minders.

Have a care, Mountford, she told herself. Life's never going to be the same again.

Three

Suzie turned and smiled. Make a good impression, she thought.

'WDS Mountford, Guv.' The smile turned into a grin that did no good. Oh bugger, she thought.

He looked through her, moving towards his door, 'Oh! Yes! Well! Okay, Sergeant Mountford! Yes!' Ignoring her outstretched hand he walked straight into his office behind the opaque partition.

Subtle as a Molotov Cocktail. Damn! Confound it! The only oaths she had ever heard from her late father's lips.

He left the office door open, threw his overcoat on to a chair, sat at his desk and began talking into the telephone. She heard him ask the internal operator for a number, then his voice became an indistinct murmur.

'Sarn't Mountford?' Shirley Cox said quietly. 'Yes?'

In his office DCI Harvey raised his voice so that everyone could hear. 'What am I supposed to do, sir?' Then louder still, 'I asked for a real

34

sergeant, not another girl!'

'Sarn't Mountford, you'd better meet the lads,' Shirley moved a little closer, embarrassed. 'DC Magnus and DC Thomas. Philip Magnus – "Pip" – and Dave Thomas. "Doubting Dave" Thomas.'

'Pleased to meet you, Skip.' Magnus didn't look her in the eye; a thickset man with straw-coloured hair, rubbery lips and slightly bulging eyes. A boozer, she reckoned, wrongly as it turned out.

'Welcome to the team,' Thomas, sing-song Welsh accent, sure of himself, the kind of person who never admits to mistakes, a man always in the right. Cocky, prone to impertinence; she knew the type.

Conscious of a noise behind her, Suzie half turned and saw Harvey shifting his chair, the legs rasping against the linoleum-covered floor, as he continued to speak into the telephone.

'You mean I'm stuck with her for six months? Yes? ... Yes, I know there's a bleeding war on, sir. Yes, and thank *you*, sir.' His hand went to his forehead, touching the smooth, polished skin above dark, expressionless eyes. He wore a double-breasted suit, well cut, in a nice herringbone, and his shoes had that glassy shine she knew from the Major who had married her mum. This mental association with her stepfather would colour much of her short relationship with Harvey.

'Always keep your kit clean! Sparkling!' The Major barked – interminably. Suzie and Charlotte would mimic him, using the words as a code to indicate when one or the other looked particularly smart.

'*Your* kit's clean, bright and sparkling, Suze,' in her head she heard her sister. Childish, but at the time it had helped pour oil on the troubled waters of their anger at the Galloping Major.

After their mother's wedding Charlotte had quickly lost herself in a whirlwind romance and marriage to a young accountant – Vernon Fox, a boy she'd known since she was sixteen and who now had a job with a firm in the Hampshire town of Andover. Suzie – who had taken a secretarial course in the year she left school – grabbed a job as far away as possible: at a solicitor's, Jonas, Jonas & Jennings, in Cambridge, where she rented a bed-sitter, put up with the monotonous routine work and spent most of her spare time being squired by desirable undergraduates.

Finally it all came to an unpleasant end, mainly because of the ultimate dullness of the job, plus the drama of a fractured romance with Ned Griffith, an undergraduate reading law. Recently she'd heard Ned had joined the RAF and now, three, four years later, she found that she could think of him without heartache.

At the time, however, it had been emotionally traumatic. Lost and confused, she had gone home, hoping to be comforted. But her mother was not the woman she had known even a year ago, and the overbearing, autocratic bumhole of a stepfather ... well, you know how it goes. Why hadn't he taken Mummy off to a new house of his own instead of polluting the rooms that held such happy memories of childhood and Daddy? Helen, her elegant mother, remained silent, as though stunned by her new wifely duties, and Suzie quickly identified her stepfather as a bully.

'You're well out of it, Charles,' she told Charlotte on the telephone, 'Mum's married him for his money and to see James through school.'

'I know, but what're *you* going to do, Suze?'

'I want some action. Something different. A real change. I've even thought of joining the police force. At least then I could arrest the blighter.'

Which, in the end, was what almost happened.

By the time she'd been home for a week Suzie could hardly stand to be in the same room as the Galloping Major. By the same token he could sense her irritation and, like all bullies, played on it like a boxer concentrating on an opponent's cut eye. There were times when they could hardly be civil to one another. Two days later the domestic balloon went up when she accused the Major of treating her mother like an unpaid skivvy. Worse, that he was actually physically ill-treating her.

Her mother tried to be conciliatory, defending him. 'He can't help it, Suzie. The war. He was very badly shell-shocked on the Somme. I've told you before. One has to understand. He wouldn't hurt me. You have to make allowances for men like him. Brave men like him.'

'Threatening a woman is an act of cowardice,

not bravery.' Suzie was convinced that she'd seen him raise a hand to her.

She left the next day.

Nobody would ever enslave *her*. Marriage, yes. Oppression, no.

So she got a job at Harvey Nichols – 'Selling frocks to matrons from New Malden' – and dutifully rang her mother three times a week from the *pied-à-terre* off St Martin's Lane which had been one of her father's spendthrift luxuries, and her mother's great secret from Major Gordon-hyphen-Lowe.

Charlotte said she'd always thought the flat was a bolt hole. 'There if Mum needs to run away. That's why she's never told him about it.'

But, they agreed, their mother had already sacrificed herself on the altar of middle-class respectability and would never leave the ungallant Major – at least not until James had been educated.

So Suzie made the final decision about joining the Metropolitan Police. She was convinced that she could make a difference: imagining a life fighting crime at the sharp end, maybe even detecting – her head full of car chases and clues.

In the present, Big Toe finally cradled the telephone, stood up and walked the couple of paces to the door. Like a street fighter, she thought, with that rolling strut, the hands clenched and held in front of his body as though in search of a target.

Leaning a shoulder against the jamb, he gave her an amused smile. 'Yes, welcome to Camford Hill.' He cocked his head towards his office. 'A word, I think, Sergeant Mountford.'

The partition was made of a thick Perspex, corrugated so that figures seen through it were distorted: like people swimming through turbid water.

'How d'you make a good cup of tea, Mountford?' He smirked.

'I've not long had lunch, sir.' As she said it, Suzie realized she'd misheard.

'You're not listening to me, Sergeant,' he had a surprisingly soft voice and the accent of a man who had moulded himself to fit a class: sponging up the BBC English of announcers.

'I'm sorry, sir. Not listening ... I don't...' Flustered and confused.

'I asked how you'd make a good cup of tea, Sergeant. You see, Shirley's not always around and we have to be certain that at least one woman knows how to do it – make a good cup of tea, I mean.' There was an implied snigger in his tone.

'I don't think you'll have problems drinking any tea that I might make, sir. And I'll be only too pleased to make it if you teach me as much as my superintendent expects you to teach me.'

'Words a minute then, Sergeant?' he snapped.

'Words a...?'

'Typing. How many words a minute?'

'I don't see what that's got to do with—'

'Catching criminals? Detecting crime? Keeping the King's peace? Well, let me show you what it has to do with those things. Get your coat.' He followed her into the main office, waiting until she put on her raincoat.

'Sergeant Mountford and I are going out for a while,' he announced. 'We'll be having a word with those toms up the hospital. Ready then?' He led her outside, up the stairs into the garage and parking area at the back of the building, all the while reciting a monologue about the enormous amount of paper that was generated by even the smallest investigation.

'Take this morning,' he said as they climbed the stairs. 'This morning I ran Magnus and Thomas down to St Mary Mother's Hospital – our local hospital if you didn't know – to talk to a couple of girls who were suddenly taken with a spot of GBH.' He explained how they'd interviewed the girls, Cathy Watts and Beryl Pegler.

'On the game, these two. Harlots, whores, tom tarts, brass nails. You follow?' he asked, as though she might not understand the words.

'They haunt a well-known area just south of the gasworks,' he explained. 'Down by the railway line on the edge of the Cut. There's a little caff there called Amy's Tea Shoppe and don't be misled by the name. This isn't your Kardoma, or a Nora's Nook olde worlde place.'

They had passed through the garage to the white-lined parking spaces at the rear of the building and he led her to a grey unmarked Wolseley, the ubiquitous police car usually black with a blue light on the roof and a gong to attract attention or move traffic out of the way.

40

Harvey climbed behind the wheel, indicating with a nod for Suzie to sit next to him in the front. 'This is the CID transport, Sergeant. The super uses it on occasion; otherwise it's ours. If you need it, you ask me, and if you haven't been cleared to drive you get a driver from the pool. Got it? *You* have *not* got permission, because I hold a firm belief that women drivers all have two left arms and three left feet. Right?'

He glanced at her: a nasty, knowing look. 'Far as I'm concerned, women police officers are good for two things: making the tea and typing.'

'Now these two girls—' He started the engine, smoothly put the car into gear and negotiated what was known locally as Lockup Alley, coming out on to Camford High Street in front of the police station, where he joined the thin flow of traffic. 'These two girls, Cathy and Beryl, they're not your expensive bits of brass, a couple of quid for a short time in a flat up the West End. These two are more your half-a-crown bunk-up against the wall at the back of Amy's caff.'

Once on the main road he drove smoothly, anticipating the intentions of other drivers, utilizing gaps in the traffic, constantly changing gear up and down, keeping it fluid just like they taught on the Hendon Police Driving Course. You could almost hear the fury of other drivers.

'What's this got to do with the standard of my typing, sir?' She wasn't intimidated by Big Toe – after all she had stood up to the

41

ungallant Major.

'Wait-wait-wait.' Harvey repeated the words softly. 'Just a minute.'

'Well, sir?'

'All crime generates a pile of paperwork. Remember that. We asked young Cathy and Beryl – they couldn't be more than eighteen, nineteen at the outside – we asked them how they'd come by their injuries, and, guess what? Fell off their bicycles didn't they? No cycles around, mind you. Not a wheel in sight, not a pedal to push, nor a saddle to sniff. Yet one of them, Cathy, has three broken ribs, smashed nose, a ferocious black eye and a face battered out of recognition; while young Beryl has a broken arm, broken nose and assorted facial damage: maybe a chip out of a cheek bone. They've both got dental problems as well. Unusual that. Silly really 'cos they won't be able to work for a while. Cutting off noses to spite their faces. Bloody pimps.'

'And the typewriter, sir?'

'The typewriter, yes. What d'you think? It's all got to be typed and logged. Every last detail: typed, logged, sorted, filed.'

He swung the car in through the hospital gates and up the gravelled drive. In a second they passed from the busy streets and shops of Camford Hill into a country of landscaped gardens, lush with trees; rhododendrons flanking the wide driveway with its speed limit 5 mph signs.

'I've been lucky enough to have you assigned to CID, Sergeant Suzie – that's what they call

42

you isn't it, Suzie?'

'It's what my *friends* call me, sir, yes.' She wondered how he had got that detail so quickly. He knew already, she realized with a flash of clarity. He had known before she arrived. Everything since then had been carefully choreographed.

'Oh, I'm your *friend*, Suzie. Make no mistake about that.'

The best way to learn the job, he told her, is to watch and follow investigations on the ground. 'Watch, listen and learn,' he said. 'Then, when you've done that, type up the reports. That way you'll familiarize yourself with cases. You'll learn method and logic; when to push and when to stay shtum; how to make four out of two and two.'

He ran a very tidy department and was proud of it, he said. Most of all he was proud of the neat, well-typed reports he placed in front of the Station Commander each week. Other people didn't take that kind of trouble, sent reports in willy-nilly. Bad handwriting. Spelling all over the place. 'You'll learn a great deal by doing those reports,' he told her. 'Collating the evidence. Reading the evidence itself. Gruelling and laborious, but it'll pay off and you'll look back on your time here and realize that you've learned the hard way.'

St Mary Mother's (The Hospital of Mary the Mother of Jesus) was an ancient place of healing, dating from the thirteenth century, when documents described it as a refuge. It was on the original site that a brand new

43

modern hospital had been built in the 1860s: a great gothic structure standing in parkland, a huge oasis in the middle of the built-up area.

Big Toe had brought her not simply to see the two sad and injured girls, nor even to investigate their case. She had been brought here to get a squint of the vicious ruthlessness of a certain brand of criminal who operated on their patch. On any patch come to that.

'Armitage Ward,' he muttered, leading the way up the wide, uncarpeted stairs, turning left at the top and clattering along an uncarpeted passageway.

Then as they reached the entrance to the ward a short, neat woman – all breasts, bum and tight-fitting clothes – came through the doors. As she saw Harvey her small eyes widened in recognition and she all but launched herself at him.

'Oh, Mr Harvey,' she wailed. 'I've done my best with her, our Cath, I can't do no more.' She only came up to around the middle of Harvey's chest which meant she had to look up at him, her pert face a paradoxical mixture of gravity and foolishness. She wore a scarf over her head like a snood, and what hair peeped out in Victory Rolls on to her forehead showed more than a passing enthusiasm for peroxide.

For a second Suzie could have sworn she saw a look of complicity pass between the woman and the detective, and this she stored away for a rainy day. It was certainly clear that the woman knew him well.

'I can ask no more than that of you, Vera.'

The smile around Big Toe's mouth softened but never made it to his adamantine eyes and you didn't have to be Sherlock Holmes to know that Vera was Cathy Watts' mum. She had a button nose; a mouth exaggerated with lipstick, and eyebrows plucked clean then pencilled in: giving her the look of permanent surprise.

'Help her. Please, Mr Harvey, help our Cath. They'll be the death of me else, those boys.' The note was pitched a shade too high to be convincing. There was, Suzie thought, some coded subtext going on.

'How's Archie?' the DCI asked.

'Went and volunteered. At his age. I ask you.'

'He can't be much older than you, Vera.'

'Forty-six,' she rolled her eyes. 'Forty-six last September. Too old for the forces. I told him, but he would go, then of course they said not yet. Maybe next year. Now he's with the Home Guard.' She pronounced the aspirates with care, no discarded aitches here. She's been in service, Suzie considered. Some smart town house – Kensington, Knightsbridge. Brought up among the moneyed classes.

'If he's joined the Home Guard we can all sleep safe in our beds then, Vera.'

'Oh, yes ... Yes, indeed. They've been training for street fighting, climbing all over the roofs down Alma Road, near the school.'

Harvey grunted. 'Well, your Archie always did like climbing didn't he, Vera?' He grinned.

'Yes ... Well ... Yes ... I've got to get home, get his tea for him. He's out on parade Tuesdays and Thursdays. Drop in when you're passing, Mr Harvey. We all miss you down Alma Road.' She gave him a nod, then another, once more with feeling and one for the insurance. She glanced at Suzie as though she were some foreign person with two heads and scales, then left, heels clicking loud and quick on the bare stone floor of the corridor.

Big Toe was still smiling to himself as they moved on into the ward.

Both of the girls looked defeated, their faces disfigured and lumpy as though reflected in distorting mirrors. They were swollen, so that their flesh looked as though it had been fashioned out of bread dough which, in turn, had been coloured in deep violet, scarlet, vermilion and that dark blue that signifies a blow so hard that the bruise reaches right to the bone.

The flesh around both of Cathy Watts' eyes was swollen, the eyelids large, inflated and a harsh blue-black. When the girl tried to raise the lids her face contorted into almost a caricature of pain as the skin was stretched tighter.

Beryl's eyes were in a similar condition and her lips were painted with iodine, which seemed to exaggerate the deep V-shaped splits distorting her mouth in such a way that you could glimpse her teeth through the crevasses.

Both patients were in plaster: each with a damaged leg and arm, while Beryl's right hand lay immobile in a splint.

The girls seemed to listen to Big Toe, only

you couldn't really tell how much they took in. When either of them painfully pried an eye open it would gaze not at either of their visitors, but somewhere towards the doors leading into the ward, as though watching for an unwelcome arrival.

Suzie thought she could smell the fear – almost see it – and Big Toe had no comfort for them. He had only one message: we know who did this to you and we have a good idea why they did it. Just tell us...

'Cough the lot so we can take care of it.'

They forced out their stories, croaking from the throat, breaking through the pain of wounded lips: each with the same tale – 'Fell off me bike. Don't know. Just fell off our bikes ... Our bikes ... Fell off. Terrible ... It hurts,' they groaned.

'Silly cows,' he said of the girls as they drove back to the nick. 'Remember them, Mountford. Remember them well.'

She could hardly forget them.

Detective Chief Inspector Harvey took his right hand off the steering wheel and raised it, fingers splayed: a gesture of either madness or frustration.

'You've seen their injuries. To the animals who did all that it was merely a spanking. Meant very little. If one of them had died they wouldn't have thought much about it. Those girls'll probably have some kind of pain for the rest of their lives, and the men who did it'll possibly hound them for ever. These people have biblical memories – unto the third and fourth generation.'

And what had they done to deserve losing a few teeth, badly broken bones, and get their faces turned into a purée? 'Probably held back a few quid. Doing that more than twice would merit that kind of beating. But it could be that one of them had simply spoken out of turn. Very strong on getting the respect they think they deserve, the Balvaks.' He spat out the name, but it didn't ring true somehow: like a punch with no weight behind it. 'The Balvak twins, Sergeant Mountford. Charlie and Connie Balvak. Today Camford. Tomorrow the underworld.'

'And the Balvaks live right here,' he said. 'Right here in the Cut.'

The industrial district policed by Camford Hill nick was small – a radiator factory for a famous car; a printing works; and the large railway goods yard, known to the Great Western Railway as Camford Hill Yard, and to others as the Cut. The railway goods yard was in fact the reason for the district of Camford existing at all.

Within two months of war being declared last autumn the radiator factory and the printing works had moved out into the country but Camford Hill Yard was immediately enlarged, instantly becoming part of the war effort; and Camford Hill Yard lay on the western extremity of the town. Next, to the east of the Yard, was the dark, cramped, mean, huddled sprawl of grubby, dark-brick houses, each with a tiny walled yard and outhouse, backing on to each other and segmented by narrow unadopted alleys which flooded in heavy rain, or silted up with uncleared rubbish. With the coming of steam, this dense domain had been built to house the railway personnel who worked the sheds, tracks, loading bays and sidings that made up the Yard.

Three pubs served the Cut – the Thomas Picton, the Earl of Uxbridge and, naturally, the Duke of Wellington. The largest and most influential of these was undoubtedly the latter, with its long, ornate and mirrored public bar and the huge room at the back, the scene of all kinds of sporting and quasi-political events. Its first landlord had been Mullard Balvak, son of a Balkan refugee, grandfather to the Balvak twins, who grew up as the young princes regent to the predominant ruler of the locale.

Carl Balvak, the twins' father, well-known drunk, second generation landlord of the Duke, wanted to see his sons installed in his place, but never did, dying suddenly at half past six on an August evening in 1935, leaving the running of the pub to his wife, Nellie – sour, mean, brutal and foul-mouthed.

It was in the following year, Big Toe told Suzie, that the twins took over the pub, and from the moment they took over the Duke they owned the Cut. 'Loans, protection, the slate, gambling, the girls, the corner shops and every bit of villainy that went down in this manor, and quite a lot outside as well.'

He was silent at the wheel for a minute, then he announced, 'I think I'll take a trip down the

Duke tonight with Pip and Squeak. Have a word with the Balvaks and their precious wives. Not that it'll do any good.'

'Pip and Squeak, Guv'nor?'

'Magnus and Thomas. We've got another DC, Wilfred Purser. Pip, Squeak and Wilfred, we call them.' It was the name of a children's cartoon in one of the daily newspapers.

'You think you'll ever nick them – these Balvaks?' she asked.

'Well...' He tilted his hand, palm down, fingers parted, but for all his talk, Suzy thought she could detect a lack of resolution in his manner.

'Nasty bits of work, the Balvaks.'

Takes one to know one, she thought as they turned into the parking spaces behind Lockup Alley and the nick. Suzie glanced up, catching Big Toe smiling down at her. He switched off the engine and turned towards her. 'What do they call you, apart from Mountford and Sergeant?' The smile was like the smile of a cartoon reptile. Have to be careful of Big Toe, with his soft voice, the cold, dark eyes and the chameleon smile.

'So, what they call you, eh?' he asked again.

'You already know, Guv – Suzie.'

'Nothing else?'

'Susannah. That's my real name. My mum only called me that when she was cross with me.' She felt as though she was giving away a part of her soul telling him that.

' "Oh Susannah, don't you cry for me," ' he sang softly. Then: 'Well, Suzie, you can make a difference here if you use your common sense and keep your nose clean.'

'Yes, Guv.' She saw the glint in his eye, Big Toe trying to sell himself to her.

'No tales out of school, right?'

'Right, Guv.' She didn't believe a word of it.

'So, I'm taking Pip and Squeak over to have a little talk with the twins,' he told her as they walked back to the CID office. 'Just let them know that we know who did the girls. Never hurts to put it on the table, let them see we've got their cards marked. We won't get them for it of course.'

'I come, Guv?' She made it sound a bit cheeky.

'You, Suzie? No, Suzie. *You've* got to type up the day's reports, Suzie. Give me a few minutes and I'll have mine ready for you, Suzie.' Then, as they reached the office: 'Any more at home like you, Suzie?'

'I've got a married sister, Charlotte, and a brother, James.'

She could see Charlotte and James clear as day as she spoke about them. She was the second of the Mountford children: twenty-two years old now and physically the image of her sister. They could have been twins, and she was brought up with a start because she realized it was now over five years since her father had been so suddenly killed.

Resigned and *triste* with the memories, she sat down behind the big old Underwood type-writer in the CID room. If she had learned anything it was that life was for getting on with.

You didn't sit and mope or grumble. You made your own luck. So she gathered the pages of scrawl together and added Big Toe's when he came out of his office ready to take Magnus and Thomas off 'down the Cut'.

So she got on with typing the reports.

A little after six Shirley Cox came in with her coat on, gas mask over her shoulder.

'That's me finished for the day. Okay by you?' she asked.

'Sure.'

'You'll be okay, Skip?'

'I'll be fine, Shirley. You get off home and watch yourself.'

'I'm planning to go down the Palais. Get an hour's dancing in before Jerry arrives again.' Most nights you heard the warning siren wail around eight o'clock.

'Got your eye on someone?' Suzie asked.

'There's an auxiliary fireman I quite fancy.' She grinned almost sheepishly. 'It's worth hearing the siren go to see him leg it out of the Palais.'

'Enjoy yourself, Shirley, and watch out for the fireman's lift.'

WDC Cox paused by the door, then came quietly back. 'Skipper?'

'Yes.'

'Be careful, Skip. Careful of the lads. It's not my place to say it but they try it on. Pretend they're mates and that. But they're not. They don't like even the idea of women in the job. Come to that I don't think any of them really like the Guv'nor either, but he's got a big reputation and they'll always side with him.'

'Thanks, I'll remember.'

'You be careful with them, Skipper. They'll take advantage like any other bloke, and they'll have no respect for your rank either. Any of 'em'll have a hand up your skirt, or all over your tits, as quick as look at you, so take care.'

'Thanks, Shirley. I mean it, thanks.' But she couldn't meet the girl's eye. She was uncomfortable with the sexual innuendo and had the recurring thought that she really had to do something about that side of life. Even Charlotte had called her a complete innocent and she supposed she was.

'You mind what I say, Skip. Take care.'

'I will, thank you.' She was going to leave it at that, but couldn't. 'You don't think any of the lads trusts the Guv'nor then?'

There was a pause. Then: 'Not really. No. It isn't my place to say it because the scrambled eggs think he's wonderful. And, of course he has his contacts. After all, Big Toe comes from here. Went to school in Alma Street and all that.'

'He comes from the Cut?'

'No, Empire Street. Runs parallel to Alma. Nicer houses. His dad was a designer at Reveltons and his mum was a draughtswoman there. Toe really does know everyone. He was at school with the Balvaks and he doesn't like people knowing that, though I didn't tell you, Skip.'

'No, course you didn't. You take care tonight, now.'

Big Toe and the two DCs did not get back until just before seven thirty – as Suzie was getting ready to leave – so it was a little after nine before she put the key into her door, just as the sirens started their wail and the anti-aircraft guns began to thump.

Most days after that she ate in the canteen because it was cheap and easy and she was able to catch up on the latest gen around the station. She heard very little more about the case of the two girls and when, over sausages ('mysteries' as they now called them) and chips one lunchtime, she asked Pip Magnus and he told her they had disappeared. 'Gone to Cathy's aunt I think the Guv'nor said.' He chewed on his sausage, swallowed and added, 'We should have given the Balvaks a good smack when we went to see them.'

'You think that would have been wise, Pip?'

'No, but it'd make us feel a lot better. The Guv'nor's always belting suspects. Does the trick though. Calls it aggressive interrogation. Knuckle dusting.'

From the first day at Camford, Suzie suspected Big Toe Harvey of being violent. Often at the end of a day when they had successfully charged a suspect he would lapse into a kind of braggadocio, the thin, frangible coating of allure that he often put on would disappear totally, and his pugilist walk would become more pronounced. At these times Suzie thought he looked as though he was spoiling for a fight: it was the way he eyed people, the quick darting look followed by the hard glare, the eyes locking on. Yet with all her reservations she got on with him after a fashion – certainly better than she did with her stepfather, the Galloping Major.

Then on one night at the end of the first week of December Suzie didn't get home at all, and life totally changed for her.

Four

It was a Friday night when the bombs came to Camford. The warning siren sounded earlier than usual. The pattern of raids was changing, and by early December the ports and dock-yards were catching it – Southampton, Portsmouth, Plymouth, Bristol, Cardiff, Liverpool. The strategy had started to alter around the middle of November with the heavy raid on Coventry: the one that ripped the heart from the city, killed over five hundred people, left twice that number homeless, and reduced the proud medieval cathedral to a ruin.

But on this Friday night, the only bombs to fall in the London area were the ones they dumped on Camford. Tonight's raid on London was only a token force: a feint to tie up the ARP, Rescue and Fire services, make them prepare for a further heavy onslaught that would not come. Every other Nazi bomber base in occupied Europe sent aircraft to the British ports and docks. It was what the RAF called a 'spoof' raid.

The whole of Camford's CID were gathered in the nick in the late afternoon because Big Toe Harvey wanted to discuss a series of street robberies that had taken place within a triangle made up of Linden Road, Elm Way Gardens and Oakley Crescent – 'the Nobs' Hill' of Camford, a good couple of miles away from the dark, uneasy Cut.

'We've been getting more than our fair share of these muggings.' Big Toe used the old nine-teenth-century slang that formerly referred to the vicious garrotting carried out in street attacks of that time – often by women. 'Four in Linden Road, one at the corner of Elm Way Gardens and three more in Oakley Crescent,' he listed, ticking them off on his fingers. 'All women, all on consecutive Wednesdays, and all between six and seven in the evening. That's a pattern we need to look into. The streets're bad enough in the blackout without footpads skulking around.'

At night, what little traffic there was drove with feebly hooded headlights, while pedestri-ans tried to move around in pairs – girls nearly always went about locked to each other, arm in arm, usually giggling with fear. Regulations had reduced cylindrical battery torches to an almost opaque glimmer, while the chunky square ones – like miniature car headlights – had the beams blocked off except for a narrow strip of light angled downwards so that people watched their feet and, inevitably, bumped into things.

Big Toe was getting into his stride. 'This must stop, it's a return to the Dark Ages.'

Suzie thought they'd already returned to the Dark Ages with the Blitz, but she didn't say anything.

'Thin end of the wedge,' grunted Pip Magnus, taking the piss.

Kerbstones and the edges of pavements were painted white, and people took to draping light-coloured scarves around their necks, or even sewing pieces of cloth on to the back of their coats.

'Wednesdays? Why Wednesdays? Do they all have their bridge parties on a Wednesday, I wonder? Check up on that, Shirley.'

Shirley checked up and found it was indeed a favourite day for bridge. Many older women who now worked in shops took advantage of the Wednesday early closing. It was the same with afternoon whist drives. They had whist drives on Wednesday afternoons down at St Leonard's and at the Roman Catholic Church, St Thomas of Canterbury, a mile or so from Elmway Gardens. One of the victims had been returning alone from St Leonard's Parish Hall having won ten shillings and a lardy cake at the whist drive. The thieves stole her watch and handbag. Significantly they left the lardy cake.

'We've got to keep an eye on that area,' Big Toe told them. 'Next week, for instance. Next Wednesday we should mount a little operation to catch these buggers.'

'We could call it Operation Dark Horse,' Richards offered.

'Put out a stalking horse,' Magnus suggested.
'More a tethered goat I should've thought.'
Big Toe looked solemnly at Suzie. 'For instance, if Sergeant Mountford here could be persuaded to hobble along Linden Road, then across Elm Way, disguised as an elderly bridge player, we might just catch these jokers in the act.'

'How d'you disguise yourself as a bridge player?' asked Mortimer, who was pleased with himself, having just arrested a pair of dodgy grocers for knocking off a lorry load of tinned goods. 'That was good old-fashioned police work,' Big Toe had told Suzie. 'Jimmy Mortimer spent hours nosing around every small grocer in the area and discovered these two clowns popping tinned peas into people's shopping baskets and winking at them. It was the customers gave it away, gossiping about the tinned peas, beans and carrots they were getting at rock-bottom prices and off the ration.'

'Those tins weren't just for buying and selling then?' Thomas smirked.

'You want to be a bit careful, David. You're getting so sharp you'll cut yourself.' In answer to Mortimer's query about disguises he had no suggestions.

'I once took a girl to a bridge party,' said Sammy Richards. 'Her mother caught us under the bridge.'

'And you've been listening to Max Miller again, lad.' Harvey showed not a flicker of amusement. That was Big Toe all over: laughed at his own jokes but rarely smirked at other people's wisecracks.

It was finally decided that they would put Suzie out as a decoy on the following Wednesday. But that night bombs fell on the Camford Hill area and by the middle of next week far more deadly things would have happened involving Suzie. By then the attacks on elderly bridge players were relatively small beer.

The warning sirens sounded just after seven that evening – a good hour earlier than normal – just as Suzie was getting ready to wrap up the day's work and head back to Upper St Martin's Lane. Nobody in CID was aware of the aircraft noise or the incendiaries coming down. Then the high explosive bombs dropped and everybody knew what the target was.

Five Heinkel 111s were involved, one flying some five minutes in advance of the other four, dropping flares and incendiaries. When the main force made their appearance over the target the flares still burned and several fires were taking hold. The ornamental bandstand in Revellers Park was half consumed and a steady blaze had begun in the building that had once been the printing factory. Worse, some houses deep in the Cut were well alight, as were two sections of trucks on the railway lines. One of these was an ammunition train loaded with mortar bombs, hand grenades and boxes of .303 rounds standing adjacent to Number Three Bay; the other had four wagons stacked high with thick rubber aircraft tyres and an additional four trucks contained tea. These trucks had come up from Portsmouth only that morning, having been delayed by the raids earlier in the week. They had only just been shunted to the far end of Number Five Bay.

Six incendiary bombs hit the Earl of Uxbridge public house at the corner of Oporto and Barrosa Streets. These shattered the roof tiles and smashed their way into a dry, dusty attic where only two exploded, bursting into searing white flame and igniting a couple of old suitcases and bits of furniture. In seconds the fire drove its way through the top storey of the pub.

Then the high explosives began to rain down.

Suzie Mountford came out of the main doors of the police station and winced in the glare of the white lights hanging in the sky, the orange and red glow away to her right and the singe of burning in her nostrils.

She had been called up with the others, by the station sergeant, 'Loamy' Lomax, and she was conscious of the throbbing note of desynchronized aircraft engines, her stomach turning over, rippling with the familiar butterfly roll of alarm. Some of the bombs screamed as they came down. All of them produced a terrible jarring of the ground and a strong blast of air. She felt the pressure from the soles of her feet and the physical thump up her spine.

The first bombs straddled Revellers Park; others, including a further stick of incendiaries, dropped directly on the old Revelton Printing Factory. More high explosives fell on houses in Barrosa Street and another three plunged into

60

nearby Oporto Street.

Altogether twenty-five houses were affected, not counting the blazing Earl of Uxbridge. The remaining bombs fell, as if by design, into the Railway Yard, ripping up tracks, obliterating Number Five Bay and destroying a shed in which eight men were having a tea break before going back to load more tyres on to trucks standing ready in the bay. The balance of the incendiaries fell across a mile-and-a-half stretch, setting light to buildings within the Goods Marshalling and Shunting Yards, igniting the wooden trucks and wagons loaded with aircraft tyres and tea.

Close to Number Three Bay, several dozen incendiaries dropped in a line along the length of the ammunition train.

Everything began to burn like dry tinder.

The explosions in Revellers Park ripped up the neatly laid paths, the rose garden, several benches, the two big arbours at the far end across from the old printing works and part of Queen's Walk, the northern boundary of the park, uprooting trees and killing a stray dog.

Camford Hill Police Station lay only two hundred yards from the point where the High Street became the wide, tree-lined Queen's Walk on the edge of Revellers Park.

The deserted printing works was cut in half by the bombs, while those that landed at the northern end of the park sent shock waves funnelling back up Camford High Street.

Even as far as the police station.

You imagine it's just the impact of the noise.

61

You think it's the explosion battering your ears, Suzie thought. Then she felt the rumbling, quivering thumps, and saw the wide panels of glass on the doors catch in the safety mesh, crazing over so the adhesive netting was all that kept it from falling, or being hurled, splintered, from the doors. Even here at the top of the police station's steps she felt the pressure around her ears and the thump as the blast almost knocked her off her feet.

The entire building seemed to move and wallow as, with both hands, she clung to the edge of one of the doors as though she was on a bucking ship or a fairground ride. For some inexplicable reason she thought this was what sex must be like.

When things returned to normal she was standing in front of the doors looking at Loamy Lomax who had followed her out and appeared to be dazed, shaking his head as though trying to clear it, like a boxer who's just taken a hard knock.

She heard odd sounds, like tin cans being dropped down in the street, and a roar as though she was on a beach at the seaside with her mum and dad in the good old days.

'Sarge? Here, Sarge?' Somebody yelled, 'Sarn't Mountford!'

Pip Magnus and Dougie Catermole were shouting, while Shirley beckoned to her from the bottom of the steps. Down in the street, they were clustered around an open truck drawn up by the kerb.

Catermole yelled, 'C'mon Sarge. They need

help down the Cut.'

Suzie's mind worked slowly. Her legs felt unsteady and she was conscious of light-headedness as she went down the steps. Coming to Catermole she muttered, 'Don't ever call me "Sarge" again.'

Close proximity to the Blitz was not a new experience. From the start of those nightly attacks, Suzie had travelled from New Scotland Yard to Upper St Martin's Lane through the bombing. Because she had worked in uniform she had sometimes been called to help on her way home. One night, a group of ARP wardens and a team of rescue workers had made her go with them up to Belgravia where she helped clear a house that had suffered a direct hit; another time she stayed with some casualties on the Embankment until ambulances arrived. But on this Friday evening in Camford she found herself with Shirley Cox in the thick of it.

They had cadged a lift on the ARP truck, and for twelve hours worked together, in the eye of the storm that came to the Cut. Later when she thought of that night it became a kaleidoscope of events and horrors punctuated by explosions, the stench of smoke dry and clinging at the back of her throat and in her eyes. She tasted the tangy savour of explosives, and the terrible cloying scent of burned pork: the sweet smell of violent death. And on that night everything appeared to be lit by red and blue dancing flames and the occasional white glare of burning magnesium. Around her there were shouts, cries, the sound of pumps and engines and the crackling of blazing buildings – a horrible, frightening incidental music to the scene.

The air about them sizzled heavy with the charred smell of scorched earth and brickwork. People stood around in the narrow streets between the little terraced houses; there were broken windows and small children crying, others standing silent and cowed as though waiting for some horror not yet identified in the symmetrical streets.

In Oporto Street about ten fire-fighters battled to save the Earl of Uxbridge. Two engines were pulled up on the corner with Corunna Street, their ladders extended with men at the top hosing water into the burning red and white cauldron that had been the roof. The bare beams were black and shrivelled as the fire ate its way through the building, cracking tiles and sending showers of sparks down the bulging front walls.

On the ground floor more hoses played into the public and private bars, trying to dampen the threatened building.

As their truck slowed in front of the pub someone shouted to Shirley, and Suzie saw a young fireman turn towards them, his face shining with sweat and grime.

'How's it going?' Shirley's voice croaked, nearly drowned by the noise and roar of the flames.

'Like pissing at a thunderstorm,' the fireman shouted back. 'You'll be more help along there.' He pointed up Corunna Street, where a huge gap and piles of rubble signified the destruction of three or four of the houses, with more further away in Barrosa Street.

'That was Bernie. My auxiliary fireman.' Shirley smirked a shade too proudly.

Suzie nodded. Lovely command of English, she thought, and for the next three hours they worked, digging in the rubble, dragging out bodies, and people who were miraculously still alive.

Eventually, weary and bone tired, Suzie and Shirley trudged up Corunna Street where they could just make out more figures working ahead of them. Already they felt filthy, their faces burning from the heat of the fires, their hair soiled by the charred remains of material and wood that floated with the dust like obscene dark and poisoned snow.

Further up the street there was an ambulance pulled to one side of the bruised and shattered buildings, and as Suzie paused she felt something tug at her sleeve. Turning, she realized a little straggle of children had shuffled up behind her and a boy of about ten or so had pulled at her sleeve.

He was dressed only in a long striped shirt, much too big for him with tails hanging down to his ankles. His hair was tousled and white with dust and he led a small girl by the hand. The girl walked with him, unprotesting, occasionally looking up at him searching for reassurance. The pair were followed by three other children: a boy and girl of around seven

65

or eight and another little girl in a torn blue dress covered by a cheap fawn coat with little velvet tips on the lapels. This last child carried a small teddy bear dressed in a dark coat with brass buttons.

'Please miss,' the boy began. 'Please miss, they've taken my mum away.'

Suzie dropped a hand on to the boy's shoulder, asking him if the girl was his sister. 'Yes, miss. It's my sister Vi-let, but they've taken my mum away.'

'Well, I'm sure they'll bring her back,' she said automatically.

'What?' His eyes opened wide. 'What? From the fucking mortuary?'

For a moment she was more shocked by the language coming from a child than the chaos around them.

A nurse picked her way towards them, around the edge of the crater from the ambulance.

'You local?'

'Detective Sergeant Suzie Mountford. Camford Hill nick.'

'Staff Nurse Pilbeam – Hannah. I don't know what we do with the kids. We pulled nine people and the kids out of there,' she said, inclining her head towards the ruined houses. 'Could you, perhaps, move them up to the Martha Revelton Hall? We've got to get them out of here.'

Together, Suzie and Shirley organized the children. The little boy, whose name was Jack, was put in charge of a rag, tag and bobtail group of small kids.

'Right. Jack, do you know where the Martha Revelton Hall is?' Shirley asked him.

'Bottom of the 'igh Street, innit?'

'That's the one. Where they have the scouts meetings. You a scout, Jack?'

'Nah. Scouts're for poofters, my Dad says. For fucking goodie-two-shoes.'

'Enough of the language, Jack. There're ladies here.'

'You're not a lady – you're the filth en' cher?'

'Maybe, but the nurse and my sergeant are both ladies. And the other girls. Well, they're—'

'Wat' cher want me to do, then?'

'Take charge, Jack. You're to take these smaller children to the Martha Revelton Hall. It's the rescue centre. There'll be nice ladies there. They'll give you tea and something to eat. See you've got somewhere to sleep – in the warm.'

'They've taken my mum away ... in another ambulance,' he repeated. Violet still cried.

'I know, Jack, but you've got to be brave. You've got to think of these kids. Now, will you do it? Take them to Martha Revelton Hall?'

'Yea, awright.'

She told the children that Jack was their leader. 'He's taking you up the Hall. Will you do that, listen to him?'

There was a mumbled affirmative response. 'Off you go then,' she said sharply. 'Quick as you can and, Jack, no matter what, you go straight there, right.'

Jack nodded bravely. 'Right you lot, follow me.' He seemed to have taken to authority, and the children went off uncertainly in the direction of the park, the boy leading them, fussing and giving orders like a tiny drill sergeant. 'Keep up can' cher, Vi-let, and you two little buggers, keep up. I'm re-bleedin-sponsible for yer, so keep up.'

I just hope young Jack'll keep them together, she thought. They're so small. Vulnerable. Christ, how can all this happen? Suzie wondered.

Then the young nurse asked if they could help with a particularly unpleasant job. Many of the dead had lost limbs and other parts of their bodies. These were marked where they had fallen and now needed to be retrieved.

They had no option but to assist. Someone had to walk around the crater and look under the bits of red and bloodstained blanket that covered the sliced and decimated bits of humanity, dropping them into specially lined sacks. Afterwards, they both felt it was the most unpleasant half-hour of their lives. That was to change, but this was more than normally bad: they collected parts of several legs, arms and a hand, all jaggedly ripped from the bodies. Suzie even had to handle a decapitated human head, a woman, henna-haired, so that it was difficult to distinguish what was dyed hair and what was blood. When she picked up the head she found it unbelievably heavy, as though it was made of solid metal. She thought of what a bloodthirsty young nun, the history teacher at St Helen's, had told them when they were doing the French Revolution. Sister Mary Innocent had gone into bizarre details about the guillotine and said that the executioners learned to wait several seconds before scooping the severed head from the basket. The brain, she said, can remain active for up to half a minute or so in a severed head, and could reason that when deprived of all other means of defence it would use the only thing left – its teeth, snapping and biting at anything that came dangerously close until the blood stopped pumping and life drained away. All this had given her a couple of unpleasant nightmares.

'Not as bad as some,' Shirley Cox said later. 'My uncle was there when they had that direct hit on Sloane Square Underground station last month. There were two girls stripped naked hanging by their feet, trapped somehow in what was left of the roof. Took two days to get them down.'

The light was bad, only a steady glow now coming from the Yard, reflected off the clouds. But even that glow was soon damped down by a thick pall of dark smoke rising from the tracks, making a slow, engulfing sooty shroud over the buildings.

'What the hell d'you think that is?' Suzie asked.

'Burning rubber.' Shirley glanced up. 'I've seen it before. It's certainly what it smells like, and the smoke's thick enough. You could cut that cloud into slices and serve it on a plate.'

'That nurse okay?' Suzie asked, gulping air.
'Didn't bat an eyelid.'

'Hard-hearted Hannah.' She straightened up, and as she did so a brilliant flash lit up the sky from the direction of the railway tracks. The flash was followed by a thunderclap explosion that made the ground ripple and sent a double shock wave slamming through the streets.

The silence after the explosion was eerie and seemed to go on for a long time, followed eventually by grating noises and more faint shouts and cries from the area of the railway lines.

'Jesus!' Shirley straightened up. 'You think we should...?'

Suzie's ears pulsed, as though she had just come up from a deep dive. For a second she was back at St Helen's, in the big swimming pool that smelled of unidentified disinfectant. Summer, childhood and little in the way of responsibility. She heard the calls, echoed shouts and splashes of girls enjoying them-selves, slicing to the bottom, leaving silver plumes of water behind them. Then she was back in the present, listening for the sound of the aircraft that had dropped that last bomb.

There was no engine noise.

There were shouts and calls as they started to run towards the Yard.

Corunna and Oporto Streets emptied into Boundary Road, the most obviously named thoroughfare in the whole of Camford, mark-ing the edge of the long stretch of railway lines running the two-and-a-half-mile perimeter of

70

the Marshalling Yard. A panorama of destruction waited for them: a terrible inferno that made them pull up and, for a second, clutch at each other in horror.

Fires blazed from destroyed loading bays and long snakes of flame streamed from wooden trucks on the tracks. The ammunition train close to Number Three Bay had been hit by a line of incendiaries; the goods vans and trucks engulfed from the moment the first bombs had fallen. Now, in spite of the constant spraying of water, the ammunition – mortar bombs, hand grenades and boxes of small arms rounds – had finally detonated in that last violent explosion they had taken to be another bomb.

The railway tracks close to this last conflagration were now twisted and turned upwards, tangled around the scattered bodies of firemen and ARP people who had been caught in the blast.

The two women headed along the scorchingly hot, jagged metal of the walkways that stretched out over the railtracks, sheds and loading bays. Smaller detonations surrounded them – hand grenades and small arms ammunition still exploded from the heart of the flames, throwing up flashes and thuds in a variety of colours – deep red, orange, blue-white; thick belching smoke rose from shattered trucks that contained aircraft tyres.

At the edge of the walkway, where cast-iron steps descended into a turmoil of what had once been an orderly collection of rail tracks, turntables, platforms, cranes and loading ramps, a four-man team of firemen stood braced against each other, trying to direct water on to ruined wagons from which a different, thinner, kind of smoke rose almost languidly – one that smelled strongly sweet.

'That's tea, isn't it?' Suzie asked, sniffing.

'Yes, love,' one of the firemen laughed. 'All wrong innit, spraying it with cold water?'

They began to make their way across the splintered, wrenched, twisted rail tracks and were met by Pip Magnus and Duggie Catermole carrying a stretcher on which an unconscious fireman lay, his head bandaged and his uniform jacket ripped and bloodstained down one side.

Both Magnus and Catermole looked dirty and wide-eyed. 'Sarge, we need you,' Magnus said. 'There's about a ton of dead and wounded down there.' He nodded his head back towards where the ammunition train had blown. 'Maybe more than a hundred. We're trying to get them out to ambulances and crews up on Boundary Road. We've got to lift these people out.'

'We got anyone in charge?'

'They say the Chief Super's up on the road, but I can't find him. And I don't believe it anyway. He's about as much use as a wet weekend, Sarge.'

'Right, and don't call me "Sarge".'

'Sanders of the River's down there though. He particularly asked me to get you. I told him you were around.'

Hallo, she thought, what's old Sanders of the

River asking for me for?

As though reading her mind, Magnus called back and said that Sanders had said she was more use than a dozen uniformed sergeants.

'Praise indeed.' Shirley said, raising her eyebrows.

So that was one of the ways the night became a landmark for Suzie Mountford. She worked, with Shirley Cox, the other DCs and some of the uniformed men from Camford nick, until around two in the morning, helping to lift, comfort and calm the casualties from the Yard, getting them into ambulances and off to St Mary Mother's. They had been working for a further hour or so when news came that Big Toe Harvey had been injured in a bad fall as he was helping to move a critically wounded man from a pile of metal half-a-mile or so down the tracks. He had been taken to hospital, and Magnus said he was sorry for the nurses who'd have to look after him. 'He had a bad bronchial infection last winter.' He grinned. 'Chrissie – Mrs Harvey – had one hell of a time. Not the best patient in the world, our Toe.'

Around half-past six in the morning they began to wander back to the nick, calling in at the Martha Revelton Hall to rest, have a cigarette, or get tea and a sandwich from the Women's Voluntary Service people on duty.

Tired, shaken and deeply troubled, Suzie saw a pile of odds and ends in a corner: bundles of clothing, a couple of suitcases, and an umbrella. Among them she spied a teddy bear dressed in a little navy-blue coat with

73

brass buttons.

'What's this then?' she asked one of the women, recognizing the bear dragged along by the girl who'd been on her own, tagging on to Jack's little group of children.

'Oh, don't.' The WVS woman pursed her lips and tears started in her eyes. 'Children,' she said blankly. 'Five kids. Terrible accident. They were up on the corner of Queen's Walk when a fire engine ploughed into them. It was so dark and the driver didn't see ... Terrible. Driver's in hospital: shock. Apparently he knew one of the kids.'

'So did I,' Suzie muttered, pushing herself towards the door as though she was about to vomit. Outside, she leaned against the wall and lit a cigarette, the flame from the match waving around like a piece of corn in a breeze. She pulled on the cigarette, taking in a great drag of smoke and letting it settle in her lungs until she felt it had done its job, calming her nerves. She took another drag and held the smoke in until she began to get over the immediate emotion. Her hand still trembled so much that she thought she would drop the cigarette, and she realized her face was wet with the tears running down her cheeks.

At least Jack West would be with his mum again. She mopped at the tears. They'd be together at the mortuary and wherever the dead went on that extraordinary journey someone had once called the adventure of eternity.

Depressed, she went back to Shirley's digs to have a bath, and the landlady, Mrs Gibson, gave them both breakfasts, bustling around and bringing curses down on Hitler. Suzie wondered where she'd got the extra bacon and sausages from, though Shirley did say of them that she didn't know whether to put marmalade or mustard on the sausages because the main content seemed to be bread.

After they'd eaten and bathed Shirley offered Suzie a change of underclothes and for the first time in her life Susannah Mountford found herself wearing black silk. Until then she had retained what her mother called 'sensible unmentionables', which meant some of her blue serge schoolgirl underwear. Vaguely she believed only tarts wore stuff like Shirley had produced, but she found it quite a pleasant sensation. How odd, her mother had always said that nice girls only wore white cotton – 'And you should never ever wear black.'

'Parachute silk,' Shirley said. 'I can get some for you if you like, Sergeant. I have a source in the RAF.'

'And the elastic?'

'Well, that's a bit more difficult. I can do you some lace, but miracles take a bit longer as they say. We do a nice line in mother-of-pearl buttons though, like the ones on those.'

Back at the nick, Sanders sent for Suzie. 'DCI Harvey's not going to be back with us until at least early January, Sergeant. And what with the shortage of manpower and the rest I'm not going to be able to get anyone else in to take his place. Can you manage?'

'As long as we don't get too many nights like

75

last night; and as long as there isn't a sudden crime wave.' To herself, she wondered if she could perhaps get something on the Balvak brothers before Big Toe came back.

She had actually seen the Balvaks only a few hours ago. She had been with Shirley, heading back into the Yard after delivering yet another shattered body to an ambulance. They stood behind the vehicle and shared a cigarette, taking a short break before going back into the debris, dodging the fires and occasional explosions. A group of men – civilians – had come to gawp at the scene and Shirley nudged her and whispered, 'The Balvaks.'

'Where?'

Shirley nodded towards two men, smart but a little racy in camel-hair coats and snap-brimmed trilby hats, standing close together with three older men, big, broad, heavy-set bully boys with roving eyes, constantly looking over their shoulders.

As Suzie edged closer to the group she heard one of the heavies murmur something about, '...the filth!'

'Look at all that damage and destruction, Connie,' one of the camel-haired commented, raising his voice.

'Charlie, look at all them flames. A lot of people're going to need help after this. Some won't be able to meet their debts.'

'The flames, Connie.'

'All the colours of the rectum, Charlie.' And they both laughed again: Connie had a soft wheezing chuckle while Charlie's laugh was deep and barking.

Suzie moved away with Shirley Cox at her elbow. 'I expected something a little more fearsome,' Suzie said as they negotiated their way back towards what had once been Loading Bay Three. 'They're little men. Short, vulgar little men.'

Shirley agreed. 'Chunky and Plush,' she laughed. 'But make no mistake about it, Sarge, they may be vulgar little men but they're dangerous little men. I've seen some of their handiwork.'

'Don't call me "Sarge",' Suzie said, still very interested in the two Balvak brothers because, at the time she expected to have a lot of dealings with those two men. Other things would get in their way. 'And what d'you mean, "Plush and Chunky"?'

Shirley just smirked and muttered something inaudible.

But other things lurked in the wings for Suzie Mountford. Things far worse than the Balvaks. Five days further on, unknown people were ready to enter her life and make it a waking nightmare. Some of them were here, not five minutes from Camford Hill nick. Others lived up West and around Soho.

One of them was David Slaughter...

Five

David Slaughter sits at his desk in the offices of Jewell, Baccus & Dance, on the second floor of a Regency house near Albemarle Street: a street that empties into Piccadilly some way up from the Circus that is London's hub. It used to be said that if you stood on any corner of Piccadilly Circus for long enough you would eventually see everyone you knew.

Jewell, Baccus & Dance are property management: an old established firm that has much to win and lose in wartime London now the bombs are falling.

It is night and David Slaughter sits at his desk with only the green student lamp washing across the leather inlay and his large radio – the one with the fretted sunburst on the speaker – playing softly. Everyone else has gone home long ago; the two secretaries, Miss Burrage and Miss Holroyd, left hours before. Miss Holroyd only began work in September and she had scuttled off, heading back to Hammersmith at five. Miss Burrage is older and has worked for Jewell, Baccus & Dance since 1934. She thinks Miss Holroyd will soon leave because Miss Holroyd has been talking about joining the WRNS – the Women's Royal Naval Service. 'Personally I think it's the uniform that's the attraction,' she told Mr Slaughter. 'These girls think the uniform will get them a man. Not that Miss Holroyd has cause to worry. She could make herself very attractive, don't you agree, Mr Dance?' That's what they knew him as: Joshua Dance.

Mr Slaughter is alone. Among other things, he has listened to Carol Gibbons and the Savoy Orpheans broadcast live from the Savoy, and tonight the bombs have fallen steadily all evening, from around eight o'clock. It is now one in the morning and he has tuned to a foreign station. Listening to jazz and the scholarly commentary that goes with it.

From childhood David Slaughter had sensed that he'd inherited the right name; knew he was an infinitely more sinister member of that group comprising dentists called Fang or Rinse, doctors named Bones or Body, and a verger he'd known long ago called Jim Tombs. Once he had also been on nodding terms with an undertaker called William Coffin. These were amusing names, but David Slaughter – who had long since changed his by deed poll – had little sense of fun or humour.

'There are ten or twenty Slaughters in the London telephone directory,' he occasionally says to himself, 'and I'm not one of them.'

On this night in mid-winter he senses that maybe life is about to take on a new clarity for him. But is life that important? We're all on the same train, he tells himself, the express to Death Junction with its first, second and steer-age classes. He has already been face to face

with the old Grim Reaper, and there was really
nothing to it. He knew that and smiled.

The radio station still plays its late-night
jazz as Slaughter smokes a cigarette and sips
brandy.

'O love, O love, O careless love,
You fly into my head like wine.
You wrecked the lives of many a poor girl
And you nearly wrecked this life of mine.'

He did not recognize the recording.

Slaughter looks at his watch and thinks that
maybe tonight he'll have to wait a little longer.
He wonders if the time will come when he'll
never have to concern himself with careless
love ever again.

Soon maybe he'll have to leave: go out and
play old Jack Nasty again. And then? Well—

Jack shall have Jill
Naught shall go ill,
The man shall have his mare again,
And all shall be well.

Oh yes.

As he waits, Emily Baccus comes into the
room. This perks him up.

She was not surprised to see him because she
was aware that he often came back into the
office to finish paperwork late at night. After
all, he lived on the premises. She gave him her
usual distant smile, then turned her back to
him, adjusting her stockings. He suspected that

80

she was teasing him when she went through this little ritual. With her back towards him she would lift the skirt of her severe dark suit and do something with the tops of her stockings. First one leg and then the other. Running her hands up and down her long thighs, making sure the stockings were just so, straightening the seams so that they ran true: like pathways from heel, up calf and disappearing under the skirt, true as a bullet. He could rarely see anything – sometimes a flash, an occasional hint of silk and lace. He could imagine it, though. Oh, he could imagine it all, for Emily Baccus was striking; tall, slender, long legs; with a wide mouth, a serious mouth, negroid lips also, large brown eyes, button nose and neat chin. Very dark hair, sleek, black, dark and deep as the woods at night. Emily Baccus wore her hair long, her eyebrows pencil thin and her fine, long lashes curled upwards. Slaughter was always one to fantasize and could spend entire nights dreaming that he was with Emily Baccus, fondling her, running his tongue over her juicy breasts, stroking her velvet thighs. If she had been that way inclined, David Slaughter would have wasted weeks serving Miss Baccus, getting into her body.

Tonight he should have anticipated her arrival back at the office, because it was the second Wednesday in the month and she always worked late, going out and physically claiming her rent from the two Soho properties she personally owned: the two buildings close to Rupert Street which were divided into small

81

apartments – one- or two-room affairs right for only one thing.

'You're going to collect your rents then, Emily?' Slaughter asked.

'You know me, Josh. Always collect them in person.' That's how Emily spoke, with a lisp. Slaughter likes her lisp. The lisp is a special shade in her voice. Very attractive, that lisp.

'On the nose,' she said. 'Hit them late on the second Wednesday in the month: don't mess around, then we all know where we are.'

That is what Jewell, Baccus & Dance did. They managed properties, renting them out to businesses and individuals. Properties, large and small. They dealt with keeping up the fabric; settling small dramas; improvements; renovations; legal matters, and the cashflow from the tenant to them and from them to the owner.

'Like me to come with you, Emily?' he asked, and she gave him a supercilious smile, eyes going sideways, not looking at him directly.

'Want to frighten the girls off, Josh?' At the door she paused, turned back. Josh she called him, didn't know him by any other name.

He undressed her with his eyes and made a quick appraisal as she shrugged herself into the long coat with its big fur collar. Her suit, blouse and shoes had to be worth a few hundred at least – say two – while the little diamond pin she wore in her left lapel added a further two. The coat he had seen advertised as an exclusive from Fenwicks for a hundred and fifty. Six hundred and fifty quid or more on legs, he thought. Plus the items he couldn't see. Add another fifty or so. And she had the guts to walk into the territory of whores.

Slaughter's admiration for Emily Baccus bordered on the obsessional, and she knew it. She was thinking about it as she made her way into the black, early morning streets of London, still smelling of the bombs and the anti-aircraft fire. A van being used as a makeshift ambulance clattered past, its tiny pinpricks of masked headlights hardly reaching down to the road.

Far away there was a crump that shook the pavement and the buildings she walked past. She crossed Regent Street and took a short cut up Brewer Street. She wondered if she would see Golly tonight. She hoped so. Emily liked Golly.

Golly Goldfinch remembered the dream that had hustled him into the cold day lurking outside his window. The clouds were dark pewter and the air froze the skin even as he lay for a moment in the cramped bed.

He remembered that it wasn't a dream, knew it was a nightmare that had wakened him shivering and troubled; stomach churning and the rivers running down from his hairline even in the chill room. And he remembered what had wakened him. The voices were back. There had been bombs again last night. He wasn't afraid of the bombs. It was the voices that scared him. Particularly the lady who gave him orders.

Golly didn't like to think of the cold night sweats and the terrors that regularly held him captive and came with the voices. Kill Joe Benton, the dominant voice had commanded with its distinctive and chilling throatiness. Kill with the wire, and it worried Golly because he didn't know who Joe Benton was, though he remembered the name and knew what he had to do.

He loved that voice, the woman's voice, persuasive, powerful. He also feared it, because if he didn't do as it commanded he knew that he would be tortured and something terrible would happen. Nobody had told him this, but he knew it. He didn't have to be told something like that. It just was. Any fool could see that.

Before, the voice had not been so specific. Just things like: 'You must take the train to Cambridge. A girl will be there for you to kill.'

He got up, disturbed about the familiar name – Joe Benton – unable to link the name with a face or body. The person was just out of sight and he wondered why he was being told to kill a man. Before, it had always been a woman. A girl even – well, a couple of times it had been a girl. Like two weeks ago, and afterwards he'd seen her picture in the paper. She looked a pretty little thing, nothing like she'd looked when he left her.

Golly washed, shaved and dressed, did the usual things, cleared the blankets from the bed, stored them away in the cupboard, opened the window just like Lavender told him. The same

84

as he did every morning. He liked the order she brought to his life. Golly had problems if the routine was changed or altered in any way. Kill Joe Benton, he remembered.

Lavender was good to him, very good. Yes, she was his cousin, and he did give her protection of a kind, but he thought she was better than anyone. She even gave him a ride now and again. 'Don't be sad, Golly,' she would say. 'I like to help, and there's no other woman would open up her honey for you, baby.'

He brought the carpet sweeper in from the tiny room off the equally tiny kitchen and ran it over the carpet – straight strokes across the room, like the lines of a well-mown lawn. Then he went out and did the hall, then Lavender's room.

Golly liked doing Lavender's room and he took great pains with it. He dusted the brass head of the small bed before he moved the mat so that he could get the sweeper under the bed, then plumped up the big coloured cushions she liked. Nobody else was around, so he sneaked a look in the drawer: held the silky things to his face. He liked the things she wore.

He dressed with great care, put on his mask and the hat before getting into his coat. A new mask every morning. An oblong of white cloth with strings of cotton at each corner. Doctors used them when they were doing operations, so that they wouldn't breathe germs on to the patients, or on to the open wounds as they performed the surgery.

But for Golly this was a mask to hide his

lower face from the nose to beneath his chin. It was ideal for him; necessary. People who had known him all his life still preferred him to have his nose and mouth covered and the large-brimmed hat on. They said that they could take seeing him without the mask, but they did not like the reaction of folk who were not used to him.

Lavender would say that he was better than any guard dog. 'One look at Golly's face and they'd beat all records running from the flat. Beat Jesse Owens even,' she used to say.

As well as looking after her when she was working, and being her cousin, Golly was Lavender's friend and he was worried. The girls were leaving earlier and earlier these days to get out of the way of the bombs. There was plenty of trade but it was usually all over by five o'clock.

Lavender said she didn't know how she was going to manage if the Germans didn't stop their bombing. If it wasn't for her hardy annuals she'd be in Queer Street, she moaned. 'You're one of my hardy annuals, aren't you Golly? You come up real nice.' And Golly would laugh at that. Sometimes it would be his snorting laugh, on the brink of losing control, so that Lavender had to speak sharply to him. She was never cross with him for long though. She really understood him, knew him inside out.

When he went out, Golly crossed Brewer Street, under the arch and on into Berwick Street Market, where he helped out some of the stallholders; not serving of course, but humping boxes and crates around, tidying up, getting rid of spoiled stuff, feeding the rabbits they sold – not for pets, but to be nurtured for the table. He liked the rabbits.

Lavender started at noon: midday. She started at midday and before the war she had often still been in the flat, working at midnight. But that had all changed. Even Edith the Maid liked to leave early. She had to go all the way back to Camford Hill and had two teenagers and a husband who had been at Dunkirk. 'Lucky to get back in one piece,' Edith the Maid said. Life was hard for Edith, and Golly was worried because Lavender had a place over in Camford as well, and Edith the Maid said she ought to come over to Camford Hill permanent and work there.

'Safer,' Edith said and Lavender had told her she'd think about it. 'You'd get well looked after in Camford,' Edith told her. 'You'd be really safe.'

'It's safe when old Golly's here,' Lavender would say. 'One look at Golly and they think the monsters are around.' Golly could make anyone wince. You just had to look at that face without the mask, scarf and hat. It made strong men feel cold shivers up the short hairs on the back of their necks.

Mind, Lavender didn't sleep in the flat. Her first rule was never to live over the shop. She had a nice little house, buried away in the outlying Borough of Camford. Quiet street where she lived, with plane trees sprouting from the pavement. It was modern and had every possible convenience, and she'd bought it after she left off living bang with Gilbert Carpenter who got sent down for life. Such a nice young man, Lavender's nan used to say. Always so well dressed and smart. Gilbert Carpenter was in fact a petty criminal. Bit of a gangster really. Golly had been over there, to the house, once and thought it was lovely. You'd never know what Lavender did near Rupert Street if you had only seen her at home. It was so nice, and now she lived with another bloke – Laurence. Laurence Lattimer. Same name as some bishop who was burned to death at the stake, but he only had one T. Lavender said that he was one of Laurence's forebears, and he 'chose the steak because he didn't fancy a chop'. Bit of a wag, Lavender. A bit of good as well with her blonde hair bright as a brass button.

Golly was glad now that it was winter. In the wintertime he could wear a hat and keep a muffler over the lower part of his face with a comfort that wasn't possible in summer. Golly was no fool. A little unbalanced, yes. But not a fool.

About twelve forty-five he was all done and walked back up Berwick Street to the private bar of the Blue Posts, where they knew him. He'd have a beer, then get back to Lavender.

'Ey up, it's the man in the iron mask.' Mickey the Mangle leaned against the bar. The 'public' was chock-a-block with people, but the usuals were in the 'private' – the regulars.

Mickey, Bruce and Billy Joy-Joy were on their

own in the 'private'. When he was quite young, Golly had asked Mickey why they called him 'the Mangle' and he had laughed, ruffled the back of Golly's hair and said, 'Don't you worry your pretty little head about that.' This had caused much hilarity at the time. Pretty little head. Very droll.

Bruce the Bubble and Billy Joy-Joy still laughed about it when they'd had a few. 'Remember the time Mangle told Golly not to worry his pretty little head about it.' And they would cling on to each other and laugh.

'Usual?' the Mangle asked Golly.

'Yes,' he said, distracted, because the wireless was on, turned up loud for the news. After Dunkirk, when everyone said the German parachutists would come any day dressed as nuns and priests, they made the announcers and those who read the news start giving out their names first. Up until then it could have been anyone announcing. Nobody knew. Now it was 'This is the news and this is Alvar Lidell reading it,' or Bruce Belferage, 'or Kumquat,' Billy would say. They even had ladies reading stuff.

Golly knew all that.

He listened now to the lady as she said, 'It's one o'clock. This is the news from the *Home and Forces Programme*, and this is Jo Benton reading it.'

Oh, *that* Jo Benton, Golly thought. Now he understood. Yes. Kill Jo Benton. Kill with the wire, he thought. Of course. Jo Benton the announcer. And he knew where she lived because both Lavender and Edith the Maid said she lived out in Camford Hill. He'd ask Edith the Maid for the address. She'd know.

Then he'd do it.

Six

The noises dissipated: the scuffles, croaks and the retching cries had gone. Now the house was cold and silent except for the thudding of his heart and the sound of his hard breathing. Both seemed to fill his ears, so when the door-bell rang it was like something ripping through him causing him to flatten himself against the wall.

His head moved to the right, slowly, like a turtle's head, and he sensed the person on the other side of the front door. In his mind he saw the visitor as a man, huge and looming. Then the doorbell slashed at him again and once more he felt the shadow moving against the blackout material.

In his head with the rasp of the bell he had a vivid picture of a village green and rooks flapping upwards in a great cawing flock from skeletal trees. He wondered if this was a real memory or something conjured from a dark corner of his mind. He couldn't remember being in a village with trees like that, and the big sinister rooks flying up, though his mother had told him often of the place where he was

90

born back in 1901: a village in Dorset where she had been sent to have the baby. He thought that this might just be a stored memory, tucked away from one of those first nipple-sated pram rides.

He stood still as stone, mute as a maggot: terrified. It was terror that gave him the buzz, the best thrill ever. Unforgettable.

The shape at the door fussed around, moving, getting larger, bending down to rattle at the letterbox, using the knocker. Shave-and-a-haircut-me-next. Then calling through the flap:

'Jo? Jo? It's me. I know you're back. I know you're home.' A young voice. A girl.

Then – 'Maybe you're in the bathroom. I'll come back in five or ten minutes.'

The shape grew, then vanished. Nobody there. Nobody home, he thought, as he tapped at the kitchen door with his gloved knuckles, letting it swing back softly, allowing the sliver of light to stab into the hall. If this was a film it would have been carol singers at the door, so close to Christmas.

She lay just inside the kitchen door as though she was asleep, hands above her head which lolled sideways, the hands palm out as if she was surrendering; agreeing to her death. Below, her dark skirt fanned over the floor. His shoulders ached from the exertion of killing her and the room still seemed to be full of the violence.

It was hot and sticky as well because of having the pan of water boiling on the gas hob. She'd known something was wrong as soon as she came in through the back door. 'Oh,' she'd squeaked. 'What on earth? Someone's left a pan on... Who...?' Then he was on her. Hadn't expected her to come in the back. Thought she'd come in the front.

He bent down from the knees, taking a bunch of the material in his hand. Lifted her skirt for the final indignity. God, he thought, I wish she'd close her eyes. He'd do the eyes later. He put his knife on the carpet. Like a bookmark. Remind me where I'm at.

But the caller would return. There was no time to wander through the house, or sniff out Jo Benton's secrets. 'Where the bee sucks, there suck I,' he sang softly, so nobody could hear.

In his head he again saw the rooks rising, agitated from the trees, and heard their cacophonous caw.

Suzie Mountford came down the steps of Camford Hill Police Station with Pip Magnus desperately attempting to match his stride to hers. He found this difficult because while he was a tall man, his legs were short. He reminded Suzie of one of those toys for toddlers: the ones with a wheel of legs below a plywood Goofy or Donald Duck head and body. Small children pushed them along with a stick, and little bells jingled as the legs whirled round. Ben had one in Overchurch but he couldn't walk with it of course.

Suzie, on the other hand was blessed, or cursed, with legs that went up for ever making her shoes into fairytale seven-leaguers. The shoes were sensible, a present a year ago from the Major. Clarke's, she thought. A *present* from the Major? She thought, strange. What was he after? She'd wondered at the time.

It was just after eight in the evening. She had been about to leave when Sanders of the River had sent for her. Now God knew when she would get home: probably not tonight. Shirley would offer her a bed at her place but she would probably stay at the nick. She'd try to get home though, she decided. Depended on Jerry really. If he came over tonight or not.

'You want me to drive, Sarge?' Magnus dangled the keys to the unmarked Wolseley, swinging them like a hypnotist doing the business. She had given up telling them not to call her "Sarge" and it crossed her mind that Magnus was being sarcastic: extracting the urine. Who else would drive?

She gave him the look and he shook his head saying, 'I mean Skipper! Sorry, Skip!'

Her hand came up automatically to tidy an imagined unruly strand of hair. 'We could walk it in five minutes, Pip, Coram Cross Road.' As she said it she went resolutely towards the car which had been brought around to the front. It wouldn't do to arrive at a murder site on foot, and Loamy Lomax had thought it a good idea to have the car out front in case of the reporters. 'There are reporters up at the house,' Loamy said. 'It's going to be in the papers this one.'

'Drive it in two,' Magnus opened the car door for her, then went round and got behind the wheel. 'There was this penguin walked into a pub—' He turned the key in the ignition.

'I know it.' She didn't even smile. 'The penguin says, "Have you seen my dad?" and the barman says, "I don't know, what's he look like?"'

'That's the one.' Pulling away into the light traffic, Magnus glanced at her in the mirror and wondered if he was going to have to hold her hand through this? Suddenly it's all gone and she's got no confidence, he thought. Tremendous in the Cut the other night when the bombs were falling. Today it's all gone. Aloud he said, 'This duck walked into a pub.'

She sighed.

'Said to the barman, "Can you spare a piece of bread for a hungry duck?"'

Within herself Suzie was troubled. Here I am, she thought, Detective Sergeant, twenty-two years old; healthy hair and teeth; walking into a nightmare. Even Shirley said it was a nightmare when she spoke on the phone. 'Sammy Richards has just lost his tea. It's a hundred times worse than those bodies down the Cut, Skip!' Shirley said.

Suzie'd had her hair cut short after what they were now calling the Blitz of Camford Hill, because it had constantly blown across her face and into her eyes when they were bringing people up from the Cut. Now it was sleek and short and heavy, what her mother would have insisted on calling *en brosse*. She reflected as she worried her bottom against the passenger seat thinking, Bloody hell, did it have to be today?

Did this have to happen on one of my bad days?

The bad days had lived with her since she was a teenager; sudden depressive plunges into total lack of confidence. They seldom lasted more than twenty-four hours, but when they struck, the world went from bad to worse and she felt useless: fat, ugly and totally useless.

Back in the nick, fifteen minutes ago, Sanders of the River had looked at her with flickering, weak dirty-grey eyes and said, 'I don't like it, Suzie, but I don't have any option. Everyone else is tied up. I've been on to the Yard and they can't spare anybody. I told them this is a relatively "known" victim – an announcer: BBC – but they've still said no. Just haven't got the manpower. Tony Harvey won't be back until the New Year, as you well know, so I have to put you on it. Suspicious death.'

'You won't be calling in the Yard?'

'Did you not listen to what I said? The Yard can't spare anyone. However, once you've started the investigation you must telephone Detective Chief Superintendent Livermore of the Reserve Squad at the Yard. Take his lead. Take his advice. If things get very difficult he'll come down, but that's a last resort because he's on three cases up west at the moment. He'll guide you through things and step in if it's really necessary. Experienced man, Tommy Livermore, but we're bloody short of bodies. You'll have to do the best you can. You're getting on famously, Susan, and I'm always here if you need me.' He was the only one who called her Susan, though a couple of the uniformed sergeants called her Sue.

'Very good, sir.' It wasn't very good but Suzie would have been stupid to point that out. She reckoned Sanders of the River knew it already.

She had yet to meet the senior officer at Camford Hill, the Chief Superintendent. He was away again on another course. 'He's been round more courses than Gordon Richards,' Catermole observed. Gordon Richards had already been a champion jockey a number of times.

Wilf Purser came out with it straight and said he thought the Chief Super was bomb happy and had been ever since the Blitz of Camford Hill, when, they were reliably informed, he had locked himself in his office and refused to come out. 'He's not on any course,' Wilf said. 'He's on indefinite leave and we're going to be landed with Sanders of the bleedin' River as senior station officer, and he's about as much use as a wet weekend. It's absolutely porous.' Nobody had sighted the Chief Super anywhere on the night they bombed the Cut.

'Porous?' Suzie asked.

'Porous piss,' Wilf explained.

That was probably what they thought of her, Suzie imagined. Sergeant Porous Mountford. For WDS Mountford to be put in charge of a murder was about as useful as putting her in charge of a Spitfire. Come to that, putting her in charge of anything in police work more daunting than a typewriter was a long shot. Suzie was suffering from a complete breakdown of confidence. It was something that happened every few weeks.

Magnus went on with his duck joke. 'This duck goes into a pub, says to the barman, "Can you spare a piece of bread for a hungry duck?" The barman says, "No, I've got no spare pieces of bread. We don't like your sort in here. Get out." '

Today she was convinced that Sanders of the River knew it, and most of her colleagues knew it as well. When she was like this she would wonder why they put up with her at all.

'Half-an-hour later the duck comes back,' Magnus cheerily went on. ' "Spare a piece of bread for a hungry duck." Again the barman tells the duck to get out, but half-an-hour later he comes back. "Spare a bit of bread for a duck down on his luck." The barman gets really angry. Says, "Out! If I catch you in here again I'll nail your beak to the bar." Half an hour later the duck comes back. Says, "Got a nail?" The barman says, "No!" "Good," says the duck, "Got a piece of bread for a hungry duck?" '

Suzie snorted.

'Number five, was it?' Magnus asked.

'Five, yes. Five Coram Cross Road.'

'Yeah, we've arrived. Coming up on the left. There's a bloke with a camera and one or two other people. You all right, Skipper?'

'Not really.'

'It'll be okay. Just do everything by the book, right?'

At least Big Toe had made her read the notes

on the system. Everyone in CID had studied 'The System Relating to a Murder Investigation'. Harvey had put it together from three separate papers written by senior officers of the Met.

They were large detached Victorian houses in the kind of street that stank of nice middle-class respectability. Suzie reckoned they would have four bedrooms, drawing room, dining room, study, kitchen, bathroom and a nice, well stocked, mature garden. Bigger than your average semi, but still built close together. The people who had done them in the 1870s obviously wanted to cram as many into the space as they possibly could.

Now, in late 1940, Coram Cross Road balanced itself between being middle-class and upper professional, with St Leonard's Parish Church at the far end: dark and sooty with a spire fingering its way to God.

'Don't pull into the drive,' Suzie told Magnus, thinking they might need to look for tyre tracks or footprints if it *was* murder. The little cluster of people by the gate was being kept back by one uniform. The other uniform stayed by the door of the house.

Magnus parked the Wolseley in the street, close to the kerb and they both got out while the knot of people stood and gaped.

'Who's she?' someone asked.

'Stand back. Let the officer through,' said the uniform, and Sergeant Mountford walked – a little slowly Magnus thought – towards the house.

The other uniform was by the little gabled porch in front of the door. Of course there was no light in the porch but just enough moon for Suzie to make her way up the sedate path, past the cold flowerbeds and a couple of scabrous, spidery trees. She recognized Sergeant Eric Osterley's tall, stooped figure by the door. Because of the stoop, his angular face and the large spectacles they called him 'the Prof'. She had worked a theft with 'the Prof' just after she arrived at Camford Street. 'Hello, Prof,' she said raising her eyebrows to make it a question. Her body language said, 'What's it like inside?' Then she said it aloud.

He gave a little shudder. 'Not for the faint-hearted. Very unpleasant, Sue.' In his head he was saying, Christ what's Sanders thinking about letting Suzie loose on this? Aloud he told her to take care. 'There're a lot of fluids about in there.'

'You got the shout at the nick?' she asked.

'I was in the area car. A civilian phoned in. Friend of the deceased – Winnie Tovey's with her. In number three. Next door.'

'WDC Cox?' she asked.

'Inside with DC Richards. I sent Winnie next door.'

'Right.' Winnie Tovey? She searched her memory. Tovey? Was that the little blonde WPC? A bit common? Dumpy? She thought so. Certain of it. Nodded to herself.

'Okay.' She shrugged and called out for Magnus to join her.

Magnus had the murder kit: the black leather

99

case holding portable fingerprint equipment, tweezers, cellophane evidence bags, rubber gloves, knives, glass cutter, steel pull-out measure, magnifying lenses and the other essentials of on-the-spot evidence-collecting gear. At the Yard she'd heard it referred to as the John Bull Printing Outfit, after the child's toy.

As Magnus was getting it out of the car someone again asked, 'Who is she?'

'WDS Mountford.' It took him off guard, then he thought, Oh bugger it – doesn't matter.

'Know how old?' The press were obsessed by age.

'Twenty-two, twenty-three, but I didn't tell you that.'

As Magnus came up the path, the police surgeon's car pulled up short of the drive and the doctor got out, nodding curtly towards Suzie: an older man; the one she had seen with the ambulance down the Cut the other Friday night. Dr Jimmy Blatty, Shirley Cox had told her later – stocky, leathery, thickly Scottish, a no-nonsense man with a brittle manner and little sense of humour. That was all she knew about him except that under normal circumstances he'd be retired by now.

He's over the hill and doesn't approve of me being here, she told herself. Well, he's in good company because I don't approve of myself being here either.

'Let's do it,' she looked Magnus in the eyes, square.

'By the book,' he said again. 'By the system, Skip. It'll be fine.'

'Absolutely.' She swallowed and they went inside.

To the horror.

You could smell it as you came through the door, the heavy abattoir reek of gore, the electric and metallic stink, thick as pig shit along the passage which ran to the left of a wide staircase into the large kitchen. Dominating the hall was a tree, half decorated and with a scattering of tinsel and little candles in tin holders, the Ghost of Christmas-Never-To-Come scattered about. Green crêpe paper round the base of the tree.

Love the carpet, Suzie thought. Really like that blue. Light blue, darker than the Cambridge blue, but a lovely bright colour that worked down the stairs and across the broad stretch of hallway. On the stairs it was secured by shining brass rods, and the wooden border was stained dark and shiny: neat and clean as a new pin.

'Oh, Christ!' She was on it before she realized and it sucked the guts out of her, made her head spin. She opened her mouth and thought she'd vomit. As Osterley had advised, there were a lot of fluids.

Pip Magnus' hand dropped on to her forearm, but she roughly shook him off. Whatever else she was not squeamish. Not after the Cut. It was one of the few things she was proud of, being able to stand unflinching at a really bloody crime scene, even though she found this particular body very hard, from the skewered eyes to the wired throat and right down to the detestation: the bloody mess between her spread thighs.

Even when she turned her head away, she still had a clear picture imprinted on her mind's retina. The revolting thing was that you felt you knew the girl. She put that down to seeing her photograph in last week's *Radio Times*, and knowing her reputation: the story they all knew.

'Tomorrow it's going to be the start of a very cold snap. Winter drawers on.' And she knew what she had said. Signalled it with a small smirk in her voice. That's the winter drawers girl, Suzie Mountford thought. Wonder the BBC didn't give her the push like they'd done to that naval commander who was drunk describing, 'The Fleet'sh lit up; everything'sh lit up.' Now what's her name? Benton. Jo Benton. Jo Benton's dead.

Metal meat skewers plunged into the dead jelly of her eyes, the face disfigured into a new dimension by the skewers sticking out and the rictus of death, the tongue over the drawn-back lips, showing her teeth. Then the terrible swelling around the neck. Last, the first thing the eye was drawn to, the bloody entrails and mess between her thighs. The belly ripped open with one deep upward slash. And above, the hair unblotched by blood, still a full cap of thick gold. Close up it looked as if it had needed some help from a bottle.

The doctor had come in behind her, fumbled with his bag, dropped it but was now kneeling, taking a good look before he spoke, clipped, matter-of-fact. 'I'm pretty certain the eyes and the other thing are post mortem.'

'What—?' Suzie began.

'She's been strangled with a piece of wire,' he said, trying to make it sound as though this was something he encountered every day. 'Looks like piano wire. About two and a half feet long; maybe three feet; ends wrapped with insulating tape. Penetrated the flesh in a few places and smashed the windpipe. Not the nicest way to go. I'd say she probably tried to fight back but gave up pretty quickly. I'll tell you what pictures we'll want and then I'll take samples *in situ* and others when appropriate.'

Suzie saw Shirley hovering with the camera, and not looking at all shaken by the revolting mess that had been Jo Benton only an hour or so ago. Behind her, Suzie heard movement, turned and saw the ambulance men with their stretcher. She lifted a hand, indicating they should wait. 'Go through it with a fine-tooth comb...' She glanced back and saw Sammy Richards looking haggard, face like parchment. 'Go through it, and then go through it again. I want it really sorted with the Home Office people, the people at Hendon, by the morning. Will he not be coming, the Home Office—?'

'Home Office Pathologist?' Blatty looked up at her, hard and irritated. 'The senior pathologist has enough to do. I'm going to remove the body when I've got all the pictures and samples we need. Maybe he'll be over for the post-mortem; maybe not. It really doesn't matter.'

'I hope so. I hope he will.' She hadn't pleased

the doctor. She could see it and somehow didn't care; didn't really like Doctor Blatty, moving past him going to the door into the kitchen.

'Why's it so damp in here?' she snapped, seeing condensation on the kitchen windows and the opaque panel in the kitchen door. The wall also had a coating of condensation.

'There was a pan of water boiling its head off in the kitchen when we arrived, Skip.' Sammy retreated from her, backing into the kitchen.

'What did you do with it?'

'Turned the gas off and—'

'Make sure you check that pan for prints, and put the whole thing in your report.' Something had clicked on like a light bulb in her brain. She glared around and realized that the bad day stuff seemed to be leaving her.

'We think he just walked in. This door was open.' Sammy pointed to the door that led straight into the kitchen from the side of the house. 'People don't lock their back doors as they should.'

Suzie thought, no. No, they don't. It's near enough the same as she remembered it from the file she'd seen. She'd ring Rex Fulbright in CRO and get him to look. It was round the end of the summer: August, September time. Cambridge, she thought. Somewhere up there. She'd ring him tomorrow, Rex. She could call him Rex now: sergeant to sergeant.

Magnus was behind her in the kitchen doorway. She dropped her voice and told him, 'We'll go and see the witness who found her then come back here and look upstairs.' As they passed the doctor she said something about getting samples from under the victim's nails and seeing they got to Hendon with the other things. The Forensic Laboratory was at Hendon.

Then she again said something about the Professor – the Home Office Pathologist. 'Young woman,' the doctor almost snarled trying to stay dignified, 'you're obviously unaware that I'm an accredited Home Office pathologist. We don't *need* the Professor. I know my job.'

'Sorry, Doctor.' She felt an idiot. 'I'm very sorry.' Then, 'Can you give me a time of death?'

'Not very long ago.' His tone was still disapproving. 'I'd say between six and half-past. Six forty-five at the latest.'

As they got to the door she said to Magnus, 'What price your bloody duck now.'

'Doc Blatty's very good, Skip.'

'No doubt. Why didn't you tell me?'

'Thought you knew. Why rattle on about the Home Office? He plays golf, belongs to the same club as Sanders of the River. Used to be head of the Path Lab at St Mary Mother's.'

'I really don't care if he plays cricket with Donald Bradman. I know we're stretched and doctors are scarce, but I'm not mad about him.'

'Don't think he's got much of a crush on *you* either, Skip.'

'No. Well.' She remembered Sanders of the

River's caveat. Suspicious death, he'd called it. 'Does that look like a suspicious death to you, Pip?'

'Looks like murder to me, Skip.'

'Very little doubt about it is there?'

'No doubt at all.'

'Then we need good forensic stuff and I don't get the impression that old man Blatty's all that good. Looks slow and plodding to me.'

'Skip, we're not going to—'

She shushed him sharply. 'A tough old copper once told me that detection is ninety per cent keeping your ear to the ground and ten per cent having ideas.'

'So?'

'So I just had an idea, right?' She hoped she *was* right; prayed that she had remembered correctly: a young girl, thirteen or fourteen, choked with a piece of piano wire in a Cambridgeshire village; a pan of water boiling on the kitchen hob and access through an open back door. The kid had just come home from school on her bicycle. She thought it was the end of August; what if it was last year though, or even the year before?

'Right, Skip.'

Outside someone stuck a camera in her face and a flash bulb plopped. There were four reporters and a couple of photographers.

'Damn!' she said. 'No!' she said, and, 'Pip...?' hoping he would do what you saw at the pictures, up the Odeon: whip the camera away and break out the film. But Magnus just hustled her through, pushing the reporters off

106

the path and on to the meagre little garden with its winter flowerless cherries and the hard empty beds.

'The Prof' – Sergeant Osterley – started to ease her through the little throng. 'Was going to warn you,' he muttered, and Magnus now moved in front of Suzie as though he planned to guard her with his life.

'You *have* made sure there's nobody else in there?' she inclined her head back towards Number Five.

'Of course. We went into every room.' He was breathing hard. Not used to the exertion.

'You moved nothing?'

' 'Course not. Didn't touch a thing.'

'What time did you get here?'

'Just after seven. The call to the nick was six fifty-seven.'

'You must've just missed him.'

'Who?'

'The bloke who did it. The quack said she was killed between six and six-thirty. Not later than six forty-five.'

'Bloody hell.'

'Not now. Later,' Magnus said to one of the newsmen.

Then the reporter slipped through to block Suzie's way, his long raincoat flapping around his legs. Muffler flying. It was a navy blue raincoat, like the ones she had worn at school, only hers had been dark green. He had probably worn the navy blue coat at school himself a couple of years ago.

'There's a rumour that the owner of this

107

property has died. If so, she's a colleague of ours: a radio journalist. Please tell us.' He wound his scarf about one more time. Later they would tell her his name was Meadows from the *Camford Herald*. In the nick they called him 'the Daring Young Man on the Flying Trapeze'. Chris Meadows was his name and he was out to earn himself a bit of lineage from the nationals.

Suzie Mountford faltered, stopped, then spoke quietly, 'There has been a death at this house. It *is* suspicious. The person has yet to be identified.'

'Not now,' Magnus muttered again. 'There'll be a statement later.'

'That's all,' she said and they jostled closer again. They wanted her name and rank. Was she in charge? Was the dead person a woman? What killed her?

'That's it,' Magnus said louder and, with his hand on the small of her back while Sergeant Osterley became the outfielder, they murmured and elbowed a pathway through.

She moved forward, turning, sideways, using her shoulder to get through the knot of people, thinking, 'O Jesus, I'll be in the papers tomorrow. Mum and the Major will see it and they'll be on the telephone in no time.' The Major didn't hold with getting in the papers. He thought it was vulgar.

At Number Three Winnie Tovey had a quiet sparkle about her and was totally in command. 'I got her mum to send for the doctor,' she said as if to explain the trembling, sheet-faced, quaking young woman slumped in an easy chair close to the fire, surrounded by cosiness. There were incongruous chocolate-box pictures on the walls, a tinted mirror big over the fireplace, chirpy chintz covers on the easy chairs and a little sofa, the antithesis of the house next door, the death house.

'You've had a terrible shock.' Suzie reached out and touched the young woman's shoulder.

'Doctor's given her something to quieten her down.' Tovey looked at her, one eyebrow raised. The subtext was clear. Don't expect too much from her. Suzie had been right, Winnie Tovey was a bit common.

'I'm WDS Mountford,' Suzie began.

'Woman Detective Sergeant,' the constable translated. Then, 'Sally.' Tovey had a husky voice: like the film star Jean Arthur. 'Sally Grigson.'

It was an introduction.

'Right, how are you, Sally?'

The girl gave a long, tremulous sigh.

Suzie had seen the policewoman leaving the nick yesterday wearing a long and stylish wine red coat with enormous lapels and a lot of brass. Tovey tried to be modish even in uniform, but it didn't quite work. Suzie wished she could have afforded the coat. Boyfriend? she wondered, or is she from a well-off family? Now, Suzie could have carried that coat. It needed her height. All it did for Tovey was swamp her.

'Sally, I'm sorry to bother you but I have to ask a couple of questions.'

The girl nodded, raising her head. She had lank dark hair and her eyes were large, round and, at this moment, teary. Sally was thin, insubstantial as the proverbial wraith. Looked eighteen or so, but Suzie never trusted her own assessment of people's ages.

'I'm sorry,' Suzie repeated. 'You found her, yes?'

Sally Grigson gave a long shuddering nod, then shook her head, once, then again and then twenty seconds of continued shaking. 'Horrible,' she croaked. 'Oh God, horrible.' Her hand lifted from her knee. It was trembling violently.

'It was Jo Benton wasn't it?' Suzie prodded.

'Jo, yes, Jo.'

'Definitely?'

'Jo, yes.' She raised her head. 'It was Jo.' Tears again and the juddering.

'Sally, how did you get into the house?'

An older woman had come into the room and seemed about to say something, but Suzie looked up and gave a tiny shake of her head. Just looking at the two women she knew the older one was Sally's mother, she had the same straight nose, lankish hair, the large pools of eyes and the flimsy frame. Looked so thin that she might break like a stick.

'She was coming round here for a meal. Looking forward to it. We were going to listen to *Happidrome*, then probably go out if Steven came round. I went over at half-past six and couldn't get a reply. I came back here and after a while I rang her. She didn't answer. I knew

110

she was home. So...' She gave another shudder, a sob. 'So I went to the back door. The kitchen door. She often leaves it open. It was. I went in and...'

'That's enough, isn't it?' Sally's mother said with a catch in her voice. Then she came forward, wrapped her arms around the girl and held her, rocking, crooning to her.

'I'm sorry—' Suzie tried to sound firm and resolved. 'I'm sorry but there are things that have to be done, things that have to be said. It may sound harsh but we must move quickly. This is a murder, Mrs—'

'Grigson,' Tovey supplied.

'Grigson,' Suzie repeated. Then, switching back to Sally, 'You saw nobody?'

Shake of the head.

Suzie thought, I've missed something here. She said something I didn't understand. Now it's gone. Damn.

'I'll have to ask someone to come over and take your fingerprints. They'll be dusting that back door and inside. Could there have been someone else in the house when you found her?'

Another shake of the head. 'I don't know ... I really don't ... It was ... it was...'

'Horrible. A shock. I know, Sally. Leave you alone in a minute. Did she have a boyfriend, Jo?'

The eyes opened wide and brimming. 'Of course. Steve. Steven Fermin.'

'The announcer?' That was it: Sally had said the name, Steve.

'Oh, poor Steve, yes of course.' She gulped air as though coming up from the depths of a pool. 'Of course, Steve. They're engaged ... getting married ... Oh God ... Christmas ... I was going to be her...' Her eyelids were drooping and her mouth went slack. The medicine was kicking in.

Magnus touched Suzie's arm. 'Let her sleep, Skipper.'

She nodded and went into the hall with the elder Grigson. 'I'm so sorry about this, Mrs Grigson. I wouldn't do this unless it was absolutely necessary. Can you tell me anything about the victim? About Jo Benton?'

'I can't believe it.' Sally's mother looked strained. Her eyes had crow's feet, deeply etched, and the forehead was lined, which gave her the look of a woman living in constant concern. 'She's so nice, Jo. Full of life and devilment. Always laughing, I should get to Steve, tell him quickly, you don't want him hearing it on the what's-its-name ... thing.'

'Bush telegraph...?'

'Grapevine, yes. They're, were, so attached. In love. It's... it's...' She gave up the struggle and sobbed as though her entire world had come to an end. In her head Suzie heard Judy Garland singing 'Over the rainbow', and she struggled not to cry also. No, she told herself, severely. No, a police officer doesn't cry at death.

Outside she told Magnus that she was going to track down Steven Fermin. 'I'll get him through the BBC.'

Fermin had a weekly interview show – *Fermin*

and Friends – for the BBC; very popular, a kind of mid-week *In Town Tonight* which went out on a Saturday before *Palace of Varieties*. She often listened to it. *Fermin and Friends* was broadcast on Wednesday evenings.

'What do you know about Fermin?' Suzie asked as they ran the gauntlet back to Jo Benton's house next door.

'Same as you. Listen to *Fermin and Friends* when I can. I listen to the news, *In Town Tonight*, *The Brains Trust* and *Fermin*. It's about all I do listen to. Sometimes a play when I'm in, oh and Henry Hall of course.' Henry Hall was leader of the BBC Dance Orchestra. Dance music was the rage and orchestras even topped the bill at variety shows – Roy Fox, Maurice Winnick, Harry Roy, Billy Cotton.

'Did you know about the girl and Fermin?' Suzie asked, teeth gritted.

'There was something about it in the paper. A little piece in the *Evening News*, I think.'

'I didn't see it.'

'You probably don't read the right papers, Skip.'

'True.'

They reached the shelter of the porch and Sergeant Osterley said they were almost ready to take the body out.

'Not while the press is here.' Suzie scowled.

'What else d'you suggest, Skip?' Magnus asked when they were inside.

'Well not until I've made sure the boyfriend's been told. And her parents, of course. Oh lord, her parents.'

113

Inside, the ambulance men stood by the kitchen door blocking the view with their stretcher. The doctor was still there, and Shirley was very active with the camera, the flash lighting up the kitchen.

'Okay.' Suzie made for the stairs. 'Let's try and find an address book and stuff.'

They were only halfway up when the front door opened below them and 'Sarn't Mountford,' Osterley shouted, 'a word please.' There was urgency in the call, and she turned and started back into the hall.

Osterley blocked the doorway with his drooping shoulders against door and jamb, left hand on the brass knob as though trying to hold back a wall of pressure. Outside, through the space of the open door a flashbulb exploded and, as Suzie reached the uniformed sergeant, so he was pushed forward into the hall. The constable was behind him talking, 'Sir, you can't go in there. Please sir...'

Suzie raised her voice, 'What's going on? What is it?' and the uniforms gave way, allowing a third person to butt into the hall. Highly glossed dark brown shoes, cavalry-twill tailored slacks, a houndstooth-checked jacket, green-flecked on dark grey, a rollneck sweater.

He was a shortish man with a flop of dark hair, longer than fashionable, pale-faced in the hall light. 'Are you police?' he asked. 'What're you doing here? Is it true?' The questions boiling out of him.

And she recognized the voice. 'Steven Fermin?'

'Yes, I'm Fermin.'

'Is *what* true, sir?' Suzie asked.

He made a useless gesture with his arms.

'Is what true?' she asked again.

'Jo? Jo Benton? They say she's dead.'

Osterley stepped forward, touched his arm, trying to make up for allowing him to slip through and into the house. 'Sir, I think you—'

Fermin's head came up, eyes widened. Suzie Mountford saw what had happened. He had smelled the scent of blood and death. His eyes opened wide and a little choke came from the back of his throat as he lunged forward, gagging.

'No!' Magnus shouted and, to her surprise, Suzie slapped a hand around Fermin's wrist and brought her weight forward and then back, the other hand coming up so his feet stuttered backwards, then stopped off-balance.

'No, sir!' she barked, surprising herself. She swung in front of him, close. 'Mr Fermin, I can't let you...'

His face crumpled and he took a deep breath. 'I'm sorry. Of course—' he couldn't look her in the eye. 'I don't know what – I'm so sorry.'

Magnus was already helping her as they shepherded the man into the big living room to their right. The uniformed constable slipped past her and quickly drew the curtains.

Fermin took a pace towards a settee and Suzie put out a hand and pulled him back. 'We can't sit down. I'm sorry, we shouldn't even be in here until my people've examined—'

He turned, 'I thought...'

'The forensic people've got to go over it. In fact, Mr Fermin, I'd really prefer it if you went back to the station where we can talk, and I suppose I might need you to identify the victim later if you feel up to it. Pip?' She turned to Magnus, 'Pip, can you call up another car?'

'No, I've got my own car.' Fermin turned away from her. 'I've got my own car here. I'll drive myself to the station. I'm allowed petrol.' He seemed to need to explain how he was able to drive from the West End to Camford. He raised his hand, brushing the side of his face and she saw the nervous tic in his right eye and the way his hand trembled.

'Camford Hill,' she said. 'Camford Hill Police Station. You know where...?'

'Yes, of course. Can I park there?'

'Yes, look, I'll get someone.' She turned to Osterley. 'Get Winnie Tovey over here. Send her with Mr Fermin.'

Osterley nodded and disappeared while Suzie went on explaining unnecessarily.

'Go round the back: down Lockup Alley; we'll follow you. Ten minutes or so. I'm obliged, sir.'

He brushed away an imaginary piece of lint from the sleeve of his jacket. 'It's better for me to be with someone.'

WPC Tovey appeared in the doorway.

Suzie nodded. 'Look after Mr Fermin,' she said to Tovey. 'You know who he is?'

'Oh yes, Sergeant.'

'I'd be grateful if you didn't speak to the

press,' she said to him.

Fermin gave a thin smile. 'I'm one of them really, I suppose.' He bit his lip, looked Suzie in the eye, nodded and left. There was a burble of talking as soon as he got out of the main door.

Suzie had glimpsed the pain in his eyes, was excessively upset by it and could not understand why because she hadn't really taken to Steve Firmin.

Seven

There were letters, an appointments diary and a small notebook, all thrown higgledy-piggledy into a drawer in Jo Benton's bedside table. The victim had been reading *Gone with the Wind*. It was lying on the bed, and she'd got to page 208: she had marked it with a postcard from Canterbury showing a picture of the west elevation of the cathedral. On the reverse side there was the current address – Miss Josephine Benton, 5 Coram Cross Rd, Camford Hill, London; and a scribbled note about how wonderful the cathedral was and what a calming effect it had on Aunt Beatie.

Suzie did a quick search of the other drawers in the room and found nothing immediately interesting. A heavy nineteenth century wardrobe with three doors and inlaid mirrors took up almost an entire wall. She opened the doors. Suits, skirts and frocks hung in neat rows, almost filed by colour. She trailed the back of a hand along them, as a child would run her hand along railings. Her right hand went up separating a dress, lifting it out on its hanger. A nursing sister's uniform. Was Benton doing part-time nursing?

Downstairs again, she riffled through the two drawers in a little mahogany Victorian desk with red and gold skivers. In one she found an address book. In the hall she saw a green patent leather handbag lying as though thrown from the kitchen.

'You been through this?' she called to Sammy and Shirley who were still talking quietly in the kitchen, working with fingerprint powder.

'Haven't looked yet,' Shirley was harassed.

'I'm searching for address books, diaries, things like that.'

'Take a look, but be careful, Skip.'

She used a silver propelling pencil, a birthday present from Charlotte, to pry open the bag and then push things aside to see what lay at the bottom of the usual handbag clutter. Between a driving licence, identity card and some letters, she detected the flat grey shape of a Letts page-a-day diary/address book that she fished out using the first and second fingers of her right hand. Sammy Richards dusted it and there were no clear prints so she logged it together with the other items and took them all back to Camford Hill nick.

Pip Magnus had used the house telephone to make sure Fermin had somewhere to park when he got to the nick. His car was at the back and they'd put him in one of the interview rooms down in the basement.

At her desk in the CID office Suzie opened a murder book, just as Sanders of the River had told her to do. She used a bound ledger that the super had given her, writing the date and the victim's name – Josephine Marian Benton – on the first page taking the name from the diary that was in Jo Benton's handbag. She listed her own name together with WDC Cox, then Magnus and Richards. She gave cause of death as choked with wire, and left a space for the more detailed descriptions of the mutilation when Dr Blatty's PM report came in.

Then she telephoned DCS Tommy Livermore at the Yard. It was almost half-past nine and he'd long left for the day but they said he could be reached at a Flaxman number so she got through to the exchange and a couple of minutes later was speaking to Livermore, who sounded quietly avuncular.

'Yes, Sergeant Mountford,' he began. 'I spoke with Mr Sanders. Don't say you want me to come traipsing over to Camford Hill at this hour.' He didn't sound like a man who'd want to take the mickey out of her like most of the senior officers in the Met.

'No sir, I'm managing.'

'Glad to hear it. What've we got?'

'Nasty, sir. Josephine Benton the BBC announcer—'

'The winter-drawers-on girl?' They all knew her because of that. It was like a schoolboy sniggery thing in this middle-class world of

119

comparative innocence.

'That's the one, sir. Dr Blatty's doing the forensics to send to Hendon. PM in the morning.'

'You done one before, Mountford?'

'No, sir.'

'Well it's not obligatory if you don't feel up to it. You say it's nasty?'

'Strangulation – more choked really – with piano wire, cut into the flesh of her throat. Then mutilated.'

'How mutilated?'

'Meat skewers in her eyes, then the stomach ripped open: low down; genitalia ripped up really. Reminded me of the old Jack the Ripper details.'

'Unpleasant.' He sounded a little shocked for a hardened older officer. 'Any ideas?'

'I've got the boyfriend here, sir. Going to talk to him. Steven Fermin.'

'The radio bloke, Fermin?'

'Yes. He's probably well out of the frame, Guv, but—'

'Don't say that till you've talked to him. Ninety-nine per cent of murders are committed by close friends, relatives, husbands, wives. Handle him gently. Not too friendly, and don't give him the full strength. Got a time of death?'

'Dr Blatty says between six and half-past, and not after six forty-five.'

'Well he should know. Good man, Blatty.'

Oh hell, Suzie thought.

'Where're you going after the boyfriend?'

'Got some address books and diaries. I

thought I'd look through them. There is one thing though, Guv.'

'What?'

'Pan of boiling water. There was a pan of boiling water on the gas hob in the kitchen. Unexplained. She wasn't cooking anything.'

'Ah. Then you might have a robbery gone bad. It's an old thief's trick that: put a pan of water on the hob as soon as you get into the property, then you have a nasty weapon you can use if you're disturbed. Was there a definite break-in?'

'We think he used the back door – leads straight into the kitchen.'

'It could still be a robbery buggered up.' There was a silence and she could hear him at the distant end. Sucking on a pipe, she thought. Don't tell him. Not yet, even though she was certain this wasn't a disturbed thief because of what she had remembered.

'Right, anything else, Sergeant Mountford?'

'Not yet, Guv'nor. I'm going to talk to the boyfriend now.'

'Well, be one of Fermin's friends, eh?' he chuckled. 'Telephone me any time. Anything you want, ring me. If I'm not in my office there's a WPC who does the secretarial stuff. She'll usually answer the phone, WPC Abrahams, Terri Abrahams – with an i, got it? Good girl, Terri. She'll usually know where I am. And listen – be orderly; take it one step at a time. You've opened a murder book?'

'Yes, Guv.'

'Keep it current. Note everything, even when

you change your socks. Okay?'

'Right, Guv.'

'I'm going to have my supper now then. Ring me tomorrow. What they call you, Sarn't Mountford?'

'Suzie, sir. Susannah, but they call me Suzie. With a zed, sir.' She grinned.

'Right, Suzie with a zed. Happy dreams.'

And you, Guv, she thought.

Magnus was having a quick cigarette outside the interview room when she got down to him.

'Chummy doesn't smoke?' she asked.

'Like a chimney, I'm just taking a break. Okay?'

'How is he?' she nodded at the door.

'Winnie Tovey had a hard time getting him here. He suddenly broke down on her. In the middle of the High Street. Just started crying and leaning on her shoulder. His car, still in gear, stopped dead in the road.'

'I should imagine she coped, Winnie Tovey. Looks like a girl who can cope.' She thought of Winnie in that expensive and showy wine red coat. Wondered where she'd bought it. Suzie had put on her hard exterior. She knew well enough about grief and the ways it could take people. The night after her father died she had heard noises downstairs, at two in the morning. Her mum was cleaning and cooking a three-course dinner. 'I needed something to do,' her mother had said.

'How do you rate him?' she now asked.

'He's either the best actor in the world, nerves of steel, or totally innocent and just starting to realize what's happened. The last two get my vote.'

They got Suzie's vote as well. Where before she had seen pain in his eyes, Fermin now looked as though someone had punched him full in the face so that instead of the confident young broadcaster he was bewildered; dazed and baffled by what had happened.

'You know I've got to make this official?' Suzie began.

'Official?' Steven Fermin asked uncomprehendingly.

'I have to interview you, so it may as well be now. Is there anything you want? More tea—?'

He shook his head. 'Mind if I smoke?' He patted his pockets and brought out a packet of Players. The familiar slim cardboard packs had gone in November: the new ones were made of light blue paper. Insubstantial. They crushed easily. There were already signs that cigarettes were going to be in short supply.

'Could you give me one?' Suzie smiled at him. 'I've left mine on my desk.'

'Want me to get them, Skip?' Magnus moved.

'Later. Leave it now, thank you.' Fermin leaned over and lit the cigarette for her. Swan Vestas matches. The smokers' match: little, thin waxed sticks; different. Magnus waved away his offer of another cigarette.

'You said I had to do the ... the identification.' Fermin drew on his cigarette, inhaling deeply, then letting the smoke trickle out of his mouth.

'Later. No. No, it may not be necessary.'

123

Pause; swallow; a short puff on the cigarette. 'I'm sorry, Mr Fermin, but we're ninety-nine per cent certain, I'm afraid.'

'Sergeant, please.' He looked up at her. Spaniel eyes. 'Please will you tell me what's happened. I know Jo's dead, but...'

He's desperate. Be careful, she heard Livermore's friendly voice in her head. *Don't give him the full strength.*

She took another draw at the cigarette. 'No, sir. No, Mr Fermin. No we haven't told you everything, and that's because we haven't got the whole picture ourselves. From what you saw in that house, sir. From what you saw ... Well, was that Miss Benton?'

He nodded. 'Yes.' Hardly audible.

'Okay, we think someone got into the house and was in the process of a robbery when Miss Benton disturbed him. Mr Fermin, did she, did Miss Benton, ever leave her back door open?'

'The one into the kitchen?'

'Yes. The one round the side of the house.'

He shook his head again as though trying to rid his brain of thick cobwebs. 'I can't believe...'

'I know, sir.' Pause again; drag on the cigarette. 'Miss Grigson has more or less con-firmed—'

'Jo was going to have a meal with Sally, tonight. Jo's like an elder sister to her.' He stopped, suddenly coming up against the brick wall of the past tense. '*Was* like an elder sister. We used to take Sally out sometimes. With us, you know; little treats. We'd take her into the

BBC club. She was thrilled to bits when some-one well-known came in. Tommy Handley always used to come over and talk to her.' Handley was the biggest name in radio: the star of ITMA. It's That Man Again.

'You'd met Miss Benton through her work, then? Both of you at the BBC: at Broadcasting House.'

'Yes. Last year after I got the programme.'

'*Fermin and Friends?*'

'*Fermin and Friends.*' He nodded. 'We were introduced—' a momentary little smile – 'she was introduced as "the winter drawers-on girl". She nearly lost her job through that you know. Poor Jo, she had this roguish sense of humour. There are elements within the BBC who have little in the way of humour.' The sad smile again.

'You mean dirty?' Shouldn't have said it. Suzie silently drew in breath through her mouth: couldn't believe she'd been so crass.

'No. No, not dirty. Cheeky, roguish, mis-chievous.' He raised his head looking her straight in the eyes. Then with a tinge of anger, 'No. Not dirty. If you'd known her ... Oh...'

Suzie felt like an animal trapped in head-lights. 'I'm sorry, Mr Fermin. Perhaps you'd tell me about her: about your courtship perhaps.'

It was an ordinary story. A middle-class romance different only because the partici-pants were figures in the world of entertain-ment. Both of them were avidly listened to four or five times a week on the *Home & Forces*

Programme which had taken the place of the *BBC National Programme*. Their voices would be recognized on a bus, or the Tube or by people sitting at the next table in a restaurant. Though people hearing them might find the voices familiar it was possible that they wouldn't actually be able to put names to voices. Rarely would they put names to faces.

They had met because they both worked for the same organization, among the same kind of people. When they were introduced, Steve Fermin had immediately thought – in his own words – 'Hello?' but did nothing about it for a week, and even then when they met again it seemed accidental. They were both guests at a dinner party given by mutual friends: Andy and Valerie Wilson. The same Andy Wilson who directed *Fermin and Friends*. Only later did they see that the Wilsons were match-making.

'I thought I'd been invited to make up numbers,' Fermin said. 'Later we discovered that we'd both been fed the same line-shoot.'

'And when was this?'

'Oh, before the real war started. February – back in the Stone Age.' This was the kind of language Fermin used on his show.

'And you just fell in love?' It didn't sound right, the way she said it. Came out as a sneer. Damn, she thought.

'If it's not too trite or slushy, yes. I invited her to the show – we do it live, you know, almost like a comedy show. In that little theatre next to the Hungaria.'

'In Lower Regent Street?'

'Yes. We had dinner at the Hungaria afterwards. That became a regular thing. We used to eat there or at Choy's in Dean Street, or Gennaros – though Papa Gennaro had been taken away as an alien by then because he's still an Italian citizen. The younger Gennaros carry on, but there's still a lot of ill feeling because of Papa being detained.'

'And you finally proposed?' Again she heard a bit of a sneer in her voice. Why was she doing this? she wondered.

Yes, he had proposed. 'All in the April evening,' he said and tears started at his eyes for the first time.

Glasgow Orpheus Choir, Suzie thought. *All in the April evening*. Her mum loved the record. Then, 'Men are April when they woo,' she remembered. Shakespeare, but she couldn't have told you which play. 'Men are April when they woo, December when they wed.' Had Fermin turned early to December? Had he had a cold snap?

'And you were getting married when?'

'Soon. Quietly. Christmas probably, because I'm joining up in February.'

'And she knew? Miss Benton knew that?'

'Of course. I feel strongly about it. I'm twenty-seven next week.' As though that explained everything. 'I'm going into the Raff. February twenty-second.'

'Is the BBC happy about that?'

'Not really. They could have got me deferred: reserved occupation and all that.'

She looked at him again, examining his face,

expecting to get answers from how he looked. All of eighteen, she considered. Dark, rather craggy looks, the kind of features you expected to find in the face of a rugger player, or the hero of a comic book. Her brother read the *Wizard* and there was a weekly story about Rockfist Rogan of the RAF. Above the two- or three-page tale there was a drawing of Rogan. Fermin could have modelled for it – square jaw, tough, untidy curly tousled hair.

'Your relationship with Miss Benton. Was it still happy? No problems?'

'No problems? What kind of problems? What do you...? You don't think I had anything to do with...? No. No problems. We were as happy as anyone else.' A touch of anger. There was a stiffening of his body, sounding an alert. She saw that his eyes were still moist.

'Lovers are known to quarrel.'

'We weren't lovers, Inspector. Not in the accepted sense. We aren't – weren't – married.'

'It's Sergeant, not Inspector, and it *is* 1940, Mr Fermin. Nowadays you don't have to be married to be lovers.'

'We were waiting.' He turned cold, astringent. She got a sense of him holding back; maybe of hitting a raw nerve. 'We were waiting.' In her head she added, 'We were saving ourselves for each other.'

'You hadn't had a row about that? About sex, or lack of it?'

'Sergeant, I really...' He *was* angry now, and not trying to hide it. Magnus flashed her a look.

'Can you think of anybody who might want to harm Miss Benton, Mr Fermin?' Trying to change the subject.

Hesitation. The anger and emotion quite clear in his eyes and the way his mouth had become a hard little line. 'What d'you mean, hurt her? Hurt Jo? No, nobody.'

'Well, somebody did, sir.' Again, why was she doing this? It was as though she couldn't control herself. Fermin? No, she didn't think for a moment that he had any part in the killing at 5 Coram Cross Road, but there was something there; something she didn't like. 'You said she left that door open. Around the side; the door into the kitchen.'

'All the time. I don't think she ever locked it. She was brought up in the country; her parents never locked any doors; she felt uncomfortable if the place was locked up and she was inside. I warned her that in a city you couldn't live like that.'

'Then anyone could walk in.'

'I suppose so. But who'd want to harm Jo? I mean, why?'

'It's happened, Mr Fermin. Somebody did want to harm her, and they killed her.'

He shook his head as though denying she was dead.

'Who's Aunt Beatie?' she asked, surprising herself.

'Who?'

'Miss Benton's aunt. Aunt Beatie.'

'Oh? Oh?' Frowning, uncomprehending. Then – 'Oh, yes. Her mother's sister – older sister – Beatrice. Much older. She's an invalid. She's ... Oh, her mother and father.' With sudden realization of something left undone. 'Have you...?'

'No.' Suzie felt the jerk at her conscience. Almost a physical thing tugging at her shoulders. Damn! Oh hell! The victim's family.

'It'll be dealt with, Mr Fermin. In the meantime I'd like to know where you were between six and quarter to seven tonight.'

He was in the clear, of course. She should have known better, but what was it Livermore had said? *Ninety-nine percent of murders are committed by close friends or even relatives.*

Fermin had been in a planning meeting until almost half-past six. Walked down to the big swing doors of Broadcasting House with a couple of gag writers and his producer, Andy, who walked with him to his car parked in Wells Street.

Suzie had seized on a possible inconsistency, asking Fermin why he had driven over to Camford when he knew Jo Benton was going to have a meal with the Grigsons.

'On a whim,' he said. 'I often used to go over and see her – even just for ten minutes. People in love do that.'

Of course there was no way he could have got to Camford during the critical period. There were ten respected people who were with him at the meeting, would swear to it. She didn't just take his word but tracked three of them down, hunched over the telephone for twenty minutes, including Andy Wilson: asked all of them the same question, then, 'You'd swear to that? You'd sign a statement to that effect?'

'Of course,' they all said.

'Don't like him, do you, Skip?' Pip Magnus said.

'Does it show *that* much?'

'Got hostile with him pretty quickly.'

'Sorry, I shouldn't ... Yes, Pip, yes, I can't say I like him. Can't tell you why. Can't put my finger on it, but no, I don't like him. Doesn't make him a murderer though.'

Then, quite suddenly it came to her and she knew why. For all his personality on the radio, Steven Fermin was weak and it showed. Whatever her father's faults, Suzie had been brought up to face facts head on, and she did that most of the time – well, except on her fat and ugly days. Fermin, she felt, shied away from the unpleasant facts and it was clear in the way he spoke, the look in his eye, even his choice of words and phrases. She had never really liked his radio show either, she thought. He seemed to be a bit of a prude as well. Suzie thought there was always something false about prudes. Then she seriously started to wonder if she was a prude as well.

Pip had gone back to the canteen with Fermin, to give him more tea and a sandwich – 'Sardine, actually, Skipper. They're quite good an' all. They must've picked up a new batch of tins.'

'I've been on to Farnham nick,' Suzie now told Magnus who had come back to the office to see what she wanted to do next. 'They're

131

going round to the parents' house. A superintendent's going to do it, with a WDS. Break the news.' She pursed her lips, glancing away as though she couldn't look him in the eyes. 'Bloody hell, how do you do that? Break that kind of thing. Where do you start?'

'They're in their sixties, Fermin said. Very proud of Miss Benton, what she's accomplished. So what's next, Skip?'

'Address books. I want to throw names at Fermin.'

'I'll get him,' Magnus bustled out, clumping along the passage.

Suzie started turning the pages of the address book she had found in the mahogany desk: the one in the living room. The living-room carpet was crimson with a great squirling pattern and a decorative border; it was laid square in the room, surrounded by an even perimeter of polished boards. These floorboards were stained to a dark brown gloss. She had lifted a corner of the carpet and seen that it had been laid over old copies of the *Daily Mail*. She had seen a headline about Mr Chamberlain announcing the declaration of war. Last year, she thought. Hasn't had the carpet long. Her head was still crammed with doom and the horror of the woman's death. She remembered a record that Charlotte had listened to – ages ago – 'Ain't it grand to be blooming well dead?' She didn't like it and couldn't understand why her sister listened to it all the time – this was a long time ago when they were kids, when Daddy was still alive.

In the back of her head she heard it again–

Look at the tombstone, granite with knobs on,
Ain't it grand to be blooming well dead?
Look at the parson, in his white nightshirt,
Ain't it grand to be blooming well dead?

Then Shirley came in, back from the crime scene. She looked as though she had been listening to the same ghoulish popular song. Ain't it grand to be blooming well dead.

'Richards is still over there, Skip, and Dougie Catermole's giving him a hand, if that's okay.'

'You had enough?' Suzie asked and she saw the WDC flinch as if she'd been hit.

'Sorry, Skip, but yes. Worst thing I've ever seen. How d'you manage?'

'I don't really.' Long pause. 'Fermin's in the clear.'

'Good,' Shirley nodded. 'How's he taken it?'

'Don't think it's real yet. To him I mean. Unreal. Her parents live near Farnham.'

'Oh.'

'Surrey,' she added unnecessarily.

'Oh?' Shirley repeated.

'They're sending a chief super over.'

'Yes?'

In the back of her head Suzie knew it was happening even as they sat there. Might just as well have had a bomb land right in their front room. Better if it had been a bomb because killed in action was more acceptable these days. None of it was easy, but everyone lived with it now. Lived with it; died with it. Now

Magnus was ushering Fermin in, and Shirley was making a discreet exit. 'See you in the morning, Skipper.'

They sat around her desk and Suzie explained what she would like to do: go through the names in Jo Benton's address book and see how many of them Steve Fermin knew or could pinpoint. She was doing it correctly, she knew. This was by the book, check the circle of friends and acquaintances. And catch the boyfriend now because tomorrow he would be at sixes and sevens. Wouldn't be able to think straight tomorrow; that was her personal assessment.

Some he had never met, only knew of. Some were relatives and people from Jo's previous life. Suzie marked the book with slivers of paper, noting names they should follow up:

'Hetty Pinhorn?'

'Yes, an old school friend. She sees her regularly. Hetty's an actress. She's in a play at the moment, I think. Can't remember, but yes, you should talk to her. Very old, close friend.'

'Norman Weaving?'

'Met him once. Old family friend. A kind of uncle, takes her to lunch occasionally.'

'A kind of uncle?'

'You know, honorary uncle.'

'Older?'

'Oh yes, much older. Late fifties.'

Better take a look, she thought. Older men and lechery, she thought. She had read about that. Had a few uncles herself and knew the way they had looked at her as she became a woman.

From the BBC there were several names – people Jo Benton had seen every day – tagged by Suzie: Andy Wilson who had his eye on Jo Benton's future, had plans for her; Penny Hargreaves, an old chum now in contracts; Michael Dalton from accounts; Richard Webster, her agent – you never thought of announcers having agents. Maybe she should start with him first thing in the morning. Yes, she copied his telephone number into her own book with a notation.

There were people she dealt with in business. People who had easy access to her home. Arthur Dove, the odd job man; Minnie Shotten, who did bits of typing for her; Josh Dance, estate agent. She rented the house from Mr Dance; Daniel Flint, who had an antique shop over in Kensington Church Street. Daniel was a friend and advisor. She was learning a lot about antiques from Daniel: antiques and paintings. Another older man, Barry Forbes, who was the elder brother of a school friend: did something in the city and saw Jo from time to time.

'Yes, I've met him, know who he is now, of course. Now he's popping in and out of Downing Street,' Steve Fermin replied when she threw the usual question at him.

Lord, she thought, he's *that* Barry Forbes. Advisor to the Prime Minister. Advisor to Churchill.

'Yes,' Fermin continued. 'I went over to Coram Cross after work one night and he was there, having a drink with Jo. I was surprised. She'd never mentioned him before. He had a girl friend, a stunner, Emily Baccus, and that was odd—'

'Why odd?'

'Emily is another part of the firm Jo rents the house from.' He was still speaking of her in the present, Suzie thought. It would take time. 'Yes, I suppose they moved in similar circles, property and that, Barry Forbes and Emily Baccus...'

'And the firm was?'

'Jewell, Baccus & Dance.'

'And Forbes? Apart from his advisory capacity, who does he work for?'

'Himself, I think. The City, I gathered. Big-wheel financial advice.'

'And when was this?'

'Oh, just after we got engaged, and I've seen him again since then. Jo had people in for drinks, two, no three months ago. Barry Forbes was there. Knew her very well indeed, they talked about his sister, and he knew Jo's parents.'

Barry Forbes, Emily Baccus – yes there was an address and telephone number – then Gerald Vine.

'Gerald Vine?'

'The actor.'

Of course, she thought, she knew the name. 'Gosh, Gerald Vine's a friend?'

'And Betty Tinsley, Gerald's wife. Don't forget that Jo did two years at the Royal Academy of Dramatic Art before she came to the BBC.

Betty was a contemporary, she's a good deal younger than Gerald.'

Gerald Vine had recently starred in a swash-buckler made out at Pinewood studios. Gerald Vine and Betty Tinsdale both. Suzie had at one time been a shade star-struck and remembered Gerald Vine from his great early success, *Ball at the Palace*, in which he had played a dark, brooding landowner in the Mr Rochester mould.

She also remembered Dorothy Wood, Michael Judge, Harry Henton, Roland Gee, Mavis Truebridge, Leonne Carter and Elizabeth Briggs. The names were in Jo Benton's address book and Suzie could put faces to all of them, huge faces as seen on the silver screen.

'Before RADA where did she go to school, Mr Fermin?'

'Farnham Place in Surrey.'

Suzie knew about Farnham Place because St Helen's had played hockey against them. Farnham Place was one of those schools that girls at St Helen's longed for: an experimental mixed boarding school where, so all the stories went, the pupils ran the discipline and went to the classes *they* chose; where everyone was known by first names. Teachers and pupils.

The members of HM Forces who were in Jo Benton's address book had all been school friends; all the right age: Leading Wren Monica Parker; First Officer Maureen Riseque; Section Officer Polly Smythe; Lieutenant Commander Jock McCormick RN; Captain Martin 'Midge' Fowler MC; and not least Squadron Leader

Fordham O'Dell DFC. Each one, she presumed, had played a significant part in Jo's life. School friends you keep up with usually did, and that night she travelled back to St Martin's Lane with lists of names running through her head. It was like the end of the film *Goodbye Mr Chips*, she thought, where the old man lies dying and the long lines of boys he has taught are superimposed on the image: their voices running on the soundtrack. She laughed because Ned Giffith had called the film *Auvoir M. Pommes Frittes*. She had thought that was very funny.

Now, she could also see the names: long columns of the names, their addresses and telephone numbers running inside her head.

Jerry wasn't over tonight. He was bombing Liverpool with the lights of the Republic of Ireland pointing the way, and markers set up by patriotic Welsh Nationalists on the Pembrokeshire coast – though that didn't get into the papers at the time.

Suzie walked, lonely, back from Leicester Square tube station without any contact with humanity except for a warden who told her to watch it with her torch. Bloody little Hitler.

It was a crisp night with more than a hint of frost there among the buildings, the pavements glittering like diamonds from the compound they used, and the music in Suzie's head straight from her teens – 'He dances overhead/On the ceiling near my head/In my sight, through the night.' She had seen the film – *Evergreen* – with a bunch of school friends on a

Saturday afternoon, back in the early '30s. Jessie Matthews was the star and Suzie had longed to be just like her: an all-singing, all-dancing beauty full of confidence, drawing men to her like the proverbial flies to a honey-pot.

She got into the flat just before midnight and the telephone was ringing.

Eight

It was Suzie's sister, Charlotte. She had been ringing every fifteen minutes since ten o'clock and she was concerned. She had even rung Camford nick, then lost her nerve and said it was a wrong number when she got through. 'It's the number you asked for,' the operator told her accusingly.

'You okay, Suzie?' There was worry in her voice. 'I thought something had happened to you.' They knew each other inside out; not only did they look like twins, but also they could read each other's minds, think each other's thoughts.

'Charles. Yes, I'm fine and no, nothing's happened to me. It happened to somebody else.' She told her sister about the murder, the victim and her part in the inquiry.

'What, the winter-drawers-on girl?' Charlotte squeaked, proving that it was not just men who remembered Jo Benton for her one tiny lapse of taste. 'How? How was she killed?'

'I promise, Charlotte, you really don't want to know. Change the subject – how's Vernon?'

'That's one of the reasons I've been ringing you. I had a letter this morning. He's not going to be home for Christmas like he thought.'

'Oh, Charles.'

Vernon was just completing the recruit training at the Royal Marine Depot at Deal. He had been coming home on leave for Christmas, before going to the pre-Officer Cadet Training Unit (Pre-OCTU), at Exton, in the New Year.

Marines from up North and from Scotland were getting the New Year leave not Christmas, Charlotte told her, 'Then they suddenly needed an extra two marines to cover guard duties over Christmas and they drew straws for it.'

'And Vernon lost?'

'He's pretty chocker about it, but there's nothing he can do, and now I'm getting pressurized by Mum. She wants me to go to Newbury for the whole holiday and I really can't face the bloody Galloping Major with the kids. Lucy would be okay but it upsets Ben to be away from home. He needs routine and familiar things, he finds it very difficult at grandma's. The Galloping bloody Major doesn't help either, treats him like a mentally defective.'

'I know. I've seen it.'

Ben would be five on his next birthday, their firstborn, a cerebral palsy case who was profoundly and incurably deaf; therefore couldn't speak and had his legs twisted, so that he could not walk. As so often with such cases, Ben was alert for a lot of the time and picked up some skills quite quickly, but he needed constant care and could do very little for himself, locked as he was into his own private world. His big problem was that he could not communicate.

But he showed emotions: tears, misery, unhappiness and pleasure. He expressed delight and happiness by rapidly jerking his arms about – sometimes an involuntary action – and making little hooting and tooting cries as he flapped his hands, something that gave him great joy. He could colour things with crayons and he was also showing skill at doing jigsaws. Suzie would sometimes weep at the thought that this lovely little boy was unlikely ever to talk or have any real understanding of the life so close around him.

'Anyway,' Charlotte said, 'I wondered what you were doing. For Christmas, I mean.'

'Don't know if I'm going to get any time off.' Then she began to sing quietly, 'Bumpety-bumpety-bumpety-bump...'

And Charlotte joined in, 'Here comes the Galloping Major.'

So they both had a short laughing fit.

Christmas had once been the most joyous day of the year for the girls. When Daddy was alive he seemed to be the very spirit of Christmas, infusing everyone around him with the delights of the season. Even now, in her early twenties, Suzie experienced a thrill of anticipated pleasure and excitement as she lay in bed on Christmas Eve. Until now that is, she reminded herself.

'If I do get some leave I'll have the same kind of pressure from Mum. She'll want both of us in Newbury.'

'And you'd want to be there?'

'I'd like to see Mum, of course, but the bloody Major, well, he's not your Ghost of Christmas Past or Present, is he? I can really live without him banging on about Christmases when he was a boy, and yule-tide on the Western Front – in the trenches – and what unrelieved hell it's going to be when Hitler finally invades.' The Galloping Major had been sunk in gloom ever since Dunkirk, talking himself into believing that it was the end for Britain and the Empire.

'Well, I thought you could probably explain my situation to Mum better than I can do it myself.' There was a long pause at Charlotte's end. Then – 'Listen, Suzie, if you do get time off, could you come down here? That's what I'd really like: a great Christmas together, the two of us with the kids: especially now Vernon's not going to be around until the New Year. You really can't be looking forward to spending time with the Galloping Major.'

'Charlotte, yes, of course that's what I'd like to do. Tough on Mum, but if I do get time off ... Well ... Yes, I'll spend it with you, Ben and Lucy.'

'You promise?'

'Of course, and I'll explain it to Mum. Leave it to me.' She had this idyllic dream of Christmas at Falcon Cottage, real holly and a real tree, decorated with an angel at the top; going to Midnight Mass in the village church; Ben and Lucy excited, though Ben wouldn't have a clue about what was happening. Oh, Suzie thought, let me get a couple of days off just to be in a normal home – even one with a badly handicapped child – just for a couple of days.

She would ring her mother tomorrow.

But tomorrow her mother was ringing her all day. She wanted to talk about the murder and ask if Suzie was really investigating it like the papers said.

The *Daily Mail* had a photograph of her with Magnus outside 5 Coram Cross Road, and the headline SUZIE OF THE YARD? The *Express* had one photograph of Suzie – a close-up of her face looking concerned – and next to it one of Steve Fermin arriving at the house. Their headline was WOMAN LEADS MURDER HUNT. Several other papers had stories on their front pages and the *Herald* ran part of its leading article under the title IT'S MURDER FOR WOMEN.

We are all aware that, in the current international situation, women are being called upon to take over traditional male roles. Women now labour in factories doing men's jobs. Nightly in London we see the frail sex in action with the barrage balloons, the anti-aircraft guns, the ARP and the AFS. We see them in factories and in uniform on our streets, but we draw a line at allowing them to go into battle at sea, in our aircraft or in the front line in tanks or side by side with our foot soldiers.

But yesterday evening, following the murder of the nationally known broadcaster Jo Benton of the BBC, it was a woman who went to the murder site and was in charge of the investigation. We wonder if this is either right or proper. Murder is a serious, unpleasant and, more than often, sordid business. Last night concerns were being expressed that leading a murder investigation may not be a fitting role for young women, who, by the nature of their sex and upbringing, are probably unfit for this kind of duty.

New Scotland Yard would make no comment except to say that the officer concerned, an acting Temporary Woman Detective Sergeant, was working under the direct control of a more senior officer at Scotland Yard, the well-known Detective Chief Superintendent Tommy Livermore – 'Dandy Tom', as he is sometimes called. DCS Livermore has yet to visit the site of Miss Benton's death.

And that put the cat among the pigeons.

'This is serious,' Sanders of the River glared at her across his desk. 'It's not the kind of publicity we either like or countenance. The Yard has already been on to me three times this morning. One very senior officer talked to me about the possibility of the public losing its confidence in the Met if they believed women

144

were being put in charge of sensitive cases.'

'Sir, I—' Suzie began.

'So what've you got to say for yourself, Sergeant Mountford?' He was embarrassed and plainly ill at ease.

'What can I say, sir? I told them there had been a death at the house and that the victim had yet to be identified. I did *not* give them my name and I did *not* say I was in charge.'

'Oh!' Sanders of the River sounded quite pleased. 'Oh, you didn't? Good. That's excellent.'

'No, I did not, sir. You can ask DC Magnus, who was with me all the time; or Sergeant Osterley, who was with me outside when the reporters were asking questions. In fact DC Magnus told them there would be a statement issued later – and it was, sir. Under your signature I understand, sir.'

'Yes. Well, yes, Mountford. Now you have to understand that from now on you're not to speak to the press. We're so damned short-staffed that I really cannot raise a more senior officer to come out here at the moment. Carry on, but quietly and gently. Don't make a fuss, and don't tell anyone you're in charge, because you're not.'

'Sir.'

In the CID Office there was a message for her to ring DCS Livermore at the Yard.

'He's not here at the moment,' a female voice told her.

'Is that Terri? Terri Abrahams?'

'Yes, who's—?'

145

'Suzie Mountford. WDS Mountford, Camford CID.'

'Oh, Sergeant Mountford, yes. He left a message for you.'

Her stomach sank. She was going to get a roasting second hand.

'He said, take no notice of the newspapers. They'd make up things about their grandmothers if it helped sell papers, and they'll make up things about you. He says he's been there, so he knows. Right, WDS Mountford?'

Smiling to herself, she rang Rex Fulbright at CRO. 'Look, Rex,' she began.

'Careful,' he said. 'Don't get too matey just 'cos you got your picture in the paper.'

'I'm not getting matey, Sergeant Fulbright, but I need some help.'

'I know,' he said, not unkindly.

'The current crimes files, Sarge.'

'What of them?'

'I was looking at one a few weeks ago. A murder, somewhere near Cambridge. A girl; thirteen/fourteen years old. Choked with piano wire. About two and a half feet; ends bound with insulating tape. The murderer got in through the back door, and they found a pan of boiling water on the hob in the kitchen.'

'Apart from that you can't remember a thing about it, eh?'

'Come on, Sarge. I need to know the facts and who I should get in touch with. This is a dead ringer for the Jo Benton thing.'

'I'll get one of the chorus girls here to take a look,' he said. 'And, well done, Miss

Mountford.'

'If I'm not in the office I'll ring you back. *Don't* leave a message.'

'You're learning a bit sharpish, aren't you?'

'I've had good teachers, Sarge.'

'Yes, right.'

'Oh, and I've just remembered something else—' She was trying to pin it down: something she'd seen on her first ride out to Camford.

'Well, the day I was posted out here, to Camford, there was a report in the paper – the *Evening News* – about a young girl.' She foundered, trying to remember the name. 'Bachelor, I think she was called. Early teens. In Acton. Went missing one day and then found dead in her home the next. Strangled with piano wire.' She remembered the report said some of the girl's clothing was missing, which usually meant only one thing.

'I'll do my best young Suzie, okay?'

Magnus and Shirley had come in and they sat waiting for the day's instructions. Before telephoning Sergeant Fulbright, Suzie had sent Sammy Richards off to chase the fingerprint evidence; Catermole was still interviewing people concerned with the attacks on elderly women in the blackout, while Pinchbeck, Mortimer and Wilf Purser were dealing with a serious robbery that had happened overnight. The local council offices had been broken into and hundreds of pounds' worth of ration books and petrol coupons had been stolen. Ration books and petrol coupons had become more valuable than money.

'I'm going to interview Jo Benton's agent,' Suzie told them. 'I gather that an agent is usually someone very close to his clients. So close he takes ten or twenty per cent of his client's salary.'

'Who told you that?' Magnus asked, in an interrogatory mode.

'Fermin,' Suzie answered. 'Before he left last night.'

Magnus had been slightly withdrawn ever since she had first seen him that morning. Jealousy? she wondered. Just because she'd got herself in the papers. And just as she thought it, again her mother was put through to the office telephone. 'I'll ring you later on, Mum. I'll certainly call you this evening, only it could be late.'

'I've seen your picture in the papers,' her mother said. 'So has the Major. He doesn't think it's very nice, you having anything to do with a murder like that.'

She wanted to tell her mother what she should do with the Major, but wisely didn't. No point in aggravating things at this stage. There were going to be ructions about Christmas anyway.

'I can't talk now. Sorry, Mum, I'll have to phone you later.'

Her mother reluctantly hung up and Suzie asked the operator to get her Richard Webster's number: Richard Webster of Webster and Broome, Personal Representatives – the late Jo Benton's agent. She was put through to Mr

Webster with great speed and it was obvious that both the telephonist and Webster's secretary knew exactly who she was.

'Sergeant Mountford?' His voice had the slightest touch of cockney. 'I was expectin' you to ring.' Gs were dropped at the end of some words, but not others: no logic to it.

'I think we have to talk.' Suzie got down to work straight away. Best to present him with a businesslike exterior.

'When would you like...?' he began.

'Really as soon as possible, sir.'

'Will it take long?'

'Depends how much you have to tell us.'

She could hear pages being turned. Like a radio play, she thought.

'As it happens I'm free just before lunch. Say twelve thirty?'

'That'll be fine, Mr Webster.'

She put down the phone and, on cue, it immediately rang again.

'Rex Fulbright. I have those details you wanted.'

'Great.' She grabbed for a pen and note pad. 'Shoot.'

The victim had been a thirteen-year-old girl called Marie June Davidson who had been found dead, and mutilated, in the family home at 4 Heartfarm Terrace, Nr Trumpington, Cambridge. Her father worked on a nearby farm, and her mother was in hospital, at Addenbrooke's in Cambridge, following an appendectomy. It was the father, Norman Davidson, who had found her and, naturally,

149

he had been the first suspect – quickly ruled out with a cast-iron alibi. Norman Davidson had been with other farm labourers from five thirty that morning. He had returned with a colleague who lived next door. Davidson had gone into his cottage and almost immediately called his colleague back, hysterical with what he had found.

The kitchen door had been left open, victim strangled with a 2ft 6 inches length of piano wire, the ends of the wire sealed off with 4 inch insulating tape. The victim's genital area was slashed with broken glass, some of it embedded deeply along the walls of the vagina, eyes were slashed straight across with a kitchen knife – one cut – and a large pan of water was boiling in the kitchen.

There was a queried link to a similar case near Stratford upon-Avon – the village of Snitterfield – in the spring of this year.

Enquiries were directed to Detective Inspector R.E.G. Giddings at Cambridge Police Station.

'And the Acton business?'

'I'm coming to that. Barbara Bachelor. A couple of weeks shy of fifteen. Yes, she went missing overnight. I spoke with their CID. They suspect an uncle fancying her. 'Bubbles', they called her and I gather she was a handful. Father came back the next day, found her dead. Piano wire round the neck.'

'Well?'

'Well there's a DI in Acton seemed quite pleased you'd brought the matter up. DI

Prothero. Ernie Prothero. Says thank you and he's looking into it. Phone him if you want. I gave him your name, so he may just telephone you. Okay?'

'Okay, thanks, Sergeant. That's Acton nick, is it?'

'Well it's hardly likely to be Bermondsey if the offence took place in Acton, is it? The girl's body was found at Fifteen Layer Street. Got it?' Acton was way out the other side of Kensington. Not too far from Camford.

DI Giddings was in when Suzie telephoned Cambridge.

'Oh yes, I've been reading about you in the papers.' He sounded amused and ready to take the mickey.

'Don't believe all you read, sir. I'm not in charge of this case.'

'Glad to hear it.'

Insufferable, she decided and got on with asking the questions. The family lived in one of four tied cottages belonging to the farm and Norman Davidson had cycled home with his colleague. 'Went into the cottage. Bounced out again like a Jack-in-the Box,' Giddings told her. 'Bob Evans cycled to and from work with him every day. Lives in the next cottage. He was putting his bicycle away when Norman called him back. Marie June Davidson hadn't been in long herself: she'd come back from school. Usually got home about quarter to five. Norman arrived back at ten past.'

Marie June had been next door to see if a parcel had arrived for her father – the postman would leave it there if nobody was in at number four. Evans' wife said the girl was fine, full of chatter about the school play and the summer holidays. She planned to work on the farm for part of the holidays, helping to get the harvest in when it was time. That was it. Norman Davidson arrived home, found the dead girl. Nobody had seen anything.

'No strangers. Nothing,' Giddings said. 'I thought it was probably a casual. A tramp, or worse, a bloke from one of the aerodromes, but casual all the same. She put her bike away, went next door to Evans' wife then straight back to the cottage.'

Giddings thought the killer was probably there all the time, going through the place, seeing what he could lift. Old dodge, the boiling water. Villain's trick. 'They had one of those big ranges in the front room and a little kitchen like a cubby hole out the back. The whole place was small. A door to the stairs. Two bedrooms above. Bath night on Friday when they filled a big old tin bath from the copper out in the little wash house next door to the outside lav. No electricity. Gas lights and a hob. Wireless runs on a big battery. They have two. One they're using and one down the garage getting juiced up. Change over Thursday evenings. Wonderful isn't it? Modern times out in the country.'

'There are a lot of people still live like that in the cities as well,' Suzie said, but he did not respond.

'All along I've thought it was a crime of

opportunity – crime of necessity. She caught him at it and he killed her, then made it look really ugly with the cutting. Broke the bottle right there in the kitchen.'

'What kind of bottle?'

'Wine. They made their own wine, the Davidsons. Elderberry, damson, blackberry and a concoction they call Pear Brandy. Lethal stuff. Round here the farm labourers make a lot of wine – or, I should say their wives do. It's the cheapest way of getting pissed.' A short pause. 'I'm sorry. Forgot I was talking to a lady.'

'I'm not much of a lady,' she lied.

'Oh, well.'

The murderer had smashed the bottle holding it by the neck then gouged it into the girl's genital area.

'Really very nasty. Vicious,' Giddings said.

'Post-mortem?'

'Oh yes, she was well and truly dead by the time he did the nasties.'

'And you've got absolutely no clues?'

There was a long, slightly uncomfortable pause. 'Not really. No. I think we missed out badly. Well, I missed out badly.'

'Why so?'

'Because I think he was there all the time. I know he was there all the time. I should've had the dog brought out ... If I'm honest I suppose I wasn't quick enough on my feet.'

She waited for more, and eventually he told her. They had been so puzzled that the next morning they brought one of the two dogs run by the Cambridge Police. 'We had no ideas. No leads, and I thought what I've already told you: that it was a crime of desperation on top of a crime of opportunity. But nobody had seen a thing. No strangers, nobody lurking around, out of place. Nothing. The same people rode along there on the bus that do it every day.

'The cottages have a few yards of ground out the back. About ten or eleven yards and as wide as each cottage. They grow potatoes, sugar beet, lettuce, carrots, peas, beans, you know the kind of thing. Running along the bottom, well it's their sort of boundary really, is a line of poplars. We let the dog sniff around the kitchen and he was suddenly off up the garden. Behind the trees there was grass that had been trampled down. Someone had been stood there for some time. I've no doubt about it. When it was good and dark I think he wandered off the way he had come – across the fields. There were some cigarette ends there. De Reskie cigarettes – geezer with a monocle on the packet, right? Great long cigarette holder, all that. The killer came in that way, and waited in the trees after he'd done it, then made his way back to Cambridge or wherever. Slept rough and got lost. I still think he's some kind of travelling man. Maybe a didicoi.' There was another pause. 'Except for the Snitterfield business.'

'Tell me about that.'

'Beginning of May. Just before the *Blitzkrieg* began. Eighth or ninth, you'll have to get that from the Stratford nick. Snitterfield's quite a small place, about three miles out of Stratford.

Another girl killed in her kitchen. Well, not a girl. More a young woman. Twenty, I think she was. Just married.'

There is no railway station at Snitterfield. You can get there by bus, but on the afternoon of that particular murder the only clue they had was a man seen on the two o'clock bus. He got off at the stop before the village. Then he was spotted walking across the fields. A stranger. Nobody had seen him before, or since.

Giddings said they did not have a decent description, but two people saw obviously the same man. 'Wore a scarf, muffling himself up, and a wide-brimmed hat. Dark overcoat. Some reckoned it was a navy blue raincoat, but you'll have to get the full strength from Stratford All I recall is that the bus conductor gave a description. Also a woman walking her dog, saw him crossing the field. The bus conductor was in the frame for a while. The victim was on his bus. He was chattering away to her and couldn't give a description of me-lad-oh.'

'The times fit, though?'

'The Snitterfield murder? Oh yes. Yes, right on the button though nobody saw him leave. It's a kind of dead end, if you'll excuse the expression.'

'And the MO?'

'Wire and the eyes this time. If it was the same bloke he didn't do his Jack the Ripper thing.'

'You thought that as well, did you?'

'Yes, very much so. If you've read the descriptions of the Ripper's victims you can't really miss it. I thought of it straight away. As soon as I saw Marie June, I thought, Hello, it's Jolly Jack. Now, anything else I can do for you, Sergeant?' This last spoken very quickly.

She couldn't tell if he had been stringing her along about Jack the Ripper, but by his voice she thought he probably was. Having a little joke at her expense – 'That tart with the Met,' he'd tell his mates. 'She give me a ring about the Marie June Davidson business. I really got her going; said it was just like the Ripper.' And they'd all have a good laugh.

'Yes, sir. Yes, did you get any prints?'

'One set of unknowns. Could've been chummy, yes. Not one hundred per cent certain, but it's possible.'

'They matched them with Snitterfield?'

'None at all on that one. Smudges, gloves, but all the other prints accounted for.'

'Could you send the ones your chaps lifted, sir?'

'Of course. Who do I send them to, your guv'nor?'

'No, sir. Send them direct to me, would you?' She parroted the Camford Nick details, thanked him, then got off the line. She felt that DI Giddings had been stringing her along on more than just the Ripper stuff. There was something else just out of reach. God these blokes really disliked having a woman doing the job. Women for them were good only for cooking and breeding: in the kitchen and up the spout, as she'd heard 'the Prof' say to his mates in the canteen.

She tried DI Prothero at Acton nick, but he wasn't around, so she spoke to his sergeant, a man called Simon Finton, who told her that his guv'nor was quite excited about her possible connection with the Cambridge, Stratford and Jo Benton cases. Alas, Finton did not sound as enthusiastic as Mr Prothero.

Yes, he'd seen the body; no, there were no other intrusions – that was the word he used, intrusions. No, the eyes were intact, which was more than the girl was. They were waiting for the tests to come back but his guv'nor, and by association Sergeant Finton, thought she had been raped. She was certainly not a virgin.

Finton's money was on Bubbles' uncle, Peter Bachelor. 'Shifty,' the sergeant said. 'Dead shifty and rattled.' That was about it. Suzie asked one more essential question. 'What pan of water?' Finton said. Yes, they'd keep in touch, and they would report progress.

She really wanted Shirley to come to Richard Webster's office with her, but she didn't have permission to drive the Wolesley either, so it had to be Magnus. It was either Magnus or go by tube and she knew which would be better.

Webster and Broome had their offices deep within the warren of streets that ran between the Strand and Covent Garden. There was a polished brass plate by a non-committal door straight off the street. You went up a flight of steep linoleum-covered stairs to a tiny landing and a door with a typed card that said, KNOCK AND ENTER, WEBSTER AND BROOME.

'Like a tart's parlour, I bet,' said Magnus and looked visibly surprised at the carpet, leather chairs and smart secretary manning a reception desk.

Webster was in his mid to late fifties. Smooth as a baby's what's-it and – as Magnus put it later – sleek as owl shit.

He wore an obviously bespoke suit, more suitable for the country, Suzie thought, with a classy yellow waistcoat sporting brass buttons. His shoes were ox-blood, the socks matched the waistcoat, and the tie was also a yellow silk. Sulka, Suzie bet herself. Yellow with a red pattern.

He waved them into chairs, offered them cigarettes from a silver box, and asked if he could get them something to drink.

'I'm knocking off. Lunchtime, so I can allow myself a teeny gin and it.'

They declined in the time-honoured manner of police officers.

'I should offer my condolences,' Suzie began. 'You've lost a good client.'

'I don't know about good–' he flashed her a quick smile, there and gone in a second – 'but, yes, we had great hopes for Jo. Expecting trouble, mind you, but nobody thought it'd be as serious and as final as this.'

'What kind of trouble, sir?' Suzie asked.

'In my business there are two staple troubles.' He lit their cigarettes with a table lighter that looked like real silver. 'Two staple troubles. Money and sex. If it isn't one it's usually the other.'

'And there was a money problem?'

Richard Webster looked at Suzie with an amazed, slightly stunned expression. 'No. With Jo it was sex.'

'Ah.' Suzie did not know what to say until she heard more. 'Sex?' she asked, feeling the colour rush into her cheeks.

'She was trailing around young Fermin, who was bound to find out in due course. When I heard you had him in for questioning I thought he'd found out and killed her in a fit of pique – only pique would be a shade extreme for young Steven. I can't think why the silly girl actually said yes to him. She told me it was to seduce him, but here we are, months after the event, poor Jo's in her grave, well almost, and Steven hasn't laid a hand on her. From a sexual point of view, I mean.'

'Let me get this straight.' Suzie was conscious of her jaw drooping, and Magnus was leaning forward as though he was about to learn the secret of life. 'You're saying that Jo Benton ... er ... well...'

'Put herself about?' Webster leaned back in his chair and laced his fingers behind his head.

'Yes, I suppose that's what I'm asking.'

'Twenty-four hours a day,' the agent said without a smile. 'If a male swam within her ken and was the least bit respectable then she had him. The engagement didn't seem to slow her up either. In short she was the BBC bicycle and I can't think how Steve Fermin didn't know it.'

'Husbands and fiancés,' Magnus muttered.

'Quite right.' Webster nodded. 'Last to know.'

Suzie felt completely ineffectual. I just haven't got the experience, she thought. I haven't got any real experience of life, or of this job. I shouldn't be sitting here. I'm probably drowning.

Nine

'She was a ticking UXB.' Webster settled back in his chair. 'D'you know, it'll be a relief to talk about things now she's gone. She could've pulled the plug on so many people.' He looked up at Suzie. A coy kind of look. 'But of course she wasn't that kind of girl.'

'You mean she could've blackmailed people?'

'Oh, the full works. If ever a girl had dirt to dish it was Jo Benton. The problem was that I was her agent and agents are known to be the receivers of secrets. Now I know most of what she knew, and that makes me rather uncomfortable.'

'I have a list of some of her friends. Can we start by going through that, Mr Webster?'

'One minute, Skipper,' from Magnus. 'I don't know if I'm slow, but I'm not sure I follow all this. Mr Webster, are you saying that Jo Benton was some kind of – what would you call it? – a nymphomaniac?'

Suzie frowned: I thought I was thick and inexperienced, but Magnus really *is* a plod.

160

'I don't know that I'd call her that, Mr...?'

'Magnus, sir.'

'I've known some nymphomaniacs, Mr Magnus. They're rather sad people who get no real enjoyment out of life. They certainly don't enjoy what they're after most of the time. You couldn't say that of Jo Benton. No, she *really* enjoyed what she did.' He smiled and appeared to be thinking back to times now gone for ever. 'I warned her,' he said.

'In what way, sir?'

'Jo had this – how can I describe it? – this lust for sex: it wasn't the itch that nymphomaniacs seem forced to scratch, an addiction. And it wasn't about bragging – showing off, kissing and telling. I think I'm the only person who shared all her secrets, but I suppose she was still playing with fire. If she fancied a man, she'd have at him and wear him down – in very little time as a rule.' He took another long pull of his cigarette and blew out a stream of smoke. 'But with the exception of one or two special friends, that was it. She'd have them once and never again. There were some ugly scenes because people *did* fall in love with her. Some of her targets couldn't understand how she could have an inspired three or four incredible sexual hours with them, then wave goodbye. There were some who got pretty angry, thought they had done something wrong, offended her; thought they'd let her down sexually. Played havoc with some men – and not only men—'

'You mean women—?' Suzie began.

'Oh, yes,' he nodded. 'Most definitely, yes. In one case I know of anyway.'

Magnus still looked puzzled, while Suzie thought she really ought to take a course in sexual encounters. She didn't even know what it was like, because she'd never done it. Now she felt her virginity was shining blankly from her eyes.

'I saw it in action,' Richard Webster continued. 'I remember giving her lunch one day at the Savoy. A very famous American film star was at the next table – I won't mention his name.' Webster flashed his shy smile again. 'When he got up to leave, the movie star, Jo excused herself and followed him out. I didn't see her for three days. I phoned her at work, but she'd called in sick. I saw her again on the fourth day when she turned up uninvited in this office. Insisted we go out to lunch during which she gave me a blow by blow account – if you'll excuse the expression.'

This went right over Suzie's head. She had no idea what he was talking about. She had never even heard of fellatio let alone the slang for it. 'And you say Steve Fermin had no idea?' she asked with hesitation.

'I think I'd have known if he'd found out. I suppose those in the know really didn't want to widen the circle. Those who worked at the BBC, that is.'

'Even the ones who were angry with her?'

'Close to home she was careful. "It's our little secret" kind of thing. When Jo wanted to control people she usually could, and she had a sixth sense of who was dangerous and had to be handled with care.'

'Yet she was still a time bomb?'

'Of course. She wasn't infallible. She had some serious blind spots: usually about people she had known for a long time.'

'My list of friends, no—' She changed her mind. 'You said she had one or two people with whom she carried on long-standing relationships.'

'Four, to be exact.'

'Are you willing to—?'

'I don't know the morality of this, but yes, I'll tell you. I've wanted to share it with someone for a long time. Anyway, I think you should know.'

Suzie took out her notebook and the silver pencil that had been a birthday gift from Charlotte.

'I'll start with the ones whose names you'll recognize. The actor Gerald Vine; the fighter ace Squadron Leader Fordham O'Dell DFC; the antiques expert Daniel Flint, and one you might not have heard of, Barry Forbes – he's a financial wizard, one of Churchill's confidants, he's—'

'Yes, I know who he is.' The man was rarely out of the papers these days: advising the government, counselling Churchill. There was a desperate need for all kinds of specialist opinions and Churchill surrounded himself with a glittering court: Anthony Eden; Brendan Bracken; Beaverbrook; Professor Lindemann and, for financial advice in the country's darkest hour, the young, mercurial Barry Forbes. 'He has a steady girlfriend, I'm told.' As she said it, she realized that Fermin was the only person who had mentioned the girl. What was her name?

'Has he?' Webster frowned.

'A young woman called Emily Baccus.'

He shook his head. 'Can't say I've heard of her.'

Suzie was conscious of Magnus giving her a warning look. Quite right, she should not have mentioned something that could be privileged information. 'So these are the secret four?' Too quick, Susannah. She had blurted it out.

'Pretty much, yes. What about your list now?'

'Can we stay with those four for a moment, sir?'

'If we must, yes.' Having spilled the information without a hitch, there appeared to be slight resistance from Richard Webster. Was he suddenly regretting it? she wondered.

'For the time being, sir. Let me ask you, is there any specific reason why we should be suspicious of any of these men?'

'Jo talked to me about some pretty intimate things.'

'That doesn't answer the question, Mr Webster. You're being a bit of a tease. First you come out with the victim's four long-term lovers, then you close up: put up the shutters.' Suzie had heard this last expression from her young brother who was an avid cricketer.

This time Webster's smile was more enigmatic than coy. 'I think you should know that each one of those men has what you might call strange sexual habits.' He paused and looked, Suzie thought, a bit shifty. 'Well they had odd sexual ... er ... sophisticated tastes.'

She didn't want to hear; didn't want to know; wondered if she could ever possibly understand. 'Would you say that knowledge would put her at serious risk?'

'Normally I wouldn't have thought so, but ... Well, she's been brutally murdered, so...' Webster made a little waving gesture with his right hand.

'So I suppose you'd better tell us.'

Webster gave a long sigh. 'I feel a shade embarrassed, talking to a woman.'

'You came by the information talking to a woman.'

'Yes, I suppose, yes. But we were very close.'

'Were you her lover as well, sir?'

'No, alas.'

There was a pause, a long silence stretching across the room.

'Okay.' Suzie had to steel herself. 'The squadron leader. The Spitfire pilot. Battle of Britain ace. What was his particular problem?'

'He liked being beaten. With a cane, like a schoolboy. On the backside with her in her undies.'

She tried not to look shocked. 'They actually were at school together weren't they? Miss Benton and Squadron Leader O'Dell?'

'Yes. She was at school with two of them, O'Dell and Flint, and the school – Farnham Place – didn't believe in corporal punishment.

He used to joke that he felt he'd missed out. It's not an unusual sexual predilection.'

St Helen's had played hockey against Farnham Place, she reminded herself.

'It isn't? I mean, no, it isn't,' she said quickly. 'What about the antiques expert.'

'He had a thing about women's high heeled shoes. A shoe fetish. Foot fetish as well, I suppose.'

Suzie felt totally uneducated. 'And the actor, Gerald Vine?'

'Similar to the squadron leader, only he preferred to be tied up and whipped. I gather that was pretty extreme. It was the one that amused her – and I think gave her a little pleasure also. In many ways I think Gerald Vine was really the love of her life. It was still going on.'

'Okay, and Barry Forbes?'

'More complex and strange.'

'How strange?'

'He likes dressing up in women's clothes. He also likes to take two women at a time: loves dressing in smart underwear.'

'And she supplied the other woman?'

'Yes. Another old school friend – that's the lesbian relationship actually. A young woman by the name of Monica Parker. She's a leading Wren in HMS *Daedalus*. That's the Royal Naval Air Station at Lee-on-Solent. In mythology Daedalus made the wings for Icarus and—'

'The wax melted close to the sun and Icarus pranged. Yes, I know who Daedalus was.'

'Ah, right.' He sounded surprised that a

detective sergeant knew anything about Greek mythology.

'And Leading Wren Parker got as much fun out of it as Miss Benton?'

'I gathered it was all mutually satisfactory.'

Suzie wondered quietly how these people felt about Jo Benton getting killed. Wondering if she'd taken their little secrets to the grave. 'I wouldn't have thought those kind of...' She scrabbled around her mind searching for a word not quite as pejorative as perverted. She wondered if she was being a bit of a prude. '...those kind of games,' she supplied, 'I wouldn't have thought those kind of games would've been too embarrassing.'

'No, I suppose not.' Webster still had the remains of a smile on his face.

'I think, for the time being we should go through my list,' Suzie added quickly, deciding that she really had to do some digging, and had to read a few books: talk to Shirley perhaps. Shirley seemed a pretty knowledgeable young woman.

It took the best part of two hours to check and cross-check the names she had brought with her, from the long night with Steve Fermin, against Richard Webster's experience and memory.

In the end Suzie and Magnus came away with a muddled picture of Jo Benton's amorous exploits. She had been the lover of many famous stage, screen and radio stars; she had seduced, or been seduced by, a large number of powerful men. She also discovered that through Jo Benton's affair with the fighter pilot Fordham O'Dell, Jo had met a number of high-ranking military, naval and air-force officers whom she had slept with, then discarded. Nor did it stop there. At the time of her murder she could count three members of parliament, and even one member of the cabinet, within the circle of her undoubted charms.

'Whatever else,' she said to Pip Magnus, as they drove up through Kensington on the way back to Camford, 'I think there were a few people around who would benefit from her early death.'

'Is it all that important, Skip?'

'It's pretty indiscriminate behaviour. Animal really, isn't it? Just taking your pleasure anywhere you fancy. I'm surprised she hasn't caught something.'

'Maybe she has. You didn't ask Mr Webster, and I got the impression that you really had to ask the right questions, Skip.' Again he repeated, 'Was any of it all that important? He's a pouf, isn't he?'

'Webster?'

'Yes, he's a screaming pouf. A homosexual.' He pronounced it as two words, homo sexual.

'I don't know. Is he?'

' 'Course he is, Skip. Sticks out a mile. You can tell at once.'

I can't, she thought.

'Bugger,' she said under her breath.

Before going over to the offices of Webster and Broome, Suzie had sent Shirley off to take statements from what they were calling the hired help – Arthur Dove, the odd job man; and Minnie Shotten, who was a sort of secretary and had done bits of typing for Jo Benton.

She had seen both of them and was now back writing up her notes and getting the statements typed.

'They're devastated,' she said. 'Real old family retainer types: hearts of gold and all that. Minnie's in her sixties but was pleased as punch to do Miss Benton's typing – private letters and such. Bit mysterious about them. Wouldn't say what kind of letters she did, very loyal, just spoke of them as 'private'. And old Arthur Dove, I got the impression that he did a lot of stuff around that house without even being asked. Now, what's up, Skip? You're in Never-Never Land, aren't you?' Astute, that was Shirley.

'A bit shaken up,' Suzie acknowledged, 'and I've got to report to Sanders of the River again.'

'This is bloody rough on you, Skipper. Being landed with a visible murder like this. You want to take the evening off, come up the Palais with me and Bernie.'

'That's where you're off to tonight, is it?'

'Once I've got this finished.'

A constable from the front counter came down with a large, thick sealed envelope containing the post-mortem and forensic reports from Hendon.

'Ugh! She was raped after death,' she read aloud. 'Male sperm in all the usual places. Cutting and the eyes were also *post mortem*, that's

169

the gist of it.'

Suzie was sickened, wanted to throw up just thinking about it. Oh Jesus, she thought, then turned it into a kind of prayer.

Shirley asked her again if she was coming out with her and Bernie the Fearless Fireman. She dropped her voice so that nobody else could hear.

Give it a minute, Shirley. She didn't actually say it. She closed her eyes. All she could think of was the razed body of Jo Benton. Her hand was visibly shaking as she held the PM report. Like a bloody aspen leaf. Christ, she was thinking in clichés.

'Skip?' Shirley waiting for a reply.

She slowly opened her eyes, then thought, Why not? Bugger it, haven't been to a dance for months. 'You got a dress I can borrow? In my size, Shirley?'

'Certainly, Skip. We're much of a muchness.'

'Then you call me Suzie once we're off duty. And you can lend me a pair of those ritzy knickers as well, in case I get swept of my feet.' She grinned, swallowed, banished the lurid picture from her head.

'Down, girl,' Shirley growled.

'D'you think I can sneak out without seeing Sanders?'

'It's pretty late, Skip. Don't you think he's already left?'

'Definitely, and we'll go off to see that Josh Dance without coming back here in the morning.' She grinned.

★ ★ ★

170

Golly had gone into the Blue Posts at midday. The landlord told him they hadn't been in this morning, his friends Mickey the Mangle, Bruce the Bubble and Billy Joy-Joy.

'Probably be in later, Golly. I think they were out of town last night. Said they had something quiet on out Wimbledon way.'

Golly understood, ordered a half-pint and took a look at the *Star*. He recognized the photograph on the front page. It was that girl from last night. And there was another girl's photograph, taken in front of the house. He knew it was the house because he had been there a couple of times looking it over.

He read the piece carefully. They had her name there, this other girl, and she was a policeman. They had her name, Woman Detective Sergeant Suzie Mountford. She was investigating the murder.

It made Golly quite angry. His murder. His murder being investigated by a woman. He wanted to tell someone, but knew he couldn't. Maybe he should go into the church and say a prayer. Best thing really. Tell God about it. God would understand. Golly sometimes thought that the voice he heard was God's voice: God telling him to do what he was told to do.

He walked all the way up to All Saints, Margaret Street. He liked the smell of incense and he talked to God for a long time.

Suzie and Shirley enjoyed the Palais de Dance. Bernie brought another friend, Ernie, with him and Suzie danced almost every dance with him. Not really her type, she thought, but what the hell, you're only young once and she wanted to let her hair down tonight: wash away the dirt of the murder and of Jo Benton also. She had known Jo Benton was a dirty cow by just looking at her photograph. That's why she had asked Steve Fermin if she had a dirty sense of humour. He got angry of course.

She danced a dozen foxtrots and waltzes with Ernie, and they all went round together doing the Palais Glide as the band played 'Poor Little Angeline'. They also did 'the Lambeth Walk' and 'the Gallop', prancing around as the band played faster and faster. Then 'the Last Waltz', when they danced very close to one another, and she could feel him quite hard against her as they one-two-threed it around the polished, bouncing floor, and the big glitter ball slowly revolved sending splinters of light across the waltzing couples, flicking colours through the haze of cigarette smoke.

Ernie wanted to feel her up, Suzie knew that, and she abandoned herself after a manner of speaking. She let him plunge his tongue through her lips, and she responded, let him feel inside the blouse she'd borrowed from Shirley, but pushed him away when he tried to get further, against the wall outside Shirley's digs.

'You're a bloody little tease,' Ernie whispered. 'Come on, let me have a feel.'

'As long as it's only your hand,' she said and let him. But no further. Then later, sharing Shirley's bed she wished she had. It was terribly difficult. But that was the way she'd been brought up. Also, of course, she was terrified. No way could she afford to get pregnant and you couldn't trust men.

Tomorrow, she thought, I'm going to take a look at this Josh Dance from whom Jo Benton rented her house.

Out in the street some soldiers, well away, sang:

'Oh, this is number one
And the fun has just begun.
Roll me over, lay me down and do it again;
Roll me over, in the clover,
Roll me over, lay me down and do it again.'

They wouldn't half get some stick from Sister Martha Mary at St Helen's, she thought. Sister Martha Mary taught English and she was dead hot on some things. 'Hens lay,' she would say. 'Hens lay, and you can lay a table, but you don't lay something down; and you don't lay on the bed. You *lie* on the bed.'

Oh, but you can get laid on a bed, Sister, Suzie whispered silently. I just wish I could find the right person. Am I consumed by sexual thoughts? I think I must be. Just once, God. I want to know what it's like. I just want something to remember it by.

And she drifted off to sleep.

To dream of a handsome young bloke she'd yet to meet...

David Slaughter wondered why Emily Baccus

had come back to the office at this time of night. Couldn't understand it. It wasn't usual and she was all dolled up to the nines in a long dress, and her evening cloak and bag.

'Been dancing at the Savoy, Josh. Now you turn your head away 'cos I've got to get changed. Got some business to do.'

Bold as brass she was tonight and Josh turned away, but made sure he could see everything reflected in the mirror by the door. Oh, he thought. Oh my. Oh, if only, oh. And he saw the long legs and the suspenders. Everything. And of course she knew it. She winked at him as she went past wearing her smart suit and the little hat; fur coat over the shoulders and, 'Goodnight, Josh,' she said, and blew him a kiss.

'Oh, if only. But that was the reason for restraint...'

'Golly, you know there's a lady policeman looking for you now?' It was the beautiful, soft voice that he had to obey. He would come to great harm if he didn't obey.

The voice came spearing into his head, cutting its way in through the dark and un-knowing sleep.

'Golly, listen to me. The lady policeman will do terrible things to you if she catches you. You must catch her first. Be afraid of the lady policeman. She can do away with you. Her name is Sergeant Suzie Mountford. Remember her and be afraid. I will give you the place where she lives when I come to you next time.

Golly, be aware and beware. The lady policeman is terrible. You will have to get rid of her.
I will tell you how and when.'

Golly had very troubled dreams that night.
In the morning he was afraid.

Afraid of the lady policeman called Suzie. He
would kill her when he was told. But he was
frightened. He wanted his mum. It was coming
up Christmas and he always liked to see his
mum round Christmas time. His mum lived in
what they called an almshouse in a village not
far away from a town called Andover. Not as
big as London, no, but it was nice in the
village. They had ducks and everything. His
mum had been born there. Goldfinch her
name was. Ailsa Goldfinch. Lived near Laverstoke. In a cottage off the main road. Yes, he'd
like to see his mum. He'd arrange it when the
throaty lady gave him the orders.

Ten

Joshua Dance walked with an almost imper-
ceptible limp. The right leg. Suzie noticed it
immediately because it was more pronounced
as he showed them up the stairs, walking
ahead, halting a little on each tread.

Jewell, Baccus & Dance inhabited the entire
second floor of a lovely Georgian house just off
Albemarle Street in the heart of London's West
End. The building's ground floor was a select-

looking dining club called Sur la Table. Later, Shirley checked the club's details and said it was one of those places where men could take women for lunch or dinner and feel safe from the wrath of their wives – 'And so they should at fifty pounds a year membership and ten pounds for lunch or dinner – men-only membership of course.' It was pretty steep because you could get dinner at the Savoy for around a fiver, give or take a couple of quid. But maybe the dinner at Sur la Table was better than the one you'd get at the Savoy. Some people would say that wouldn't be difficult.

Suzie had telephoned Dance from Piccadilly Underground to make certain he could see them, and they found him waiting for them outside on the pavement, as though he wanted to be certain they didn't go astray: into Sur la Table or up to the third floor, the offices of Grayling Green Associates – whoever they were.

At first glance, Dance seemed to be a slightly effete though pleasant enough young man. Suzie had been with him for a while before she realized, good looks apart, there was a self-possessed hardness about him, from the cold blue eyes to his highly polished shoes, shades of the Galloping Major. His neat light hair was worn a little longer than the fashionable short back and sides and he had an attractive stutter that manifested itself in occasional hesitations before words he found difficult. Suzie guessed that he was in his early thirties. But what do I know? she reflected.

'We're not usually very busy just before...' his lips framed the word, opening and straining; pause, stumble, continue, '... Christmas.' He smiled. Charming. A girl could get used to being smiled at like that. He seemed to envelop her with his smile. Suzie was quite smitten. Shirley had been sent to interview the secretaries, Miss Burrage and Miss Holroyd, so Suzie and Dance were alone.

'But you did rent 5 Coram Cross Road to Miss Benton just before Christmas last year. Christmas '39.'

'Not me personally.' The smile again. Ought to come with a warning. 'People don't normally buy or rent property just before...' pause, control it, continue, '...Christmas. Business usually picks up after the holiday. Old Mr Baccus used to allow everybody in the office to take a whole week off at...' hesitation, '...Christmas.'

'Old Mr Baccus?'

'Founder of the firm. Alas no longer with us.' He indicated a deep leather chair, inviting her to sit, as he limped – not so marked on the flat – to his desk. The desk was the size of an aircraft carrier. What was it they said about men with big desks? There was another smaller desk directly behind her, diagonally across from Dance's. With a quick sweep her eyes took in the telephones, student lamp with the deep green shade, the big wireless set, the long mirror, the comfortable leather chairs and the copy of a Breugel on the wall directly behind him. If he turned his back, standing behind the desk, Suzie reasoned, a glance in the long mirror would give him a clear view of the other desk and the area surrounding it. It was a matter of angles, she thought, and the setting up of the mirror was not a question of chance.

'Old Mr Baccus?' she prompted.

'Old Paul Baccus. Founder, originally a Greek family, came to London in 1901, I believe. Had a great talent with property. Knew what to buy and what to leave alone. What would sell and what was good for development. A natural in this business.'

'So Emily'd be his daughter?' she asked.

'Emily?' he looked up, his eyes widening and an expression of surprise flitting across his face: there and gone so fast you had to be equally quick to spot it.

Whoa, she thought, what's *that* all about? 'She was mentioned somewhere; by someone.' Suitably vague. 'Isn't she part of this firm, Emily Baccus?'

He took his time. 'Yes. Yes, Emily's the only Baccus left with the firm.' Pause, teeth together, stumbling, and over. 'She has a few properties of her own. Deals with them on her own as well. The finance goes through the business, but we really don't see her very often. I hardly...' hesitation, '...see her at all. A tough young woman.'

'A lot of properties?'

'Who? The firm?'

'No, Miss Baccus.'

'She has two very good ones. Right on the edge of Soho. Close to Rupert Street. They're converted into flats.' A low single laugh. 'A very tough lady, our Miss Baccus. She goes round the flats and collects the rent herself. Usually the second Wednesday in the month, but she's in and out of those properties at all hours. I personally wouldn't like to do that.'

She nodded, thinking that she wouldn't be happy going in and out of some of those places at odd hours. 'I presume you're the Dance.'

He inclined his head in an affirmative movement.

'So, who's the Jewell?' she asked.

'Morecombe,' he said, then repeated it, 'Morecombe Jewell. A sleeping partner. To be honest, Miss Mountford, I'm the reality of Jewell, Baccus & Dance. The two ladies assist me: Miss Burrage keeps the books, sometimes does the lettings, follows up if rents aren't paid, and Miss Holroyd does the letters. Grayling Green do the legal stuff when we deal with a leasing contract.' The S again. Teeth, tongue, lips and over, 'Solicitors, Commissioners for Oaths. We don't have to go far.'

She glanced around her. 'Looks as though you haven't got to go very far for anything.' The door to his left was half-ajar and she could see the back of a sumptuously covered armchair on a thick carpet and a picture hanging just inside the door. Nice. Looked like a view of Venice: a painting of the Salute from St Mark's, she thought. She was an expert on Venice, because in 1932 they had all gone to Venice for a week. A real treat. Charlotte was fifteen and she was fourteen. One day, on a

179

vaporetto they both had their bottoms pinched, which upset Charlotte, but was a reasonably pleasurable experience for Suzie.

'No, not far to go for anything.' He smiled his sweet embraceable smile again. 'I've one room through there–' nodding at the door – 'and there's a staircase to the rest of the apartment at the top of the building. What used to be the attics. Handy for the firewatching now. Would you like to see?'

The offer was so unexpected that Suzie found herself grinning and nodding. Like a monkey, she thought. Grinning like an ape. Is Mr Dance flirting with me? Maybe? Her hand came up automatically to tidy away an imagined unruly strand of hair.

'Come.' Rising, he gestured with one hand (long rather beautiful fingers, she thought) showing her through into a large room with wide bay windows looking down on to the street. There was a deep-pile cream carpet and a silk wallcovering: a watery blue with lozenge-shaped flecks of gold that matched the coverings of two button-backed easy chairs and a long Chesterfield. The picture inside the door was, as she'd thought, Venice and two other paintings – one of the Mall with members of the Household Cavalry passing towards Buckingham Palace; the other of the Champs-Élysées looking towards the Arc de Triomphe – hung on adjacent walls. All three were framed in gilt with light grey mountings.

'My father was an artist,' he said as though that explained everything.

'He did these?' she asked.

'Yes, these and many others. I only have these three originals.' He hesitated and then suggested that she might like to see upstairs. 'This is my drawing room. It is an unconventional arrangement. Above here I have a dining room, kitchen and bedroom.' He led her along a passage punctuated by a cloakroom door, and from there up a wide staircase, carpeted, like the passage and the drawing room, in the same deep cream pile. The stairs turned acutely, doubling back on themselves, so that eventually they led to the room directly above the drawing room. Three windows up here, originally dormer windows now framed with heavy, dark green curtains. The smell was of wood and polish and money. A long, heavy oak table with six high-backed matching chairs occupied a central position while an equally heavy oak sideboard held silver chaffing dishes, a tall engraved slightly bulbous tea pot, two trays and other dishes, all in silver. On the table candelabra winked, the candles pristine and loaded into the holders: seven to each set – Georgian, she thought, but that was a guess. What she knew about silver could be written on a postage stamp.

His bedroom was directly above the firm's office. The door stood open and Suzie saw right in to the wide, large bed covered in scarlet, dotted with gold fleurs-de-lis, the scarlet echoed in the bedside lampshades. She glimpsed books on a table and a small oil painting of a large country house – sixteenth century, she'd say – in golden Cotswold stone with a clutch of chimneys at one end, mullion windows, leaded lights and an elaborate iron-bound door, the whole place glowing at dusk on a summer's evening. In the distance, behind the house, cornfields rose to meet a stand of trees and she half recognized the view, there was the tip of a church tower showing above the corn on the left. Through the rest of the day she kept trying to place it, just over the lip of her memory.

Next door, the kitchen was professional and businesslike, a modern gas oven and hob, stainless-steel sink and brushed steel fronts to the cupboards below a marble work surface. 'You cook, Mr Dance?' she asked and he smiled, nodding, muttering something about it being his hobby, his passion in life.

On their way back he slid an arm around Suzie, pausing for a second, resting a hand on her waist allowing it to remain there for a count of five sending a little shock through her, a sparkle in her loins. There, standing at the top of the stairs.

To the left there was another door that he opened to show it led on to the roof, giving a staggering view of London to the west.

'You can walk right around the block and it's perfectly safe,' pointing to the balustrade that came up to her thighs. 'Right round,' he repeated and she turned back looking up the sharp slope of the roof, slick and grey tiled. There was a space of a good two and a half feet between the rise of the roof slates and the balustrade: enough room to walk with some comfort in spite of the shallow runnel to carry rain water down to the gutters below. 'Builds up when it's raining,' he said.

'This is where you firewatch?' she asked.

'The post's two buildings along.' He nodded up the street towards the corner with Piccadilly. 'Best view in London and I've got a personal entrance to it.'

They went back, and down through the drawing room and into the office. Suzie felt her cheeks red from the short time on the roof; excited by being shown the rooms of his apartment; impressed by the veneer of wealth that hung over the décor and furnishings.

Now it was rather tame to be back asking questions when she would much rather be frittering time away with Josh Dance.

'Where were we?' she asked, and he said something about the Coram Cross Road lease.

'Yes, if you didn't do the lease, who did?'

'I'd have to look,' he replied. 'Emily possibly. She was here full-time while I was away.'

'Away?'

'Yes.' He looked at her with the same smile, hands slightly apart as if he would embrace her if she came close enough.

'Away where?'

'At the war. I came back on a st-stretcher, via Dunkirk.' He tapped his leg significantly as if to say that's where I collected the limp.

Her heart all but went out to him. Like everyone, she'd seen the newsreel film at the cinema: the defeated army wading out from the

183

beaches, and along the Mole, being taken aboard the fleet of small ships. Men lining up in disciplined rows; the Stukas howling down and thick oily smoke pumping in the background.

'I'm sorry.'

'I was a territorial soldier. Went as soon as war...' He trailed off. Enough said.

'You've been invalided out?'

'Not much use as a soldier if you can't run.'

'No, I suppose not.'

'I'm on indefinite leave.' Pause, then a puzzled look. 'Is this something new?' He frowned, perplexed.

'New?'

'You're a girl. A lady. Do ladies investigate murders nowadays? Is it the war?'

'Something like that. Shortage of coppers.' Dunkirk, she thought.

Eventually, she asked, 'You knew Josephine Benton though?'

'Hardly.'

'Your name and number're in her address book.'

'Well, I'd met her, dealt with a query she had about decorating. I even went to a Sunday lunchtime drinks party.'

'And Emily? She had Emily Baccus's address and phone number.'

'Oh yes. Yes Emily knew her, of course. A good name to drop.'

Suzie raised an eyebrow.

'Emily likes names she can drop,' he said with a slanted smile.

'Like her friend, Barry Forbes?'

Dance's face conveyed that he was searching a long way back in his memory. 'I expect so. *That* went on for quite a long time I believe.'

'Went on? Miss Baccus isn't seeing Mr Forbes any more?'

'It was always a bit on and off. One was never quite certain. May I ask what this is really all about? You can hardly think that her leasing agents had anything to do with her death.'

She smiled, nodding, a deprecating movement of hand and head. 'Background, Mr Dance. Looking at her friends and acquaintances. But you say you hardly knew her, Jo Benton?'

'I really didn't know her at all. Let me see if we can find out who dealt with her lease.' He picked up one of the telephones and spoke briefly – 'Miss Burrage, do you know who handled the lease for the Coram Cross St-Street property ... Yes, yes Miss Benton, that's what it's all about ... Oh, really? One minute.' Covering the mouthpiece with his hand he spoke to Suzie. 'Sh-should Miss Burrage bring the details up here? She's just been over them with your colleague.'

'Why not? Yes.' And as he hung the earpiece of the tall telephone back on to its Y-shaped rest she added, 'Could you also give me Miss Baccus's address so that I can check it against the one I've already...'

'Yes, of co-course.' He rattled off a flat number in a service block off Marylebone High Street. 'Three-twenty Derbyshire Mansions.

Sounds grand doesn't it?'

'And is it?'

'In a rather vulgar sort of way. All art deco and such. There's a big cubist picture in the foyer and a laminated pink mirror in the lift. Not my kind of place.'

Suzie reached into her mind realizing that the address was the same as the one she had copied from Jo Benton's book. 'And she rarely comes in to work here these days, Emily Baccus? Any reason for that?'

'I hardly think,' Josh Dance began, then, 'Well, there's not much for her to do. As long as she keeps her own properties ticking over.'

Suzie thought she wasn't getting very far. Not with the case anyway. There was little that either Dance or Miss Baccus could contribute, though it had been nice to meet Dance ... Josh. He started talking again.

Then Shirley arrived with the two remaining employees. Miss Burrage was a plump, fussy woman with thick spectacles and the manner of a gossip. Next to her, Miss Holroyd looked positively slender and alert, a girl of around eighteen or nineteen. They were both agog about the murder, eager to assist in any way. But in effect Suzie had lost interest: there was little they could add. She simply went through the motions, getting the details of how Miss Benton had come to take out a lease on the property.

'Josephine Benton actually came into the office?' she asked.

'Oh, yes, with a nice Raff officer. A squadron

186

leader with a host of gongs – that's what they call medals in the Raff,' Miss Burrage supplied. 'I have a nephew in the Raff, in Norfolk, only we're not supposed to know where he is. We write to this number, but we know. I believe he's engaged in something hush-hush.'

Engaged, Suzie thought; something hush-hush. 'A senior officer is he, your nephew?' she asked.

'Oh, no. A pilot officer. But he's highly thought of, I gather from his mother, my sister.'

'That bloody woman.' Shirley wanted to let off steam as they walked away, back to Piccadilly Underground Station. 'She maundered on and on; gave you the far end of a fart.'

'Shirley!' Pretending to be shocked, but with a smile.

'Well. Middle-aged, chatty spinster.' Then, as they were going down the steps, hurrying through the tunnel past the Gents convenience, the reek of urine like a wall, 'That Dance seemed a gent.'

'Asked me if I'd like to have dinner with him sometime, actually.' Suzie was like the proverbial cat who'd had the cream. Before Shirley had brought in Burrage and Holroyd, Josh Dance had apologized for not being able to be of more assistance. Then, 'If you're ever free, perhaps you'd care to have dinner one evening – when we haven't got the Luftwaffe in of course. You've seen where I live; uncovered my secret passion. Cooking. I'd give you dinner any time. Just ring me.'

'He didn't?' Shirley drew in a hiss of breath. 'There you are interviewing him and he asks for a date? Cheeky beggar. I thought he was a bit chummy, even with Misses Burrage and Holroyd there – all that stuff about hoping you had a good Christmas, and were you going somewhere nice? And oh yes, he has friends near Overchurch. I noticed that.'

Suzie told her about the apartment. 'Got the guided tour,' she said, and described the luxuries, the table and sideboard, the silver, his father's paintings. 'Only I'm not sure he's telling the truth about his father. The signature looked like Charles Slau-something to me.'

'They get things in that business. Perks,' Shirley said. 'My mum's brother works in an hotel out near Esher. He gets perks. Mr Joshua Dance could get good furniture, pictures and that on the q.t. Perks.'

They took the Tube out to Marylebone where workmen were adding more metal bunk beds to those ranged along the Underground platforms. More and more people were sleeping down there every night, and there were even men who would queue for tickets from early in the afternoon. The line was popular because they were good stations, with nearby toilets. If you didn't have male and female toilets you had to make do with piss buckets which became pretty toxic after a few hours.

The air normally smelled strongly of soot, even deep under the ground. It was part of any memory of London: the soot smell and the roar and clanking of the Underground trains as

188

they arrived or left the stations. Suzie could remember her fear of them as a child, shrinking back from the platform as the train came blustering in, or listening with awe to the echoed sound borne in on decreasing waves as it grumbled its way on through the endless tunnels.

At the block of service flats – Derbyshire Mansions – they found the apartment on the third floor. The place was Edwardian, purpose built, Suzie considered. Big apartments for business bachelors of the naughty nineties. Lots of mouldings. If these walls could talk, she thought. Nobody challenged them. 'Could've jemmied our way in and nicked the silver, no problem,' Shirley said. 'These people think they're safe from everything except a Nazi bomb. I bet some of them don't even lock the door.' She tried three-twenty. A Yale lock. 'Bet I could loid that easily. But there's probably a dead bolt as well.'

'What's that mean?' Suzie asked.

'Crikey, Skipper! You don't know what a loid is? Stiff piece of celluloid. Flexible. You can slip it into a Yale lock. If the sneck's not down, or if it hasn't been double locked, the bolt just slides back. Easy as pie.' Her fingers obviously itched.

They rang Emily Baccus's doorbell three times with no result.

'You want me to—?'

'No.'

'I think she could be away,' the porter told them when they dug him out. 'I haven't seen

189

her for almost a week. Don't know where she is.' He was a grizzled, nutbrown little man in his sixties who carried himself well, obviously a former NCO.

Suzie showed him her warrant card and he asked if it was something serious, obviously longing for her to tell him to break into the flat. 'I told you, I haven't seen her for a few days, maybe a week,' he said, his grey nicotine-stained moustache quivering as though vibrating of its own accord. He wore medal ribbons on the green uniform jacket that appeared to be *de rigueur* as porter of Derbyshire Mansions. Suzie recognized the Mons Star because the Galloping Major wore the Mons Star among his medals on Armistice Day.

'People go missing without warning in this bombing,' the porter said darkly. 'Take Mrs Evans from two-four-one. There one day and just not around the next. That was Mrs Evans all over. Nobody knows what happened to Mrs Evans. Two-four-one.'

Suzie took the porter's name for future reference. It was Russ, Cyril Russ. In her head she christened him Cyril Nutkin.

She thought about letting Shirley have a go with a loid, but in the end, she left her card with a scribbled message asking Emily Baccus to telephone her at the Camford Hill station. They left and made their way up Marylebone High Street to a British restaurant where they had lunch. British restaurants were about the cheapest you could get and it was patriotic to use them.

'We have meat today,' the waitress said. It was amazing how quickly shortages had set in.

Shirley scanned the menu, realizing there was no real choice. It was either Hot Pot or Hot Pot.

'We'll have the Hot Pot,' Suzie decided.

'Good choice.' Shirley grinned. 'We going to have the Spotted Dick as well?'

'I've spent most of my life avoiding Spotted Dick,' Suzie scowled.

'Oh, so have I,' Shirley smirked with glee.

Then she told Shirley that her father used to say the French pronunciation of Hot Pot was Ho Po.

'I thought that was the Chinese?'

'No, Chinese is number sixty-eight.'

It didn't take them long to realize that the Hot Pot had been given only a quick glimpse of the meat.

'Should've had the fish,' Shirley said.

Later, Suzie bemoaned her lack of training. 'I'm doing it by instinct, Shirl. I'm amazed they're allowing me to investigate this but I do need help. Please, let me know if I'm being stupid.'

'Well, at least you now know what a loid is.'

After the Spotted Dick, she said, 'I'm going to concentrate on Benton's secret four. When we get back to Camford I'll ring the antiques fellow...'

'Daniel Flint?'

'He's got a business in Kensington Church Street, so we should be able to see him early on. Then perhaps you'd get Gerald Vine's address and Barry Forbes, right?'

'Okay.'

'And ring the Air Ministry. See where the Squadron Leader's stationed. Perhaps I can fit them all in by Christmas Eve when I'm going to stay with my sister, Charlotte. Did I tell you about Charlotte?'

It was Thursday. Christmas Eve was the following Tuesday. It was going to be very tight.

'I suppose I'd better ring Stratford nick,' she mused, muttering under her breath. 'The Snitterfield thing.'

Back in the CID office at Camford Hill, Suzie spoke to a DI Eagles in Stratford and he took almost an hour to get her genned-up about the Snitterfield murder. Then she got down to putting her notes in some sort of order and writing her report while Shirley started to telephone the people her sergeant wanted to see. Suzie had not done one page when she got the telephone message from Sanders of the River. 'I want you in my office now,' he said. 'Pronto.'

'Pronto, sir,' she repeated.

'I've been waiting since yesterday afternoon, Sergeant Mountford.' Sanders had a bit of a high colour and she noticed that his right hand was clenched: the skin stretched; the knuckles white. She found it difficult to meet his eye.

Nobody really took Sanders of the River seriously; certainly she didn't: until now, when it quickly became clear that he was put out.

'I waited for you to come and see me last

night. I know you got my message. Then I discovered you'd left the station without a word. And you didn't come in today until this afternoon. Three o' clockish.' All little sentences, yapped out at her, a fine spray of spittle forming. 'I understand, of course,' he said in case she thought he was sitting in judgement. 'I gather you had to interview someone. Can't be easy with Tony Harvey away.'

Sanders had always seemed inoffensive, lacking in so many graces, but now he seemed to be roused.

'Responsibility, Sergeant–' he made a shrugging motion – 'responsibility comes with promotion. You're only an acting WDS, but you still have the responsibility.' He made the shrugging movement again and she realized that he had a new silver insignia on his shoulder. Sanders of the River had been made up to Chief Super. They'd been right, Sanders of the River was now the senior officer at Camford Hill.

'Sir, I...'

'I hope you haven't got a problem with authority, Mountford. I wanted to tell you that I'd had a long talk with the press liaison officer at the Yard. They suggest that you try to steer clear of reporters, and newspaper cameramen.'

'You've been promoted, sir. Congratulations.' She had learned the trick long ago when she was still at St Helen's.

Sanders of the River blushed. 'Thank you, Sarn't Mountford. Thank you...' The pause was a shade long. 'Thank you ... er ... Suzie. I was wondering...'

'Yes, sir?'

'Wondering if you'd care to have dinner with me sometime. I was going to ask you last night, but you ... Well.'

'I'm afraid I couldn't have last night, sir. But, yes. Well, yes, I'd love to.'

'I know a place near Richmond. The Silver Fox, perhaps you've heard of it.'

'No.'

'Ah, well it doesn't matter. Perhaps...?'

'After Christmas, sir? I'd love it.'

It did wonders for her confidence, to be chatted up twice in one day. To be invited twice in one day.

'Yes, that'll probably be best.' He smiled.

A nice smile, she thought. Lights up his eyes and makes him look terribly young.

'Things'll be easier all round after Christmas. DCI Harvey'll be back on January 1st.' He smiled again and licked his lips.

'Sanders's asked me out,' she muttered to Shirley back in the CID office.

'Never!'

'Wants to take me to a place near Richmond.'

'Not The Silver Fox?'

'Yes. Why? D'you know it?'

'The Silver Fox's noted for it.'

'Noted for what?'

'It's where businessmen take their secretaries, Skip.'

'Oh my God.'

'The restaurant's dead expensive and they do rooms – by the hour I'm told.'

'By the hour?' She'd never heard of such a thing. 'By the hour? Never heard of such a thing. I don't believe you. Why would they do ... Oh. Yes. Oh. I see. Yes.'

'You want me to get you some of that parachute silk, Skip?'

'Mmmm, yes. And some of those little mother-of-pearl buttons, yes.'

'Lace?' Shirley knew the signs. When a girl started to take courting seriously she first looked to her underwear.

'Please, yes.' She had already decided that Sanders would be the one. She wished it could have been Josh Dance, but with Sanders ... Well...

Shirley had arranged for them to see Daniel Flint the following morning and Barry Forbes in the afternoon. 'Gerald Vine's rehearsing in London at the moment and he's offered to see you tomorrow evening.'

'Okay, fix that, and what about the Squadron Leader?'

'He's at Middle Wallop. 609 Squadron. Just up the road from Overchurch, isn't it?'

'Not far. I could go there – train to Andover – on Monday, then get a bus to Overchurch when I've seen the Squadron Leader. Can you arrange that now?'

'You won't need me.' It wasn't a question.

'Why not?'

'Air Ministry says that no aircrew personnel from 609 have been off the station, except to one of the local pubs, in the past month.'

When she got back to St Martin's Lane,

Suzie rang Charlotte. 'I'm coming on Monday. Got to see a Raff officer at Middle Wallop, so I'll get the bus down to you after.'

Charlotte told her that she'd had their mother on to her again. 'I had the feeling that she's been trying to get you. One of us has got to tell her.'

Suzie knew what Charlotte meant was that she – Suzie – had to tell their mother. 'Let's compromise,' she said.

Her mother was very disappointed. 'I'd made up my mind that you'd both manage to come down. I thought how wonderful it would be, with the children and everything. I mean Ross has brought in a wonderful tree...'

'We're going to come over on Boxing Day, Mum – if I can get away. It'll be my treat, so keep your fingers crossed.'

'We've got a turkey. Well, Ross got a turkey, so we'll save it: have our Christmas on Boxing Day. Shall you stay the night?'

'I doubt it, Mum. I'll let you know, and don't save your turkey till Boxing Day. Please. I really am terribly busy. It's murder here.' Then, 'You'll never guess.'

'What?'

'A chief superintendent asked me out.'

'Out? Where out?'

'On a date out, Mum.'

'A chief superintendent?' Her mother made it sound like a rat catcher.

Then she rang Detective Chief Superintendent Livermore, and they talked in detail about the people she was going to interview tomorrow. He was careful, wise and patient. Livermore of the Yard, she thought.

That night, Suzie dreamed that she was walking in a field of ripe golden corn. Suddenly her daddy came striding towards her. She noticed that the corn didn't move as he went through it. 'Daddy—' she tried to hug him and it didn't quite work – 'Daddy, what's it like being dead?'

'Oh, not so bad,' he said. 'But there's a terrible lot to do. We don't get a minute's peace. Talk about eternal rest. It's just the opposite.'

As that night's raids developed it became clear that the Luftwaffe was attacking the ports again: the ports and northern cities. Early in the evening stray German aircraft came in high over London, above the balloons, nuisance bombers, spoof raiders, dropping random bombs. The All Clear sounded just after nine.

Golly didn't like being down the shelters. Golly had nightmares when he was still awake. The nightmares made him shake and sweat. Sometimes he would scream. What he saw were terrible creatures conjured from his own mind. He knew they were not real, knew they were like parts of a dream, but that didn't stop them frightening him. If he was going to be frightened then he'd rather be frightened in private, so he made his way back to Lavender's flat off Rupert Street, leaving a lot of people settling down for the night in the shelters and the Underground.

Lavender had left a note for Golly saying she

was over in Camford, where she had a nice little house in Dyer Street. She'd had it done up beautiful, furnishing it with bits and pieces she bought from people who had flats around Rupert Street. So many people were moving out of the metropolitan area now that you could pick up stuff for a song and Lavender had made the house in Dyer Street really nice with some lovely pictures she'd bought – paintings of country cottages with hollyhocks and roses round the door. She even had a beautiful lady in a woollen crinoline to go over the telephone – a telecosy, she called it – because she didn't like the telephone. Said it reminded her of work.

Golly was downcast after he spelled out the note. He felt deserted and lonely. He groped his way upstairs and across the rooms that had windows looking out on the street. He stood and allowed his eyes to adjust, then groped around again, this time looking for the black-out screens: the big wooden frames to which thick blackout material was stretched and tacked. Then he crept around the flat doing the blackout. After that he went into the bathroom, turned the light on and took off his hat, unwound the muffler from around the lower part of his face, then untied the white surgical mask, leaning closer to the mirror and looking with loathing on his reflection.

There was no continuity to his face: it was like a jigsaw puzzle assembled by an idiot.

Golly was a man with two faces.

The top of his mouth was a harelip that went

upwards like a lightning flash, dividing his nose, slashing between his eyebrows, cleaving his face into two separate portions as neatly as an axe stroke. The left half of his nose was smaller and more straight than the right half, while his lips were of different sizes.

His reflection was not just bizarre; it was horrific, like looking into a cracked mirror. Some days, Golly had to hang cloths over all the mirrors because he could not bear to look at himself with the two different shaped mouths, one reaching wide into his left cheek; the two noses, set askew, and the eyes at an angle to each other, so that at first sight the impression was that the left eye inhabited his forehead – the incision dividing his face running right up and disappearing into his hairline. This deep jagged trough looked red raw.

'An abomination,' Golly muttered quietly. 'I am an abomination.'

And he began to weep as he did so often when he saw his reflection.

He went over and turned the light off, stumbling back to Lavender's empty bed, clasping the teddy bear she always left on the counterpane. He held the bear close like a child as he hunched his body up and rocked to one side, whimpering. His knees drawn up to his cleft chin.

Then Golly thought about what he had done to Jo Benton. The nice voice would be pleased with him. The beautiful, soft voice he must obey. He muttered to himself, 'I'll come to great harm if I don't do what I'm told. Oh dear ... Oh dear what will become of me? ... Oh dear.'

And he fell asleep, but did not dream of killing.

Then, in the dark he woke trembling, knowing that all the creatures were there, in the room, gathered around him. Moving close so that he could hear their stealthy muted shuffling. They sounded like dry sticks being moved across the floor, and in their midst the worst image of all: a rat-like creature that walked on its hind legs, carrying a flag or banner over its shoulder and constantly glancing behind it. He had never seen the device or wording on the banner, yet Golly thought that if he saw it disaster would soon follow. The creature whined and whistled, making horrible noises. Golly thought of it as the Banshee. He couldn't sleep after the Banshee came into the room.

Eleven

The Underground train rattled on towards Knightsbridge on the Piccadilly Line.

'Shirl, do you really? Truly, I mean, do you?' Suzie asked.

'Do I what?'

'You know. With your fireman.'

'Suzie, you're so naive for a sergeant. You're

bloody exploitable.'

'Exploitable?'

'Yes, it's a good job I'm me. If I were some-one else, some Nazi woman, I'd exploit you to hell. You're the Met's equivalent of Pilot Officer Prune.' She pronounced Nazi like Churchill did – Naa-zi.

They started to talk about men, and Suzie said something about natural desires and how difficult it was. 'I'm so afraid I'll get pregnant. It's the one thing that stops me. But come on, Shirl. Tell me. Do you? Do you really? With the fireman?'

''Course I do, Skip. What d'you think? There's a war on. Death is coming down twice nightly with matinées Thursdays and Satur-days. Neither of us have any excuse to get inside out of the bombs. It's the luck of the draw. We've been born and come to maturity in the middle of a damn great war, and I'm not going to my Maker without knowing what it's all about. Most fundamental thing in life, sex. When I finally catch a bomb with my name on it I don't think God's going to hold it against me, because I've had a man out of wedlock – regularly – and I've had him for pleasure not procreation. Suzie, you really ought to...'

'I know.'

'Do you? Or do you believe your mum: that you've got to lie back and think of England on your wedding night?'

'My Mum's never said that.'

'Well mine did. Said it's only for the man's pleasure. Used to say to me, "That's all a man wants of a woman, his conjugals." '

Suzie thought of her mum and the Galloping Major. They share a bed and they do it. Kissing that moustache. Ugh. At her age! Double ugh.

'Do you really want to enjoy it?' in the swing and rumble of the train Shirley shouted and a businessman, deeply engrossed in his news-paper, glanced up, then quickly looked away when Shirl gave him her Evil Eye.

'You know I do.'

'So you're going to do it with Sanders of the River?'

'Do you think we ought to have another session with Steve Fermin?'

'Don't change the subject, Suzie. I've got some advice for you.'

'What?'

'Well, if you're at last determined to become a woman—'

'I am.'

'Suzie, how old are you?'

'I'll be twenty-three on April 3rd next year.'

'I'm nearly two years older than you.'

'Sometimes it seems like a century.'

'Listen Suzie, take Sanders of the River by all means; let him chase the hell out of you and catch you and marry you. Make a man out of him – but for the first time, for your virginity's sake, get your arms around Josh Dance stick your tongue down his throat and open your legs for him.'

'Why?'

'Because I reckon Joshua Dance has more experience than Sanders, and for that first time

202

you need to have a man with experience. I'd lay money on Sanders of the River still being a virgin, like yourself, and it would be a good idea to know a bit so you can teach him a thing or three. And it's so worth it. The sheer pleasure's a two-way street, and that was lost to a lot of women in our mums' generation.'

'And do you think we should talk to Fermin again?'

'About what?' Shirley shouted.

'About if he knew his future wife was playing bury the bone with people she bumps into, like the entire BBC Symphony Orchestra.'

'Why, Suzie?'

Suzie waited, then didn't look Shirley in the eye. 'Because I'm marking time, Shirl. I haven't the first idea about investigating a murder.' Silently she said, I've had one good thought – that the killer has done this before – and that's it. 'If I can hang on until the New Year, just over a week, Big Toe'll be back, and he'll take over. I've simply got to question people and type up the reports.'

'You mean you don't really want to solve this? You don't want to find whoever's behind this?'

'I don't really believe I could even manage the Ovaltiney's code, let alone a murderer.'

They got off at Knightsbridge and walked up past the sandbagged Albert Hall and on to Kensington Church Street, with its antique shops all looking a little lost because their owners had taken the precaution of moving their best stock out of town.

'There it is, over there – Flint's.'

Across the road there were two large double-fronted antique shops: flamboyant in a stylish sort of way. Sandwiched between them was this one bay window with a black painted door to the left. Above the door was a swinging sign, like an inn sign: black with white gothic lettering.

'It's the Admiral Benbow,' Shirley said. 'Jim Hawkins is going to come out any minute. You can almost hear them singing "Yo-ho-ho and a bottle of rum".'

'Daniel Flint,' Suzie read. 'Antiques. By Appointment.'

'I told you. Cap'n Flint. Pieces of eight, pieces of eight.'

As they approached the door, Shirley murmured, 'Considering Flint's predilections regarding footwear I hope you've got your sensible shoes on, Skip.'

'Shut up,' said Suzie. She opened the door and a catch hit a bell above the jamb. The bell pinged.

Jim Hawkins wasn't there, neither was Long John Silver, Blind Pugh, Billy Bones or Israel Hands.

'You must be Detective Sergeant Mountford,' said Daniel Flint, no relation to Cap'n Flint, and many miles from the Spanish Main. Daniel Flint was tall, sleek, dark, moderately handsome and not altogether likeable. 'Before you ask –' he shook hands with both of them, squeezing and holding a little longer than necessary – 'before you ask why I'm not in uniform, I should tell you that I have a dicey heart.'

He gazed at Suzie's feet and she felt a blush creeping up the back of her neck. Then he switched allegiance and looked longingly at Shirley's size sevens.

Suzie suggested that they find somewhere to sit down, so Flint led them through the long, narrow and elegantly furnished shop into a dowdy little apartment at the rear – scuffed carpet, an indifferent circular dining table, scratched and ringed, surrounded by half a dozen stand chairs of differing sizes and indifferent condition. On one wall – she could hardly believe it – a print of Edward Landseer's *Stag at Bay*.

'A drink?' he asked. 'Tea? Coffee? I'm afraid that's all I have to offer.' Once more he glanced down: first at Suzie's shoes and then Shirley's.

'No, thank you. This shouldn't take long.' She sat down and took out her notebook. Flint sat opposite and Shirley pulled a chair out and put it near the door, as though she was ready to block his escape if he made a run for it.

'Daniel *Elbow* Flint,' Suzie read.

'That's me.'

'Elbow? Odd. Elbow, that's a strange name.'

'Elbow. Yes it *is* odd. My mother's maiden name. Every male child in the family has that as a second name. My initials are DEF as in deflate. That's what I was called at school: Def.'

'That's what Jo Benton called you then.'

'Yes, as a matter of fact. You're well informed, yes we were at school together.' The light went out of his eyes. 'That's a terrible business. Are you anywhere nearer?'

'Nearer what?'

'Catching the man who killed her? Motive, all that.'

'How do you know it's a man?'

He gave a wry, off-centre smile. 'Assumed. Also I read a scholarly article saying women kill with poison, occasionally a knife, rarely with a gun and uncommonly by strangulation. The manner of Jo's dying seems more like a male act.' He coughed, nervous. 'Progress, Sergeant?'

'We're asking a lot of questions, that's all I can say at the moment.'

Flint looked serious. Even a little emotional. 'I still can't really believe it. Jo being dead, I mean.'

'You've known her since school?'

'Yes. I suppose since we were both around eleven years old.'

'Then you knew about Miss Benton's predilections.'

He gave her a little two-note laugh. 'That her hobby was sex? Yes. She's been like that since Fordham O'Dell first tupped her one Saturday night in Glenbervie Woods. We were all free spirits in those days and I suppose that was what Farnham Place was all about – being free, doing your own thing, learning through life's little surprises. It came naturally enough.'

He started to fiddle with a box of Bryant & May matches. Then – 'Some people were into being entrepreneurs. I remember one guy bought eggs, bacon, sausages and potatoes cheap then cooked them; got orders for them, sold at almost a hundred per cent mark up. No surprise that he's now a colonel buying most of the food for the Army. Brilliant idea because the food at school was pretty atrocious: he did a roaring trade. Others were into the demon drink, and some of us were into sex quite early on. Jo had a talent for it; enjoyed it immensely; said it was the nicest thing you got for free – only she used it as a business in those days.'

'You mean she—?'

'Oh, yes. Half a crown a pop, as I recall it. Unless you were a special chum.'

Lawks, Suzie thought, a million years from her days at St Helen's with its regimentation and strap-wielding nuns. Farnham Place was definitely different. The discipline was by the pupils for the pupils, and you chose what subjects you wanted to study: though the impression given was that study was a word not encouraged by the staff.

'You see–' Flint seemed to think he had to explain matters – 'with most people these days sex is one of the prizes for getting married. But to people like Jo it's always been for fun. I know that's not the general view, but it was her slant.'

'A lot of people would disagree with her.' Suzie knew she sounded prissy. She cleared her throat and continued. 'I presume she made a lot of enemies.'

'Particularly with her ideas about free love and having a lot of men,' Shirley Cox chimed in. 'I mean it follows that there could well be people who might be driven to harm her?'

Flint gave a snort of laughter. 'She'd be the last person to understand that she was causing offence, jealousy or whatever. Jo had a really bizarre view of life: almost the view of an innocent.'

'But she did have a number of regular lovers, yes?' Shirley avoided her sergeant's eyes.

'I don't know if "regular" is the right word. She had people with whom she was on sleeping terms. I think that's how you'd put it, and I suppose I was one of those.'

'That's what we understand,' Suzie said quickly, wanting to change the subject.

'Funny that. I didn't see her for long stretches of time, but when we met up again it was always as though we'd never been apart.'

'You were seeing her regularly over the last year or so?'

'No. Over the last six months. She turned up here one day without warning. Waltzed in all merry and bright, said she'd a proposition and that she'd tell me after we'd been to bed ... only she put it a shade more frankly than that.'

'Which you did.'

'Like a couple of stoats, yes.'

'And the proposition?'

'BBC'd offered her several ideas for programmes. One of them was about antiques. She said she didn't know an antique from a badger's whatsit. Needed advice and a good teacher. Said she'd get me a regular spot with her on the show.' He gave a sketchy little laugh. 'As she was leaving, she told me she'd got engaged to this wizard gem of a bloke called Steve Fermin. I'd heard of him of course. Well, I'd heard of his programme, *Fermin and Friends*.'

'Did it shock you? That she was engaged and yet had, well, just been to bed with you.'

'Not at all. That was Jo. All the fun of the fair. I doubt if marriage would ever have changed her.'

'Fermin didn't know she was promiscuous. Still doesn't.'

'So I gathered. She said she wanted to keep him unblemished. Though I suppose he was bound to find out sooner or later.'

'You saw her again regularly after that? After she tagged you for the antiques programme?'

'Of course. We went to it and at it. Job to be done. Met a couple of times a week. I taught her about antique furniture and a little bit about paintings. We worked out what she called a format; and we had a couple of meetings with BBC people. The accent seemed to be on fake antiques – how to identify iffy pieces.'

'You're an expert on iffy antiques, Mr Flint?'

'Anyone in the antique business for more than ten years is an expert in dodgy wood. I suppose I've had my fair share of experience.'

'So, the radio programme on antiques was going ahead nicely?' Suzie smiled sweetly to push things along.

'Yes, until last week.'

'Last week?'

'She telephoned me. Said it was all off: there wasn't going to be a new show about antiques.

Powers-that-be thought the listeners weren't in the right mood for it. They could be right with what else is going on. Consigned the show to oblivion. I remember I asked what they were planning and she said probably German classes – her idea of a joke.'

This was new, Suzie thought, and tried not to show it.

'She sounded bitter, then, Jo Benton?'

'She wasn't best pleased,' Flint agreed. 'But neither was I. I'd invested quite a lot of time in teaching her. Casualty of war, of course.'

'Of course. And that was that?'

'She said that was what happened in radio. Said she'd see me around.'

'And you felt a bit let down.'

'Of course I felt let down. In fact I sent an invoice to Broadcasting House.'

Suzie thought that if it had been her she'd have been as chocker as hell. Wondered if there was enough of a motive there.

'So, she was having a bit of a carry on with you, and—' Shirley Cox sounded like someone who desperately wanted to know all the sordid facts.

Flint held up a hand to stop her, 'If you're going to ask if I felt jealous or something, don't even start. That was Jo. We'd known each other a long time and it was how Jo was.'

'I was going to ask if she mentioned other affairs, other friends.'

He thought for a moment. 'One day, oh, a month or so ago – no, beginning of November, end of October it would be, she said she'd seen

Fordham O'Dell. The way she said it you knew what she meant. Old Fordy was a live wire. You knew what she'd been up to with him. "Saw old Fordham last night," she said and you knew immediately what she meant.'

'Anyone else?'

'Oh she said she'd been out to dinner with Gerry Vine and he'd been in splendid form. She liked to name-drop Gerry.'

'You know him? You know Mr Vine?'

'Yes, I've sold a few pieces to him.'

'And, when she name-dropped Gerald Vine that meant the same thing?'

Flint pondered for around twenty seconds. 'Not sure. Not so certain about that one. I think she mentioned that Betty was there, Vine's wife, Betty Tinsdale. Medusa, as she's known in the trade.'

'Medusa? I know who she was, but why?'

The laugh again, 'Because that's what Betty is – a gorgon with the ability to turn people to stone. In the case of Gerald, people say she turns only one part of him into stone.' Cough, laugh again. 'People're quite frightened of her.'

Suzie wondered if, in some ways, people had been a bit frightened of Jo Benton as well.

'What about Barry Forbes?'

'Yes.' Distracted, unsure of himself. 'Yes, turned up here with him one day.'

'When?'

'End of the Battle of Britain. Late September. He looked decidedly fishy and finally left muttering something about having an appointment at Number Ten. Got to see Winston, he said. Good excuse that, an appointment with Winnie.'

'Chummy with Miss Benton, Barry Forbes?'

'More of a case of *her* being chummy with him. He seemed a bit uncomfortable. He's a long-term sleeping partner as well, isn't he?'

'So the story goes.'

Suzie asked when exactly had he last seen Jo Benton – 'Been with her, I mean. No, I don't mean *been* with her, as in sexually. I mean when did you last see her physically.'

'December twelfth. Lunch at a nasty little place in the High Street. She arranged it. Didn't come here. Thinking back, I'd say she already knew the idea of a programme on antiques was just about washed out.'

'Ah, yes,' Suzie murmured. 'Washed out.'

'Think so,' he said. 'Looking back, the writing must've been on the wall already.'

'Well, Mr Flint. We'll probably speak again.' She rose gathering up her notebook and pencil.

'It'll have to be after Christmas, for me.' A shade too quickly. 'I'm going to the country for Christmas. Off tomorrow.'

'Somewhere nice, I hope.'

'Relatives. West Country. Huge house. Tradition. Big tree in the drawing room. Carols, mince pies, Father Christmas arriving with the local hunt. Used to be servants waiting on you hand and foot. I gather that's changed.'

'Well it would have to be after Christmas anyway. I'm off on Monday.'

'Somewhere jolly?'

'Hampshire. To my sister and her children.

Husband's off keeping Hitler at bay.'

'Hampshire's nice. Good part?'

'Overchurch. Village the other side of Basing-stoke.'

'Know it well. Lovely part of the world. There's a good pub there, the White Hart, right?'

'All the pubs in Hampshire seem to be called the White Hart,' said Suzie and her feelings lifted at the thought of a couple of days with Charlotte and the children, maybe a visit to the pub if her sister could get someone to look after the kids. A good old-fashioned pint on Christmas Eve, she thought. Well, half-pint if we're talking about me.

Twelve

'Flint's got the motive.' For a change Shirley sounded serious, not a smile in sight.

'I didn't like him either–' Suzie took another mouthful of Cauliflower Cheese – 'but that doesn't make him a killer.' She mumbled, trying to chew the Cauliflower Cheese and talk at the same time. The cheese was stringy and tasteless and had begun to go claggy around her teeth.

'This is the original Cheddar that was cheesed off.' Shirley pulled a face that made her look like Dopey of the seven dwarfs. When Shirley started being silly like this Suzie felt great warmth towards her. At times she imagined they were almost forging the same kind of relationship she had experienced with her sister, Charlotte, during those last years when they were at home; when their father was still alive.

They had done so many stupid silly things together; a month or so when they only spoke to each other in a cleft-palate-like language; and again they'd had a primitive kind of sign language that now seemed dreadfully out of place given the reality of Charlotte's little boy's – Ben's – total exclusion to the hearing world. Theirs had been a coded lifestyle punctuated by catchphrases from BBC comedy shows.

Now Suzie Mountford and Shirley Cox discussed Daniel Flint over lunch at an anonymous restaurant just off Trafalgar Square. The bottom of Nelson's Column was sandbagged and boarded off with big signs that said, GET YOUR OWN BACK; LONDON! THE WORLD IS WATCHING; LEND YOUR MONEY TO BUY WAR WEAPONS, NOW!

Suzie wondered if this was part of Barry Forbes' advice to the government: get the people to pay for the war now with promises to repay them with interest when it was all over. She wondered if she should actually ask him that outright when they saw him in his plush office near Marble Arch.

'Do you think Cap'n Flint meant the BBC had just given up on the antiques programme; or was he suggesting they'd given up on Miss Benton?'

'Nobody's mentioned that, but if the BBC had pulled the rug from under the fair Jo – well, that might make a difference.' She thought of Jo Benton's photograph. The last one she'd seen was in the agent's offices: Josephine Benton leaning forward, one hand cupping her chin, a smile on the full lips, and a deep twinkle in her eyes, the right eyebrow slightly raised – quizzical they'd call that. Her hair looked gold, fine and shimmering even in the black and white print. And there was something else Suzie Mountford remembered – Jo Benton had been wearing a wooden brooch, a sword-shaped piece fashioned out of bleached wood: more a scimitar than a sword. It was slightly fuzzy and out of focus.

But it was a publicity photograph, she reasoned, so why was she wearing a little wooden ornament? Was this some special keepsake, the wooden brooch? A lucky charm? Did it matter? Jo had been a devious woman, a meticulous planner: the kind of person who would choose carefully for a publicity picture.

'You think I should ask the agent? Ask Webster?' She meant ask about the intentions of the BBC, but part of her wanted to find out about the wooden brooch as well.

'Tiny details.' On the day before he had been injured, Big Toe Harvey had said to her, 'Never underestimate tiny clues, Susannah. Query anything you find odd – even the smallest thing should be looked into if it doesn't feel right to you. Develop your sense of constant suspicion.'

'You're the detective, Suzie,' Shirley said, 'but

yes. Yes, I think you should talk to him. Find out what the BBC were doing.'

'I'm no more a detective than I'm Pilot Officer Prune.' She laughed. Then, making up her mind to phone Webster, she held out her hand. 'Pennies, Shirl. I haven't got much in the way of ackers, and I've no change. None at all. We can claim it back, though. All contributions gratefully received.'

They raised four pennies between them and Suzie went down the stairs to where there was a public telephone to call the Webster and Broome Agency.

Richard Webster wasn't in. 'Gone out to lunch with a client,' the receptionist told her.

'When're you expecting him back?'

'I've no idea. It's an important client so he could be out for the rest of the afternoon.' She sounded exceptionally snooty.

'Would you tell him that Detective Sergeant Mountford wants a word. I won't be back in my office today, but I'll try to ring him later.'

'Who?' the girl asked with all the charm of a King Cobra.

Suzie all but spelled it out for her. A moron, she considered as she went back into the restaurant where Shirley had ordered rice pudding with raisins and sultanas – the dried fruit was a real treat. The war was just over a year old but as they approached Christmas it was clear that there was a serious shortage of dried fruit for cakes.

'My mum used to make rice pudding with cocoa and sugar. Called it chocolate rice. Only

216

way I'd eat it,' she told Suzie.

'My mum once took me out for a meal when I was a kid and I read through the menu. The joke she always told was that I said very loudly, "Do you have to *pay* for rice pudding?" I was flabbergasted that you had to part with money to eat rice pud. Not my favourite choice.'

'You've got no choice here. It's rice pud or cold wait-and-see pudding.'

They took the Tube to Marble Arch at the top of Oxford Street, then spent twenty minutes searching for Barry Forbes' office. Finally discovering it in a little mews house tucked away in one of the streets behind the Cumberland Hotel.

At the mews house a thin grey woman – uncertain age and very indecisive clothes – answered the door when they rang. Suzie showed her warrant card and said they were here to see Mr Forbes.

'You're the police?' The woman sounded surprised, bewildered, as though she didn't really believe them.

'I've just shown you my authority.' Suzie exuded gentleness, and the woman gave Shirley Cox a piercing stare as though uncertain of what or who she was – or why. Shirley smiled sweetly and said, 'I'm police as well. Who might you be, madam?'

'Miss. Miss Poulter. Mr Forbes' personal secretary.' She was all business with a touch of bustle. 'He can give you fifteen minutes. He's off to Chequers soon. Mr Forbes is going to Chequers with the Prime Minister.' Miss

Poulter was important by association. 'Come,' she snapped, leading them across a tiled floor, pausing in front of an oak door, which she tapped and then immediately opened. 'There are two policewomen to see you Mr Forbes.' It was as though she was telling her boss that a pair of illiterate tarts had forced their way in, uninvited and with dog dirt on their shoes.

'He can give us fifteen minutes, Skip,' Shirley whispered, deadpan. Suzie raised her eyebrows and stepped into the office with Shirley at her heels.

A polished military desk stood on a wine red carpet. On the wall behind the desk hung a large oil painting of a naval battle: men o' war pounding each other, a lot of smoke and a dark brooding sky. Barry Forbes rose slowly to his feet: around five-ten; neat straw-coloured hair, the kind of hair some people would envy; thick and heavy; the sort of hair that would always drop back in place, perfectly. There was no doubt that physically he was an attractive man, deep blue eyes, smooth skin and a scrubbed complexion.

Makes you sick, Suzie thought, introducing herself and Shirley, leaning across the desk to shake hands. All very civilized. He had soft hands and she caught a glimpse of well-manicured nails. I know you, she thought. I've seen you somewhere, in the flesh and, no I'm not thinking of seeing your picture in the newspapers. What had Richard Webster said? 'Enjoys dressing up in women's clothes. Also likes to take on two women at a time: loves dressing in fancy underwear.' How do the girls dress up? she wondered. Uniforms, she reckoned. That's what he'd like: the three of them: the Wren in her uniform, and Jo as a nurse. She remembered the nursing sister's blue uniform in the Coram Cross bedroom. Should have followed up on that. Inwardly she blushed and wished she'd had more experience. She really found it difficult to understand why people would want to do things like this.

She had a vivid picture of him rolling around a double bed with the women shrieking with laughter at the fun and frenzy of it all. Today though, Barry Forbes was dressed in a Harris Tweed jacket with big leather buttons like small conkers, and cavalry twill trousers. He wore a double-breasted waistcoat and the jacket hung open showing off his slender figure. Not all men have waists, she thought. Suzie remembered an old Etonian – a friend of Ned Griffith – who had taken her dancing in Cambridge, at the Dorothy Café, making some remark about 'not trustin' a fella who wears double-breasted weskits or two vents in the back of a hackin' jacket'. Where do I know you from? she thought again.

'You've come about this dreadful thing that's happened to Jo Benton.' He was making more of a statement than a query, the voice fiendishly ruling class with what Suzie thought of as a wha-wha overlay.

'Yes, about her murder.' She sounded like a blunt instrument.

A look of concern passed across Forbes' face:

there and gone in a blink. 'Odd, isn't it?' he said. 'So much death out of the skies every night, yet we have to differentiate –' He had a melodic voice, and knew how to pitch it. She thought she detected a bit of Welsh in there.

'Differentiate?'

She didn't like him; didn't like his type. Ruling Class came off him like some cheap, obvious scent. I am someone to be reckoned with, his manner said. Suzie had met his type at Cambridge. Public school, trained from birth to run the country and the Empire. Great charm and ability no doubt, but everything taken for granted. I'm going to deflate you, she thought. (Where the hell do I know you from?)

'Differentiate between legal and illegal murder.' He moved his hands a lot: a series of controlled gestures that said there was a bit of an actor in him; that he knew what he was doing.

Businesslike, she said they had to ask him some routine questions.

'Yes?' He looked at his watch as if to tell her to be quick about it.

'You were a close friend of Miss Benton's?'

Deep in his eyes she saw the fear move again, then his right hand twitched on the desk while his left came up across his body to rest for a second below his right shoulder.

'Well. Yes. Well, I don't know about a *close* friend. I did know her, of course.'

Not close? You bloody little liar, Suzie thought. 'Known her for some time?' she asked, casual; soft as a child's kiss, and as treacherous.

'Oh, several years, yes.' A shade of uncertainty in his voice, slinking in and mingling, moving up to his eyes. Remember, Suzie thought, remember that he'll think he's fireproof, being one of Winston's special advisors with his name in the papers all the time.

That's what DCS Livermore had told her when she'd rung him last night. 'You've probably heard him on the wireless, Suzie. He's a relatively young man but he sounds a bit of a Charlie to me: bit full of himself, if you know what I mean. Probably thinks he's real; thinks you can't touch him either. Most of these fellows believe that. Advisors and politicos. Because they get important jobs they take it for granted that they're above the law. In Germany they probably are, but not here. If he gets cheeky slap him down. He's only a glorified bookkeeper after all, not the real financial McCoy like John Maynard Keynes. But take care because Forbes can probably still bite, and the newspapers'll make a right mess of you because Forbes is on the side of the angels. Difficult, it's always bloody difficult to find the right tone. Walk the right line.' The DCS had paused then said he wondered if they were ever going to meet in the flesh. Then he laughed, told her to be careful.

In the present she queried, 'Several years? What's several years mean exactly?'

There was no response and she didn't press it. Waited in silence until he volunteered, 'She was an acquaintance. Five, six years maybe. Yes, an acquaintance,' he repeated as though he had found the form he wanted.

'An *intimate* acquaintance?'

'Well, I wouldn't—'

'Mr Forbes, we know you had an intimate relationship with Miss Benton.' There, it was out in the open, sprawling on the carpet between them.

'Oh.' For the first time he sounded embarrassed. The arm moved defensively across his body again and the flicker of uncertainty recrossed his face. 'No,' very firmly. 'Oh no, certainly not intimate. I must deny that absolutely. I find it objectionable. Offensive.'

Stung him, Suzie. Wounded him.

'Miss Jo Benton *and* Miss Monica Parker.' Shirley spoke from behind Suzie's shoulder.

Forbes flushed and his eyes moved, looking towards the door, over her shoulder. 'No,' he said. Then again, 'No.' Shaking his head. A vigorous, aggressive rejection.

'You deny knowing Monica Parker?' Suzie asked, leaning forward, her body language full of hostility. 'Miss Monica Parker who is, we understand, a leading Wren serving in HMS *Daedelus*, a shore station at Lee-on-Solent. What the navy calls a stone frigate.'

'Miss Parker was a friend of Jo's, yes.' He looked Suzie straight in the eyes. 'Yes, I knew her as well. Foolish. Of course I knew her.'

'Leading Wren Parker would make up a threesome with you and Miss Benton.' Shirley Cox gave him a big friendly grin. Come inside, dear – oh, what lovely teeth you have, grand-mama.

Suzie heard herself make a tiny guttural sound in the back of her throat. Oh my God, watch it Shirley.

'No!' He scowled. 'No! You're reading far too much into this.'

Suzie imagined that in his head Forbes was assessing his situation. Asking himself if he was in trouble. He wouldn't want the press tipped off. Probably had enough clout to keep them off, though maybe he was frightened and trying headlines on for size. A couple of the Sunday comics might just have a go – WINSTON'S SPECIAL ADVISOR MET WREN AND WINTER DRAWERS GIRL IN THREE-SOME LOVE NEST! On the whole the press didn't like printing rumour and government scandal, so he was probably right to think he was untouchable.

'You knew both Miss Benton *and* Leading Wren Parker?' Suzie asked, bringing it all down a bit.

'Yes!'

'Knew them in the Biblical sense,' needled Shirley, delighted at Barry Forbes' confusion.

Oh, Shirl, no.

'No! No, *not* in the Biblical sense.' He sounded very positive. Roused. Even angrier.

'When did you last see Miss Benton? With or without Leading Wren Monica Parker?' She flashed a look at Shirley Cox.

'Some time ago. Some time...' Rattled but still sure he could stop his reputation going for a burton. 'But it wasn't ... I can swear on oath that I didn't know them in any improper sense. This is quite outrageous.'

His denial was so vehement that Suzie now really wondered if Richard Webster, the agent, had made some error. 'You'd swear on oath?' she asked, and the doubt was there in her own tone.

In the pause that followed, Suzie told him that this information was confidential. 'We're anxious to clear any really close friends. Personally we think Miss Benton's murder was a crime of opportunity.'

'For now, that is,' Shirley added and Suzie could've killed her.

'Mr Forbes, we're not interested in morality. We're only out to catch whoever killed Josephine Benton.'

Barry Forbes gave an exasperated sigh. 'Well, yes. Yes, all right I knew them. Both of them. Jo and Monica. But there was no impropriety. I must stress that. A bit of foolishness from time to time but not—'

'And when did you last...?'

'See them? Oh, I don't know. Maybe three weeks ago. End of Novemberish. I don't have much time these days for—'

'Three-in-a-bunk?' Shirley supplied and this time Suzie gave her a look designed to puncture her sense of humour. She put out a hand as if to signal Cox to slow down, take it easy.

'I find that distasteful, disrespectful and embarrassing.' Then low, almost under his breath, Forbes said it was all very childish.

Suzie was about to ask him what that meant when Shirley chipped in again – 'And there's somebody else. A Miss Emily Baccus?'

'Yes?'

'You know Emily Baccus?'

'I did know her, yes. We went ... We were...' Having regained his equanimity, Barry Forbes had started to get flustered again. This time he crossed both arms over his chest for a moment – big medicine to ward off the evil spirits. 'Yes, of course I knew Emily. But...!'

'You had a relationship with her...' Suzie spoke quietly, calmly, dropping her voice.

'*Had* is the operative word.' He fiddled with his tie then looked at his watch. 'I really must...' he said, then stopped short, looked at his watch again and – 'The time. I have to be with the PM.'

'Emily Baccus?' Suzie prodded.

'Emily Baccus, yes. Yes. There was a time when I thought we could become engaged. Marry. Emily and me.'

'Not any more? You don't see her nowadays?'

'So busy,' he said and it didn't ring true. 'We had a falling out. She became distant. We drifted. I don't really see that it's any of your business, Inspector.'

'Sergeant,' she corrected. 'Detective Sergeant, and I'm afraid it *is* my business, Mr Forbes. We know you've had a sexual relationship with Miss Benton, and—'

'No! No!' Very firm. Outraged even. He took a deep breath and little white patches of skin showed high on his cheekbones. 'No, I want to

225

make this quite clear. I don't have to stand for this. And I did *not* have a sexual relationship with Miss Benton,' he insisted, raising his voice. 'Not in any accepted sense. Anyway, it's none of your damned business.'

'We could do this at the station if you'd feel happier.' Immediately Suzie knew that she had gone too far.

If there was any bluff to be called he called it. 'If you feel we should speak formally. At the police station. Then we can do just that, and I'll bring my solicitor. When would you like to arrange that, Sergeant ... er?'

'Mountford...'

'When would you like to do that, Miss Mountford?'

Quite suddenly, Suzie became aware of how incredibly aggressive they must have sounded. Livermore, on the phone last night had summed it up – 'It's a difficult line to tread. Difficult, the line between accusation, rudeness, and what's within the bounds of decency. You learn it by doing it. If you overstep the mark, then for God's sake apologize.'

'I'm sorry, Mr Forbes. Sometimes in a murder inquiry we go too far. A formal interview's probably not necessary, sir. If you could just tell us where you were on the evening Miss Benton was killed? Between around five and seven?' Sounds like a radio play, she thought. I was proceeding in a westerly direction when I came upon the accused and all that. She hated the unimaginative construction of standard police jargon.

'As it happens, I was at Ten Downing Street for most of that day. In fact every day this week up until today. I think you'll find the staff there will bear me out. Prime Minister as well if you like. I was at Ten Downing Street from eleven in the morning until well after nine o'clock at night. Monday, Tuesday, Wednesday and yesterday.' He sounded smug about the witnesses he could call, and she was tempted to go on the attack again. 'Professor Lindemann as well if you need more,' he said. 'Professor Lindemann and Jock Coleville also should you have cause. Chief of Air Staff Portal was there on Tuesday, and I saw General Ismay on Wednesday and yesterday.' The pinkness of his cheeks darkened, turning quite florid, with the white patches still clear. Little white triangles.

Suzie thought of Harlequin, then asked, 'And Miss Baccus, sir?'

'No. I don't think Miss Baccus has ever been in Number Ten.'

'That's not really what I meant, Mr Forbes. Could you give us her address, sir?'

'Of course.' He parroted the address near Marylebone High Street – Derbyshire Mansions. He shook his head, gave an agitated sigh. 'Really, I've had enough of this. Insinuations, and these disgusting accusations.' He continued to shake his head, and there was a kind of violence in the gesture.

This wasn't getting her anywhere. She'd tried to be conciliatory and if anything she seemed to be treading towards more trouble. She really did not have the right to be as hostile as this.

227

Anyway, Big Toe would be taking over directly after Christmas. She'd give him the notes and let him do the work. She'd made a complete lash-up of this, and Shirley hadn't helped. 'Very good, Mr Forbes,' she said. 'Thank you, Mr Forbes,' she said.

'Is that it? Satisfied are you?' Like one of those nasty little snapping dogs.

'Not really, sir. You'll probably have to sign a statement. My senior officer'll almost certainly want to see you after Christmas. I'm really sorry to have bothered you, sir.'

He looked at her with unashamed dislike. 'Yes. Yes.' Tilting his head to one side as though examining her face, eventually he said, 'Not a woman's job this, is it?' Then another pause, and – 'You were in the papers weren't you?'

'Sir?'

'Read a piece in the paper, didn't I? Didn't seem to approve of you doing a man's job.'

'Free country, Mr Forbes.'

'Thank God for that. Let's hope it remains so. Now you must excuse me. I really do have to meet Winst— the Prime Minister.'

'We'll probably see you after Christmas. Where will you be, sir? In case we need to speak before then.'

'With the Churchills.' Smug. 'I've no family and he's kindly asked...' He trailed off. Then, 'And where will you be, Sergeant? Just in case I need to get hold of *you*.'

'Overchurch. Hampshire. Falcon Cottage. Telephone Overchurch 358. I'll be with my sister: Mrs Vernon Fox.' Suzie was angry again.

It wouldn't do, she should get out of here. Forbes was unbelievable.

'Know it well, Overchurch,' he said calmly. 'Used to stay with the Bartholemews. The local doctor, his son's an old chum of mine, Paul. Maybe you...?'

'I'm afraid not. No.' Everyone seemed to know the bloody village, she thought. That lovely Josh Dance, Daniel Flint and now the odious Barry Forbes.

The two women took the Tube back to Piccadilly, planning to walk through to the Corner House in Coventry Street.

'For crying out loud, why d'you let him off the hook like that?' Shirley Cox asked as soon as they were out in the street and out of Miss Poulter's hearing. She looked like a woman with incredibly acute hearing.

'The man's a big gun, Shirley, and you made a dog's breakfast out of it. We really didn't have the right to be as belligerent as we were. He could make trouble, and I could be back directing traffic.'

'He's a little turd.'

'Maybe, but it won't be my job in the end. Big Toe'll take over fast as a Spit once he's back. I agree there's something unpleasant about Forbes.' Then – 'What's a turd?'

'Oh, Suzie. A stool, as in shit! Yes, he's a jumped up little—'

'Shirley, I couldn't be bothered,' she said calmly but very firmly. 'Just couldn't be bloody bothered. He spells trouble – trouble for me, I mean.'

229

'Oh, come on, he's been messing around. If this death has got something to do with sex I'd put him in the frame.'

'Pretty intense about it, though.' She deepened her voice, did an imitation Forbes' accent. 'I did *not* have a sexual relationship with Miss Benton!'

Shirley Cox smiled, a little patronizingly perhaps. 'Of course he's going to deny it. He'd swear his mother was an Eskimo if it'd help him. He's one of Churchill's advisors. I wouldn't trust someone in his job even if the Pope himself gave him an alibi. He thinks he's fireproof because he's built himself a sinecure next to the most powerful man in England.'

'Big words, Shirley, but I know that bugger from somewhere. Not from pictures in magazines and papers.' She shrugged. 'Anyhow, it's not going to concern me for much longer.'

'Quite frankly, you don't give a damn. Why?'

'Big Toe'll be back on New Year's Day.'

'How d'you know that?'

'My high-ranking would-be boyfriend told me...'

'Sanders of the River? He told you Big Toe's coming back on New Year's Day?'

'Yep.'

'Then I bet Big Toe'll put you straight back on to him. On to Forbes, I mean. Way of the world. I can see him saying it – "Sarn't Mountford, you'll go and talk to Winston's friend, Forbes, right?" '

'Then forewarned is—'

'Forearmed, yes. Was your mum as full of clichés as mine was? A problem shared is a problem halved. Look after the pennies—'

'And the pounds'll look after themselves, yes. Full of it. A stitch in time and all that rot; a fool and his money; laugh and the world laughs with you—'

'That one's right, Skip. Cry and you cry alone. I've cried alone many a time and usually on my own.'

They spent the journey to Piccadilly trying to outdo each other in the homespun philosophy stakes.

'Many a mickle makes a muckle, what the hell did that mean?'

'Don't ask me. Let's have tea and you can brief me on Gerald Vine.'

They walked up to Coventry Street and into Suzie's favourite Corner House. 'You'll be charging me rent next,' she said when the nippy arrived to take their order. She had served Suzie on countless visits but had little sense of humour. 'Yes, miss,' she replied all straight-faced. They ordered tea for two and toast. 'No butter,' she said.

'Jam?' the nippy asked.

'Yes, please.'

'It says greengage and ginger on the jar but I don't think it's been near a greengage.' Nowadays all kinds of things masqueraded in jam – turnips for instance.

'It's being so cheerful as keeps her going,' Shirley said once the nippy was out of earshot.

At least the tea was strong, though they both

231

agreed about the jam.

'So what's the gen on tonight?'

'Tonight you're on your own, Skipper.'

'You're not going to be with me? I've got to have someone with me.'

'Not asked. His secretary specifically said he'd meet *you*. If there's not a raid he'll be at the Ivy: six o'clock.'

'I can't do that.'

'Why not? Who's to know?'

'I can't accept the man's hospitality and interview him at the same time.'

'He has to be there – at the Ivy. It was either meet him there at six or leave it 'til after Christmas?'

'I can't.'

'You'll have to. Just sit and talk to him, then leave. No need to order. He's a catch, so get to meet him, Skip.'

'I suppose so.' She did not feel good about it. It would be awkward. 'Dinner at the Ivy and you're not coming?'

'No option. Anyway I'm seeing Bernie the Fearless Fireman.'

'What if there's a raid?'

'You're to ask for him at the Garrick. They'll direct you. He probably has a private shelter there with Noël Coward and John Gielgud.'

'I meant you and Bernie.'

'We've got our own private shelter.' She gave a little leer.

'You're a wicked girl, Shirley.' The good middle-class girl speaking.

'Whatever, it's going to be an early night.'

Shirley grinned. 'I'm on duty first thing tomorrow. Unlike some.'

For a good minute, Suzie appeared to be wrapped up in her own thoughts, gnawing away at something in her mind. Finally she once more asked Shirley if she should see Steven Fermin again before she left for Christmas.

'You've got things you haven't asked him?'

'Don't know. I feel that I'm missing something. After all we didn't know about Jo Benton and her predilection for musical beds.'

'Or bury the muscle,' Shirley said cheekily. 'So?'

'So I feel I ought to take another walk through his paradise gardens and listen to him: see if it makes more sense now. I can hardly believe that he didn't have an inkling that she was...'

'If you'd be happier, then you should. You're in on Sunday, aren't you?'

'All day.'

'Why not work out what you want to ask him and phone him from the office.'

She had no clear idea of what she wanted with Fermin: just a vague feeling that she should see him and ask the questions all over again. 'Heard anything about the funeral?' she asked.

'Not yet. You want me to ring him tomorrow, or is that a good excuse for you?'

'Yes, leave it. I'll phone and ask him on Sunday.' She thought they'd never get it done before Christmas. The coroner hadn't finished with the body yet; it was still early days. Maybe they'd do it by New Year. New Year's Day was an ordinary working day, except in Scotland where they celebrated Hogmanay.

'If it's going to be at the end of next week you'll represent the nick? When're you back?' Shirley asked.

'I'd thought of coming in on the 27th – Friday – and then perhaps going to see my mum for New Year's Eve. I'll make up my mind before I go to interview the Squadron Leader on Monday.'

'Won't be able to make your own mind up once Big Toe's back.'

'You don't know. I may have a secret weapon by then: I may have started going out with Mr Sanders.'

Before they went their separate ways Shirley told her not to get too tough with Gerald Vine. 'Get out the whips and he'll say, "Yes please." And you'll get nothing out of him.'

The sirens had not sounded and Suzie got her timing right, walking back along Shaftesbury Avenue, going through the doors of the Ivy dead on six o'clock.

Before leaving the Corner House she phoned Webster & Broome and got Dick Webster just as he was leaving the office. 'I tend to nip off a little early these days,' he explained. 'Like to be back in the nest before the ferocious Hun starts getting aggressive.'

She asked what the BBC's future plans had been for Jo Benton.

'Plans?' Webster whooped. 'They were full of

ideas. She had a long-term contract for five years, and we had a clause that gave me the option to renegotiate money after two. They certainly indicated that they wanted to keep her. Her chosen career was in broadcasting and the BBC was the one place to go.'

'It's just that I'd heard they cancelled this antiques show thing they'd been planning.'

A pause, then a little chuckle. 'Oh dear, she *was* a naughty girl. There were no plans at the BBC for an antiques show. *Jo* had the plans and was trying to get the BBC involved. They had meetings about it, but I don't think they were ever serious. Didn't think she could do that kind of show. Humoured her though.' He lowered his voice. 'I've told you how she operated. She'd fancy someone, have fun, then drop him without any reason. Then pick him up again a couple of years later.'

'And this time she gave a spurious reason?'

'You're talking about Dan Flint?'

'Naturally.'

Another pause. 'She was spending a lot of time with him. Learning a lot as well. I know she was very keen to do a show on antiques and she was going to bed with Daniel as well as learning from him. Difficult to say whether she got fed up with antiques or Flint or if the BBC gave her a firm private no. Bit of each probably.'

'That's a great help, Mr Webster.' Then, as though just remembering – 'Oh, one other thing. That photograph of Jo in your office?'

He remained silent.

'She's wearing a little wooden brooch in that picture. A sword I think it is.'

Still no response.

'Was it anything special, do you know?'

'I know Gerald Vine gave it to her and I think it had some significance – a small romantic object, I suspect. That's all I can tell you. She never talked about her jewellery. Sorry, can't help you.'

Well at least she had an opener for the conversation with the country's greatest living actor, Gerald Vine OBE.

She was going off to meet him now – to meet the famous Gerald Vine. She thought of her mother and her mother would have said, 'DV', which meant *Deo volente* – God willing.

'We're going to the pictures tonight, Mummy?' the girls would chorus.

'DV,' Mummy would say. Took the joy out of everything. Mummy could be a pain in the neck sometimes. Quite often actually.

Thirteen

Suzie's heart did a little flutter as she walked into the Ivy and told the headwaiter she was meeting the actor Gerald Vine. And why shouldn't it? Vine was undoubtedly Britain's number one heart-throb across the board because he did it all, stage and screen and everything in between: regularly played the

West End, the Old Vic and the Shakespeare Memorial Theatre at Stratford, so that's all one.

She got the impression that the headwaiter knew exactly who she was and why she was meeting the actor.

He had not yet arrived, Mr Vine, but was certainly expected. This was his table, if you would like to wait for him here. Mr Vine would wish her to have a drink. A cocktail perhaps?

'A small gin and vermouth, please.' She knew she shouldn't; she was on duty, but she'd read an article about Gerald Vine in *Woman* – on that browny-grey newsprint they were all being forced to use nowadays – and it said his favourite tipple was gin and vermouth.

'An excellent idea, I'll have one as well.' And there he was, standing in front of the table, large as life, twice as natural, in a beautiful grey suit, a silk shirt from Jermyn Street and a Sulka tie, all soft blues and old gold. Immaculate, skin glowing, incredibly healthy, bronzed, the famous hair sleek from *Trumpers* ministrations, and the voice as magical as it had been in *The Squire of Bovey Hall*. She'd seen that film last year with her mother and Charlotte. Black and white of course as so many Pinewood films still were, yet now here he was in person, and in glorious Technicolor.

Certainly he was not as tall as Suzie imagined, but the features, gestures and especially the voice – 'clipped silk and honey' as the critic James Agate had once described it – were all now immediate to her.

The pit of her stomach rolled over, and there was a ferocious twinkling in her loins. When he leaned over to shake hands across the table she only just managed to stop herself from standing up as a mark of respect. He locked eyes with her, dragging her down to Lord knew where.

The waiter fussed, holding the chair for him. About his drink he said, 'You know how I like it, heavy on the gin,' and asked if they still had any food left.

'Noël eats them out of house and home at lunchtime,' he said. The waiter made some secret moves with his hands and shoulders that indicated Mr-Vine-is-such-an-amusing-man, then scurried off in search of the gin.

'Fortunately for you, sir, Mr Coward is in Australia.' The headwaiter was also twinkling. (But probably not in the area of his loins, Suzie thought. Though you never could tell these days.)

'I'm Gerald Vine,' the actor said loudly and quite unnecessarily, 'and you must be Miss Mountford.'

'Yes.' Gosh, she thought, he's gorgeous. I wouldn't last five minutes.

'I think you London police are wonderful.' He smiled and it puckered his lips and let fly a force ten on the twinkle scale. He took out a slim silver cigarette case from inside his splendidly cut jacket, flicked it open and offered it. 'Virginian on the left, Turkish on the right, but they tell me we won't have the choice in a few weeks time. It'll be camel droppings on the left and dried herbal mixture on the right, and we'll be glad of it.'

Suzie took a Virginian – Players Navy Cut – and he leaned forward again, deftly operating a thin silver lighter and she almost choked as the smoke hit the back of her throat. It's all like a Warwick Deeping novel, she thought.

'You alright?' He looked up at her through half-lowered eyelids as he fitted a cigarette into a jet holder and lit it.

She blew smoke out of both sides of her mouth – like a bloody dragon, she later told Shirley – and nodded yes, fine, okay, wonderful, and yes, any time, and how would you like me? Lightly grilled? Without dressing? Suddenly she knew what the tarty underwear thing was all about. Pray that I'm not too late for it.

'So, what do the Metropolitan Police Force want with me? That business with Desdemona is it? Or perhaps the Scottish king, eh? Old Duncan? Or that fellow Clarence drowned in a butt of Malmsey. I deny everything of course; and my wife'll deny the Scottish thing.' He chuckled. He had played a young and passionate Othello a couple of years ago at the Old Vic, and six years or so earlier he had been an acclaimed Macbeth with Betty Tinsdale as Lady M: directed by the great Tyrone Guthrie. He had married Miss Tinsdale during the run.

There was also his Richard III just before war was declared. He had broken the rules with Richard and appeared skulking on stage while the assassins murdered the Duke of Clarence by dumping him in a barrel of Malmsey wine –

only Suzie didn't know that because she rarely got to the theatre.

The waiter returned with the drinks and placed menus in front of them.

Suzie sat there with a goofy smile as though the idea of the Met investigating the murders of Desdemona, the Scottish King Duncan and the Duke of Clarence were the funniest things she'd ever heard. She only stopped chortling when he inquired what she'd like to eat. 'Have you got any of the liver?' he asked the waiter with another of his smiles and a quick flash of the teeth.

'We kept some, Mr Vine, especially as we knew you were coming in tonight.'

'They do the most divine liver. Try some.'

'Really I can't, Mr Vine. I can just about get away with accepting a drink from you. But I'm on duty, sir.' She felt her muscles tighten as she faced up to what had to be done, even though Gerald Vine couldn't possibly have had anything to do with murder.

'Oh, but surely—?'

'No, I'm sorry, I can't.' Quite proud of herself.

He gave a little pout, playing the teenager. 'Oh, what a shame, I wanted to pump you about police officers.'

'Seriously, Mr Vine, I can't.' For a second there she managed to keep her composure and immediately regretted it.

'Well, if you're sure.' He told the waiter he'd order later. 'I'm expecting Miss Tinsdale and a friend, but let's have a bottle of the 65.' He turned back to Suzie, giving her another of his twinkles. 'We have to go on to a Christmas party. Very full diary at Christmas time.'

'I haven't bought a single present yet and I leave London on Monday.' She couldn't believe she was saying this.

'Somewhere nice?'

'Oh, just Hampshire. My sister's place.' That makes it sound like a manor house. Now he's going to ask me where.

'Nice county, Hampshire. Whereabouts?'

I'll tell him and he'll say that he knows half the village, including the cowherd's grandmother. 'Overchurch.'

'Don't know it,' he said in the kind of voice that means complete disinterest. 'And now what do you really want with me?'

Her throat was dry and she had to keep wiping her hands on the napkin she'd picked up. 'This is all wrong,' she shook her head. 'I'm sorry, I should have spoken to you officially, maybe at a police station. Or my detective constable should have asked if I could see you at your home, and I really should have another officer with me. I'll have to make it informal and get back to you after Christmas.' Pause. Count to seven. 'It's about Josephine Benton,' she said, taking a quick sip of her gin.

The smiles and twinkles faded and he seemed to transform himself into Friar Lawrence discovering the dead Romeo. 'The horrible conceit of death and night,' he muttered.

Suzie almost asked him what he had said.

'What can I do to help?' He had a slight

frown and didn't quite look her in the eye. 'I was terribly fond of Jo. We were terribly, terribly close.' For a second he sounded like Noël Coward, and insincere. 'It was a great shock. Words become inadequate...'

'I have to ask where you were on Wednesday evening between five and seven. That was when Jo Benton was killed.'

He looked aghast. 'But you don't think I...? We were the best of friends.'

'A little more than friends I think.'

'What...?'

'Mr Vine, I have to tell you that we know exactly how friendly you were with Jo Benton.'

He laughed. Like someone discovered in some small mean act. 'Then I'd be obliged if you didn't mention it in front of my wife. She should be here soon and I really wouldn't—'

'There's no reason to concern your wife with this matter yet, Mr Vine. Unless of course she has to confirm an alibi. Where were you on Wednesday, sir? Especially between five and seven in the afternoon.'

'Rehearsing. Chekov, *The Cherry Orchard*. I'm directing as well as playing Gaev. Every day this week from ten in the morning with a short break for lunch, between one and two thirty. On Wednesday I lunched with Ralph and Edith. You said between five and seven. Wednesday?'

She nodded.

'Wednesday, we didn't break until about six. Any of them will tell you we were all there. Had a bit of a bust-up with Edith actually. She was being a little difficult and I told her that as Madam Ranevskaya she was supposed to be vague and uncaring, not hysterical. Then she was rather rude, asked what she was supposed to do during the pause. I said what pause? And she said the pause while Ralph is speaking.' He gave a little snort. 'Sometimes she can be difficult. I mean she wasn't trying to be funny.'

'You left at six, then?'

'More like half-past. Went on to the Garrick. Home about ten. Betty joined me at the Garrick and Ralph was there. But surely—?' He stopped short and then gave a little shake of the head. 'You say you know? Josephine and I? Yes?'

'Yes.'

'She was indiscreet?' He sighed and there was a tiny tic visible in his right cheek. 'Jesus Christ, then everyone'll know.'

'I'm sure it was contained.'

'That wasp Webster?'

'I can't comment, Mr Vine. But I'd like to ask you something else. Unofficially. Something just to satisfy a personal curiosity.'

'Well?'

'Jo Benton's current publicity photograph?'

'Yes?'

'She's wearing a small brooch. A little wooden sword, bleached wood.'

'Mmmm?' Happier.

'On the left side of a dark dress.'

'Out of focus.' He was softer. 'Though I doubt if you could've identified ivory if it had been in focus.'

243

'It's ivory?'

'It is ivory and, yes, I gave it to her. You can't see the diamonds either. There are six small diamonds set in the hilt. It's a very romantic piece – a sabre by the way, not a sword. What did you need to know? That I'd given it to her?'

'I wanted to know why it was special. Jo Benton was a clever woman. She wouldn't have chosen any old thing for her new publicity photo. There had to be a story behind it. A reason.'

He nodded. 'Good girl,' he said. 'I think I was the reason. That little sabre was very romantic.' The smile was back, eyes glittering. Were those tears? 'We had a complicated and profound relationship. Lots of peaks and troughs, if you know what I mean. There was a time – well, a number of times really – when we could have run off together. Happily we didn't because it would have inevitably ended in tears.'

They had times when they simply wanted to discover things together. 'We'd talk 'til all hours; see exhibitions, paintings, sculpture. We spent a lot of time in theatres as well, and we'd read books together. Jo knew a great deal about the theatre and always wanted to learn more.' He stopped for a second or two. 'And we were lovers of course. The sex was wonderful, inventive. I shall never have her like again.'

Suzie glanced away, a little embarrassed, conscious of what Webster had told her – the extreme sado-masochism.

'We'd dress up, act out little dramas. We even went through a phase of reciting poetry while we made love. I remember one afternoon when she started to declaim Lewis Carroll's "Jabberwocky".' The smile was tender, the memory obviously thrilling—

'And as in uffish thought he stood,
The Jabberwock, with eyes of flame,
Came whiffling through the tulgey wood,
And burbled as it came!'

She was surprised again, for she could see, intuitively, how that worked. Perhaps she was starting to understand the finer points of sex without ever having any experience.

'The brooch, Mr Vine. You said it had a romantic story.'

'It belonged to my great-great-grandmama. It was bought for her by my great-great-grandpapa who picked it up from a French prisoner of war in Portsmouth. A Captain de Clessy of the – *1st Chevau-léger-lanciers*.'

Captain de Clessy was held in one of the prison hulks and allowed ashore to sell his carvings. How the diamonds were obtained was ingenious – 'They're quite small stones. Can't even see them in Jo's photograph' – de Clessy had trained a crow to steal for him, like a jackdaw.

'There are many well-documented incidents of French prisoners using birds to steal by proxy.' Vine told her of the famous one near Edinburgh. 'This was also a crow but it stole only clothes from a washing line. The crow trained by de Clessy was offered pieces of metal and beads, gold braid from his epaulettes; brass buttons from his uniform until it got the message. Eventually the crow became so audacious that it would fly up to the bedroom windows of ladies whom de Clessy fancied, and they would feed it, then wondered how their rings and necklaces had disappeared.' He said that these ladies were either married or were very young girls. Ladies who would never dare talk about the young French officer on parole, or what they were doing together.

'How wonderful.' Suzie was entranced by the story.

'It was passed to my great-grandmother and on to my grandmother, who, oddly, left it to me,' he told her. 'Whenever we arranged to meet, Jo wore it. I was most touched that she had it on her dress for that photograph, though the idiot of a photographer didn't do it justice. She was wearing it the last time I saw her.'

'Which was, Mr Vine?'

'Did she tell Webster, her agent?' It was like a sudden squall, the friendliness ebbing away in an instant.

'I'm sorry. I've told you, I can't comment.'

He gave a sad little laugh. 'That's as good as a yes. She was always gossiping with Webster and I don't trust any agent. Did she give him details?'

'I can't comment.' She sounded quite angry.

'Merciful heavens!'

'Mr Vine, if your wife's coming then we should get on. Or perhaps we should do this another time. You could, possibly, see my detective inspector when he's back after Christmas.'

'I'd rather we got this over with now.' The pleasant geniality had disappeared altogether now, replaced by an iciness.

'You'll have to see him anyway, my detective chief inspector.'

'Please get on and ask what you have to.' He was a different man.

The waiter arrived with the wine and they were held up for another couple of minutes while he went through his little routine. Suzie put her hand over the glass he placed in front of her.

'None for you, madam?' the waiter asked and she snapped, 'No,' rather rudely. He thinks I'm a cretin, she thought. He thinks I don't know how to behave at a dinner table.

When the waiter had gone she said, 'Look, sir, we're trying to speak with anyone who had an intimate relationship with Jo Benton. I'm sorry but it's important.'

'You've got your work cut out if you're going to speak to all of them. Go on.'

'When did you last see her?'

He lit another cigarette. 'Four, maybe five, weeks ago. I don't keep track.'

'Where?'

'We speak to each other every four or five weeks – about once a month. Depending on what we're doing, we meet by arrangement. I often give her dinner. Sometimes we do a show.'

247

'This has been going on for a long time?'

'Years.'

'And it was an arranged meeting?'

'No. I'm using rehearsal rooms, for the Chekhov, off Broadwick Street. I came out one evening and bumped into her. That was Jo. She appeared and disappeared on a whim. It was meant to look like an accident, but I knew she'd arranged it. Not that I minded.' He had become distant: too far to measure.

'So you spent the evening together?'

'Yes. I telephoned Betty and said I'd be late. I told her I was having a meeting with Baynard Blair – he's doing the sets.'

'Wasn't that a little dangerous? He could have—'

'Rung me at home? Of course Baynard could have rung, and Betty could have answered. That was the point. We both enjoyed the danger. It gave us an extra *frisson*. That's really what a lot of it was about.'

'Where did you go? Together, I mean.'

He smiled and his shoulders moved as though he was laughing. 'To her place, of course.'

'Out to Camford? Coram Cross Road?'

'No, of course not. We went to her flat in Derbyshire Mansions. Marylebone.'

Suzie went very still, cold inside and repeated, 'Derbyshire Mansions?' Knowing she had been there only yesterday. Trying to seek out Emily Baccus.

Fourteen

She felt giddy, and for a moment wondered if it was the drink. Then she rose above it, angry with herself for going weak at the knees.

Everything came back into focus.

'What number Derbyshire Mansions?'

'Oh–' he made a gesture, like a conjurer plucking a card out of the air – 'two hundred and twenty.'

'You're sure? Two-twenty?'

'Absolutely. I ought to be. Used to subsidize the rent. Paid it completely for a couple of years.'

Two-twenty Derbyshire Mansions, she repeated in her head. The flat, very likely, directly below three-twenty where Emily Baccus lived. Nobody had thought to tell them that the late Jo Benton, murder victim, had a fashionable flat in the centre of London as well as her nice house in Camford. Jesus! She thought to herself, and she rarely blasphemed. Nuns had made her wary of blasphemy.

'Mr Vine, I have to use a telephone.' It came out in a flurry and she had to repeat it. 'Is there one here d'you know, a public telephone?' Looking around, eyes everywhere.

'Oh? What's wrong? Have I said something I...?'

She squeezed out a thin smile. 'Really, Mr Vine, it's my own fault. I'm likely to get into some trouble. I didn't know about Jo Benton having a flat as well as the Coram Cross Road house.'

'Why should you?' He seemed to be delighted that she was so discomfited. 'She didn't rent it in her own name. At Derbyshire Mansions, she was known as Mrs FitzGerald. Sheila FitzGerald. Capital f. Capital g. It's not very subtle, I know.'

He signalled to the headwaiter, explained what she needed, so that was how she found herself using a telephone in a passage next to the kitchens.

She got straight on to the Yard and found Tommy Livermore hadn't yet left his office.

'I think we should take a look, sir,' she said after giving him the news.

'Yes, so do I. Damn it. Never mind. You've been there you say?'

'Looking for the other woman. Emily Baccus, yes sir.'

'Any contacts?'

She wondered if the little nutbrown former NCO counted as a contact – Cyril Nutkin. 'Yes, sir, the porter.'

'Right, you make your way over there. I'll get weaving on the search warrant. I'll bring a couple of the lads from here. You want anyone from Camford?'

'I rather think I do, sir. My Detective Constable. WDC Cox – C-O-X.' Sorry, Shirley, she thought. 'If you can arrange that for me, sir, please. It's difficult here.'

'Consider it done. Meet you there in about – what? An hour?'

'Right, sir.'

Vine's wife, Betty Tinsdale, had arrived at the table – Medusa, as she was known in the trade, Suzie remembered. She went over and stood waiting like a lemon and Gerald Vine didn't even look up: all his attention on his wife.

'So I said to her, "Boo, you know Binkie's never going to stand for it, not with Larry already playing the king as if it were the ace."' Betty Tinsdale speaking, loud and haughty. 'And she said, "Well it's never stopped him before!" Not even a smile out of her.' She looked up, hard glinting little eyes and a lot of make-up. Plucked and heavily pencilled eyebrows. The hair short, straight and dark. Mousy really. Suzie hardly recognized her and wondered why for a second or two. It was the hair, she decided. When she'd seen her in films or – once – with a school party to Stratford to see her playing Desdemona opposite a great star just about peaking, the hair had been long and golden. Wigs, she thought. All wigs. All a fraud.

'A new little friend, darling?' Mrs Gerald Vine asked her husband, drawling out the words.

Vine looked up, surprised for a moment that Suzie had returned. 'No, a policewoman, dear,' he said.

'Get younger every day, don't they sweetheart?' She smirked, lighting another cigarette.

Suzie did not wait for an introduction. 'We'll be in touch, Mr Vine,' she said, and, 'Goodnight, sir. Madam.'

It was quiet at Derbyshire Mansions. She hoiked Cyril the porter out and told him to stand by. 'And not a word to anyone. Certainly not the press, even if they offer you Fairy Gold.' She all but made him swear by St Peter, who held the keys to the Kingdom, so was, by default, Patron Saint of Porters. They paced the entrance hall together, Cyril Nutkin quizzing her about what was going on.

'I mean it's all right.' He walked too close to her. 'I wasn't doin' nothin' else in particular this evening. Well, listening to the play on the wireless, that's all. I love them plays. You know, I can see clearly what people look like and what the scene is when I'm listening to a good play on the wireless. I've got a wonderful imagination for them plays. See it all, vivid.' Pause. Turned with her. Like a bloody dance, she thought. 'What's all this about, miss?' Crafty, trying to catch her by surprise.

'You'll see soon enough. Got your keys?'

'Oh yes. You'll have a warrant then? For Miss Baccus' place, where you was trying to get in before?'

'You'll see. Just keep it under your hat.'

Shirley arrived in a rush. 'That was impressive, Skip. Though I don't think I should be speaking to you. I was in the middle of something quite important.' She made a coy little face, a lot of mouth and eye movement.

'Don't get stroppy with me,' Suzie warned.

252

'What was impressive?'

'They didn't ring or anything. The car just arrived: pulled up outside Mrs Gibson's. Your future gentleman friend had told them to go right ahead and bring me here with the bell going at the speed of light. And it was my night off. So, what's going on?'

She eased Shirley away from Cyril Nutkin and told her about Jo Benton's flat and Gerald Vine's long association with her – 'Directly below Emily Baccus's place. Love nest. She rents it in the name of Sheila FitzGerald. Capital f. Capital g.'

'That's not very subtle.' Shirley shook her head. 'With Gerald Vine and all. How was he by the way?'

'I thought he was a little, what's the word? Mannered?'

'Well, he's an actor. What d'you expect, a shrinking violet?'

'He was a bit overpowering. And his wife turned up. Medusa.'

'His wife's Betty Tinsdale. She was smashing in *Make Love Deathless*.'

'No, that's what Cap'n Flint said, don't you remember? Medusa?'

'Oh, well, how were the snakes?'

'Speaking with forked tongues? You amaze me, Shirley.'

'What? Knowing Medusa had snakes for hair?'

A wartime reserve constable – what they called an auxiliary constable – arrived with a thick manila envelope. 'Looking for Detective

Chief Superintendent Livermore or WDS Mountford?' he said in a soft voice when Cyril Nutkin stepped forward.

Suzie identified herself.

'Search warrants, Sergeant.' The auxiliary constable spoke low again, as if he had an obstruction in his throat, almost a whisper.

'Okay. Where're you from, constable?'

He wore a civilian mackintosh over his uniform, and he fumbled under it for his warrant card. 'Constable Christie, Reg Christie. Charing Cross.'

'DCS Livermore's casting his net wide tonight.'

'He was over with us at Charing Cross, talking to a witness on one of his cases. Now he's at Vine Street, so someone had to collect these. I was pleased to do it. Especially for the Chief Super.'

The manila envelope contained two warrants – both for Derbyshire Mansions, numbers two-twenty and three-twenty. She nodded to him. 'Thanks, Reg.'

'Thank you, Sergeant. I'm off duty now, but I can always—'

'No, we'll manage. You got far to go?'

'Notting Hill. Rillington Place.' He had a proprietary air. It could have been one of the most fashionable parts of London. 'Thank you, Sergeant.' The soft voice sounded almost knowledgeable, shaded with a North Country accent. Suzie nodded to him again, secretly relieved when he had gone.

Twenty minutes later Tommy Livermore

came in with a whole retinue.

'Orchestra, dancing girls, the lot,' Suzie murmured.

'And a male voice choir.'

He had his own sergeant, Billy Mulligan, big and very subservient; several DCs who seemed devoted to him, and seven extra people.

'Spear carriers,' Livermore called them. They were in fact three forensics officers, two scenes-of-crime constables and a photographer, plus a hard-faced WDC with short, straight, dirty gold hair, done as a straight back and sides with a parting on the left. Her name was Molly Abelard and she hardly ever left the Guv'nor's side.

Suzie was completely surprised, knocked out – she realized later – when she saw Livermore in the flesh. On the telephone he came across as a slightly jovial, avuncular individual, even fatherly at a pinch. So she had pictured him as short-sighted, stooped, with a thickening waist and probably a walrus moustache and bottle-glass spectacles.

In person, though, he looked incredibly young and rather dashing: the kind of man who could easily pass himself off as a fighter pilot in mufti. He had a tall, spare frame, which meant he was just over six feet in his stocking feet, slim and muscular, with a bronzed, lived-in face that gave the immediate impression that its owner came straight out of the top drawer.

'Well – Suzie with a zed – at last. How do you do?'

And she realized that the paternal interpretation she had put on his voice was totally out of order – particularly when she looked into his eyes.

'Sir. Mr Livermore. Crikey, you've come mob-handed, sir.'

'Well, to be absolutely honest with you, Suzie, I'm a bit of a lazy devil when it comes to detection.' The voice, when heard close, mouth to ear, was rich, and sounded like the product of a very expensive education, with an undertow of Scotland. Not the broad Glaswegian, but softer, only a hint. There one minute, gone the next. 'So what I've done,' he continued, 'is I've carved out a bit of a private army for myself.' He clocked off the names and specialist skills of his people, ending with, '– and last but not least, the menacing Molly Abelard, whom I suspect will be hauled away any minute to teach hulking great commandos the terrible arts of silent killing. Oh, my God!' He had come up against the huge cubist painting that dominated the foyer. 'That's pretty horrific isn't it?'

'Pretty, sir, no. Horrific, yes.'

'Ah.' DCS Livermore looked at the great slabs of paint – blue and white on a pale green background, interlocking squares, reaching back to infinity. 'Yes,' he sighed, '– the sound of water escaping from milldams, willows, old rotten planks, slimy posts, brickwork and the scent of rotting apples... Ah yes, sets the heart racing.'

He gave a rakish smile that lifted one side of

his mouth; and at that moment she saw two things clearly: first, that he was wearing a wonderful double-breasted overcoat. The coat was open, unbuttoned, revealing a magnificent double-breasted suit that screamed Savile Row from every inch of the heavy cloth, while alleluias to the tailor's art were sung from each stitch. Second, she realized that he reminded her of the actor Rex Harrison whom she'd seen in a film – *Night Train to Munich* – only last month, which in many ways was a lifetime ago.

On his head there was, of course, an Anthony Eden Homburg, set at the slightest of angles.

'Gosh,' she said, but not out loud.

'So, Suzie?' He touched her arm with strong, firm fingers. 'Hadn't we better go to? Shrink the distance between us and the divine and lamented Miss Benton's secret love nest?'

'Yes, of course, Guv. You did know that we have two warrants?' As she informed him of this, Suzie glanced at Shirley who merely stood there with mouth slightly agape, and eyes loaded with lust. Indeed, Suzie thought.

Dandy Tom, someone had called him. She really should take more notice, hone her skills of observation, and sharpen the talent of paying heed. During her basic training an elderly experienced CID officer had said, 'Listen to people telling you about what has occurred. Then listen again. Listen to the music behind the words.' The music behind DCS Livermore had been Dandy Tom all along, and she should have known it.

'Well–' he cupped her elbow, and it felt that

she was being gently driven in whatever direction he wanted to go – 'when you mentioned not being able to get into the other young woman's flat – Emily Baccus's flat? – I felt we could probably kill two birds with a single pebble.' The neat and pleasant smile surfaced again. 'Now, where do we start?'

'Flat two hundred and twenty, Chief,' snapped Molly Abelard who had materialized at Tommy Livermore's shoulder as though she carried a book of spells that would see him through any door or wall, over any border, and certainly dry to the other side of any lake, river or sea that he required to traverse.

'That it, Suzie?'

'Yes, Chief,' she said, still in a state of wonder.

'You the porter?' he asked Cyril Nutkin.

'Yes, sah! Sarn't-Major Russ, sah! Royal Fusiliers, sah!'

'A London regiment, that, eh?'

'Yes, sah!'

'Good man, take the lead.' And with that, they tagged on behind the sergeant-major, piling into the large lift with the hideous pink-tinted mirrors, discovering immediately that it was too small to take all of them. With exceptional courtesy, the DCS told the supernumeraries that he would send the lift back down for them. In the meantime they were to hire patience. 'I won't start until you arrive. I promise that on oath,' and he accompanied the guarantee with an extravagant gesture.

So, they ascended to the second storey, and

followed the sergeant major along the corridor to flat two-twenty. This short journey gave Suzie the chance to reflect on the extraordinary impact Tommy Livermore seemed to have on her. He was, she decided, one of those figures produced only in England. He was an anomaly, a rarity, seen only once in a generation: a gentleman detective, which is really a kind of oxymoron, like military intelligence. So far, she had only met his like among the pages of Dorothy L. Sayers and Margery Allingham.

She also knew, by some magic assimilation of Dandy Tom's personality, and his obvious idiosyncrasies, that he would be brilliant at anything he chose to do.

She was also getting the female equivalent of what she knew boys referred to as 'the Horn'. This last was rather pleasant and carnal, and at this late stage she suddenly knew by instinct that man and woman's purpose was much nicer than she had thought possible.

They marched firmly along several corridors, and stopped outside the substantial doorway of 220. DCS Livermore held up his hand; DS Mulligan pointed to both sides of the door and two DCs took up positions to left and right. Livermore indicated to Suzie that he wanted her on his left – Molly Abelard, naturally, was glued to his right side. Now, as the supernumeraries appeared, Dandy Tom waved Sergeant-Major Russ into place in front of them, keys at the ready.

The DCS pressed the bell push and from far away they could hear the muted tone of the buzzer.

Nothing.

Press again. Longer.

Nothing.

'How long, O Lord, how long?' he pleaded aloud.

'I give 'em three long ones as a rule, sah,' said Cyril Nutkin.

Dandy Tom leaned against the bell and waited.

Still nothing.

'The keys, Sarn't-Major!'

Cyril Nutkin stepped forward and slipped one key into the dead bolt and a Yale key into the lock, murmured the incantation, 'Hope she hasn't dropped the sneck,' and turned the keys.

The door swung inwards and the stench hit them. And Suzie knew the stench, she had smelled it down in the Cut the other night, and many times in the after-blitzed streets of morning London.

The rancid, sweet, raw, rotting scent of death.

'Stay back!' Tommy Livermore shouted. Throwing an arm in front of Suzie, he turned his head and called back towards his forensic people. 'David, after me, now, please. And Peter, you as well. Quick as you can.' Suzie heard one of the men gag as he got into the hallway, a fifteen feet by fifteen area done in a warm red brick paper, with cream paintwork and a deep-pile chessboard carpet underfoot. The walls were hung with old theatre posters – Mr Garrick, Mrs Woffington, Mrs Siddons – *Richard III: The Constant Couple*; *The Grecian*

Daughter; in cheap black print on old, creased paper, mounted on red board under glass in Hogarth frames.

Suzie took a step forward and saw Colly Cibber's name on a slightly larger poster. A door was wide open, to the right. She went another couple of paces feeling the draught of fresh air on her face. She was in a pleasant sitting room – drawing room, her mother would have probably called it. There were four armchairs covered in a pattern that repeated little roses. Perfectly acceptable, but not her taste. Some nice mahogany occasional tables; a couple of pictures she wouldn't have minded owning: oil, Venice, Bridge of Sighs through a romantic mist; a watercolour view of some scene from high up above a port – South of France, she thought – pink tiled roofs, white walls, a line of dark arches and a sweep of sand; last, a large canvas, oil again, a sweeping scene of moorland, grim, inhospitable with a wonderfully calculated wind blowing low over the scrub and bushes. If you looked long enough, you would feel that wind on your face and your hair would move with it.

The two long windows, with their heavy gold velvet curtains and the scalloped valance, had been thrown open, and the door to the bedroom which led off directly from the left of a fake fireplace, was open.

'It's okay. Careful. Gently with her.' The voice came from one of the forensic men. Then, 'Right Guv, you can open the windows now, we've got her temperature.'

By this time Suzie had reached the door and could see the two forensics lads gently removing a rectal thermometer from the thing with crêpe skin on the bed, inching her back into the dent she had made when she first landed there.

Suzie walked quietly to the bed and looked at the terrible face, the long jet black hair clawed and stuck over her scalp, rivers of dried sweat that had plainly formed a delta down one side of the face that was frozen in a merciless agony: the tongue starting from the open mouth, blue and suggestive, the eyes half closed, as if she was on the point of waking, and around the neck, biting clear into the flesh, the wire ligature, with the insulating-tape ends standing up obscenely from behind her shoulders.

'Well done, Sergeant Mountford,' Dandy Tom congratulated her for not showing the revulsion she felt. 'Who is she?' he asked.

In life, Suzie reckoned, she would have been attractive – a neat button nose, high cheek-bones, a generous mouth, long thick black hair brushing the shoulders, and the body, tall, slim, very attractive, though life must have left it, she imagined, at least a couple of days ago.

'I've never seen her before,' she said, sad for the corpse.

'Sarn't-Major Russ?' The voice loud, coming from the stomach and the back of the throat.

'Sah?'

'In here.' The thud of Cyril Nutkin's stamped approach.

'Seen plenty of bodies, Sarn't-Major? Not afraid of cadavers?'

'No sah.' He appeared in the doorway, all full of himself, preparing for one of the great moments in his life.

'Then tell us who this is, Sarn't-Major.'

'Yes, sah. That's Miss Baccus, sah. Miss Emily Baccus from three-twenty. Oh my Gawd! Oh Christ.' And he pitched forward in a dead faint.

'Molly,' Tommy Livermore sang out. 'Get rid of him, Molly,' and Molly Abelard detached herself from her charge's side, and with a couple of deft movements slung the little porter across her shoulders in a fireman's lift, marching out of the room stiff-legged, carrying him as though he were a babe.

'You're going to need the doctor, Guv,' one of the forensics men, Dave, had moved close to him, hardly raising his voice.

Dandy Tom nodded. 'Get everyone doing their jobs. Photographs. Fingerprints. Everything. The lot. Go through it like grease through a goose. I'll be in search of the doc. With me, Suzie with a zed.'

They sat in Emily Baccus's flat – 320: DCS Livermore at a table cradling the telephone, Suzie perched on the edge of a deep leather easy chair, not that leather chairs are ever easy, she thought.

Cyril Nutkin, still looking queasy from his brush with the corpse, had let them in.

'You'd better go and have a quiet lie down in a darkened room, Sarn't-Major,' the DCS told him.

'Don't know what come over me, sah.' It was

almost shamefaced. 'Maybe the herring I had for my tea was a bit orf.'

'I should imagine that was it. I think we should hang on to the keys of both the flats for the time being, oh, and Sarn't-Major – a word to the wise.' He stooped over Russ's shoulder, adjacent to the right ear, almost whispering. 'I would like you to understand that everything you've seen tonight is confidential; so please don't go telling any little friends in Fleet Street that there's been a death here. We like to control these things for as long as possible. A few hours at least, and even then you're deaf, blind and dumb. Understood?'

'Yes, sah. Of course, sah,' and having absorbed the lesson that the shock of sudden death is not made easier by the passing years, Sergeant-Major Russ, porter of this parish, departed in an uncertain peace.

'Will he keep, shtum, Suzie? Will he curb his tongue?'

'Only until tomorrow or at sight of remuneration, whichever comes first, sir.'

He nodded sadly. 'Cynicism is alive and well in Camford, then.'

'Upper Saint Martin's Lane actually, sir.'

Tommy Livermore gave her his quizzical look, the one with the raised right eyebrow. Her mother was able to do that, but she could never quite master the trick.

He had taken off his beautiful overcoat and the homburg and now he passed a hand over his thick dark hair. She saw the signs of frosting at his temples and thought how attractive it was. In fact, Suzie Mountford went into quite a reverie as he telephoned some secret number and asked if he could have a particular professor of pathology over as soon as possible.

'Tell him it's Tommy Livermore and he owes me a favour,' he said. 'I have a body conveniently stashed away in Derbyshire Mansions, Marylebone. Almost on the corner of New Cavendish Street.' He gave the flat number, and when the conversation had finished, he looked around him with interest. 'Well, Suzie,' he commenced, 'let's go over the easy stuff. This apartment, three-twenty, is the natural home of the lady we've already discovered sadly shuffled off this mortal coil in the secret abode of the deceased Josephine Benton. Right?'

'Right sir. Absolutely, sir.'

'Bearing in mind that you have only had a glimpse of the body, is it possible that Miss Baccus could've met her quietus at the hands of the same person who slaughtered Jo Benton?'

'That's difficult, sir. I don't really know—'

'Suzie, I just want to listen to you think it through, aloud, heart, if you would.'

'Sir, I've had no—'

'—real experience? I know that. But you have common sense and maybe a little bit of logic. Who knows? Just talk me through it; start the wheel turning for me.'

'It looks as though Emily Baccus was killed with piano wire, choking, crushing the windpipe. Insulating tape wound round the ends of the wire, and the wire doubled after one layer of tape was attached.'

'Why doubled?'

'The wire doubled so that the tape wouldn't slide off. They were all attacked from behind—'

'Who're the "they"?'

'You know, Guv.'

'Humour me.'

'In the past few months at least three other women have been choked with piano wire, and two of them were teenagers.' She reeled off the cases – the Davidson girl, Marie June, strangled with piano wire, grips at each end made out of insulating tape; the genital area had been gouged deeply with a broken bottle and there was a pan of water boiling on the kitchen range.

Patricia Cooke found strangled with wire, Snitterfield, near Stratford-upon-Avon, similar to Davidson; eyes skewered; pan of water on the range; no assault on the lower abdomen and genital area.

'Then there's Jo Benton, our Camford case. She had everything done to her – the wire, sexual assault, eyes and the wild attack on the genital area: ripped with a knife; and there was a pan of water on the hob. And last of all, this one, tonight...'

'I think we'll find out it was a few days ago, heart.'

'Right. Whenever. Emily Baccus—'

'We need that officially. I don't think the dashing Sarn't Major can be relied on, even though I think it probably is Miss Baccus.'

Dandy Tom smiled, all consuming, Suzie thought. Dandy Tom and his all-consuming smile, fresh from their success at WHItehall 1212 – this last was the well-known telephone number of New Scotland Yard. 'You know what the ripping or cutting of the genital area means, don't you?' he asked.

'Not really, sir, no.' She wanted to say that she'd rather not think about it. Then, 'You don't have to be Havelock Ellis to equate it with sex.'

'You know about Havelock Ellis, heart?' He looked suitably surprised.

'Not really, sir. No. I know he died last year and that he studied sexual aberrations. My young brother heard rumours.'

'Schoolboys think the published casework is delightfully smutty. Anyway, destruction of the genital area usually indicates something pretty disturbing to do with sex. Which is,' he added, as though listening in on her mind, 'sort of obvious really, but the old trick cyclists make a big thing about ripping the abdomen and the genitals.'

'And what about the eyes?' she asked, in spite of herself.

'Could be lots of things. Maybe it's the old idiocy about the picture of the murderer imprinted on the retina; or it could be that he didn't want the corpse to see him. Lots of primitive ideas about the eyes of corpses. We'll only really know when we get him in the nick, sitting down and talking to us.'

'Emily Baccus, strangled with wire, I presume. No eyes, no cutting. Then there's one more, Guv.'

'Bachelor?' he asked. 'Bubbles Bachelor?'

'Yes, Barbara Bachelor. Bubbles,' she nodded. 'No knives, bottles, skewers or pans of water. But a possible rape.'

'And DI Prothero was quite amazed when you added that one to the list. Gave him a new row to hoe, so to speak. DI Earney Prothero being a keen gardener.'

'How fascinating, sir.'

Tommy Livermore lifted his right eyebrow. 'Isn't it? Takes prizes for his marrows and cucumbers every year at the Harrow Flower Show.'

Suzie sensed there was something wicked coming her way.

'So, what're your conclusions, Suzie?'

She frowned, an outward sign of the struggle going on in her head. 'Sir,' she began. 'Really, sir, I can't say. I'm not a trained detective.'

'Doesn't matter a damn, heart. Apart from a few technical bits and pieces you own everything required to be a careful and conscientious investigator.'

She gave a little unbidden laugh, half-sarcastic, part disbelief. 'With respect, sir, how can you know that?'

'From your file and your school reports.' He smiled again, and, as she'd already noticed, the smile seemed to hug her. I'll burst into flame she thought – spontaneously combust.

'I always try to find out about people I'm

called to work with,' he continued. 'Particularly those, like yourself, whom I am supposed to teach. The reports for your final couple of years at school were, I thought, exceptional. The dear nuns at St Helen's were more than helpful, and from what I've seen of you already, I think you're what they call a natural.' He gave her a flirtatious wink. 'So, Suzie, grab at your confidence and tell me. What conclusions do you come to?'

She told him: that they certainly had a repeat killer who had murdered at least four people, probably five, and possibly many more.'

'Good. Go on.'

'He has some kind of sexual problem, and I'm not very good at sex things, sir. I suppose I was brought up in a sort of repressed...? Is that the word I'm...?'

'Haven't a clue, heart. Only you know what you know about sexual problems. It's enough to be aware of the sex thing. Is that why you're so certain it's a man?'

'He kills women. Yes, and I think he'll kill women until we catch him and put him away. He has a down on women, and it appears to be random. There's no link between the victims, except he seems to be more partial to very young women. Teenagers.'

'Teenagers, yes, but—'

'Not exclusively.'

'And who is he?'

'Well he's someone who can travel easily, I would think. To our knowledge he's murdered in Cambridge, near Stratford, and in London—'

'Description?'

'He's someone with a distinctive face, or some distinguishing mark.'

'Why do you think that?'

'Because our one description of him, from the Snitterfield killing, has him of medium height bundled up, his face obscured, on a day that was pleasant: a lovely spring day so he's easily recognizable; and he's strong in the shoulders and arms – the way he kills.'

'There you are. QED, as my old chemistry master used to say. Quite Easily Done. You're a star pupil, Suzie,' he said. 'Now...'

The bell buzzed throughout the flat. 'Damn, just when it was getting interesting.' He strode off towards the hall and the door, returning with DS Billy Mulligan in tow.

'The forensic pathologist is on his way, and that long rather nicely made polished oak wardrobe, facing the bed in two-twenty, is locked, and I'd earmarked you for the job of going through it, Suzie.'

He rang the porter's flat and had a stilted conversation with Cyril Nutkin, which yielded more keys. Mulligan was sent to bring them to two-twenty. 'Old Russ still doesn't sound well,' the DCS mused. 'I used to know a judge called Russ, you don't think they're related...?' Shaking his head firmly, he rejected the idea.

When they got down to the master bedroom of two-twenty it seemed terribly crowded. The forensic pathologist was there, in full fig – the razor-creased striped trousers, black jacket, grey waistcoat, starched wing collar and immaculate cravat. He smelled of some expensive lotion but it didn't completely banish the formaldehyde.

'Tommy,' he greeted the DCS with affection.

'Robert.' Obviously on friendly terms with the eminent professor. They clasped hands in what could have been some secret ceremony. Around them the forensic boys did their thing.

'Going to be a long night.' Dandy Tom did not sound happy about that, standing there with a notebook in one hand and an exceptionally slim gold fountain pen in the other.

'Couldn't we do room three-twenty tomorrow, Guv'nor?' Billy Mulligan suggested.

'You game for that, heart?' he asked and Suzie felt as though he was paying her a great compliment.

'Can't do tomorrow,' and she saw a thunder cloud cross his face, so she quickly explained. 'I'm going down to interview a close friend of the deceased.'

'Ah.' He tapped his lower teeth softly with the capped end of his fountain pen.

All men, her mother had told her, are children at heart, and if you spoil their fun and games they will often behave like *very* small children.

'Which deceased we talking about?' he asked.

'Benton.'

'That can wait. Which one?'

'The pilot.' Behind his shoulder the pathologist bent over the body, checking out this and that, prowling in her hair, ears, nose, mouth, under her fingernails: practically everywhere. A

271

tall very thin young man, with a bad complexion and roving eyes assisted him.

'I thought you were doing the pilot on Monday.'

'Yes, in Hampshire.' Oh hell, she thought, he doesn't miss a thing. He bloody knows it all. Been shadowing me all the way. 'Day off tomorrow, Guv. I'm on Sunday and I go to do the pilot on Monday; then straight from there on leave: also in Hampshire.'

'Could you rearrange tomorrow?' he seemed to be pleading.

She stood looking blankly over his shoulder watching her present-buying and happy Christmas plans go down the drain. 'Well, sir,' she said, and was conscious that Shirley Cox was at her elbow.

'Don't worry about it, we'll talk later. Now, let's see what's in the wardrobe.' The DCS nodded.

The wardrobe was a built-in fitment: probably the original well-crafted work made and polished by experts in the last years of the previous century. Suzie had been allowed a quick look around Emily Baccus's apartment on the third floor and it had a similar piece: she had felt a charge of pleasure in running the flat of her hand across the doors until the DCS reminded her that it hadn't been fingerprinted yet. But down in two-twenty, the fitted wardrobe was now painted with smudges of fingerprint powder.

Once the keys had been inserted and the doors opened to display the interior inlaid mirrors, drawers, shoe racks and hanging closets, her heart sank.

'Angels and ministers of grace defend us,' muttered Dandy Tom, crossing himself. He meant that, Suzie realized. There had appeared to be nothing frivolous about his action.

She knew the theory behind most of the bizarre items, but could not in any way associate them with pleasure: the restraints, the whips, the leather masks. The racks of clothes displaying the more obvious fantasists' dreamworld of nurse's uniforms, nun's habits and gymslips. Others were more difficult to fathom: the uniform of an Uhlan, complete with lance, or coats with belts, leads and buckles that would have looked good on a Borzoi but were obviously for use by adult males on all fours. She would never understand some of these items, but there was of course a large supply of the frills, lace and garishly coloured intimate apparel. Those she now almost understood.

'Well.' For a second Tommy Livermore appeared to be lost for words. Then – 'Who was it who said: "The pleasure is momentary, the position is ridiculous, and the expense damnable"?'

Molly Abelard coughed, 'Lord Chesterfield I think, Chief.'

'If that's true then the owners of all this are making right fools of themselves. Or not, as the case may be.' He turned to Sergeant Mountford. 'Young girl like you understand all this, Suzie?'

'Only that it's a whore's boudoir,' she said. 'I don't follow the rather absurd rituals. Don't think I care to, sir.'

'I'm very pleased to hear it. But no, Suzie. This is not a tart's boudoir. It's a very high-class tart's boudoir. All yours, Suzie.' Livermore chuckled. 'Just give me the sub-headings. Your DC'll assist.' And at that moment the pathologist sighed.

'The wire ligature was put on *post mortem*,' he said quietly. 'It didn't kill her.'

'Well, that's a twist,' Dandy Tom said, and they both laughed. They were the only ones in the room to even smile.

But Suzie understood. 'Loamy' Lomax, back at Camford nick, had said that sometimes you had to treat death as a joke or you'd go crazy. He had been talking with the Great War in mind, but similar rules applied. She wondered how many bodies the pathologist had seen that day.

The DCS and the doctor went back into the next room and presently a couple of men in white coats came in with a hospital trolley to take Emily Baccus away. Slowly the room started to empty and the drone of conversation vanished from the apartment's main room.

'Fifty-six bras,' Shirley said, finishing the count. 'Seventy dresses and fifty-six bras. Suzie, you do know who he is?' she whispered.

'Who?' Suzie was still out of sorts, angry with Livermore.

'The Detective Chief Superintendent.'

'Tommy Livermore? Dandy Tom?' Maybe

she had misread him, she wondered. He had seemed so friendly, full of praise for her. Star pupil, he'd said. Then came the sudden change.

'The *Honourable* Thomas Livermore. His father's the Earl of Kingscote. Pots of lucre. Filthy with it.'

'How d'you know?' It was odd the way some people seemed to think there was something special about anyone with a title.

'Sergeant Mulligan. Worked with him a long time. He's even been up to the family seat. Gloucestershire. Told me it was dead opulent.'

'Well, he's welcome to it.' She was somewhat surly as she helped count the remaining underwear, which took forever.

'Suzie. A word.' Livermore stood in the doorway.

She went over to him and he signalled for her to follow him through to the drawing room, as her mum would've called it.

'I'm sorry about earlier, heart.'

'About what?' Pretend it had passed her by.

'About going down to Hampshire. Interviewing the pilot. Going on leave.'

'Oh, that.'

'Yes, *that*, heart.' He had his slanting smile on, the eyebrow cocked very high. Again she wished she could do the thing with the eyebrow. 'Never try to shoot a shooter, Susannah. It don't work.'

'Well, sir, I...'

'Don't worry about it. You don't have to come in. What I really wanted to know was could we have dinner perhaps, tomorrow night? That's what I was really after.' He gave a self-effacing chuckle. 'Just to discuss the pathologist's report of course, heart.'

'Of course, sir. Yes. Why not, sir?' Crikey, she thought. That's typical of policemen. Never around when you want them, then several arrive at once. Sanders of the River; and now Dandy Tom. 'Where, sir?'

'I pick you up?' he asked and she looked pleased. 'Seven o'clock be okay?'

'Of course, sir.' She gave him her address and felt that old nightingale singing away across in Berkeley Square. He already knew my address, she thought.

'Incidentally,' he added, almost ruining everything, 'to state the obvious, Miss Baccus and Miss Benton appear to have been running a friendly parlour for quirky sex. And I presume you heard that Baccus didn't get herself strangled with that piano wire. Some idiot wanted it to look as though she had.'

Joshua Dance/Slaughter could not sleep. He finally got up, put on a dressing gown and made himself a cup of tea, the old standby, then brought it downstairs. He switched on one of the standard lamps, sat down and thought for a while. He had no idea why he should be restless. The recent change in the number of air raids could have something to do with it. His sleep pattern was strange at the best of times and this wasn't the best of times.

He fetched his book and seated himself in

one of the comfortable armchairs. He was reading Graham Greene's new novel *The Power and the Glory*, about a priest who was also a drunk – a whisky priest. In the Roman Catholic magazine the *Tablet* the reviewer had said that it was as though God had said, 'Love me and break my commandments.' That was a bit like himself, Josh had thought. Ever since he had met the detective, Suzie Mountford, he had found it difficult to get her out of his mind. Women detectives, he thought. Strange. Was this a sign of how things would change in the future? Women doing all the traditionally male jobs. No, he considered, that couldn't possibly work. To some extent you could understand it in wartime, but never in peacetime.

Outside, below in the street a drunk was singing, 'There'll always be an England.'

He lit a cigarette, stood up, walked around a little, then sat down again, lit another cigarette and read. For an hour or so he read and dozed, his head falling on to his chest. Once, the book slid to the floor and he woke with a start. He lit another cigarette, stubbed it out then read again, and fell asleep once more.

A noise. He was awake instantly, head jerking up, looking around. The noise again. Someone was in the office, next door. It could only be Emily Baccus and he didn't worry. Emily was a late bird. There, now her footsteps were on the stairs. She was leaving, clickety-clack, he'd know her step, in her lovely high heels, anywhere. Tick-tack-clippity-clop.

He stood up and stretched. He would go

back to bed, he thought. So he switched off the light and pulled back the curtains. There was just enough light in the street to make out Emily Baccus leaving the building. She wore her beautiful coat, the long one with the fur collar that had cost her a hundred and fifty pounds from Fenwicks – a king's ransom.

She strode off on her long lovely legs, heading heaven knew where.

In the office the wall clock struck three.

Three o'clock in the morning, Josh thought. Three o'clock in the morning and all's well.

He didn't know that Emily Baccus lay silent on a slab, waiting for the post-mortem saws and knives.

Josh went off to bed, and this time slept peacefully.

Golly was deeply asleep. He clutched Lavender's bear, and in his dreams the creatures came into the room on their dry, clicking legs, and the nightmare began. He started to whimper and the lady made soothing noises. 'Golly,' said the lady with the calming voice, 'Golly, you have to kill the lady policeman. Kill with the wire, Golly. Kill the lady policeman at Christmas. She will be in a village, Golly. Seek out the lady policeman in Hampshire, Golly. Hampshire in the village of Overchurch. Overchurch, Golly. Kill her in Overchurch. In Overchurch, Hampshire. In Falcon Cottage. Let her see your face, all the better to frighten her with. Falcon Cottage on Christmas Day, Golly.' It began to echo wildly inside his skull.

'Christmas-mas-mas-mas-mas Day-ay-ay-ay. Overchurch-urch-urch-urch. Hampshi-shi-shi-shi-shire. With the wire-ire-ire-ire. Golly. Kill-ill-ill-ill-ill-ill-ill.'

When he woke it was the first thing he remembered, the soft, honeyed voice, dripping into his head. Kill the lady policeman, Golly. At Falcon Cottage in Overchurch. In Hampshire. Kill, Golly. Christmas Day, Golly.

Overchurch was three miles from Whitchurch where his mother lived.

Golly screamed and went on screaming until the girl who worked in the flat above came down and calmed him. Later, when Lavender arrived for work, she said that Golly had been shaking with fear and it was like a child having a nightmare.

Only Golly knew the nightmare was real.

Fifteen

Half-way along Oxford Street, heading towards Oxford Circus and from thence to Marble Arch, there was a great gap where a bomb had destroyed a whole shop. It looked like a surgical job: a gap, like someone's mouth after the extraction of an infected bicuspid. Suzie couldn't even remember which shop had stood there, but it had been a recent disaster because workmen were still making the wreckage safe. They had roped off where the pavement had been and marked out a path so that little streams of pedestrians left their straight course and followed each other round in a loop back on to the trail again, moving both east and west, like opposing armies of ants being deviated from their common route.

There were quite a few people in the street, trying to catch up on their Christmas shopping during this the last weekend before the holiday – not that it was going to be much of a holiday for many people in the capital, or in the whole country come to that.

Only a handful of years ago, Suzie thought, you could have walked down Oxford Street without even brushing shoulders with fellow pedestrians: now it seemed comparatively crowded – in spite of the bombs, the regular doses of death and destruction.

She had only half-a-dozen or so Christmas gifts to buy but had not even found one by the time she got to Oxford Circus where she stood now, like an animal sniffing the air as though it would give her the scent of inspiration. After a moment she had a kind of brainwave and turned left into Regent Street, swerving from her chosen route to Selfridges, up near Marble Arch, where she had planned to pick up good gifts for Mummy, the Galloping Major, Charlotte, James, Vernon, Ben and little Lucy.

Because she felt that Christmas was a time to heal wounds and build bridges, it was the Major's present that troubled her most, but the idea that came to her in Oxford Circus had removed her concern – or to be strictly accurate, would remove it if Hamley's had what she was looking for. Her mother said that all men were children at heart and she had recalled one evening when she was trying to set her life to rights, after the Cambridge job and before the night of her row with the Major.

'Used to keep me happy for hours,' the Major had said, going on and on about his memories of childhood. Later he added, 'Best board game I ever played. Give a lot to know where my set went. Hours of enjoyment.'

The board game that so delighted him dated back almost to the turn of the century and had been updated a number of times. It was called Dover Patrol – the board marked out as the English Channel; counters to represent types of craft; dice to rotate the moves; rules so arcane that, Suzie suspected, only the Major himself could understand them.

'Kept us happy. Rain or snow. Dover Patrol. Had another called L'Attaque as well. Both good. All of us young people. Happy.' The Major had a kind of shorthand speech that one had to live with for a while before it became comprehensible, and it was at this point that her mother, now Mrs Gordon-Lowe, had said – Suzie recalled with profound joy – 'Yes, you know they still sell it at Hamleys. I've seen it there.'

Dover Patrol: the reason why Suzie now walked smartly down Regent Street with a Christmas carol in her head.

'In Dulce Jubilo'.

And coming up the street, from the opposite

direction, a lonely figure ambled along the gutter: his collar turned up, his oblong piece of cotton masking the lower part of his face, and the wide-brimmed hat pulled down to conceal the forehead. Golly Goldfinch, the abomination, came scuffling along on an errand for a bloke in Berwick Street Market.

So, among the hurrying people they approached one another, oblivious and unaware: one with his mind obsessed by the other – 'Kill the lady policeman' – the other with her thoughts dominated by the idea that she may just possibly heal the rift with her stepfather. Heal it by buying a board game called Dover Patrol.

As they came abreast, each caught a quick glimpse of the other. Golly felt as if an electric probe had reached behind his eyes, but he didn't know why. There was turmoil and panic in his head, racing through his nerves, singing with that terrible discordant scream that went through him at times when he killed: when the rooks flew up from the skeletal winter trees.

Suzie saw him. Briefly saw him. Glimpsed him and registered that he displayed no face and knew it meant something: that the powerfully moving man had some secret he withheld, kept close and unshared.

She felt a spark of danger, yet sensed only the tiniest chill of fear as they passed one another: part dread, part a frisson of excitement she associated only with the pleasure of Christmas that was almost upon them: a touch of peace in the boiling cauldron.

Half an hour later she came out of Hamleys not only with Dover Patrol tucked under her arm, but also L'Attaque: both games and with prices so reasonable that she felt it would be mean not to be generous. She also had a separate bag holding a splendid teddy bear in a velvet jacket for Lucy. Suzie Mountford retraced her steps and was quickly back on track for Selfridges, where she hoped to get a bright scarf for her mum, the book Charlotte wanted – Ernest Hemingway's new novel, *For Whom the Bell Tolls*, about the Spanish Civil War – another that would suit James, something, undecided as yet, to brighten up Vernon's military life, and a book of drawings for Ben to colour.

This last was an essential, for colouring was Ben's best thing; locked within his own private and silent world, he could sit for hours with his crayons and a book, engrossed and working with pleasure; and by chance Suzie was to find the perfect present. As she walked into Selfridges toy department, where the staff had at least made an attempt to work up some Christmas spirit by putting up a tree decked with tinsel and spun glass baubles, she saw a hastily printed notice – IDEAL XMAS GIFT FOR YOUNGER CHILDREN. FORMER CORONATION COLOURING SETS 2/6d.

Several people were showing an immediate interest while the floorwalker and a pair of assistants hovered in anticipation.

'Yes, madam, they've been discovered in one of our warehouses. I remember them at coronation time a couple of years ago. These are all we have and they'll sell very quickly, I shouldn't wonder. Now that things are so uncertain. The bombing. The invasion.'

Suzie had a vague memory of seeing these boxes on sale at the time of George VI's and Queen Elizabeth's coronation in the summer of 1937. There was a box containing about two hundred quarto-sized cards, each displaying a line drawing of some aspect of the coronation: heralds, the yeoman bodyguards, gentleman ushers, the King and the Queen themselves, the Earl Marshal of England, pages, the Archbishops of Canterbury and York, the royal regalia, the state coach and the uniformed soldiers of every possible military unit in the great procession, from the Life Guards and the Blues and Royals to representative regiments from everywhere in the Empire. The box was topped off with a set of crayons and was, as the shopwalker said, a little loudly – 'A snip for half-a-crown'.

She bought three, because of Ben's insatiable demands as a colourer. So, clutching yet another parcel, Suzie made for the restaurant and ate a dismal meal: a thin soup masquerading as tomato, then macaroni cheese, as claggy as the cauliflower cheese she'd had with Shirley on the previous day, and a rhubarb tart, that was. The cup of coffee left her with doubts about what the liquid really contained: it tasted disgustingly bitter, flavoured heavily with chicory. Suzie smoked two cigarettes while she drank her coffee, sipping the brew as though it were medicine.

She browsed away the next hour, picking up a scarf in red and gold even though she knew her mother would make a joke and say it would match her eyes. In the book department she bought *For Whom the Bell Tolls*, for Charlotte – 'You'd think people are having enough war without the Spanish Civil War as well,' said the assistant – and a new much desired *Boy's Book of Aeroplanes* that she knew James coveted. She then got a present for herself: a nice grey woollen skirt that would be splendid for Christmas morning, and she kept her eye open for a blouse in a similar shade to go with it.

Suzie was still worrying over what to get for her brother-in law, Vernon, then it came to her as she entered the gentlemen's clothing department. 'In a few weeks I'll be starved for some little luxury,' he had said the last time she'd seen him. From the Royal Marine depot at Deal he was to go on to the Pre-OCTU (Officer Cadet Training Unit) at Exton, down in the West Country, down in Devon where, rumour had it, the eight-week course was physically and mentally brutal.

Silk pyjamas, Suzie thought. That's it exactly. Silk pyjamas for the Royal Marines – backbone of the new special force, the Commandos, the spearhead troops to 'set Europe ablaze', as Winston Churchill ordered. As yet clothes were not rationed – though there were rumours that it would soon come to that – and she didn't even think of the possibility that Vernon could be ridiculed and teased by his fellow 'bootnecks'.

It was almost half-past three when she emerged into the street clutching another parcel containing a pair of red and white silk pyjamas. Day was fast turning into dusk even at this hour, and Oxford Street had started to take on its menacing night clothing. What little colour there had been was now drained from the street, and danger hung invisible in the air. Words came into her head from school. Shakespeare, she thought – 'grim-visaged war' – but she could never identify the play, even if it did come from Shakespeare. It was how it felt out in the cold and on the street that she remembered from other days and other times.

But around her there was nervousness, concern for the terror by night – as the prayer-book called it – that so often came with the throb of its engines and the shriek of its bombs hurtling down to alter the landscape and kill indiscriminately without even seeing those who died in a twinkling of an eye.

Like others on the street, Suzie now scuttled into the Underground and within ten minutes was on the train rocking back towards the Strand and her short walk to Upper St Martin's Lane. As the cold, sinewy night took over she was again aware that the war was out there, ready to bite with little warning: with no reason the sinister prancing death could leap from the darkness.

She tried to lengthen her strides through the murk ... wondering how those women must have felt fumbling, terrified, grabbing and retching as the wire bit into their throats.

Indescribable, she thought, being choked with piano wire, neck arched, mouth wide in a silent scream as the windpipe collapsed. And the picture of the rigid, forbidding body of Emily Baccus came into her head, drenching her with fright, so that she double-locked the front door of the flat behind her, then secured the top and bottom bolts, locking herself in, then feeling the dread again and going through the rooms one at a time to make certain she was alone.

By half-past four she was lying in a hot bath, irrigating her body, washing away the aches, pains and tensions. Only now she began to look forward to the evening and the novel experience of having dinner with her boss, the attractive Tommy Livermore, Dandy Tom.

In some things, Joshua Dance insisted on order. He had his own routine and, like an autistic child, he couldn't bear to have the routine upset. As a child, his morning visit to the lavatory had had within it a secret enchantment, a superstition that set in motion – bad choice of word – a spell that could ease the entire day into one of good luck. He would unlock the door, pull the dangling chain and dash with all haste down the passageway. Half-way along there was a loose board that squeaked. He had to reach the board before the toilet flushed or the day would be ruined. If he managed it then the next twenty-four hours would be serene.

Still beset by these little fortune-deciding acts, Josh Dance, one time David Slaughter –

but what's in a name? – was at times convinced that his damaged leg was the result of routine gone wrong.

Lieutenant Dance, as he was with the British Expeditionary Force – the BEF, or Back Every Friday as it was sometimes referred to – in France, had been ordered to hold a small, dusty track, a mile or so outside Dunkirk. He had eight men, five rifles, a Bren gun, several grenades and a determination to hold the line or die in the attempt. His men knew him, and worked well with him. They were aware, for instance, that Mr Dance liked his morning tea served to him promptly at eight o'clock. So he was put out when he crossed the road, on that first and last morning in June, to the little shack where they were brewing up, and found that the tea wasn't ready. In effect he had to wait until ten minutes past eight before he was given his big tin mug. In the end he was ten minutes late in crossing the road back to the barn around which he had positioned his men.

He crouched, ran and reached the middle of the chalky road at the same moment as the bullet that shattered his leg and left him sprawling on the dusty ground with all hell going on around him.

His sergeant, 'Tubby' Shaw, got a posthumous Military Medal for saving Lieutenant Dance's life, and Privates Rob Auld and Colin Knight were both mentioned in dispatches for getting the wounded officer off the road and across to the Dunkirk beaches, along the famous Mole and on to a ship and to a naval surgeon lieutenant-commander who saved the leg and got the young officer back to Blighty on that bright, warm and bloody summer's day. When he thought about it, Josh Dance remained convinced that had he been given his tea at the preferred time of eight o'clock, he would have remained with his men.

And probably died with them.

Each weekday, there was a routine with Mr Dance's evening paper which also had its effect on life, death and the future. If Josh did not get his evening paper by five minutes past three in the afternoon, danger would stalk until fifteen-oh-five the next day. So, Miss Holroyd would leave the building in Albemarle Street at five minutes to three o'clock every afternoon and walk to the junction of Piccadilly where old Nosey sold the *News*, the *Star* and the *Standard*.

Nosey was a living warning from the fleshpots of the 1914–18 war. Nosey had no nose, only two small holes where it had been: the extremity possibly lost to the creeping hell of syphilis. And it was to Nosey that Miss Holroyd walked each weekday afternoon. It was something she dreaded, yet she was more terrified of Mr Dance's wrath if she was a minute late in bringing his paper into the office.

She had been late with Mr Dance's paper on a number of occasions and his fury was one of the reasons she wanted to leave Jewell, Baccus & Dance as quickly as possible to join the WRNS, not because of the uniform, as Miss

Burrage suspected, but because one of her boy-friends, Chris – now Leading Seaman – Leach, had told her that 'the Andrew' was the only service to join. She had to ask around to find out that 'the Andrew' was naval slang for the Royal Navy, just as 'the oggin' or 'oggwash' was the sea.

On Saturday afternoons, when he was at home (he would sometimes go to a cinema matinée on Saturday afternoons), Joshua Dance would walk to Nosey himself, and stroll back with the *Evening Standard* neatly tucked under his arm.

He would sit quietly in one of his leather chairs in his room off the main office, and read the paper between three five and three thirty-five on a Saturday afternoon. So it was around three fifteen on this present Saturday that he suddenly shot bolt upright as he came to page three and the story spread across four columns headed WOMAN DEAD IN FLATS! FOUL PLAY SUSPECTED! LINK WITH ANNOUNCER DEATH SUSPECTED!

Scotland Yard has issued a statement saying that the body of a woman, identified as Miss Emily Baccus of 320 Derbyshire Mansions, Marylebone, was found dead in a friend's flat in the same building. Miss Baccus's body was discovered by Detective Chief Superintendent Thomas Livermore early yesterday evening. Mr Livermore is at the head of a team of detectives investigating a number of murder cases including the death of the BBC announcer Miss Josephine Benton.

Unconfirmed reports suggest that Miss Baccus was found dead in a flat belonging to the late Miss Benton in Derbyshire Mansions. It is thought that Detective Sergeant Susannah Mountford was with Mr Livermore's team when the body of Miss Baccus was discovered. Recently concern was expressed when it was thought Sergeant Mountford, a female police officer, was in charge of the investigation of Miss Benton's murder. At the time a Home Office spokesman said, 'The investigation of a foul and brutal murder, such as the killing of Miss Benton, does not, in my mind, appear to be the best way to use our resources. I do not think it is a woman's job.'

'No!' Josh Dance cried aloud from his chair. 'No! It wasn't. It couldn't have been. But it wasn't like that.'

He telephoned Camford Hill Police Station and asked to speak with Detective Sergeant Mountford, but was put through to WDC Cox.

'Sergeant Mountford?' he asked.

'She's not on duty today, sir. It's WDC Cox, can I help?'

'My name's Joshua Dance...'

'Oh yes, Mr Dance, we met the other day. I was with Sergeant Mountford when we came to your offices.'

'Well, yes. I wanted to speak to Sergeant Mountford about Miss Baccus, Miss Emily Baccus?'

'Yes, Mr Dance, I'm so sorry about Miss

Baccus, we—'

'I have to report something...'

'Yes?'

'The paper says that she was found dead...'

'That's right sir, yes.'

'...Found dead early yesterday. It says here! That's not possible. What happened didn't ... couldn't have happened like that.'

'Why not, sir? Do you know something about Miss Baccus's death?'

'Yes,' said Joshua Dance. 'Of course I know something about it. She was alive in the early hours of this morning. I saw her alive, so tell me they've got it wrong: the paper's got it wrong.'

He thought to himself that this was a typical police cock-up. Emily wouldn't have got herself killed like that. He knew that it would be very bad luck for her to be found early on Saturday evening.

Jack shall have Jill
Naught shall go ill,
The man shall have his mare again,
And all shall be well.

Sixteen

'Normally,' Dandy Tom said, 'I'd have beaten all land speed records to Camford when Jo Benton was killed. I'd have worn my seven-league boots and everything. But as you were one of the chosen few we decided to let you run with it. See how you did.'

They sat in the Louis Quinze dining room of the Ritz, tucked away in a corner, shaded by a large feathery plant, and a little out of place in civilian clothes amidst the sea of uniforms. 'The uniforms see civvie clothes, spot 'em a mile off and think about getting the memsahibs to hand out white feathers,' Tommy Livermore told her. 'They're uncomfortable with people our age not in uniform.'

'*Our* age? Speak for yourself, sir.'

'There's something else. As things are now, Suzie, you can get lost in a uniform: merge into the background. Think about that the next time you're chasing a felon around the back streets of Camberwell. That's my tip of the day.'

As it happened they did get some strange stares from the military diners and their ladies. But the food made up for the iffy looks.

You didn't often come across lobster in London at this point in the winter of 1940,

Suzie considered, and the roast beef was rare in every sense.

Dandy Tom made his pitch almost as soon as they sat down. He had his leather notebook to the right of his place setting, the gold fountain pen next to it. 'Not done,' he smiled. 'Not really the done thing. Business at the dinner table.' Then—

'How would you care to work directly to me, Suzie?'

'Meaning exactly what, Guv'nor?' She had dressed up for the night out: a turquoise frock with a slim skirt and a nipped-in bodice with some frogging in a slightly darker shade up the front, like a hussar, all of it done in an imitation raw silk. Dandy Tom said it suited her and that she looked very nice and tonight they'd be slumming it at the Ritz, which thrilled Suzie who had wanted to be dined at the Ritz since she had first seen its colonnade at the age of twelve.

But tonight Detective Chief Superintendent Livermore seemed to be all business from the moment the head waiter led them over, oozing charm and telling Dandy Tom that they had given him his usual table and madam looked particularly enchanting tonight. But really Suzie didn't get to savour the event. Dandy Tom was still lovely, but any sense of a flirtation had disappeared.

You old tease, she thought, got me here under false pretences. 'Meaning what exactly, Guv'nor?' she repeated: cautious and wary, looking up and seeing Tommy tapping his lower teeth with the capped end of his fountain pen, lost in thought.

'She's a very wary girl,' Tommy said later to the Commander (Crime), and the woman police super in charge of A4, the one with the kipper-coloured hands who had given Suzie her marching orders from Scotland Yard. 'Very cautious, which is a good thing.'

In the here and now, having dinner at the Ritz he answered her. 'Meaning that you'd be groomed for stardom, young Suzie. We'd be covering murder mainly, which is what I do best. We'd do the cream of the crop here in the Metropolitan area. Sometimes, out in the sticks as well.'

'Do I have any option?'

'Not really, heart. You've more or less been working for me since you got yourself posted to Camford.'

Tommy Livermore thought it was time to tell her what had been going on. It had started back in June or July. 'Some of us felt we should look to the far future.'

It was at the time when each day was expected to bring squadrons of gliderborne nuns with submachine-guns, or regiments of priests with grenade launchers parachuting into the British channel ports, and shiploads of Nazis, *Sieg Heil*-ing their way up the beaches. At first light and dusk the aged, halt, maim and the boys not old enough for the military had to stand-to with their home-made pikes and ancient weapons.

'It was before what we're now calling the Battle of Britain, and some of us felt a bit sick

295

at the way we'd been jumped. Angry about the manner in which we'd been caught off guard and the way Hitler had bounced us out with our trousers down, so to speak. After France we were left to bungle our way out. Everyone said, "There go the Brits, muddling through as usual." Not really an enviable reputation.'

'Well, there was Dunkirk,' Suzie countered brightly, 'and we seem to be left with a better reputation than the French.'

'Not difficult, but it would have been better still if we hadn't boasted about hanging the laundry on the Siegfried Line. And Susie–' a cautionary finger wagged – 'never confuse a successful retreat with victory.'

None of them, his colleagues, ever doubted victory in the end, but it was going to be a long haul – maybe eight or even nine years. One of them had said that, in order to win the war they should start building the peace here and now. It was going to be a very different world after they'd cleaned that bluebird mess off the White Cliffs of Dover.

'We expect one of the changes'll be our attitude towards women, and we should start behaving differently straight away. Now. Because when peace breaks out a lot of women're going to want the same rights as men: a real education and a chance to do the same jobs: the kind of jobs they're doing now – and more. There are diverse views of course, but a lot of people agree that's how it's going to be.'

'Who's *we*?' she asked. 'We as in those who're seeing the future in their crystal balls, telling the tea leaves, reading the runes. I mean you, sir, obviously, but who else?'

'The woman superintendent in charge of A4; the Commander (Crime); and myself to begin with. There are others, just as there are also quite a few people who don't see it our way.'

'And you're doing what, sir?'

He said that by the end of the war most large organizations, civilian and paramilitary – like the Met – would want to contain a well-trained and experienced corps of women. 'Women who've been at the sharp end. Who've got some time in, got their knees brown, their hands dirty and their brains in gear.' What they needed to do at this moment was sort out the available chaff from the useable wheat. 'We've got to steer the most likely girls on a fast track. Give them a couple of years lead. Put them ahead and see how quickly they sink or swim.'

'And you're suggesting that I'm one of the class of 1940?'

'Heart, you *are* the class of 1940. We picked six of you, pulled you in from the typewriters, the tea makers, the duty cells, the kiddie patrol, the whore minding, the nursing and doing the inspector's shopping on a Wednesday after-noon. We shoved half-a-dozen of you out into a whole rack of divisions, under some of the hardest cases in the Met. Then we sat back and watched. We're doing the same thing in January with a new half-dozen, God help them.

'As for your lot, four of the girls folded in a month, the fifth is about to crumble any minute. Couldn't take it, didn't like the atmosphere, felt they couldn't slap a detective inspector's face when he stuck his hand up their drawers; didn't like it when the men tweaked their titties, or patted their soft little bums. You name it, they couldn't deal with it, so the problems run both ways. Mind you there was one whose head was turned by the promotion. Thought it meant bitching at everyone and being an unbearable martinet.'

Some of his remarks were a bit frank and open for Suzie who felt a flush rising from behind her ears and spreading, crimson, down her cheeks.

'You, on the other hand, heart, you got a break.' Pause and a big smile for the *Movietone News* cameras. 'You lost Big Toe Harvey and took over a headline murder; and I for one think you've done bloody well.'

She wanted to tell him that she'd not really done *that* well. She'd wanted to give up on the interviews, wanted to run away and not ask the real questions. 'I didn't know what questions I *should* ask,' she said. 'Hopeless. Interviewing those blokes and all I found out was that Jo Benton was a libertine whose idea of a good time was having a roll in the hay with a new man – or one she'd known since childhood. I was about as useful as a chocolate cigarette.'

She had taken against the boyfriend, Fermin, didn't care for any of the others either, and made a lot of mistakes, antagonized people. 'As for the problems going both ways, that's not fair.' She got quite bolshie, 'Women in the Met are totally outnumbered. And the men have never been seriously challenged when it comes to the way they behave when the girls are around. The men don't really like taking orders from a woman, that was obvious. They don't even like us being right about decisions.'

Dandy Tom said that would work itself out. 'They have the same problems in HM Forces. Navy, Army and Air Force. The girls do their best. Show spunk. Damn good, the girl officers and NCOs.' He had been to a conference where they'd come to the conclusion that all they needed was time. 'Girls settled down quickly. Bit keck-handed some of them, but they had male recruits who were just as bad.'

She thought of Big Toe – *I hold a firm belief that women drivers all have two left arms and three left feet.* Then the moment when she'd got into the papers. *Not the kind of publicity we either like or countenance,* Sanders of the River had told her. She passed this on to Tommy Livermore now and he gave a deep belly chuckle.

'Idiot.' He scowled for a moment. 'Just the kind of idiot we've got to change. Sort of fellow who wants to keep women in what he thinks is their place – in bed, pregnant or chained to the kitchen sink. But the papers were wonderful, Sue. Played straight into our hands. Really lacked finesse, the silly buggers, toeing the line. Remember what I said?'

'You said they'd make up things about their grandmothers if it helped sell papers, and they'd make up things about me.'

'Quite. And now you should know that I was instructing Mr Sanders to go easy on you and let you have your head. He was obviously taking no notice of me.'

He gave a big aristocratic grin.

The Pears Belle Helene arrived. Just like any other Saturday night dinner with the nobs.

'So what happens now, Guv?'

'Nothing earth shattering. You go off and interview the Fighter Ace, what's-his-name...?'

'Squadron Leader Fordham O'Dell DFC.'

'Him. Yes. Who you don't really need to see.'

'What do you mean, sir?' Hell, she thought. The jig's up.

'Because he couldn't have been near Corham Cross Road, because there he was with his squadron at Middle Wallop Aerodrome fighting the Hun. Nobody there has had leave over the past month.'

'Yes, sir, but someone's got to have a word with him.'

'I quite agree, young Suzie with a zed.' He lifted his eyes, under the lids, squinting up in a look that said now we are in league with one another. 'You know it's not going to be the full interview with stuff being taken down and used in evidence, because you're not taking anyone to RAF Middle Wallop, someone to sit in on the interview, as it were. I don't blame you, it's only a spit and a stride from your sister's place after all.'

Then, slowly she asked, 'And after Christmas?'

'You go back to Camford, and tell nobody about this conversation. In a week or so I'll arrive and take over the investigation—'

'With the full team...?'

'With some of the team.'

'Molly Abelard?'

'Try and stop her.'

'No, thank you.'

'She's my biggest fan, heart.'

'It shows, sir.'

'Don't be too hasty about Abelard. She's my secret weapon, and she's the best-educated girl we've got – I mean the best-educated girl we've got in the entire Met. Knows every damn thing from Shakespeare to Shagnasty, if you'll pardon the expression.'

'And where were *you* educated, Guv'nor?'

'You don't want to know.'

Eton and Oxford, she thought. In the nursery they'd told him, *Tommy you're going to be one of the great rulers. Whatever you do you're going to be boss, and you're going to be at the front. Sun never sets on the Empire – the red colouring on the map. Keep the red inside the lines, Tommy.*

There were other things he asked her to do. 'Let me take a look at la Benton's address book – all the stuff you've told me about. I'll go through it and we'll quietly have a look at every one of her friends and acquaintances. I'll set the lads on them – and the lasses as well. Maybe even take a peep myself.'

'Who're we really interested in, Guv?' She accepted a cigarette, and he lit it for her.

'It's an inside job.' He sounded almost disinterested, meaning the involvement of someone close to her.

'How can you be sure?'

301

'Smells like it. I don't think some passing homicidal maniac thought, Ah, I'll try this house. Don't think it's a burglary gone wrong, either.'

'With respect, sir. You haven't been to the scene of crime.'

'I'll get over there soon. Scrutinize. Have a dig around. Let the lads have a bit of a rootle, tie up the loose ends, but it smells as though someone set this up. Somebody wanted her dead and didn't want to hang around waiting for the right bomb.' Pause, the fountain pen gently tapping his teeth again, as though he was trying to remember something.

He remembered – 'Oh yes, heart. Bit of a mystery. That fellow Dance, Josh Dance.'

'The estate agent?'

'Little oddity. He telephoned Camford nick this afternoon. Said to your friend Shirley that Emily Baccus couldn't be dead because she was in his office very late Friday night, or early this morning. Quite steamed up about it. Not urgent, but you might have a word with him. Needs clearing up.'

It was real coffee they served at the Ritz as well. Nothing like the muck she'd had in Selfridges this morning. She wondered where the devil they got all that good stuff. The lobster? Beef? Pears?

'Tinned pears,' the DCS said as though reading her mind.

'You do the Tarot as well?' she asked.

'Only when there's no R in the month.'

'And my future's mapped out then, Chief

302

Superintendent?'

'If you can do it, you stand every chance of ending up as a very senior woman officer, yes. But only if you have the application. Desire – application – attention – single-mindedness. If you can fill the unforgiving minute ... Yours is the Earth and everything that's in it ... And – which is more – you'll be a Woman, my girl. Or something like that, heart.'

'Better than old Rudyard's original.'

'Thank you.' The pause that was a part of his style. 'Now, heart–' again a pause – 'now, there's the question of Emily Baccus's death.'

He'd got the post-mortem results. She looked hard into his face, loved the tiny trembling of his lips as he smiled, saw how the eyebrows moved and the length of his eyelashes, and how they curved upwards. A woman would give a lot for lashes like that.

Using one finger, he slid a three-by-four black and white photograph across the crisp damask tablecloth. 'Picked it up in her flat and had some copies run off. Hang on to it. Just to remind you. We may need to trace her movements over the last hours of her life.'

The final face, in its hideous death grin, only hinted at the in-life attractiveness, but there it was, in sharp focus, and the snub button nose seemed to be the only flaw. A looker, possibly Greek, Turkish maybe. Hadn't delved into that, the lineage, but she was certainly attractive. Very attractive. She reminded Suzie of somebody. The face was very familiar but she couldn't place where she knew her from, this

303

Emily Baccus who owned a couple of properties on the edge of Soho and collected her own rents.

'And she didn't die from a crushed windpipe, Guv?'

'Much more sophisticated. Been dead for a couple of days when we found her. Been drinking. Quite a lot of chloral in her as well as brandy. Enough chloral to send her bye-byes. And someone topped her up with morphine. Heavy and high dose. The kind of dosage they're now giving officers and NCOs to take on to the battlefield: to kill the pain for serious wounds. That and the alcohol did it. Also some geezer had pulled hard on that bit of wire but it broke nothing. Didn't do a thing. She wouldn't have suffered. Got a bit drunk and slipped off to sleep. Woke up in the next world.'

Between discussing the way Emily Baccus had died, telling her about the course they'd mapped out for her, Dandy Tom asked about her mother, the Galloping Stepfather, as he called the Major, her baby brother and her sister.

'Like two peas in a pod, I hear,' he said.

'Heard from whom?'

'I get about, Suzie. Maybe I sent Abelard to Newbury and had her ask around. I'm prone to do things like that.'

'Nothing would surprise me, sir.'

'And what about Big Toe Harvey?'

'What about him, Guv?'

'Just tell me the truth. Nothing'll end up on your shoes.'

304

'Harvey? Local boy makes good. You know he comes from Camford?'

'I'd heard.'

'I could never prove it, but I think he does a bit of billing and cooing with childhood friends.'

'Anything I should be concerned about?'

'Not unless your name's Mrs Harvey.'

'And what else?'

She counted to herself. Twenty-five. It was something she had done most of her life. If I count to twenty-five and he hasn't asked again I don't have to tell him.

'What else d'you feel about Harvey? Like him?'

'He's a bully boy at heart.'

'And...?'

'He could be bent, sir.' She regretted saying it, so – 'I shouldn't have said that, Guv. I couldn't prove it in a month of Sundays.'

'You just have a feeling about it, right?'

'That's about the size of it. You come to the Ritz often, Guv?'

'It's my local, heart.'

'Must be a bit steep on a detective chief super's pay.'

'Don't be cheeky, Sue.' He meant it because she felt a draught of ice flick from his eyes and saw a shadow cross his face.

When they reached the building off Upper St Martin's Lane he told the cabby to wait while he showed the lady to her door. He came up with her, but stood outside.

'You alright?'

She nodded, wanted him to kiss her so much, and knew there was no chance. Wondered what it would be like. And waited in hope. Wanted to feel his body close to hers. Waited in vain.

'You have a happy Christmas, then, heart.'

'And you, sir.'

He leaned forward and put a card in her hand. She could smell lemons. Scented bath soap, she thought. How smashing.

'You'll get me there from Christmas Eve until about eight on Boxing Day evening,' he said, looking at the card.

She glanced down and saw that he had written a telephone number in blue ink. 'Thought you were giving me the Black Spot, Guv.'

'You'd know it if I was. That's just in case anything comes up after you've talked to O'Dell. Just if there's anything you feel we've got to act on immediately.'

'I'll try not to bother you, Guv'nor.' Pause. 'This the country seat, then?' she asked, and waited for the steam to come out of his ears.

Instead he gave her a kindly little smile: not the full grin but nice. 'As a matter of fact, it is. I have to go down and flog the peasants at Christmas. They'd feel neglected if I didn't keep up the old traditions.'

'Flogging the peasants; playing Father Christmas to the local children, and riding with hounds on Boxing Day?'

'Something of the sort. Have a good time, heart. It's nice to have you on the team. Oh, and...' beautifully timed, as though he really had just remembered it, '...Suzie, not a word to

306

any of the boys and girls in the Camford nick, okay?'

And he left, his hand coming up to tip the Homberg to her. Real gent, she thought. He's a real, proper twenty-four carat, gent of the first water, she thought, then went off and looked in every room to make sure the bogeyman hadn't come down the non-existent chimney while she had been out.

She thought of Dandy Tom as soon as she opened her eyes in the morning blackness. Getting out of bed she felt the cold on her feet, so hurried through to the bathroom. She remembered it was Sunday 22 December 1940. Tomorrow she would be heading for Hampshire: first the Fighter Ace, then a blessed couple of days off over Christmas with Charlotte and the kids.

It was raining and she heard the click of hail against the bathroom window. She thought of her mother. 'Rain before seven, fine before eleven,' she intoned as she performed her ablutions in the freezing cold of the six o'clock bathroom.

On the Tube to Camford she thought about the time spent last night with Tommy Livermore. The Honourable Tommy Livermore. Crime Fighter Ace. The future Lord Livermore, Earl of Kingscote, she supposed.

So there she was, on the Tube on a wet Sunday heading out to Camford nick, leafing through a copy of *Picture Post* that she had brought along for company. But she hardly saw the pictures and text about the Home Guard being trained at Osterley Park Training School. A photograph of men using a smoke canister purporting to hide them from their line of attack, but showing how incredibly inept it really was. What she saw was Dandy Tom, the lovely Detective Chief Superintendent.

Oh, when will I be experienced? she wondered, her body screaming out for what she didn't even know. Couldn't really guess at. Dandy Tom, she thought again.

She felt a touch feverish.

Pip Magnus sat at his desk with a huge automatic pistol stripped and laid out in pieces. Next to the pistol was a roll of cloth, about the width of a toilet roll, and divided up every two inches by red lines. Four-by-two. Sniggers because you get four-by-two from the armourer who has a hooked tool for getting broken pull-throughs out of the barrel. There was also a metal bottle of oil with a special applicator coming out of the screw top. Pip Magnus was cleaning the gun.

'Firearms in the CID room, Pip? I don't think so.' Suzie paused in walking towards Big Toe's office that she had purloined while he was away sick, wounded in the course of duty.

'It's evidence, Skip.' He had a sly smile and didn't look at her, just kept polishing away at the slide that he had pulled back, detached and taken apart, dropped the spring out, then removed the barrel and breech. 'I saw Big Toe last night, Skip.' Accusingly, as if she should either have been with him or visited Big Toe Harvey of her own volition instead of being wined and dined at the Ritz by Dandy Tom Livermore.

'Oh, yes? And he told you to bring a damned great shooter into the CID Room, did he?'

'More or less, Skip. I told you, it's evidence.'

It was a Colt .45 automatic pistol. She knew that from the firearms course they had sent her on immediately war was declared, where she had learned about four-by-two and the armourer's hooked tool. More to the point, she'd learned to shoot. Found that she was a natural. Did Tommy Livermore arrange that as well? she wondered.

'Evidence of what?'

'It belongs to Charlie Balvak, Skip. Or maybe it belongs to Connie. One or the other.'

'Well, you must know which one.' At last, she thought. At last Big Toe's got something on the Balvak brothers.

'No, Skip. We haven't found it on them yet. Big Toe said I had to get it ready for when he's back in harness next week.'

If she made a fuss he would deny saying it. If she didn't do something now, straight away, this minute, the gun would not be around when she needed it. This was the lads versus the lasses. There are more of them than us. That's what she'd told Tommy Livermore last night. 'There are certain things no woman police officer can ever win,' she'd told him as they drove back to St Martin's Lane. 'There's a male *esprit de corps*,' she'd said, 'and when that's in play no criminal can win and no woman police officer can win either. Black becomes white, Guv, and white becomes sky-blue-pink.'

'Is Shirley in yet?'

She'll be in later, Magnus thought aloud.

'What's she on?'

'She's feeling a few collars with the rest of the boys. Raiding party. Sherlock Mortimer's leading them into battle.'

'Whose collars?'

'They think they've got a result on those street robberies. The old ladies divested of their jewels and stuff.'

'Shirley Cox has been working with me. Not the street robberies.'

'Mortimer thinks he's struck lucky, and there're a couple of girls involved so Shirl's going along to see that nobody takes advantage.'

'And Big Toe told you to get this weapon out?'

'Yes. Wants to be sure it's in working order for him coming back next week – well, first of the year.'

'Next week.' She looked at the Colt automatic lying on the desk. 'Next week is an unexplored territory.' She walked into her office – well, Big Toe's office – and settled to typing up the reports she had drafted over the past few days. The interviews with the Grigson girl, Sally, Steven Fermin, Richard Webster, Josh Dance, Daniel Flint, Barry Forbes and Gerald Vine, which led her directly to the notes about Emily Baccus and what she had done about it.

Too late.

She typed the interview details in triplicate, using two carbons. One for the CID file, one for the nick and one to be sent over to the Yard – to DCS Tommy Livermore of the Reserve Squad – often confused with the Murder Squad which didn't really exist. When a death was announced in the provinces, foul play suspected and the Yard had been called in, more often than not it was an officer from the Reserve Squad who went tooling off to an outstation, or to a provincial nick that needed assistance in a headline murder case.

She also wrote a long note on Richard Webster about the need to question him again, quite closely and with some hostility. To Suzie's mind, Mr Webster was a prime suspect being the repository of secrets, but a lot didn't add up. She couldn't understand why he didn't know about the flat in Derbyshire Mansions. He knew every other damned thing about her, why not that? Or maybe he did know it, but was reluctant to share it with anyone. Especially the police – the Filth.

Around ten thirty Pip Magnus came in with a cup of so-called coffee for her from the canteen.

'Skip–' he put the cup on her desk, holding another in his left hand – 'Skip, look, the shooter. Well that was a kind of joke really.' She was aware that he had spent some time on the telephone while she was working. 'The Guv'nor said it'd be fun to see how you re-acted to a shooter in the CID room. And you

311

certainly reacted, Skip. I've locked it away again. You reacted though.'

Toe, she reckoned, had given him a rocket. She rang Steve Fermin at his home number and had a long conversation. Asked him how he was doing? Was he coming to terms with the grief yet? No, it *is* a bit too soon, of course. He had a brother with him. Parents were coming down for the funeral, though they had not yet fixed the date because the police wouldn't say when the body would be released. But he'd let her know as soon as they knew, though he would have thought she'd get the word before him. He sounded better, she felt. Hoped he was. Grief could be a killer. There'd be more than ever when he discovered Jo would never have been the virgin bride. A bit too late for that, seeing as how her hobby had been losing her virginity on a regular basis.

Next she set about writing a short personal letter to DCS Tommy Livermore. It was marked private & personal. Mr Livermore's eyes only.

I know it will all disappear like ice in a heatwave, she wrote, but one of the DCs here has been handling what I think is a dodgy Colt .45. He said he had retrieved it from among other evidence and suggested it was going to be planted on one of the Balvak brothers after DI Harvey returns to duty. I was alone with this officer. Name Magnus P. Number 4587. I am putting this note in with other items to be sent over to the Yard by hand in case I am involved in an accident or go for a burton.

The raiding party got back just before noon, making a row. They had brought prisoners and they whooped into CID like a clutch of school-children who had just won the inter-house hockey trophy, or whatever, and Jimmy Morti-mer came straight into Suzie's appropriated office, followed by Shirley Cox.

'Got 'em, Skip,' he trumpeted. 'Got the bug-gers. Laid 'em low. Picked 'em up and pulled 'em out. We've got a lot of the stuff back as well. Rings, bangles, watches, necklaces.'

'Who and where?'

'Three young men and two girls. We dragged them out of the Cut. Almost a dawn raid, wasn't it Shirley?'

'Almost.' Shirley sounded subdued. 'Eight o'clock in the morning is, I suppose, the dawn chorus for some people.'

'Five of them? From the Cut?'

'It's alright, Skip. We got permission and all. Went without a hitch. I suppose we'd better go and have a heart to heart with them. They wouldn't own to it, none of them. But I'm sure we'll persuade them. Got to get a coffee, Skip. You come down while we're talking. Give them the evil eye or something, eh?' And he was off, leaving Shirley looking decidedly uncomfort-able.

Had she heard correctly? Suzie asked, 'Did I hear that, Shirl, and does it mean what I think it means? *We got permission?*'

Shirley Cox nodded. 'Big Toe says that it's safer. If he'd been here he'd have marched us all down there. He isn't here, so Jimmy

313

Mortimer and Pip Magnus took a walk down the Duke last night and had a word in Charlie's ear. Well, Charlie and Connie both.'

Suzie realized that she was shaking with anger. 'And you think it's right? Going into a part of the manor we know's controlled by the Balvaks and speaking to them first. Asking their permission to pull felons out of their patch. Shirl, it's disgraceful. Disgusting.'

'Maybe it's not as bad as it sounds, Skip. Big Toe always said there was a demarcation line – Revellers Park. The other side of the park was always the Balvak territory. He always said it didn't hurt. That we'd put them away in the end.'

In her anger Suzie could only see the seeds of corruption sown by Harvey and gobbled up by his disciples in the CID room. She didn't trust Big Toe an inch and certainly didn't purchase his feeble concept that you could reach the heart of lawless evil by cuddling in to parts of it.

She wondered what the business with the Colt .45 was all about. She looked hard into Shirley's face and saw more troubles in her eyes.

'There's something else worrying you.' It was part statement and part question.

'I've got nothing to go on, Skip. The lads handled it all.'

'Confide in me.'

'Well, I have no idea if Pip and Jimmy gave any names to the Balvaks. But the lad we had sussed as the ringleader wasn't there when we called on him this morning: Freddie Kemp. And guess what? Charlie and Connie are his uncles. The father said he'd gone to join up – they're all around the right age and the three we've got already have their papers. The girls're a bit younger, and they worry me a lot.'

'Why?'

'I don't think they're good actors. They deny everything, they seemed genuinely shocked when we rumbled the goods hidden in their bedrooms, and they're cousins – cousins to the girl Watts, Cathy Watts, the one you saw in hospital the day you arrived. Remember? What I think is that we've pulled these two as a kind of reprisal for Cathy Watts and Beryl Pegler.'

To the buggers who did all that it was merely a spanking. Suzie remembered. The broken bones, the beaten-up eyes, split lips, the arms in plaster casts, the broken ribs. And, *These people have memories like the Bible, unto the third and fourth generation, and once you've crossed them you can never climb back.*

'You'd better go and help with the inquisition,' she told Shirley. She, DS Mountford, didn't want any part of this business. The more she could keep herself occupied the better it would be.

'How was last night?' Shirley asked. 'How was it with that lovely detective chief superintendent? The one with the stylish tailoring?'

'One hundred per cent business,' Suzie told her flatly.

'No larks?'

'None whatsoever.'

315

'How bloody dull,' Shirley said as she got to the door.

Suzie sorted the typewritten interview forms, her notes on the whole business, the evidence – Josephine Benton's address books and things – slipped her private & personal envelope under the last pile, scooped it up and dropped it in to a thick manila quarto envelope. She ran her tongue along the gummed flap and pushed her balled right hand across the flap, pressing it down on to the desk. As she wrote DCS Livermore's address at the Yard, she thought how much nicer it would be to run her tongue over Dandy Tom than over the thick envelope flap. She tingled at the prospect, and didn't know if it would be right, was not certain which part of him she should run her tongue over, his lips or his cheeks? In her secret life, the one that went on all day in her head, she was totally obsessed. Will someone eventually teach me? And when they do, will it plunge me from a state of grace into a state of darkest sin?

She took her package up to Loamy Lomax at the front desk.

'We got a courier going to the Yard, Loamy?'

'Next one's two thirty.'

'I want him down here, I've got highly confidential stuff for the Reserve Squad. If I'm not in CID I'll be in the canteen, with the lads doing the interviewing or with Superintendent Sanders.'

'Right, Suzie. Camford to Reserve. I heard you'd been dallying with the great Tommy Livermore.'

316

'And who did you hear that from, Loamy?'

'Your DC Cox. Said it was an education. I saw him once. That murder in Hounslow a couple of years ago. Like a dose of salts he was, went through everything in twenty-four hours flat.'

'Good. About half two then, Loamy.'

Back in CID she wrote up the murder book, filed the papers and took the duplicate file up to the admin office, where a uniformed woman police officer took it and signed for it. As she was heading down to CID again Sanders came out of his office in his best uniform with his cap and the leather-covered swagger stick he now affected.

'Oh, Susannah!' he called and she expected him to add, 'Don't you cry for me.' But he managed to control the vocal urges. 'I see from the duty log that you're off early today, heading out of town and then off on Christmas leave.' He pronounced it 'leaf' like naval petty officers, and she thought to herself someone ought to tell him about that, and knew it wouldn't be her.

He came over and stood very close to her. 'I hear your people've pulled in some hobblede-hoys for these street robberies. Good show, that.'

'If they can prove it, sir.'

'Gather they've got some of the stuff back. Bang to rights, I'm told.'

'I'll drop in and have a word with them later, sir.'

'Well, you have a really good Christmas,

317

Susannah, and don't forget our night out in the New Year. I'm told the Silver Fox is good value.'

'Yes, sir. I've been told that as well. Look forward to it, sir,' she lied in her teeth as she nipped downstairs and slipped into one of the rooms they were using for interviews. Pip Magnus and Pete Pinchbeck were belabouring a pale acne-covered youth with questions, misusing the rapid technique, their questions overlapping each other, not giving the lad a chance to even answer. In the books on interview techniques they called it establishing a rhythm, and something similar in the handbooks on interrogation. Either Magnus and Pinchbeck had read none of the books, or they just weren't trying.

She got tired of it and asked the one uniform present where Shirley was.

'Next room. Dealing with one of the girls, Fat Paula.'

So she went through and Shirley was with Mortimer and a tear-stained plump girl – Paula Potter, undeniably fat with lank ginger hair and oily skin. They were just about finished – 'I believe you, Paula, thousands wouldn't,' the woman detective constable said, and Mortimer scowled black anger.

Suzie pulled Shirley out. Took her into the corridor with its gleaming linoleum on the floor, brown and polished almost to a mirror: you could smell the wax they used on it every day. Fracture Lane they called it down here because if a prisoner was on remand they'd get him to do the corridor every day. It was slippery as ice and the story was that the floor had claimed one solicitor, compound fracture, and two police constables, tibia and fibula, plus a visiting newspaper man who did for his right wrist. 'Clutching at straws as he went down,' Sergeant Lomax reckoned.

'I'm not getting mixed up in this, Shirl,' Suzie told her. 'I've enough on my plate, and I've a favour to ask.' She spelled it out in about seven ways that she did not want Shirley gossiping to everyone in the nick about Dandy Tom. 'Just drop it all down a well, Shirl. Wrap it up and lock it away. At the end of the day I'll see you're okay. Yes?'

Shirley nodded. Agreed completely. Did everything except sign a confession. Admitted to talking to Lomax, who everybody knew was more loose-lipped than a chimpanzee.

'Okay, Shirl. Give me my moves tomorrow.'

Shirley couldn't remember all the instructions for tomorrow's journey, so came back to CID and read from her notes. 'Eight thirty, Waterloo Station. See the RTO and he'll make sure you get on the first train going direct to Andover. He'll also ring RAF Middle Wallop and they'll send a car to pick you up at the station on arrival. You're expected by Squadron Leader O'Dell. You can either have lunch in the sergeants' mess or fudge your rank and eat with the toffs in the officers' mess. If you play your cards right, they'll drive you to Overchurch.'

The RTO was the Railway Transport Officer. Every junction and central railway station had

319

an RTO and they all performed a thankless job with reasonable efficiency, assisted by enthusiastic teams of both sexes. 'RTOs are the unsung heroes,' the Galloping Major used to proclaim. 'Victoria Cross should come up regularly with the rations.' Charlotte always maintained that the Major himself had spent the Great War as RTO at King's Cross fighting the WVS.

'Sounds like you've fixed everything.'

'I do my best.' She flapped her hands in a gesture that could have meant that she hadn't really done well enough.

'Come and have lunch.'

They ate what was on offer in the canteen: boiled bacon with chips and cabbage, followed by the raspberry jelly and cream which was in effect a very rubbery flavoured gelatine covered with sickly sweet Carnation tinned milk that often had to do for cream in these dingy days. The cabbage was disgusting, but the chips and the boiled bacon weren't half bad. It could only get worse.

Suzie was just starting on the jelly when the dispatch rider – who rode the link with the Yard – came in looking for her. So she had to take him along to the office, unlock her drawer and get his signature after she handed over the papers and her note to Dandy Tom.

'Hear you took a phone call from our friend Josh Dance,' she said when she was seated across from Shirley again.

'Yes. Strange. Seemed to think Emily Baccus wasn't dead – at least wasn't at three o'clock yesterday morning.'

'But we knew she was very dead by then.'

'I more or less told him but he insisted that she'd been in his office a little before three in the morning.'

'He talk to her?'

'I don't think so.'

'Drunk?'

'Didn't sound it.'

'Just sounded irrational, eh?'

'I got the feeling he believed what he was saying.'

'I'll have a word after Christmas. Remind me, Shirl.'

'I will.'

After another minute, 'These chums you arrested this morning–' Suzie began.

'You want the truth?'

'If you'd be good enough.'

'I've already told you, Skip.'

'Tell me again.'

'I think the boys steal with monotonous regularity from elderly people in the blackout. I believe it totally because they were all far too nonchalant about being banged up. Personally I'm sure they'd prefer to be banged up than go and do their duty for King and country. All three've got their call-up papers. I've seen them and they've to report to the Induction Centre and Infantry School by twelve noon on 3rd January 1941. They're terrified of it because they know life's going to be uncomfortable and they could end up being killed. A twelve months sentence they can all do standing on their heads because they have contacts inside. It'll be unpleasant but they'll be fine. So I'd hope that we let them go, and then provide an honour guard to the station on 3rd January.'

'And the girls?'

'Fitted up. Both of them. Separately they had visits from two of the boys last night and there was plenty of time for the lads to drop the stuff on them. I only say this because I know what I told you earlier. Both the girls're related to Cathy Watts, and one of them is also related to the Pegler girl. The Balvak boys are so sweet. They never forget do they? And they're quite content to see those three lads go down the chute, as long as the girls are popped inside as well.'

Don't let it happen, Suzie told her. If it's not cast iron, make sure they go home for Christmas, but make certain those boys get their guard of honour to Catterick on 3rd January. 'Do it,' she instructed.

Then, 'Just one thing, Shirley,' and she told her to watch Pip Magnus; outlined the business with the pistol. 'Watch him like a bird of prey, Shirl.'

Then she went off to take a listen and look at the interrogations. The boys and the remaining girl were still denying everything, and everyone was telling a different story, singing out of tune, marching to a different drum. Shirley would be able to make short work of it, call a halt and send them all home for Christmas. Bah, humbug.

When she finally went along to the front

counter to sign off, there were several Christmas cards waiting for her and a small soft package wrapped in silver paper. She collected everything and opened the cards as she rode back to the Strand on the Tube. All the lads, plus Sergeants Osterley and Lomax, had done cards for her, which was something.

Back at the flat she opened the package. Shirley had put a card with the gift. *There you go, Skip. A couple of pairs of those ritzy parapants you fancied – From Mary Christmas and Shirley Cox.*

At half-past eight she was thinking about having a bath when the telephone rang.

'Suzie with a zed,' Dandy Tom Livermore said. 'Thank you for your billet-doux. It's all very interesting, but I think now's the time to distance yourself from the politics of Camford nick.'

'I just don't like pistols being waved around in the CID room, Guv.'

'Quite right. Leave it alone now unless your DI brings the matter up after Christmas.'

Stay shtum, she thought, so after a count of around ten he said, 'I've just spoken to Ernie Prothero at Acton nick.'

'Oh, yes?' Acton – the Barbara Batchelor killing. 'Bubbles' Batchelor.

'The uncle's coughed. *Not* a coincidence. Said he'd read about the Cambridge girl and got hold of the piano wire from a shop in the High Street. Bought the insulating tape at Woolworths. Prothero's confirmed both. Sounds right, so I think we can cross it off our list.'

'Right, Guv.' Why did she feel disappointed?

'So what've we got, Souze?'

'A loony who strangles girls at random?'

'Yes. Or?'

'A man who has a grudge against each of these women, and who is mad enough to kill them one at a time.'

'Or?'

She thought for almost half a minute. 'Give up, Chief.'

'Go away and think about it. Where would you hide a car, Suzie? And what would you do with a spider in a bottle? A spider with a deadly toxic bite.'

'Pour sugar on it? You speak in riddles, O Great One.'

'Have a nice time with the Brylcreem Boys. Ring me after Christmas.'

There had been no warnings and no bombs for a couple of nights. When that happened there were usually enough clients to keep Lavender happy until around eleven o'clock. She rarely worked on a Sunday, but tonight she had arranged to see two old clients. One at ten, the other at ten forty-five, so she left just before midnight. Edith the Maid didn't come in from Camford just for the two and a half hours, so Lavender made sure that Golly was around, though she told him to stay out of the way as she knew the clients. 'Don't want to frighten them, do we, Golly?'

Just after Lavender left, the telephone rang. He wasn't allowed to pick up the telephone as a rule, but Golly was sitting right next to it looking through the *Tatler*, left by a client. He automatically stretched his arm out, picked up the telephone and grunted.

'Golly?' the voice at the other end said, and he knew straight away that it was the voice he heard at night, in his ear, when he was asleep. 'Golly, you haven't forgotten have you? It's very important. What do you have to do on Christmas Day, Golly?'

He told her and got so excited that, for the first time in ages, he wet himself.

Seventeen

It was a bitter, bright morning and from the front of the car as it swung in through the main gates of Middle Wallop Aerodrome, Suzie Mountford could see a Spitfire turning in on its final approach. The car she sat in was a Humber, painted Air Force blue over all, with a RAF roundel on the offside bumper and its registration number stencilled in white on the nearside. Over the car's engine noise, she could hear the sweet throb and whine of the Spit's Rolls-Royce Merlin. The aeroplane's under-carriage was down, and the big flaps drooped below the trailing edges of the wings as it lined up with the runway.

In the distance leafless trees were hunched together on a skyline of ploughed fields, the brown, corrugated earth curving gently up to a sharp horizon. The car turned right inside the gate, driving along a grey macadam perimeter track, so now the aircraft was in front of them, to the left, flattening out and beginning to drop, nose up, towards the mowed and smooth grass strip. She could see the wide runway was not flat, as she'd supposed, but sloped in a shallow fall towards more trees and the airfield's main buildings behind her.

Over the hedge, the aircraft's engine pitch suddenly changed as the pilot increased power, lifted the undercarriage, and climbed away to go round the circuit again. She wondered why. Was there a problem? Or had the pilot gone round on a whim?

Suzie had today's *Daily Mail* folded on her lap, neatly creased with the murder story upwards. She had opened the paper just as her train was pulling out of Waterloo Station and, turning the page, she bumped straight into Emily Baccus's face across three columns, with the headline, PROPERTY HEIRESS FOUND STRANGLED.

Good for Dandy Tom, she thought. The story had not got out in time for the national papers on Saturday – though it had squeezed into one of the evening finals. This morning the dailies were trying to catch up.

Yes, well, read all about it. Her eyes went down and focused on the photograph of the late Emily Baccus and immediately saw the likeness that had been so bothering her. That's who she looks like. Oh yes, of course. Now you see it, now you don't, and she hadn't seen it until now. Plain as the nose on your face. She was startlingly like him. Susannah, she thought, you're a prune not to have seen it before.

Like two peas in a pod, I hear, Dandy Tom had said about Charlotte and herself. She wondered how he would feel about this likeness. When she got back to London, after Christmas, she'd ring Josh Dance and ask him. Might even take up that invitation to have dinner with him. She could put some judicious questions to him between the Woolton Pie and the grilled snoek and chips without making a song and dance about things. 'What was her lineage, Emily Baccus? Is she related to anyone we know, Josh?'

'This is it, miss.' The RAF driver didn't really know what to call her: ma'am? Miss? Sarge? So he had stuck at miss. '609 Squadron, "A" Flight Dispersal, miss.' It was a long, divided Nissen hut, part communal where the pilots could relax, and part office space for the paperwork. A sergeant came out through the dispersal hut door and didn't know what to do. Doesn't know whether he should salute me or paint me, she thought and got out of the car to help him make up his mind.

'You looking for Squadron Leader O'Dell?' he asked with a schoolboy grin.

'Yes, I've got an appointment with him.'

'From London?'

'Yes.'

'You're police then.'

'To see Squadron Leader O'Dell, yes.' Going around in circles like the Spit she could still hear.

When she had told the driver that she was going to see O'Dell he said, 'Squadron Leader O'Dell? Lovely man. They'd follow him anywhere, the pilots. Straight as an arrow.'

She stood on the hard, frosted grass, and wrapped her coat around her, hands snug in the pockets, pulling the skirts close, her wrists crossed, just below the junction of her thighs. For a fraction of a second she thought of Jo Benton's gaffe, 'winter drawers on'.

A ridiculously young flight lieutenant came out, wearing a Mae West over his jacket, and flying boots carelessly unzipped on his feet. 'Hey Bas,' he called to the sergeant. 'This the lady for Fordy?' and Bas called back that it was, making the flight lieutenant light up like a Christmas tree – lovely youthful grin and everything. Warmed the cockles, Susannah thought.

'If you want Fordy at the moment you'll have to use a sky hook.' He sounded like a schoolboy as well. Could've equally said, 'O'Dell's in the San. Matron won't let him come to morning prayers.'

Blade on the feather
Shade off the trees

She turned to the driver and wondered if she should take her cases out of the Humber's boot.

328

'Don't you worry about those, miss. I'm to stay close to you. At your service, so to speak, until I drive you back to Andover station.'

'Oh bother, I wanted to go to Overchurch,' she said softly.

'Easier still, miss. I can run you to Overchurch. Be glad to.'

The flight lieutenant came bounding up like a puppy anxious to please. Given half a chance he'd have put his paws on her shoulder, climbed all over her and licked her face. 'That's Fordy's crate coming in now,' he drawled.

The same Spitfire she had seen from the car was over the hedge again, dropping effortlessly towards the grass. Five more aircraft were parked in what seemed to be a haphazard fashion around the dispersal area, and mechanics were finishing off some work on the nearest one, fitting a panel back over the engine in the nose and loading long belts of ammunition into the wings. In this incomplete state, she thought it looked like a beautiful wounded bird, and she could smell the compelling mixture of oil and aircraft dope that was its particular scent.

'Simnel,' the flight lieutenant said, sticking out a hand. 'Just plain Simnel, one l, as in Lambert, the Pretender chappie. No relative. M'father says we're descended from scullions and dairymaids. Fordy's been on an air test.'

Must be glorious here in summer, she thought. The Spitfires buzzing around like big wasps and the scent of hay mingling with oil and cordite.

Jolly flying weather,
And a hay harvest breeze,

And these overgrown children had spent the summer here, fighting and dying in the cramped cockpits, showing a bravery, courage and honour far beyond their years.

The Spitfire touched down: a perfect three-point landing, the canopy open and speed bleeding off as it rolled away from them, downhill and slowing. Already there was another aircraft, a Hurricane this time, in the circuit.

'You've done a lot of fighting from here?' she asked the young officer regretting her ineptness as soon as she'd spoken.

'I should say so, yes. Had a few tangles with Jerry from this 'drome. I came here with Fordy. We're the only two left of the original "A" Flight.' And she caught just the hint of something else behind his voice and in his eyes as she looked at him. Not fear exactly, but a longing for it all to be over, one way or the other.

The aircraft noise got louder as Fordham O'Dell taxied his Spitfire back to Flight Dispersal. He raised an acknowledging hand as he bumped past and, gunning the engine, turned the aeroplane into place and stood on the brakes as he closed the throttle. The ground crew swarmed out, sticking the chocks under the wheels, a corporal climbing on to the wing root.

Just forward of the canopy, O'Dell's Spitfire

had a small painting of Jane, from the *Daily Mirror*'s strip cartoon. Jane was always losing her clothes and running around in bra and gossamer-thin pants. She lay below the canopy looking provocative, one elbow resting on the words 'Orf Again!' Below the painting were two rows of swastikas. She counted nine as the pilot unfastened his harness, lowered the access hatch on the left of the cockpit and climbed out, helped by the ground-crew corporal.

'Hello. You're from London, yes?' Public-school voice, pleasant smile, looked about eleven. Maybe twelve at a pinch.

'Yes,' she called back as he sorted out his cap from inside his battledress blouse and jammed it, slanted, on his head. It was battered and all the stiffness had gone out of it. The story was that the fighter pilots sat on their uniform caps, but obviously O'Dell flew with his tucked inside his jacket.

So here he was. The man who had led Jo Benton down the racy run that had ended in the Coram Cross Road house, sprawled dead in a passage. Of course, if it hadn't been Fordham O'Dell it would've been someone else. Flint had said it though. *Her hobby was sex? She's been like that since Fordham O'Dell first tupped her one Saturday night in Glenbervie Woods.* And here was the young Lothario now, and he couldn't have looked a less likely candidate.

Apart from being such a child, he was rake thin and wiry. He also looked slightly unkempt. Frayed at the edges. She had expected a mature figure, handlebar moustache, florid, maybe even debauched. What she got was the slim young fellow-me-lad who, at first sight, couldn't say boo to a goose, and seemed slightly hesitant in his speech, as though he was carefully weighing up the words: putting his brain in gear before committing himself.

'Been keeping the lady company, Jamie?' He grinned at Simnel.

'Ra-ther, Fordy. Wizard popsy, eh?'

Do they really talk like that? she mused, realizing that they did. Schoolboyish and slangy to distance themselves from the fire and turmoil in their natural element, the heavens where they fought and occupied their business in great vastness. These men see the works of the Lord; and his wonders in the air.

'You watch out for young Jamie,' O'Dell warned her. 'You know what they call him? No, not going to tell you. Don't want to sully the ears of a pure young girl, eh? Been giving you the scullions and dairymaids line-shoot, has he? Yes, well, many a woman's gone to her doom because of Simnel and the scullions and dairymaids line.' He slowed and now spoke as though imparting a great confidence. 'Not true. All a line-shoot. He can't cook and even has difficulty putting the milk on his cornflakes. Scullions and dairymaids indeed.'

They walked between the aircraft on their way to the dispersal hut. Close up, the aeroplanes were less perfect. In the air, their natural element, they showed off their lines and looked wonderfully clean. Close up you could see exactly what they were for – hurtling out of the sky and pouring bullets into an enemy. Platforms for weapons. Here, walking past them, you were sensitive to the wear and tear, the places where the paint had worn off, revealing silver metal underneath; the marks where the mechanics and armourers had taken off hatches, unscrewed panels, removed plates. Also there were patches hurriedly stuck over defects she didn't want to enquire about – not too deeply anyway.

They reached the door of the hut and there was a little dance of indecision. Who should go first?

'Please,' a gesture, giving way to Suzie, then the realization that he should lead the way, so O'Dell opened the door and stomped in before Suzie, with Jamie Simnel bringing up the rear.

Inside, the air was thick with smoke and a blast of hot air hit them together with a shouted chorus of 'Shut that door!' In one corner stood a Christmas tree with a model Spitfire instead of an angel at the top. Paper chains hung from the four corners of the room and there were big red tissue paper bells hanging from the light fitments. Four young men in flying kit had been reading, drinking coffee and sprawling in chairs. Now they stood and came to attention, and in performing the act of getting on to their feet they somehow managed to convey that they were doing it for Suzie's sake and not for their superior officer.

'Come on,' said O'Dell. 'Come into my office and get away from the riff-raff.' He held back the door and let her pass, then closed it behind them.

From outside somebody sang loudly, 'Come into my parlour said the spider to the fly,' and there was raucous laughter.

'Don't mind them.' O'Dell motioned for her to sit down on a high-backed stand chair, while he went behind his desk. 'They get in a bit of a state when any new face comes down here. Some days, when it all gets too much for them, we have to make the Waafs go around with paper bags over their heads. Cut out slits for the eyes. That sort of thing.'

She found him delightful and realized why he was such a legendary hit with women. With his slight figure and the hungry look, any woman would want to mother him, enfold him in their arms to stave off the demons that must inhabit his head. Suzie wanted to do just that, so most women would follow the desire, and after mothering – she thought – comes the loving.

From behind his desk O'Dell asked what he could do for her. 'I mean I know you're here because of Joseph's death, but is there anything special you want to ask me?'

'Joseph?'

'It's what I used to call Jo. Joseph. She'd call me Freddie. It was a thing we did sometimes. You know, playing games.' He actually blushed a little, avoiding her eyes.

Now, inside his office and sitting across from him, Suzie could see that the youthfulness had been an illusion. Fordham O'Dell had his full complement of worry lines and premature ageing. There were already traces of frosting in his hair and she noticed the distinct tremor of his hands. But it was the eyes and voice that gave most of it away. He looked bone tired, and deep in his eyes there were traces of severe weariness. When he spoke there was that tiny hint she had detected in Jamie Simnel. It fused together the same elements. The fear that was not quite terror and the desire for the whole business to be consummated.

If he completed the war in one piece, Fordham O'Dell would probably thank God and then, over the years, render the whole business down to a jolly, if hairy, game played in his youth in which some of his best friends had drifted away, lost for ever.

Suzie told him they were checking Jo Benton's background. 'You're an essential for us, sir. You've known her longest. Since school.'

He passed a hand over his eyes. 'Before then,' he said. 'We were mixed infants together. In the end I knew her in all possible ways and positions.' His tired smile was the cheeky smirk of a schoolboy taking liberties. 'I presume you know all about her tastes and way of life by now?'

'Practically everything.'

'We were two of a kind.' It was the start of a flood of rather cold and matter-of-fact reminiscences. Neither of them had been faithful to the other; yes, he was her first lover; yes, he was a sexual obsessive just as she was; yes, they got up to all kinds of things together; over the years they had seen one another regularly – just as she had done with Gerald Vine, Suzie thought.

He was incredibly calm, unusually so and it quite unnerved her because under the placid exterior she could tell there was a well of grief.

'I'm used to people getting killed,' he said eventually. 'They all go one at a time, like lemmings disappearing over a cliff. Everyone I joined the RAF with – except old Jamie Simnel. They've all bloody gone. Most of my year at school as well. But, dammit, I never expected old Joseph to get the chop like that. She was always there, you see. Both of us. We were indestructible. Thought sometimes maybe a bomb, but to have some bugger kill...' He stumbled for the first time. Then angrily – 'For someone to rape and kill her.'

Other way round, Suzie thought. Other way round, Fordy. Freddie.

She was raped after death. Male sperm in all the usual places. The cutting and the eyes were also post mortem. That's the gist of it. That's what she'd read to Shirley from the PM report.

'Poor old Joseph.' He sniffed and she saw his eyes were welling up, very close to tears. 'Oh Lord, I'm sorry, this isn't very dignified.' He ran a handkerchief across his eyes, swallowing hard. 'You can only afford to be undignified with your lover.' Laugh. Sniff. 'Not nice for you. Sorry. You see, I like lemmings. Love them.' His voice cracked and he buried his head in his hands and wept, as Suzie had never seen a grown man weep.

It's more than simply his grief for Jo Benton. This is for all his friends who've gone spiralling down the skies to flaming death.

She waited quietly until the tears subsided, a little embarrassed. Eventually he again said he was sorry. 'You must have a shopping list of questions for me. What do I call you, by the way?'

'Call me Suzie, sir.'

'Cut out the sir, please. Makes me feel a hundred and two.' A little more fussing with the handkerchief. From outside there was a roar as another Spitfire taxied out for take-off. Then from a long way off the barking of a dog.

'With all this death, damage and disaster going on around us, it makes a murder seem a shade insignificant, eh?'

Suzie knew what he meant.

Finally he nodded, sitting up and looking pretty much pulled together.

'Can you tell me the last time you saw her, sir?' Sounded as calm as a millpond on a summer day. That's good. Dandy Tom would be proud of you, heart. Suzie with a zed.

'Yes, yes, I can. Last week in November. All leave was stopped on 30th November and we've been restricted until last Friday, what was that, 20th December? So I've been here since the end of November. Not been off the station between end of November until last Friday.'

'And you last saw Miss Benton?' she prompted.

'Trying to get it right. Yes, was in town on November 25th and 26th. That's it, clear as mud. Spent a lot of 25th with her. Not quite all

337

night, but we managed. She was a great girl at managing—' He was about to go off again and lose himself in memories, so she stepped in—

'So, where'd you go on 25th November, then?'

Count of three while he got his thoughts in order. 'Early dinner in a little place in Greek Street. That was good. Laugh a minute. Then we went to Derbyshire Mansions.'

'Jo Benton's flat? Two-twenty Derbyshire Mansions?'

'Two hundred and twenty, yes. Jo Benton's flat – no she's not, she's perfectly rounded. Joke we had. God, Suzie I can't believe she's gone. It's like some of my friends in the squadron. Keep thinking I'll see them come marching through the ante-room doors in the mess. Sometimes do see them.'

'Derbyshire Mansions, you stayed there until when?'

He'd been on the brink of launching into another trip down maudlin memory lane. 'Anyone else there?' she stepped in smartish.

He had a wary look, eyes sliding towards the door and then back to her.

'Emily?' Suzie asked.

Dully he nodded. 'Oh, you know about Emily then?'

'Some,' she said as though there was a lot more to it than she was letting on. 'And Monica? Monica Parker?'

'Who?'

'Monica Parker. Wren. Leading Wren Parker. A little friend. Used to help out Jo on special occasions.'

'Never heard of her. No Monicas here.' He tapped his head.

She had a sudden terrible thought. 'You *do* know what's happened to Emily, I presume. In today's papers.'

'I haven't seen the papers, but I heard it on yesterday's news, yes. Same bastard?'

'We don't know.'

He nodded. Just a nod, and the vacuous stare.

Better try him on the whole gang, she decided. She told him she was going to run some names by him. 'Daniel Flint. You know him, of course—'

'From the cradle, yes. At school together, yes. With Joseph, yes.'

'Did she mention him when you last saw her?'

A more natural laugh, as though he was drawing back from the grief.

'Did she not talk about him?' Suzie asked.

'Oh, she talked about him. Flint was not in her good books. Had a real down on him. Been spending quite a lot of time with him, I gathered. Talking about antiques. She was trying to get the BBC to let her do a series of radio shows about antiques, but they weren't going to let it happen. She knew it. Didn't have to be good with the crystal ball to see who'd get the blame.'

'She blamed Flint for the BBC not showing an interest?'

'Good old Joseph. I loved her to bits. Still do.

Be in my memory all my life. Special place for her and all that kind of thing. But that doesn't blind me to her faults. Joseph was never to blame for anything. Never took the blame, never accepted it. It was always someone else. Know the score?'

'You're telling me she rather messed up the antique show thing and Flint got the blame?'

'The whole bag of worms, yes. Black mark if the BBC decided against the show. Black mark passed on to dear old Flint. Rode him out of town on a rail. I once had to listen to a fifteen-minute diatribe about how she had cut her finger. I was to blame. I wasn't within a hundred miles of her, yet I was found guilty. And she doesn't forget – didn't forget. Six months after she cut her finger. Me, I was still guilty.'

The more she heard about Jo Benton the more she disliked her.

'You were close to Flint, were you?'

'School chums. Spent time in the woods together. Drank illegal hooch. Band of brothers, that kind of rot. Dan was a great man for the rut in his time.'

'Ever meet Richard Webster?'

'Agent. Yes, nice fellow. Had Jo's welfare at heart. Bit of a woofter, but never hold that against a man as long as they don't do it in the street, frighten the horses, that kind of thing. Really good at his job.'

'Met a man called Joshua Dance?'

'Yes. House lettings. Smart firm, Jewell something or other. Emily was supposed to be part of it, but never talked about the business.'

340

'Never? Wouldn't or couldn't?'

'Tell you the truth, I got the impression that she didn't really know much about it – the business I mean.' He glanced at his watch. 'Want a spot of lunch? The mess?'

'When we've finished.' She didn't mean to sound harsh, but that's how it came out.

He looked confused and babbled apologies. 'Get so used to having my own way. Giving the orders. You know.'

She said she understood and asked where he'd met Dance.

'His office, actually. Back in October, just after Jerry stopped nipping in every day. I was being shifted around the country. Publicity exercise for the old Air House. Whizzed me on to several airfields to talk to the chaps. Then they brought me into town for a couple of days. I did a BBC interview and some things for *Movietone News*, *Gaumont British*, that kind of thing. How we blasted the Hun. Tell you what, the filming and broadcasting was much more frightening than fighting Jerry. Felt totally exposed.' He gave a great guffaw of laughter.

'They recorded me for the BBC and some Yank radio stuff. Boffins had a special machine. Records your voice on wire. Amazing. But the film news people had to do their filming twice because I messed up. Talked about a Focke-Wolf "split-arseing across the sky". They said the old ladies in Tunbridge Wells, and the vicars on Holy Island would object, and while I was at it, would I change the Focke-Wolf to a Messerschmitt, what? They

341

had already had objections because they let some fellow say, "Give in to Hitler? Not Pygmalion likely." Can you credit that? Woman wrote in, said it wasn't very nice.'

'Joshua Dance?' Nudging him back, not knowing where it could possibly go.

'What? Oh. Oh, yes. You must think me a bit of a prune. All fingers and thumbs on the ground, wonder I can do my stuff aloft. Main thing really, isn't it? Dance, yes. Other thing terrified me was being bombed. They were pasting London both nights I was up and old Joseph, well she didn't turn a hair. Wouldn't go down the shelter or anything. I was petrified. Couldn't get Percy pointing north for most of the night. Very difficult situation.'

She must have looked uncomfortable. 'I'm so sorry,' he tried the cheeky schoolboy look again.

'You met Dance in his office?'

'Yes, well, Joseph wanted to go and see him because they'd just invalided him out of his regiment. Damned unfair, I thought. He could've stayed on and shuffled the bumf for the adj or something. Anyway, we went into this smart office somewhere off "the Dilly". Frightfully nice bloke. Crutches. Got on like the old house afire. Old Joseph seemed quite taken with him.'

'Really?'

'Oh yes, I could see she was trying to map out his future for him.'

'And did she?'

'No idea.'

'And that was the only time you met him, Dance?'

'Only the once. Cross me heart. Don't do the rest of that one. Bloody bad luck, I reckon.'

Okay, Suzie thought let's try. 'Barry Forbes?' she asked. 'Know him, heard of him?'

'Heard of him, never met him. Met his brother Frank: bit of a wet, two years below us at school. Joseph knew Barry, though. Aware of that.'

'Boyfriend of Emily's, yes?'

'Boyfriend of Emily's? Don't think so.'

'You sure?'

'Think I'd have heard if the great financial wizard, Barry Forbes, had been playing footsie with Em.'

'But you never met him? Not even at a party at the house in Coram Cross Road.'

'Never.'

'Fermin?' she asked.

'Fellow she was going to marry? No, never met him.' Brusque. A mite cool.

'What'd you think about her getting married?'

'Her business. Told me she was going to change her way of life. Didn't believe her, mind you.'

'So you weren't jealous?'

'What's the point?'

'You didn't have any rows about it?'

'I didn't say that.'

'Well?'

'Yes, we had quite a few words about it. I strongly disapproved of the way she was dealing with it. I don't mind her saying they were saving it all until they became husband and wife, but in her case it was a totally hypocritical thing. I told her and she knew how I felt. I'm told he's a perfectly nice fellow who cares greatly for her – cared, I keep forgetting. Please, can we go and get some lunch in the mess?'

'I can't,' she said. 'I'm a sergeant.'

'I know, but I'm putting my blind eye to the telescope and saying, "I see no stripes." Come on.'

'And after that last time with Jo Benton, at Derbyshire Mansions, what did you do?'

He sighed, as if to say it's none of your business, but... 'Got into a cab with her at five o'clock in the morning and went for the ride back to her place in Camford. She gave me bacon and eggs, fried potatoes, a sausage and fried bread. I had brought her some coffee that I'd got hold of on the q.t. from a ferry pilot. She ground it and I had a couple of slices of toast with Oxford Marmalade. Then I kissed her goodbye at the door and, well, one thing led to another and eventually she went off like a factory whistle, which was good. Sergeant, I've been over it in my mind a thousand times.'

You should always treasure each moment you're with someone you care for, he told Suzie. 'Because you never know if it's going to be your last. I know everything about that night. I can recite every stitch of clothing she wore, and almost every word she said. Her last words to me were, "Freddie, be careful and I'll

344

see you again before Christmas." I said, "Bottoms up," and that was that. Less than a month and she was dead. Happens every day in a place like this, but she wasn't in a place like this. Let's go and get some food.'

The car still waited outside for her, so they rode to the officers' mess in style and she told him that her superior would probably want to talk to him. She didn't give him the name of her superior. She'd mentioned Harvey to most of the others, but now she knew it was going to be different.

She didn't particularly like the officers' mess. There were other women there, but they were in uniform and they were officers – except the Waafs who served the food, and presumably cooked it. Even with other women there, she felt it was a male preserve and that there was some hostility. There was also quite a lot of noise. Like a boarding school's dining room.

The food was passable. Not up to the Ritz standard, but she could've easily got drunk. O'Dell ordered a bottle of red wine – she knew nothing of wines – and drank most of it. 'Not flying again until Boxing Day,' he said, intimating that he was dreaming of a blank Christmas.

As he was showing her out, she had a sudden brainwave. 'Can I show you something?' she asked, opening her handbag and taking out the three-by-four black and white print Dandy Tom had given to her. The photograph of Emily Baccus. She handed it to him, saying nothing.

'Who is it?' he asked and she waited some

twenty seconds before she spoke.

'It's Emily Baccus.'

'It's not any Emily Baccus I know,' he said, his eyebrows arched and all quizzical. 'What's the joke?'

'There's no joke. Obviously some wires've got crossed. You'll definitely have to see Detective Chief Superintendent Livermore. My Guv'nor. I'll get him to ring you.'

'Tell him to wait until Friday, when I'm sober.' Squadron Leader O'Dell showed no concern or worries about not being able to recognize a photograph of Emily Baccus. But why should he be worried? Suzie reasoned. As far as he's concerned it's just a photograph of another woman.

He was very polite, seeing that she was only a sergeant. As she drove away in the RAF Humber he stood to attention and saluted her.

It was Suzie Mountford's day for discovering things. First she had realized whom Emily Baccus reminded her of. Now it was the painting – the one with the view that she had spent almost an entire day trying to recall. The one she'd seen in Joshua Dance's bedroom: the small oil painting of a low, long country house, perhaps fifteenth-century, in grey stone. A clutch of chimneys at one end, mullion windows, leaded lights and an elaborate iron-bound door, the whole place glowing at dusk on a summer's evening. In the distance, behind the house, cornfields rose to meet a stand of trees.

That afternoon as the RAF Humber came to what villagers always called 'the back road' into Overchurch, she saw that very view and so knew she'd seen it before, many times. It was slightly changed of course because none of the trees were in leaf and the cornfields were the dark grey of the local ploughed earth. The house was a manor house, long and elaborate, a clutch of Tudor chimneys at one end, the grey stone hit by the dying, weak winter sunlight, and she knew the place well: Overchurch Manor, now in this brutal war turned into a hospital for wounded eyes.

She caught a glimpse of this view and gave a surprised little gasp that so startled the driver that he swerved while turning to look at her, making sure she was all right. Nearly went off the road. He was shaken and slowed down to a crawl.

'I'm okay,' she said. 'It's just that I haven't seen that particular view for a long time and it looks lovely in this light.'

'That's a good old house,' the driver said. 'Nice old house. Beautiful.' His stomach was still full of butterflies. Could have had them all dead in a ditch.

That's odd, Suzie thought. Really strange, Josh Dance having a little oil painting of Overchurch Manor and the cornfields that rose up right to the village. That stand of trees was just at the back of Falcon Cottage as well. That's an odd coincidence.

Ten minutes later they pulled up at Falcon Cottage, across from what was known in the

347

village as the Keepsake – a small piece of common ground given to the village by Miss Harricky in 1919. That's where the War Memorial had been built with the names of the twenty-two lads who had gone from Overchurch in rural Hampshire to die in Ypres and at the Somme.

Already there were three names to be inscribed on whatever they decided to erect after this lot was over. Old George Bunce's grandson, Harry Bunce, had died in a plane crash while he was training for an air gunner; Maurice Axton and John Burdon – friends since their schooldays, joined the Royal Navy together – had both drowned when HMS *Royal Oak* went down in Scapa Flow, torpedoed by a submarine that had sneaked into her anchorage.

And in front of Falcon Cottage, Suzie Mountford thanked the driver, who helped carry her cases to the door where she embraced her sister, Charlotte, her nearly four-year-old niece, Lucy, and her little nephew, Ben, who struggled to the door on the knees of his twisted legs; made his 'uh-uh-uh' sounds of pleasure, grinned his tilting grin and waved his arms and hands around in delight, greeting his aunt.

She wrapped her arms around him, 'Merry Christmas, Ben.' Then, 'Merry Christmas, Lucy.'

God bless us every one.

Much later when little Lucy was tucked safely

in bed – 'Auntie Suzie, it's the Eve of Christmas Eve, isn't it?' – and Ben had been quietened, soothed and had finally drifted off to sleep; when Suzie and Charlotte had talked themselves to a standstill, and gone their way to bed, happy, safe and warm with the temperature falling like a stone outside, far away in London, in Soho, close to Rupert Street, Lavender did not finish work until after midnight. She was happy though, because there had been no raids for several days and it had tempted the punters on to the streets again. Tonight she had climbed the stairs every half-hour, spreadeagled herself for ten plus men to make use of her. So her Christmas purse was full. They were willing to pay top whack close to Christmas and she extracted almost all they had. It'd be a good Christmas if Jerry stayed away.

'He won't come. Not at Christmas, Edith.'

She kissed Golly goodnight and said she would be in for a little while tomorrow.

'Lavender. I go away tomorrow. See my mum.' He was worried about leaving her alone with only Edith the Maid for protection. But she said that she would be fine.

'We won't be staying this late, Golly. Not tomorrow. Not Christmas Eve. You want your present now, Golly?' So she led him through to her bedroom and gave him her best shot and a crisp, white five-pound note as well.

When she'd gone, Golly got into her bed, cuddled her bear and finally went to sleep.

Time passed.

'Golly...? Golly...? Golly...?' The beautiful voice whispered in his ear. Crooned close to him. 'Christmas is coming, Golly. You must go ... Kill the lady policeman with the wire ... Go to Overchurch on the train ... Kill her dead, Golly.'

'Yes!' he said aloud and sat bolt upright, his eyes snapping open, and he saw her standing by the bed. Turned his head. Recognized her and opened his eyes even wider. Looked at her and smiled.

'I go, Miss Baccus, don't worry. Thank you, Miss Baccus. I go to do what you need doing, Miss Baccus. I go.'

And Emily Baccus smiled her sweet smile on him and then sank back into the darkness from whence she had come.

Eighteen

Back in July, when the risk of invasion was very high they removed all the place names. The names on railway stations were obliterated, and every signpost in the land was taken away, which made it especially difficult for Golly on the morning of Christmas Eve 1940, going to kill the lady policeman at Falcon Cottage, Overchurch, Hampshire.

Nobody saw his face on the train from Waterloo. He kept it well covered with his mask and hat, or buried himself behind the *Daily Express*. He thought they used a lot of long words in that newspaper, so he also spent a lot of time in the lavatory, as the train rattled through the countryside, sending its plume of smoke out into the frosty air. It was a stopping train so they went through a lot of stations including Overton, Whitchurch, and Overchurch before they got to Andover. He remembered the stations from when he'd lived in the area once upon a time.

He began walking when he got off the train at Andover. Nobody bothered with him. He had his little suitcase with the underwear, razor, toothbrush, a clean shirt, two extra masks and spare pair of socks. He wore his corduroy trousers, the good blue shirt, the pullover his mum knitted for him last Christmas, and the jacket Lavender had bought for him in the summer at St Anne's jumble sale. It was a really good jacket that some toff had left for the used clothes stall. Kept him nice and warm. He also wore the duffel coat that Mickey, Bruce and Billy Joy-Joy had given him last week. They said it was Navy Surplus and that they had won it. They were very lucky lads because they were always winning stuff. Anyway, the duffel coat kept him warm as toast. He wore the stout boots that Mickey the Mangle had given him in the autumn last year. Mickey had shown him how to break those boots in, and now he didn't like wearing anything else on his feet during the winter. His mask was pulled well up so with the hat on nobody could see his face. Golly had thought of using the duffel coat's hood instead of the hat. The hood would come right forward round the sides of his face, and it would frighten people if he came on them unexpectedly with the hood up.

The new piece of wire was especially for the lady policeman, and he'd bound the ends most carefully with the insulating tape. The wire was in the right pocket of the duffel coat, and of course he wore his brown gauntlet gloves.

Soon he was striding out along the back roads of Hampshire and, as it was Christmas, he sang a carol he had known from school. It was about the three Wise Men and their journey to worship the Baby Jesus. The carol had been written by the music teacher, Mr Avery, and it had a lovely rumpty-tumpty tune that was good to march along to: Tah-rumdum-tah rumdum-tah-rah-rah-rum. Ta-rahrah-rahrah-rah-rum-rum.

Golly marched through the cold country lanes, admiring God's handiwork, seeing all sorts of wonders, like the thick hoar frost melting on the hedges, the squirrels, the voles, weasels, a lone badger near the river, even a fox; and the birds were out in force. As he walked singing, passing the fields, hedgerows and ditches, he sang to every creature. Perhaps they were all there to greet him. He felt like a god.

Over hill and over dale.
See we come together.

He knew three carols really well. This one: 'O little town of Bethlehem'; and most of 'Good King Wenceslas', because at the school – at St Hilda's Special School – they made him sing the Page's part in 'Good King Wenceslas', and Mr Gregory said he did it well, but some of the boys laughed at him and called him forbidden names and they got the cane from Mr Gregory, and one of them, Arthur Keep, cried. Well, old Gregory didn't half lay it on when he told you to bend over the big chair and gave you a good four, or even six, on the backside. When Golly got eight strokes for playing around with one of the girls, Mr Gregory made it really hurt and gave him an extra one for trying to stand up in the middle of being beaten. Hated Mr Gregory after that. Put salt in his sugar basin. Got caught out. Got beaten again. Didn't care.

He had his head up high as he walked along the lanes, and at last he got on to the back road to Overchurch, right up and through the village. Nobody took any notice of him because when he got to the Keepsake the Andover Salvation Army band was out playing carols, and people were singing and buying stuff, and there was a postman with a wicker cart delivering letters and parcels. He saw Falcon Cottage, and knew he was right because there was the sign, done in pokerwork, saying Falcon Cottage. It was one up from Rose Cottage. Everyone was laughing and telling each other 'a merry Christmas'.

We'll see.

Golly walked right on through the village,

353

along the side of the Common, then to the White Hart, down by the church where he could cut across the churchyard and over the farmland, in a wide ark across the fields until he reached the little stand of trees just behind Falcon Cottage, about forty yards away.

Below, and behind to his left was the splendid Overchurch Manor with its honeyed stone and the walled kitchen garden. Higher up the rise the old stables with the remains of a three-bedroom cottage for the head groom in days gone by, the woodwork decrepit and a door swinging off its hinges. The new stables had been built and they hadn't yet demolished the old. He could stay in that cottage: curl up and sleep there for a time. No, he wanted to see his mum. But it was there if he needed it.

But here, among the trees, he could see right into the back of Falcon Cottage, its back door round the side and everything. He would come here in the morning and maybe the lady policeman would come to him. If not he would go to her. Right into the cottage he would go, Christmas morning. He would frighten her to death with the wire. Kill her.

Over hill and over dale,
See we come together.

★ ★ ★

Suzie finally got to speak to Dandy Tom at half-past ten in the morning. She had rung him at the FLAxman number when she failed to get him at the Yard late yesterday. When she first rang, this morning, just after nine, Terri

354

Abrahams had answered and said he was out all yesterday afternoon and half the night on a murder that had come in yesterday lunchtime. A bad one in Harrow. A young mother beaten to death in her own kitchen.

'He got the whole thing sorted in twelve hours flat,' Terri said. 'Suspect arrested. Banged up. Everything. When he gets his teeth into a case his feet don't touch the ground,' which seemed to be an odd way of putting it, a good mixture of metaphors.

'Oh, Sergeant Mountford,' Terri said just as she was signing off. 'Thought I'd tell you. The Guv'nor really rates you. Said you were going to be the bee's knees before you'd finished. Brahma, he said.'

So Suzie came off the telephone very happy.

Dandy Tom rang her at ten thirty. 'You okay, heart? What's up?'

She told him about Fordham O'Dell and his claim to have known Emily Baccus, the intimation that he'd known her very well indeed – as in 'You lie there with Jo and I'll cosy up on the other side.' Then him not recognizing her photograph.

It's not any Emily Baccus I know. What's the joke?

'I'd better come down and sort him out.'

'You've got to go and flog your peasants, sir. To be honest, I suggested that you'd be in touch and he asked that you not ring him until Friday. His actual words were, "Tell him to wait until Friday, when I'm sober." '

'You think he meant it?'

355

'I'd say your best bet was to go and flog the peasants, or see to Grace Poole before she burns the place down.' This last was something she often did to men, checking out if they were readers or not. *Jane Eyre* was a favourite.

'Yes, Grace Poole is a handful. And I can't trust the servants these days. If she asks they just give her matches.'

'It's a tough old life, Guv.' Then she told him about the odd coincidence: Josh Dance having a small oil painting of a view of Overchurch Manor. 'Doesn't quite show the village, but on the horizon there's a stand of trees that're only a spit and a stride from Charlotte's back door.'

Tommy Livermore grunted, said something about taking another look at Dance, heart. Then they exchanged Christmas good wishes once more. Maybe she was imagining it but she got the impression that he was lingering on the phone. There was something uncertain, unfinished about the end of the conversation.

When she had been at home, with her siblings, Charlotte and young James, before Daddy was killed, there was a routine they followed slavishly on Christmas Eve. Their mother had been a stickler for cleanliness and they would bring in the tree first thing in the morning – it never went up before Christmas Eve – and spent most of the day trimming it, arranging the cards and such-like before cleaning the house from top to bottom, in between helping their mother in the kitchen. Helen Mountford, as she was then, prided herself in having everything prepared before she went to church late on Christmas Eve. 'It's one of the secrets for the success of a brilliant Christmas,' she would say, and certainly Suzie could not remember a year when her mother did not have the presents wrapped, the turkey stuffed, the vegetables prepared, the ham baked, mince pies at the ready and the house shining by the time they were shepherded off to Midnight Mass. Made Charlotte's and Suzie's heads reel to even think about it.

Like many people, Suzie associated certain smells with Christmases of bygone years, the scent of the pine needles of course, but the clean fragrance of Johnson's Wax Furniture Polish came a good second.

Here, in Falcon Cottage, Charlotte was trying to emulate her mother, and failing badly. Lucy had been shown how to do important little jobs around the house and kitchen, but lost interest very quickly. After all it was an exciting day for any nearly-four-year-old.

By mid-morning they all began to set about trimming the tree, with Ben cheerfully lying on the floor, colouring picture books, of which Charlotte seemed to posses an inexhaustible supply, bought, begged or borrowed from whoever she could.

One source was from the manufacturers of Gibbs' Dentifrice Toothpaste, who produced free colouring books telling tales of adventures with the Dentifrice White Knight, who fought the Demon Decay. Charlotte was never too proud to ask Mr Burt the chemist for more of these books. He had a roving eye, Mr Burt, and could have spent all day looking at Charlotte, who was well aware of the lust that could not speak its name. 'As long as he just looks,' she told Suzie. 'He can look to his heart's content.'

This morning she had told her sister that you could gauge Ben's moods from the way he coloured. 'If he's content, Ben'll take great pains to try and stay inside the lines and use bright colours: reds, blues, greens – what we call his happy colours.'

If he was put out or angry about something it would be blacks, browns and greys, with no attempt to follow the picture: just great scrawls and scribbles. 'They say he probably won't advance much beyond a mental age of five,' Charlotte said. 'But he has shown another new skill since you were here last.'

Ben, she said, had taken to doing jigsaw puzzles and was already completing puzzles with up to a hundred pieces.

'But he doesn't do them like we would. He doesn't make the straight outside framework and then fill it in. He starts at the bottom and works his way up. It's quite extraordinary.'

For Lucy this was a unique and explosively exciting day because, as the youngest in Father Harris's Sunday School at St Michael & All Angels, she had been chosen to be the one to place the baby Jesus in the crib after the Midnight Mass tonight.

Miss Palmer was coming over from Rose Cottage – where she lived with her friend Miss Wren, inevitably 'Jenny' Wren – just to be in the house while they were at church. Miss

Palmer was a Nonconformist and went over to the Baptists at Whitchurch on Christmas Day. 'Ben knows her so he won't be frightened if he wakes up. Which he probably won't, but you never can tell.' Miss Palmer was a small woman with a smiling rosy-cheeked face. A Mabel Lucie Attwell woman.

Long before mid-morning, when the Sally Ann came calling, Charlotte and Suzie had just about given up any hope of having the house clean and tidy, or getting everything ready in time for Christmas. 'At this very moment,' Suzie declared, 'our mother is sitting down to morning coffee with the Galloping Major in a house that's almost blinding them it's so clear and bright.'

Just after eleven the Salvation Band – Lucy called it the Salvanation Band – arrived on the Keepsake. People gathered around to sing carols, and the children became even more excited. 'He knows something's in the air,' Charlotte said, nodding towards Ben, who was bobbing up and down in the front room window seat, his eyes gleaming. 'It's times like this that I long to be able to explain things to him.' He was making happy tooting noises while his arms moved wildly, flailing the air in an independent, uncontrolled spasm. Suzie felt a stirring of emotion as the band started to play 'Good Christian Men, Rejoice' and she realized this lovely little boy heard nothing of the band playing carols or the people singing. It was so sad that it was unlikely Ben would ever have any inkling of the Christ Child's birth, the ageless story of Bethlehem.

In the afternoon, while the house seemed to get even messier, their conversation inevitably turned to past Christmases.

'Do you remember—?' became a standard opening to a flood of recollections from childhood.

'Were they good Christmases in the olden days, when you were little?' Lucy asked, and they all laughed, munched mince pies and sipped tea while they prepared to make this one a good Christmas.

When Suzie looked at Charlotte's face as they talked and trimmed the tree it was like looking in the mirror; and when she looked at the whole person it was like looking in a long mirror. As children their twin-like personalities were woven together, their minds plaited, so one could almost tell exactly what the other was thinking. Their love for one another surpassed the normal blood-sharing of sisters. If anyone had seriously asked if one would give her life for the other, they would have immediately replied yes without having to stop and think. Yes, of course, they would both have said. Naturally.

On the road to Overton, just outside Laverstoke, a couple of miles out of Whitchurch there is a long stretch of thatch. This length of thatch is the longest in England, covering an entire row of cottages. There are gardens in front, with a picturesque well. A colour photograph, preferably taken in summer, could easily adorn a box of chocolates, or make a pretty jigsaw puzzle. One that poor little Ben would adore trying his hand at.

These cottages are often mistaken for alms-houses, granted to impoverished and impotent folk of good character from the parish for a peppercorn rent, and to any others deemed socially acceptable to occupy a granted cottage in perpetuity. But these are not in fact the almshouses associated with the Whitchurch/ Laverstoke area. The Laverstoke ones lie down a turning to the right, just past the thatched cottages. Two pairs of small 1850s red brick cottages, with a little gloss-painted brown timber thrown in for good measure. A porch at the front and a garden round the back, with a tiny bit of grass out front and room for a flowerbed where you could grow hollyhocks and lupins in summer and generally make the place a shade more attractive than it is in reality.

Having reached the first of these cottages after a long and circuitous tramp over lanes, across fields, through ditches, 'o'er bush, o'er briar' as Puck has it in the midsummer play by W. Shakespeare, Golly ceased singing and marched up to his mother's front door, knocking loudly with his gloved right hand.

Soon, he thought. In the bleak midwinter.

There was the sound of shuffling feet and the door opened, allowing the pungent scent of cabbage to be released into the porch.

'Hello, Mum,' said Golly. 'Surprise! Merry Christmas.'

361

'Bugger me,' said the small, slightly stooping, stick-clutching, thin, frail, smiling elderly lady. 'Well, double bugger me, if it en't our Golly.' She turned her head and shouted over her shoulder, 'Kath. Our Kath. Come here, it's our Golly.'

Under his breath, Golly whispered, 'Oh shit, that's torn it. Our Kath's here.'

'Why didn't you warn me, Golly?' The elderly, thin and frail lady reached forward to clasp him in a Christmas hug. I squeeze too hard and I'll snap her in two like an old bit of stick, Golly thought as she hugged him as tightly as her strength would allow, which he reckoned was about equal to being sandwiched between two aggressive cabbage whites. Over her shoulder he saw our Kath skulking by the kitchen door. Golly kicked back and closed the front door behind him.

'You're a sight for sore eyes, Golly, and there's no mistake,' said Mum, noticing that Kath had sidled along the passage that stood in for a hallway. Mrs Goldfinch turned her head again. 'Isn't he, Kath? Sight for sore eyes, our Golly?'

'Soothing balm and no mistake. Do you the power of good if you'd got a bad dose of pink eye.' Kath was always thought to be the joker of the Goldfinch family.

'Conjunctivitis,' her mother corrected.

'That an' all,' Kath said nodding.

Mum Goldfinch, baptized seventy-four years ago in the name Ailsa Austin, wreathed in smiles, like a cat's anus, proudly led Golly into the kitchen and then through to the back sitting room with its scenes of Regency men and women on the wallpaper: powdered wigs and fans and all that. She put down her stick and reached up with her trembling and twisted old hands to remove Golly's hat; then his mask. She looked at him with her big old black eyes and saw the two faces, the deep lightning-flash red ridge, and the thunderstone scar running from chin to hairline. She gazed at his contorted mouth, saw the divided, wrenched nose, and the kinked eyes one above the other. She looked on his ruined, frightening mask of a face, and felt nothing but love for him, her only son, who had come so hard and early into the world.

'You don't half look well, our Golly.' She grinned her toothless grin and remembered all those years ago. 'He looks well, our Kath, doesn't he?'

'Spectacular. Don't know how you do it, Golly.'

'Eff off,' he muttered wittily.

'Why didn't you give me some warning, Golly? I got nothing in the house. Hardly nothing at all.'

It didn't matter, he wanted to say, but Kath's dark eye was on him. It's not my fault, he thought. It's not fair. What had Mr Gregory said when he'd caught him with the girl? 'You are an abomination, boy. You are the abomination of desolation spoken of by Daniel the prophet.' And as if he were back in the school, at that time, Golly clutched at his ears and gave out a keening wail. 'Stop it,' he shouted. 'Just stop it,' he screeched so loudly that his mum stepped back and Kath cringed. They knew Golly's rages.

Then the calm returned. 'I come to see you, Mum. Christmas, I come to see you and I couldn't warn you because I'm not supposed to be here. I come on a job for Idle Jack Hobday at the market. I got to do something for him, fix something. Anyway you've got nothing in the house.'

This was stupid. If he knew his mum she had enough for forty days and forty nights in the house, Christmas. Always stocked up at Christmas, and rationing wouldn't have changed a thing because when they still lived in London people said that if it was out there Alisa Goldfinch knew where to find it.

'Doing something here for Idle Jack down Berwick Street Market? You haven't been going around with that Mickey Mangle again have you, Golly? Or that Billy Joy-Joy and Bruce Bubble? They're a bad crowd. Only get you in trouble.'

'Give me me duffel coat, they did. And Mickey give me boots.'

'Yes. Found before they was lost, I'll be bound.'

Here we go. Always the same with Mum. I always gets this everlasting gramophone record about people who're good to me. Always asking questions. No wonder they used to call her Beaky. Beaky Goldfinch, always getting her nose into things, and the nose *was* like a beak as well.

'Beaky,' he said now, almost under his breath. 'I'll give you Beaky, my boy.'

'Oh, Mam, come on.' She'll get her nose stuck in something one day. Specially with that damn great wen on the end. A cyst, they called it, and she never gets anything done about it. Doctor said it was a herbaceous cyst and she wouldn't have it done. Could've had it off. Proper. In the hospital, same as she could have had his problem fixed, but no, his mum wouldn't have it done even. Mum wouldn't let them touch her cyst and wouldn't let them operate on his face. Go into those places and you never comes out again, she said. 'Golly, I couldn't risk it, having you in there. In hospital. You don't know what people get up to in them hospitals when they've put you asleep. They admitted to me as how they'd be using you as a guinea pig. Practise on you, that's what they were going to do.'

He was building up a head of steam. Now, here in her back sitting room he asked if they had rooks where he was born.

'Oh, yes,' she said. 'Something terrible the noise of the rooks when they rose from the trees across the cricket pitch, Golly. You remember that? You remember the rooks cawing out of them trees? Never, you was but a tiny babe.'

'I had a dream. Rooks flying out of the trees.'

Kill Jo Benton, and when he did, when she was struggling against him as he pulled on the wire, and gave the final tug on it and felt her body go limp, just as those big black rooks came flapping from the skeletal trees. Whatever else, Golly had a sharp intelligence and a dramatic imagination that helped remove him from any accountability of his actions. To Golly, in the black ingenuity of his mind, he was simply obeying orders. Killing was his bleak reason for being. He was an executioner in the human abattoir.

'It's alright then, Mum. I won't be any bother. Just sleep here. Have a bite to eat and sleep for a bit. Then I have to go out. Tonight. Late.'

'Poachin'!' Triumphant, full of glee, lips drawn back, gap toothed in a grotesque grin. 'That's what you're on, innit, Golly? Poachin'. They got you poachin'.'

'Yeah,' he said with a big, long-drawn laugh. Relieved she'd got a reason for him being there. 'Yeah, Mum, I go poachin' alright.'

'Well I don't want the police round here. We're respectable here. Respectable house, I got. Make sure you en't seen going out in the night and coming back in at all hours.'

Kath was starting to get agitated. 'I got to be off, Mum,' she said. 'I got to meet Keith.'

'Who's Keith?' he asked.

'Who d'you think, Golly?' His mum being sarky now. 'She's got a man over the other side of Whitchurch. At *her* age? You be careful, my girl. You shut the gate of the field when you get in there.' She dropped her voice. 'On your back.'

'I'm not goin' in any fields, but I have to go

now. I'll miss my bus else. You take care, Golly. And you, Mam, and have a merry Christmas.'

'Kath, you listen to me before you get out that door. You never seen Golly. Right, my girl? Never seen him?'

'Course I haven't, Mam. I'll bring Keith over Boxing night.' Raised her voice. 'You'll be gone by then, Golly, won' tcher?'

'Well gone.' He would be an' all. May be gone long time before that. He'd go out around four o'clock in the morning. Maybe see Father Christmas finishing his rounds. By six he'd be in the trees back of Falcon Cottage and he'd stay there as long as he wanted. Stay there. Bide his time. Then, when she was alone, he'd either entice her out ... No ... That'd be more dangerous. No, he'd just wait, then when she was alone he'd be on her and kill her with the wire. Kill easy. Kill easy as falling off a log.

He looked around the room. She'd pictures of the King and Queen framed, over the mantel; and another one, print of a painting, sort of Victorian looking, big wagon load of hay stuck in a ford. There was good thick curtains at the window, blotting out the weather and peeping Toms. She had a nice sofa an' all. He could kip on that. Then, when it was done he'd hide up here in the warm for a day. Maybe two days. She'd have food alright.

'You just sit there, Golly,' she called through from the kitchen. 'I'm making you a spot of tea. I've cooked a nice tongue. Cooked it the way you like it, done with leeks. And I've got some brawn. Really nice. The butcher give me a bit extra. You just sit there quietly and rest, Golly. Lovely to have you here for Christmas.'

'Right, Mum. I may be back later in the day tomorrow. Christmas Day.' Might not get back to her for a long time though. He knew the art of waiting when it was all over; afterwards. He'd learned that, waiting. Like the one outside Cambridge. When he was there he stood, silent, in the clump of trees and bushes, behind that cottage. He just stood, stock still for hours after he'd done it.

He could smell the summer dust in the midst of those trees, heard the father come back, heard him cry out and come running outside again screaming.

Then the police came and he waited still as a stone. Like a rock in the middle of an arbour.

The doctor came and more police, swarming all over the place, but they didn't cross to the other side of the garden, right out to the trees. It was as if there was an invisible wall and they couldn't cross it.

Then the ambulance came and went away again. Sunset and they all went, leaving two uniformed men. The father had been taken away. Taken to a relative, the papers said next day. He liked to read about it in the papers. Gave it a sense of reality somehow.

He stayed there hours into the night. When it was safe he left, stole away. Crossed the fields, smoked a fag, remembered the way she died. Pretty little thing. Died like a bird in his hands, with the wire. Snared her with the wire. Waiting, that's the secret.

'Nice bit of tongue, Golly?' His mum came in from the kitchen and lit the lamps and switched on the wireless. 'Runs on a battery, Golly. I got two batteries. One gets juiced up at Dave Cox's garage and I change them round every Monday when Dave brings the paraffin for the lamps. That tongue good, is it, Golly?'

'Yes, Mum, I like a bit of tongue.' He laughs and it hurts his throat. 'Like a bit of tongue and pickle.'

'Always did, didn't you, Golly? Bit of tongue was your favourite. Tongue pie and cold shoulder, that's what you got,' and she cackled with mirth. 'It's so good, Golly. So good having you here even for a little bit of Christmas.'

'Yeah, Mum. It's good.' Got to stand in the trees later. Maybe a long time. Kill her dead, and he remembers the very first time. The time the man saw him and said he would send a lady in the night to give him his orders, and now, at last he knew the lady's name 'cos she used to buy fruit from Idle Jack's stall in Berwick Street Market. 'Yes, Miss Baccus,' Idle Jack would say. 'A nice pair of pears. You got 'em, Miss Baccus.' Twitting her, and she would laugh with him, and she would smile at Golly. 'How are you, Golly?' she'd ask. 'And how's your cousin, Lavender?'

Miss Baccus was Lavender's landlord. Always in and out of Lavender's building.

'You've got enough to feed an army, Charles.'

'I know, it's always the same, isn't it? I've been storing up what I could lay my hands on since the summer in the hope we'd all be here for Christmas. Thanks, Suzie. Thanks for coming, Suzie. It's so good to be together for Christmas.'

Suzie had been upstairs, wrapping presents. Doing little name tags. Making the parcels look interesting. A piece of ribbon here, some sealing wax there. Now she was in the kitchen again, watching Charlotte going through everything for the umpteenth time. Just like her mother. The difference was that the house was a rubbish tip and they hadn't really finished the tree, the kitchen was awash and – oh, everything.

'Oh, confound it!' Her father's daughter. His dying words. 'Brandy. I haven't got any brandy for the brandy sauce. I meant to go into the White Hart this morning. Oh, confound it.'

'Want me to go down and get some?' Suzie was almost into her overcoat before Charlotte replied.

'Would you? Suze, would you really? I hate not to have everything in before Christmas Day.'

'Won't take me more than fifteen minutes. I'll be down there and back in no time. Might even have a glass of sherry.' Might even get picked up, she thought. When will I get a man of my own? She thought of Dandy Tom. She could easily – don't even think of it, Suzie.

'Don't have more than one,' her sister called to her. 'I've got a bottle of Dry Fly. Thought we'd have a drop of sherry after I've got the children to bed.'

It was stingingly cold outside. Cold and dark. Most people were inside doing their last bits and pieces for the great day, and the blackouts were up. She had her torch though and in a few minutes her eyes grew accustomed to the blackness and she could see in the dimness.

Don't have more than one. Not a chance, Suzie thought. Her inner, private, life was stuck like a magnet on the sex she'd never had. Nor was likely to at this rate. Oh Dandy Tom, she pined. You'd be the catch of the season. Mustn't eat or drink after nine, though. She wanted to go to church fasting and in a state of grace.

She came to the edge of the Common and passed the white walls of the vet's surgery, then Dr Bartholomew's house with its beautiful windows. Seventeenth-century, Charlotte said. Bartholomew, she wondered. Was it the odious Barry Forbes who'd said he was a friend of the doctor's son? Yes, was it Paul? She could do without people like Forbes. Money men. Smoothies. Silk ties. Heavy tailored suits. The chink of money.

Ahead of her she saw a light come on and off as someone went into the White Hart.

Yes, she'd have a sherry. In the saloon bar. To hell with it. It was Christmas. And she fumbled at the door, opened it and stepped into the warm twinkling, friendly bar. Faces turned towards her. A couple of locals were talking, heads close together, to a flashy looking young man – wide boy, she immediately noted – and a group of four RAF officers were carousing in the other corner. Jovial, pilot's wings on their left breasts, medal ribbons below on three of them. Top buttons of their jackets undone. Fighter pilots.

'Tally ho! Popsy behind you, six o'clock. Look out... break Jem!' One of them called, laughing. It was in no way offensive. Boys. Boys, who could die tomorrow fighting for the skies. Come to that we could all die tomorrow, that was the nature of war these days. Every one was in it now, everyone's a target now.

'Suzie?' Out of the past, her name rushed towards her, carried on a familiar voice.

'Tally ho. Ned knows her. Popsy identified. Friendly.'

She hardly recognized him, he had changed so much. Seemed to have grown, aged from the young, rather cocky undergraduate. Grown into himself, her mother would say. Ned Griffith whom she'd loved and lost in a blazing row outside his rooms in New Court – the Wedding Cake – in St John's College, Cambridge.

'Golly. Ned. Gosh, Ned, how incredible.'

'What are you doing here?' Tentative. Not the cocksure U/T lawyer, as they'd say today. Lawyer Under Training.

'Gosh, and you're a pilot. I'd heard you were in the Raff...'

'How on earth...?'

She gathered up her wits. 'Bumped into Pat Patton. You remember her? Nurse. Addenbrooke's. Bumped into her in London. She's an Army nurse now. Queen Alexandra's. Very smart. Pips on her shoulders – everything.

You're a fighter pilot.'

He gave a self-deprecating smile, combining it with a nod, not looking her in the eyes. 'Spits,' he said. 'Up the road. Middle Wallop.'

'Gosh, I was there yesterday.' I sound like the schoolgirl I was: gushing. Her hand came up to tidy away an imagined unruly strand of hair.

'What on earth were you doing there?'

'Seeing one of the officers. Squadron Leader O'Dell.'

'What, Fordy O'Dell?'

'Hawk Eye O'Dell?'

'O'Dell o' the dell?'

'Squadron Leader O'Dell. 609 Squadron.'

'We're 609.' A baby-faced pilot officer with a medal ribbon she could not recognize under his wings. 'Hey, you're not the policewoman that came to see him yesterday?'

'Policewoman?' Ned sounded aghast. 'You're not a policewoman, Suzie, are you? Can't be?'

'Wait a minute.' A tall string bean of a flight lieutenant looked at her as though he could see through her clothes. X-ray eyes. 'You are, aren't you? You were in the papers not so long ago. Some murder.'

She nodded and Ned said, 'Suzie?' somewhat perturbed. 'Look, I'd better introduce you.'

They all had schoolboy names: Jem, 'Topher, Rich, Barny – 'It's Barnabas, actually,' he said, near to blushing. Children, overgrown children, trained to kill in the air, sleek for the slaughter.

Ned said, 'This is an old friend of mine, Suzie Mountford. You haven't got married or anything have you?'

No, Ned. Negative, Ned. You should've given me a little more time, Ned. You pushed too hard and we ended up a thousand miles from each other.

'You are the one though, aren't you?' 'Topher was the string bean flight lieutenant. 'The one the papers made a fuss about. You were investigating a murder, and some idiots didn't think it was woman's work.'

On her side, she thought. How wonderful.

'It was that BBC girl, wasn't it?'

'Yes. Jo Benton.'

'The "winter-drawers-on" girl.'

'That's the one.'

'Is O'Dell mixed up in that?'

'I had to ask the squadron leader some very dull and routine questions.' Must give some explanation.

What was she drinking? they wanted to know, and there was some argument about who would pay for her drink. Puppies. She thought of Simnel, bounding up outside 'A' Flight Dispersal. Eager, breathless.

'Should've arrested him and taken him off to chokey.' Barny had one of those machinegun laughs, a series of little chuckles, quite high in the register, a bray.

'Oh, I don't think there was any harm of that. He was a friend of the deceased.'

'A friend of Jo Benton's?'

'They were at school together.'

'How are things in London?' Ned asked.

'About the same. Plenty of lost sleep. There

seems to be a bit of a lull on, Jerry's going for the ports and places up north.' The words felt stilted to her.

'You in London during the Blitz? The bombing?' Rich asked.

'Yes,' she told him. 'Most of it.'

'Well Manchester's getting a pasting tonight. Bad. The IO told me before we left.'

'I got stuck in London for one night,' 'Topher said grimly. 'I had to make a dive down into Swiss Cottage tube station. Never been so frightened, and they had nowhere to pee except buckets. If you wanted to go properly you had to take the Tube on to Finchley Park.'

'You should've tried Tottenham Court Road,' Suzie said. 'That was horrible. Very pungent.'

They thought that was a witty remark and there was some further banter.

'Hated being bombed,' Jem said, shyly. He had blond hair with a lock that fell over his eyes. 'Loathed it. Much rather fight the Hun in the sun.'

The others set up a chant – 'Oh, yes. There I was upside down in a cloud, on fire, nothing on the clock but the maker's name and that was blurred.'

They went quiet after that, splitting up, engrossed in a story, a joke, that Jem was telling. He came to the punch line, 'And little Audrey laughed, and laughed and laughed.' They fell about with laughter. Again, she thought, children; schoolboys behind the bike sheds. Eventually Ned shepherded her into the corner. 'Suzie, I'm so glad to have met you again.' She smiled up at him. 'I never had the chance to apologize. I was a stupid ass. I regretted it terribly.'

'I got your letter, Ned.' *Dear Suzie. I'm sorry about the May Ball. I'm sure you thought me very silly so, perhaps, it's best if we don't see one another again. Yours, Ned.*

'I'm the one to apologize,' she told him. 'I didn't even have the grace to reply. I gave in my notice and they let me go immediately. Spun them a yarn. Said there was a family problem. Left Cambridge at the weekend. Went home. Had a bit of a bust-up there. Went to London and got a job – perhaps it was my year for bust-ups?'

'The job was in Harvey Nicks, wasn't it? My sister saw you in there. Remember Eunice?'

'Yes, lawks, she saw me serving people?'

Tall ungainly girl. Came to see Ned on some flying visit. They'd spent all of half-an-hour together in his rooms, munching crumpets, toasted in front of the gas fire. She had only met Ned on the previous night. She wondered how Eunice could have recognized her? The photograph, of course. Ned had asked her to get a photograph done and she went to PolyPhoto and had one of those huge sheets, they chose the best two and she had a couple of enlargements mounted. Her Mum and Charlotte had copies, and she gave the especially nice one to Ned.

'Another sherry for Suzie,' one of the boys called out and she had to refuse and tell them why she was there. She explained to Ned that

376

she was staying with her sister. 'You on leave?' she asked.

He was off for two days. 'We've been stood down from tonight until Boxing night. Can we meet again, Suze? Please, it'd be so nice?' She had forgotten that he had always called her Suze or Sukey.

She was uncertain at first, then thought, they're flying most days – and nights – bumping up against the *Luftwaffe*. Constantly fighting the war. 'Look, Ned, why not come to lunch, Christmas dinner, tomorrow?'

All the uncertainty filtered in – well, isn't it a bit of cheek? Be foisting myself on your sister. Are you sure? His defences broke very quickly. Yes, he could get a lift over, which house was it?

'I'll pick you up here. Then I can walk you back. We can go in together. Better that way.' She told him about Ben and his enslavement to routine. Tomorrow at twelve thirty, then. Yes, of course it would be fine, and she almost left without buying the half-bottle of brandy.

It had churned up old feelings. She stood outside the White Hart letting her eyes adjust to the blackness again, and became indecisive, ambivalent. Should she have asked him? Was it going to upset her being with him for more than an hour or so? How would he fit in?

She walked back through the cold and decided that, whatever else, it was the right thing to have done – invited Ned to Christmas lunch.

Charlotte thought it was wonderful. She knew all the details of the break-up in

Cambridge. Back in those days Suzie didn't believe in second chances, but Charlotte had always felt that Suzie should have tried harder. Should never have accepted the inevitable and left. 'Who knows,' she said now. 'There's mistletoe in the hall, so maybe...'

'Oh, Charles, don't be silly, it was a long while ago. We're different people now.' But she wondered. He had changed. He was a warrior now. A warrior on the wings of the morning.

The children were electric with excitement, little Ben catching a sense of anticipation from his sister. They put Lucy down on her bed for an hour or so to get rested before her big duties after the Midnight Mass. Charlotte baked another batch of mince pies, Suzie tidied her room, wrapped the last few presents, and before she knew it she had to leave for church.

Father Harris heard confessions at eleven o'clock.

So she knelt at the prie-dieu next to the priest's chair and poured out all the petty sins on her conscience since her last confession: the unfulfilled lust, the uncurbed tongue, the evils in thought, word and deed; and he gave her a penance – to say the Collect for Christmas Day and read the Corpus Christi hymn – then, with the purple stole hanging round his neck, he absolved her in the name of God the Father, Son and Holy Ghost. And so she went to the Lady Chapel, where the Blessed Sacrament lay reserved, and said the Collect for Christmas and the hymn written by St Thomas Aquinas—

Therefore we before him bending,
This great Sacrament revere;
Types and shadows have their ending,
For the newer rite is here.

Soon Charlotte arrived with Lucy and they all sat together in the same pew, and the church filled up, the verger going around and checking the huge blackout screens that were fitted over the great stained-glass windows.

There was the scent of incense and all the truth of Christmas memories. The first notes of 'Once in Royal David's City' sending a thrill chasing up the back of their necks; Father Harris solemn in the gorgeous cope that had been made by the Wantage Sisters specially for this parish. So the service moved slowly through its various stages, and as the choir sang 'O Little Town of Bethlehem' Suzie was able to exchange smiles with Charlotte when they came to the line, 'And Christmas Comes Once More'. Something they had done down the years almost every Christmas.

And when it was over, they watched as the acolytes escorted Lucy carrying the Baby Jesus to the crib, placing Him lovingly in the manger. Then Father Harris knelt in front of it, blessed it with incense and Holy Water, and they all sang 'In Dulce Jubilo'. Outside, the smiling priest shook hands with everyone and they all wished each other a happy Christmas. And so back to Falcon Cottage and bed.

Christmas had come once more.

At four o'clock in the morning, Golly got out of the makeshift bed on his mother's settee and lit the lamp on the table. It was cold and he dressed quickly, went through to the tiny scullery and sloshed water on his face, then dried himself and finished dressing. The back sitting room again smelled of paraffin from the lamp. Paraffin and the warm cosy smell of safety: his mother. He did not want to go out into the cold early morning, but he had his orders. He must obey.

Fully dressed, Golly turned out the lamp and let himself out of his mother's house. Now he began the long walk to Overchurch. Nobody is about. Not even the police.

Not even Santa Claus.

Golly, at the beginning of his journey, sticks to the roads. His plan is to go most of the way by walking through Whitchurch then on to clip Overchurch near the graveyard.

His eyes soon adjusted and he went right through the villages, walking on the verges – hard as iron under his boots – all the way into Overchurch, down through the graveyard, then out across the fields and into the stand of trees fifty or sixty yards behind Falcon Cottage.

On the way, particularly as he went through the villages, he silently chanted:

Wee Willie Winkie runs through the town,
Upstairs and downstairs in his nightgown,

Rapping at the windows, crying through the
   lock,
Are the children all in bed, for it's now eight
   o'clock.

Now he waits, still as a standing stone among
the trees, waits like a bridegroom for his bride.
And at eight o'clock, after it gets light, a lone
Salvation Army man marches through the
village playing a trombone, repeating the first
few bars of 'Christians Awake, Salute the
Happy Morn'.

It is a glowering and bitingly cold morn.
Earth as hard as iron; water like a stone.
In the bleak midwinter.
Now.

Nineteen

Suzie changed into the grey woollen skirt she
had bought in Selfridges and the blouse
Charlotte had given her that morning: her
Christmas present. Charlotte asked if her old
blue dress was all right for lunch, and Suzie
told her it didn't look the least bit old to her,
and how were they having it? Boiled or fried?
Weak jokes apart, the 'old blue' was very smart
indeed. Being an accountant's wife obviously
had its compensations.
   At exactly twelve thirty, Suzie walked into
the saloon bar of the White Hart. Ned was

381

already there. The string-bean flight lieutenant, 'Topher, had driven him over and they'd arrived early, forgetting that under the vagaries of the British licensing laws, the pubs couldn't open until noon. The law demanded that Sunday opening times applied to Christmas Day.

'We had to cool our heels by walking up London Road and back down Church Street.' Ned chuckled as a horde of people crowded into the bar signalling that church was over. The choirmaster and the tenors led the way and the saloon bar started to fill up, the landlord making the most of it as they'd all be off for their Christmas dinners within the hour; unlikely to return again until Boxing Day at the earliest, and maybe not even then.

'Did the sprogs get good presents?' Ned asked.

She told him the children had wakened them early – 'Too damned early. We only just seemed to have gone to bed when they came pounding in. Even Ben, who really doesn't know what any of it is about, was in a high old state. Crawled in brandishing his stocking. Lucy beside herself with joy.'

Almost immediately Lucy had dragged them all downstairs to open the other presents that had been put under the tree. Suzie was relieved to see that the coronation colouring sets were a great hit with Ben, so much so that he wanted to colour all three of them straight away and had to be restrained by Charlotte; while Lucy would go nowhere without the big teddy bear with the brown waistcoat, who now answered, or not, to the name of Mr Gherkin.

'Why Mr Gherkin, sweetheart?'

'Because he's always burping Mummy,' followed be a gust of ferocious laughter. Lucy was going through the phase of experimental, surreal humour, known to all small children. In telling Ned about the morning, Suzie felt the happy warmth of having been with her sister over the past thirty-six hours.

When they shared a room as children, Charlotte had worn what Suzie still wore in bed, simple, sensible cotton night dresses and, sometimes in winter, thicker ones of flannel that prickled something terrible. But now, in the bedroom at Falcon Cottage, Suzie discovered Charlotte the married woman. She saw the black, pink and blue sets of underwear with a lot of lace panels and trimmings, neatly folded on the wardrobe shelves. Then there was the silky nightdress, fresh for Christmas, sheer and reaching to the floor, exciting, diaphanous and revealing her nakedness underneath when the light broke through.

'Ooh, your kit's very clean and bright, Charles.' Suzie used their old code words filched from the Galloping Major, and Charlotte did a mock pose, a turn, stopping in the ballet first position they'd both learned as children, modelling the nightie.

'When did you start wearing tarty stuff like that, Charles?'

'It's not really tarty, but one learns, Suze. One learns quickly, even before you're married you'll find out that you have to dress up for them, men. Actually I thought you'd have found out by now. And it's really quite nice. You soon get very used to it and you can manipulate a man with a quick flash of lace, or a glimpse of suspender.'

Just as she was shocked at her own secret preoccupation with sex, Suzie was disturbed by this seemingly esoteric change in her sister. This was a Charlotte she had never met before: one she never dreamed existed.

Suzie and Charlotte were not only sharing a room, but also a bed – Charlotte's marital bed. 'Bet you wish I was Vernon, not your rotten old sister.' Suzie poked her in the ribs and Charlotte giggled. As children they had often shared beds. Certainly they had, for a long time, shared a room.

Now, in the early hours of Christmas morning, they hugged each other silly with delight, and they wished each other a merry Christmas and remembered all the years gone by when they had been together as young girls.

'You're really happy with Vern, aren't you, Charles?' Suzie had forgotten that Charlotte's hair smelled vaguely of strawberries. She reckoned it was probably the shampoo she'd used almost all her adult life.

'He's the best bloke in the world, like my children are the best kids in the world.'

'Ben as well?' Some women, even in this supposedly enlightened age, would have put Ben in a special private hospital, to be looked after and cared for by professionally trained staff. In some circles a woman was thought of as a failure if she had borne a handicapped or sickly child.

'Ben's great. The best. He has a lovely sense of humour and he's cheerful most of the time. He'll make it, Suzie. I'll never doubt that. He may not win any prizes, he may never speak, but he'll be a delight to everyone.'

'And you never feel angry. Having given birth to an imperfect child?'

'God's given me a handicapped child because He knows Vern and I are strong enough to nurture him. And if only one of us was left, the job would still be done.'

While Suzie remained a devout believer, there were times when she was uncertain about God's personal involvement in individual lives. She just couldn't see it. But then, she would think, she couldn't envisage eternity, or a space without end, or an infinite depth.

So the sisters moved quietly into their dreams, slipping away into untroubled sleep.

For the last time.

Golly waited, and the hours ticked by. He aimed himself at the kitchen window which meant that he concentrated on watching the window and what was going on inside the house. It was as if he could project himself into the house, only he wouldn't have used the word 'project'. It was a word he didn't know.

For all morning there had been two adult people inside the house. He already knew there were two children. Eventually the mother of the children would take them out. That stood to reason, for all children were taken out to run off their excess energy on Christmas morning. The lady policeman was staying with a relative, he thought. The children belonged to the relative. Wait, Golly.

It was cold, and occasionally he had waggled his toes violently inside his boots, or would take a slow step backwards or forwards so he wouldn't keel over when he really wanted to move. He would also bend his legs, one at a time, lifting his foot up and bending at the knee, or lowering his bottom by bending both knees and straightening up slowly.

He had learned these things from Mickey the Mangle. Mickey taught him how to exercise surreptitiously. Mickey had taught him that long word and Golly would show off by using it in front of people like Idle Jack up Berwick Street Market.

'I got to go off for a surreptitious pee,' he would say to Idle Jack Hobday, and Idle Jack would laugh at the way Golly spoke. 'I'm going surreptitiously up the Blue Posts,' he'd say and Idle Jack would tell him to go secretly as well.

Now, as the morning wore on, Golly still waited. He was good at this. Waiting. His hand regularly strayed to the right outside pocket of his duffel coat, to make sure the wire was still there; that he could grasp it easily.

There was a bang. A door closing at the front of the house. He couldn't see the front door but knew someone had gone out. That must be the relative taking the children out. He knew that's what it was. Then he saw the back door open and the lady policeman came out to empty things into the dustbin against the wall outside.

She's pretty, Golly thought. He could do it all with her in that blue dress. But he couldn't take advantage of the prettiness, the long legs he could see as she walked back inside the house, into the kitchen. There wouldn't be time for any of that. He grasped the wire. The windows were blank. Nobody moved against any of them now. Only in the kitchen window could he see movement. The lady policeman was at the sink, doing something, alone. Now, Golly. Go.

He ran. A little unsteady after all that standing still and the cold.

In the kitchen, Charlotte heard the footsteps and wondered what they were. Someone running out of the Manor grounds and along the side of the cottage. She felt no alarm.

As he reached the back door his hat went flying. He grabbed the wire from his pocket, dragged down his mask, his hands holding the wire tightly. He pushed at the door, turned the handle and there she was, the lady policeman standing at the sink, running water from one of the taps. He was in. Kill.

Charlotte saw his face and screamed, turned, making for the door to defend her children. Deep from within the cottage a child cried out a questioning, 'Mummy?' and Golly launched himself at her as she turned and tried to run. Screaming.

He was on her. Wrists crossing as he looped the wire over her head and began to drag her back.

'Oh, God,' she cried. 'Help! Help me. Oh dear! Oh dear me! Oh! Oh! Help me. Help. Help...'

'Mummy?' Lucy called again from the front room.

He gave a great heave, took a pace back, braced himself against the wall, near the door, and used all his strength. So strong, he was. He thought the wire was going through her neck he pulled so hard. He felt the crack in her neck, heard it, and the gurgle. Sounded like life was being expelled from her. She slumped against the wire and he held her up, then let her lower body fall to the floor, and as he did so this child crawled through the door leading to the rest of the house. The child was laughing and burbling as he came in, crawling, dragging his legs behind him. Smiling, thinking it was some kind of game.

They locked eyes, man and child, and instinctively knew one another; aware that each had some profound defect, something malformed that made them brothers. The little boy reached out towards his silent mother, then looked at Golly again and intuitively recognized the evil in the devastated face. Stopped laughing. Assumed the face of rage.

Golly let go of the wire and the upper part of her body went down to the floor, her head jolting with a thump, a sickening lifeless roll. Her eyes were open as the head rocked to one side, staring into the limitless future.

The child raised itself on its arms, lifting its head, the face twisted in pain, distress and fear, teeth bared. From the child's throat came a rising growl: a howl that encapsulated anguish, torment and dismay. It rose in a discordant fanfare of anger, a shriek of outrage as the child pulled itself to the body.

It frightened Golly. The anger frightened him. For a second he knew remorse, then wrapped in fear he lunged for the kitchen door, pulling his mask back into place and leaving the door open, swinging, as he swept up his hat from the path and scampered through the low hedge that separated the cottage garden from the meadow and the stand of trees.

The screaming followed him, snapping at his heels, trying to bring him down. And in his head the rooks clawed for the air from the bare skeletal trees.

Suzie and Ned were half-way up Church Street, almost at the Common, heading towards the Keepsake with Falcon Cottage on the right, when they heard the screams.

Later, Suzie would maintain that it was at this moment she knew. She held Ned's arm tighter, and slewed slightly to the right, pulling him on.

'Quick,' she said in a hollow empty voice.

And, 'Ned, for the sake of Christ.'

From the screams and the shouts of female voices Ned also knew that something terrible and urgent had taken place.

The children had started the screaming, Lucy, giving way to hysteria on recognizing her mother was dead, yet not quite comprehending the enormity of the fact; Ben's happy tooting turned now to this awful howl. Later, somebody – Suzie didn't know who – said it was the sound that you could associate with King Lear as he vented his great howls on his daughter Cordelia's death.

Howl, howl, howl, howl! O! you are men of stones ... She's gone for ever!

It had all moved wretchedly out of control. 'The poor mites' shrieks could've lifted the slates off,' little Miss Palmer said. On hearing the screams she did not hesitate, but ran, summoned by these dreadful cries to Falcon Cottage. Miss Wren followed, both of them a shade ludicrous still wearing the garish paper hats they had got from the crackers pulled over Christmas lunch.

Miss Palmer, a former nurse, had gone straight through to the kitchen and seeing the death and its violent nature and the certainty of it prised little Ben from his mother's body, and with the certainty and common sense of a mannish woman, swung him up, taking Lucy by the scruff of the neck, transporting both children to the safety of Rose Cottage.

Jenny Wren was in the hall, talking on the telephone when Suzie and Ned arrived. 'Yes,' she was saying. 'Yes, the police, a doctor and an ambulance. Quickly.' And thus occupied, she could not stop Suzie from going along the hallway to the kitchen.

Charlotte's face was hideously contorted, tongue lolling, lips pulled back as though she had purposely slid her thumbs into her mouth to make some ghastly children's joke horror mask. She heard a gasp from Ned behind her, then Miss Wren's quiet voice: 'I shouldn't touch anything, dear.'

But all she could ask was, why is Jo Benton lying in Charlotte's kitchen? And she looked up fully expecting to see Shirley Cox with Pip Magnus and 'the Prof' at the door. Then the facts reached into her mind and shocked her worse than anything she had experienced since her father was killed in the car and she'd rushed to get him from the wreckage. This was wreckage of a more unbelievable kind. This was a life's total disaster.

When she looked again, Ned and Miss Wren had gone and Constable Chris Long, the good dependable village bobby, stood in the doorway. 'I think you should come out of here now, miss,' he said, softly in his local burr.

They had met a couple of times. Yesterday he had said, 'You got promotion then, I saw in the paper.' Chris Long, who kept the village safe from crime, knew everyone by name and a couple or three winters ago had walked five miles in snow up to his belly button from the police house to Overchurch Manor to make certain they were alright after the great blizzard because the telephone lines were down. Then, he'd gone on to every home in the village.

Now he smothered her in his arms, helping to get her from the appalling sight in the kitchen. She allowed herself to be led away and seated in the front room, where only yesterday with Charlotte she had watched the Salvation Army Band playing carols, and Ben bouncing up and down on the window seat, with Lucy near to levitation with Christmas excitement.

She couldn't quite grasp it all; it was as though the facts were just within reach but kept eluding her, and the next thing she knew was the doctor being there – not Dr Blatty as she had somehow expected, but a young doctor with a calm, quiet manner who suggested they should take her upstairs and give her something. 'Something to tranquillize her,' he said.

Only then did she realize that she was sobbing uncontrollably, weighed down with grief.

Golly didn't stay. Didn't stand silently in the trees until the people went away. That had been his plan: what he had thought best, but he stayed only a handful of minutes before his inner voice had told him to go, get out, and he had this horrible sense that something was wrong. He thought he could hear Miss Baccus calling to him.

His legs seemed to have lost their ease. He tried to walk quickly and it became the toddle of a child. Then he tried to run and it became what it had been when he left Falcon Cottage – a scamper.

It was as though, for the first time, he faced the enormity of what he had done. Taken a life. Stopped the lady policeman in her tracks. Stopped her dead. For ever. It was that child who had done it. Looked at him with the evil eye and would have caused him greater grief if he had stayed.

Golly didn't watch where he was going, didn't follow the long, curving arc that he had come in by, but perhaps that was a good thing because he didn't want to show himself on the streets or in the villages. Not yet.

Overchurch Manor lay below him. He kept above the big house now, scrambling along on the edge of the rise until he got above the ruined stables and the dilapidated cottage that had once belonged to the head groom. Now, Golly took care even though his heart was thumping like a big drum. Slowly he made his way down, realizing that he could easily be seen from the top of the slope if anyone bothered to come right to the edge of the graveyard, or stepped beyond the gardens of the big houses in Henry Lane. The doctor's house and the vet's surgery, close to each other.

At the broken-down cottage door he rolled himself into a ball and somersaulted in. Safe, he reckoned, out of breath, wheezing, safe with the smell of apples around him. They were still using the cottage to store apples: arranged in rows, none touching each other. Golly liked a nice apple. He reached out, took one, pulled down his mask and bit into the green fruit, then chewed the sour flesh, and shivered at the sharpness of it, but he went on eating it just the same.

He would stay here, curled up, eating apples and thinking until it got dark. Funniest Christmas he'd ever had, this Christmas.

Back in a corner of his mind, Golly saw the woman's eyes, staring out into nothing. He had done that, not once but many times, stopped a human being from living, cut off life.

'You must always do as you're told, Golly,' Lavender had said when he first went to live with her, after his mum had been ill and said she couldn't cope any more. 'Just do as you're told and everything will go well. Get stupid and people will be really difficult. And you wouldn't like that one bit.'

He got on fine. They let him help in Berwick Street Market and other places, and he did exactly what he was told to do. After a while he saw Mickey the Mangle, Bruce the Bubble and Billy Joy-Joy again, and they were kind to him. He'd known them years ago, when he'd lived with his mum near the John Snow public house. The only one he didn't get on with was Spellthorne. Manny Spellthorne, the one Lavender had to pay. Half of what she made went to Manny Spellthorne, and he beat her up rotten.

He remembered how Spellthorne beat her up.

He went to see her one morning soon after she had arrived at work.

Lavender sat on the bed wearing only her wrap and he spoke to her. 'Lavender, you okay? Lavender?' She didn't move, just sat there, back towards him, shoulders shaking a bit and her hair out of place, untidy.

'I'm okay, Golly. But I won't be working

today. Anyone comes, tell Edith the Maid that they're to go up to Dawn on the third floor.'

'Dawn's been down here, Lavender. A little while ago. Just after Spellthorne left.'

'I know. I asked her to come down. Spellthorne hasn't been very nice, Golly.' And she turned around and he saw her face. For him it was worse than looking in the mirror. Both her eyes were all but closed and her lips were puffed out and split, a long deep split with a lot of blood, and a deep cut over her right eye.

'Who done this, Lavender? Who done it?'

'Never mind, Golly.'

'Who done it? I'll do them.'

'No, Golly. Just put on your mask and hat. Then take me down the hospital.'

Lavender was off work for over two months. 'Contusions,' was what one of the doctors said. Contusions, and that bone broken in her face. Nine weeks and they all near starved. If it hadn't been for Golly doing the odd jobs they would've starved.

In the Blue Posts one night, Golly told Mickey the Mangle about things. 'I want to help her, Mickey. It's that Manny Spellthorne.'

'Ah, now, Golly, you take care. There's a rule. You never come between a girl and her pimp. Manny Spellthorne's Lavender's pimp. You have to tread dead careful with pimps.'

'Will you help me, Mickey?'

'Don't ask, Golly. Don't ask me that, lad. And don't ask Bruce or Billy Joy-Joy either. It's not fair on them, see. We're in a different kind of work. We don't meddle with the pimps. Take my advice and just sit back. Wait for your destiny.'

But he didn't give up.

September 1938 and Spellthorne was hanging around again. Didn't hit her face this time but he bruised her and said he wanted more of her money. 'You're getting so as you're not worth your keep any more, Lavender,' Manny Spellthorne said to her. Golly knew because he stood near the door, listening every time Manny came up for his money.

She rarely had problems with clients. Very rarely. But there was this one man. 'Bugger can't get it up,' Lavender said. 'Waste's my time. Says he'd do anything for me, and I know what'll happen in the end. This'll go on and finally he'll say it's my fault and he'll want his money back. Then Manny'll beat me up again, maybe kill me even.'

Dawn said, 'I don't think he'd ask for his money back, Lavender, he's a gent after all.'

Later she threw the client out. A week or so later. 'You're an empty skin. Do anything for me, would you? Well do this, bugger off. You're trouble.'

Three weeks later. End of October and she said to Dawn, 'I'll swing for Manny Spellthorne. I wish he was dead.'

That was when Golly found the piano wire in a dustbin at the bottom of Beak Street.

You must always do as you're told. Golly.

That's what he was going to do. It was the right thing.

It was his destiny.

Twenty

She realized it was Christmas afternoon as she struggled up from sleep. The curtains were not even drawn and it was already getting dark. The big, clumsy blackout frames stood propped against the wall between the windows. Why had Charlotte let her sleep like—? Then it came to her, hit her, the terrible, sobbing, grief-riven truths dropping into her head one by one: the nightmare. Only it wasn't a nightmare. Charlotte was dead.

She's gone for ever.

Suzie stumbled out of bed. Dizzy. Disoriented. Fumbling for her skirt, patting the bed with her palms. Who'd undressed her? The doctor? No, Jenny Wren, she remembered.

She stepped into her grey skirt, did up the buttons at the front then slid the waistband round to the side.

Still unsteady, with her head feeling twice its normal size; mouth dry, her tongue like a piece of sandpaper. Once before in her life she'd felt like this. A party in the school holidays when she was sixteen. She had drunk too much, was so ill. Never again.

She struggled in the dark with the first blackout frame. Finally got it up, twisted the four little wooden blocks holding it against the old casement window frame. When she lifted the second frame it slipped and fell, the bump reverberating down through the whole cottage. She hauled it up again and fastened it in place. Rapid footsteps on the stairs. Someone must have heard. A tap at the door. She went over, switched on the light and pulled the door open.

Molly Abelard had her back to the door, right hand in her raincoat pocket, a classic body-guard pose. Tommy Livermore gently dropped his hand to Suzie's shoulder and pushed lightly, walking her back into the room. Abelard remained outside, reaching in to close the door after her chief.

'Suzie, I'm so, so terribly sorry,' Dandy Tom said, eyes on her, and his face like the face of an undertaker. 'Can we sit down?' He indicated the bed, pulled the stool from Charlotte's little dressing table and sat on it, opposite her and close.

'What's Abelard up to?' she asked.

'Being dramatic,' he smiled. 'You know Molly. I've told you before, heart, don't under-estimate her. She could take your ears off with a revolver at thirty yards and have you on your back with a flick of the wrist.' He paused, wait-ing, and Suzie felt the dreadful events enfold her again, tears welling up. She swallowed and bit her lip in an attempt to stop it trembling.

He reached out and squeezed her shoulder. 'Heart, I'm so sorry, there's no easy way to do this.'

She nodded, swallowed again, nodded once more.

'We have to talk about it, I'm afraid.'

'I know.'

'Facts. Did you see the bastard?'

Mute, she shook her head, and as she did so the greatest truth of all sank home. 'It was me, sir, wasn't it?'

'Quite possibly.' Detective Chief Superintendent Livermore did a little sideways bob of his head. 'She was very like you, so it's certainly on the cards.'

'Why me?'

'We can't be sure, but possibly because you were tagged as the investigating officer on the Jo Benton murder. If he's unstable, and that's pretty high on my list of probabilities, he could well have taken exception to a woman investigating what he thinks of as *his* private work. That's one of a number of likely explanations.'

Pause and she almost automatically started counting. She could see it in his eyes. His manner told her that he was here to deal with important issues, and she didn't know if she was ready to have serious questions flung at her.

She remembered a lecture during basic training – 'Handling the Bereaved'. People who have just unexpectedly lost someone very close, through a traffic accident, a sudden illness, even murder, are at their most vulnerable. Try to take advantage of this. People involved will almost certainly give clearer answers when they are questioned close to the event. Also, their first reactions are probably the most truthful ones.

Yes, she was vulnerable. She had no doubt about that.

'Heart,' he began once more, 'I've put myself on the line here and we've got to make up our minds quickly. Normally you'd be sent on immediate leave, but I've got the power to keep you on the team...'

'Yes,' then again, 'Yes.' She could hear the anxiety in her own voice.

'Heart, let me give you a rundown of what's going on...'

'I want to stay on it. I want to get him...'

He raised a hand. 'Of course you do, but in the end it'll be up to me.' Once more he paused, holding it, waiting and signifying that he wanted her to wait. 'There's confusion downstairs. There are two small children – one of them seriously handicapped...'

'Ben.'

'They're being looked after next door by two ladies who appear to be very competent.'

'Miss Palmer and Miss Wren.'

'Right. Now it's possible that Ben actually saw his mother being killed, so that's going to be another mental hazard for him, but small children can be resilient. They come through this kind of drama with fewer scars than older kids or adults.'

He looked at her as though he required her to acknowledge what he had just said. Then, after a few seconds, 'We've got your mother and stepfather downstairs.' He raised his arms from his sides and dropped them back again as if to say they were here, that was a fact and there was little he could do about it.

'How's my mother taking it?'

'As you'd expect, she's devastated, but putting on a bold front.' It was a mark of her mother's strength that she was capable of absorbing a blow like this. When Daddy had died, Helen Mountford had been the strong one, the one who cried only in private and refused to wear her grief on her sleeve.

Of course now the war helped in a strange, abnormal way. Sudden death had become the norm, and the sense of every family being somehow in the front line was making people more stoical.

Her mother's view, Tommy Livermore told her, was that they should take the children to Newbury and look after them there, until something more permanent could be arranged. 'At the moment they're keen for you to go with them, and your brother-in-law as well of course. He's on his way from Deal.'

'How's Vern taken it?'

'I've spoken to the chaplain who broke it to him. In shock of course. But he'll come through alright. Has to, he's only got seven days leave. After that it's back to his squad and the rigours of the Pre-OCTU course.' Vernon Fox's immediate concern would be the children. The Fox family were old county people. County and country. Their view would be almost Biblical – 'Let the dead bury their dead.' Vernon would say, life must go on. Particularly for his children. Mourning was something Charlotte would not have wanted to go on unchecked. You honour the dead best by living your life well.

Suzie pondered this for a few seconds and drew huge comfort from it.

'What do you feel?' the Detective Chief Superintendent asked. 'About the children going to Newbury?'

She didn't hesitate. 'Of course. It's the obvious thing. Certainly Vernon should go there – quite quickly as well. I don't think he should be left here for long. Too much to remind him.' She had surprised herself by her own practical view. 'How's my stepfather dealing with it?'

'Exactly as you would expect. He's a retired career soldier, and he's dealing with it in the way we'd expect. Calmly, using common sense, pragmatism. He's leading with his brain – that make sense?'

For the first time since he'd been in the room she smiled. 'Not really. I've always seen him as a pompous little man.'

'That's what he may well be. But he can also be a pompous, *experienced* little man, Suzie. He really does love your mother, and you should be aware of that. And by extension he loves you, your sister, and your brother.'

'Is James here as well?'

He shook his head. 'There's some aunt, came to your ma for Christmas.'

'Aunt Alice, yes. She's a distant cousin of my mother's.'

'It's not all going to be plain sailing. Your ma's in some shock and your stepfather's naturally very upset. Now, what of you?'

She took a deep breath, then expelled it as though breathing out all the sorrow that appeared to be flowing through her veins: inhabiting her thoughts. 'I think it's my duty to help find whoever did this. It's what I should do. My job.'

'Good. Your former senior officer wanted to come down.'

'Big Toe?'

'DI Harvey, yes. I've told him what your status is now: that you're working directly to me.' He gave her a conspiratorial smile, almost a wink. 'I've rather let him think you've been consciously working with me for some time, and he sounded a shade sheepish. But he was prepared to leave his wife and children on Christmas Day because he felt he should be at your side: felt it was his duty to be there for one of his officers.'

Touching, she thought. Then, what's in it for him?

'I've asked him to send WDC Cox to the team.'

'Shirley?'

'Yes. I don't think Harvey's the happiest man in Camford today. Having two female officers taken from him, plus losing the investigation.' He put his hand back on her shoulder. 'Everything's up to me now. I've got to make the final decisions, and nobody can make them for me. It's up to me whether you stay on this inquiry or go on compassionate leave to Newbury with the children. Up to me if the team stays here or whether we use the local force to do a restricted follow-up on the spot. They know the area better than us.' Yet another pause, then with a smudge of emotion, 'Up to me when we arrest some bugger for several murders.'

'I want to stay on the investigation, sir.'

That pleased him and made it easier. He thought her voice sounded firm, in control, but he couldn't be completely certain. Nobody could. He really considered that he needed a doctor's word on how fit she was. He wondered if the local police doctor had any knowledge of psychology. Probably a little, precious little if he knew anything about it.

He looked her straight in the face, into the big green eyes that didn't flinch as he waited. He tried to recall what her dossier said, if anything, about staying power. Nobody could know how she might stand up to the strain of chasing a killer, let alone the killer of a sister who'd possibly died because she was mistaken for Suzie. He pondered for less than a minute.

'Get yourself washed. Put on some warm clothes, pack your case, then come down and see your parents and the children. Try not to break down in front of them, or the kids. Keep a level head. Don't let the grief get too deeply into your soul. I'm going to see if the team's got anywhere. Then I'll make up my mind whether we're going back to London or not. Okay?'

He had given her all the right reasons for controlling her emotions. Reasons for going on, though he didn't really have her down as someone whose world appeared to end with the sudden death of a beloved sister. He saw her as someone with reserves of pride, of self-control.

She was someone who could put steel into her own soul.

By four thirty the light had all but gone and Golly was ready to set off. He had fought the cold all afternoon, lying low, watching and trying to adjust his eyes to the approaching darkness. In his head he had worked out what to do. He had seen people up near the stand of trees in which he had waited for the lady policeman to be alone.

He reckoned they were already searching, but they wouldn't know who they were searching for. They'd have to be very clever to know who to look for. So he made his way up the rise, keeping the village to his right so that he would only skirt the graveyard, keeping to the fields on the south of Overchurch.

His breathing was laboured and his heart pounded in his ears, but finally he stood between the graveyard and an open field leading down towards the road that he needed to follow in order to reach and bypass Whitchurch. The climb had warmed him, and he felt the familiar glow, the elation he always felt when he had been successful. When he had obeyed the orders. When he had killed someone.

Eyes like cat's eyes, he thought. That's me.

See in the dark. He could now; his eyes were fully adjusted. He'd seen clearly enough in the dark on those stairs a couple of years ago. The stairs above Lavender's flat. It was like a wonderful release from tension. Made him smile.

Back in 1938 he had waited. That time it was for Manny Spellthorne to come up the stairs to the rooms Lavender used for work. Two rooms, the tiny kitchen, bathroom and the little bolthole where Edith the Maid waited. When Lavender came back up the stairs from the street with a mark, Edith the Maid had to hand Lavender a towel and look threatening, which Edith the Maid could do quite easily because she was a big woman.

Edith was never there when Manny came because he wouldn't have anyone else in the place when he arrived to see Lavender. Golly wasn't allowed either. It didn't matter when Miss Baccus came for the rent, or to talk about what they called 'the fabric'. But nobody else could be there when Manny Spellthorne came for what Lavender called his pound of flesh.

I wish he were dead.

You must always do as you're told, Golly.

So he was there, Golly waiting on the turn of the stairs that went up to Dawn's flat.

'Lose yourself, Golly. About an hour. Go off up the Blue Posts.'

'Manny Spellthorne coming up then, Lavender?'

'Just go, Golly. Go.'

And he had slipped out, through her door then off up the stairs instead of down. He had the wire and he had bound the ends tightly. He had his leather gauntlet gloves, and he had the wire ready.

He hoped Dawn wouldn't bring a client back. But he knew as he stood there in the dark of the stairs, that he could tell Manny's tread from Dawn's steps. Manny coughed as well, when he came up. Smoker's cough. Knew his tread and knew his cough and all, Golly did.

And here he came now. Ready to be rough with Lavender, late on a Monday night when trade was slack.

He was just going into Lavender's rooms when Golly, light on his plimsolled feet, came behind him, slipped the wire over his head and pulled tight. Manny was dragged backwards, and Golly brought up his knee, hard against Manny's spine. He pitched through Lavender's door, grunting and heaving, but Golly had him tight and off balance. Kicked the door closed with his heel. Manny was so taken by surprise that he simply scrabbled at his throat, reaching up with his hands trying to pull the wire away, but the wire was already deep into the flesh of Manny Spellthorne's throat.

He made two long throaty growls as if he were trying to say something and couldn't get it out. Like he was trying to clear his throat. Then he died, and Golly was surprised how quickly it had happened. Sixty seconds, seventy-five at most. Wire over his head then around the throat. Very quickly he went from life to death. Like pulling a switch.

At first Golly couldn't believe he was dead,

but he was and Lavender came out of her bedroom, hands over her face. He saw she was going to scream so he shut her up.

It's what you wanted, Lavender, he said. You said I had to do as I was told. So I did.

'Jesus!' Lavender said. Then, 'Jesus Christ, Golly. He's dead. You've topped him. What am I going to do?'

'You got plenty of friends with cars.' Golly had it all worked out. 'Get one of your friends to come and take him away in a car. Put him on the rubbish tip. Gone. Finished. Dead, Lavender. Ring one of your friends.'

Slowly she came round to the idea.

'You said anything,' she talked into the telephone. 'Said you'd do anything, well this is it. You got to do it for me... Yes ... That's it ... Yes, then I will. If you do this, I'll do it ...Yes...'

'He's coming,' she told Golly. 'Got a client coming, going to help. Golly, I can't stay in here with his body. Can't look at him no more.'

Manny did look a bit rough, skin a yellow whitish, mouth slack, eyes staring. So Lavender stayed in her bedroom, then left to go home when the man came. She talked to the man first. 'Nobody else must know, Golly,' she told him. 'Nobody at all.'

'Nobody'll know, Lavender. Only him.' Looked at the client, the Mark, and the Mark smiled back.

'You did this all by yourself, Golly?' the Mark asked him.

'Course.'

'Well, you're very good at it. Maybe I'll get a

pretty lady to come and whisper in your ear.'
The Mark smiled. He was nice and kind, the
Mark. 'Maybe sometimes a man,' he told
Golly. 'Sometimes a woman. You'll get your
orders. You'll do that?'

'Why should I?'

'Because if you don't, Golly, something bad'll
happen to you. Very bad.' Golly could tell by
the Mark's words and the way he spoke that he
was deadly serious about this. He could tell by
the man's eyes that what he meant was if Golly
didn't do as he was told the police would be
tipped off and he would be arrested. Put in a
hole.

What all that meant was that they'd hang him
by the neck and then put him in a hole. 'That
nine o'clock walk with Mr Pierpoint,' Mickey
the Mangle said. 'You do something really bad,
like kill somebody they'll take you on that nine
o'clock walk with Mr Pierpoint.' Mr Pierpoint
was the public hangman. Albert Pierpoint.

Then something strange happened. Golly
thought he knew everything about the flats
where Lavender lived, but the Mark knew
something he had never imagined. There was a
front door to the building, and you went into a
long, narrow passage and straight up the stairs.
Lavender worked out of the rooms on the first
of three landings and there was no back
entrance. Clients came and went the same way.
Up the stairs. But after Lavender had left on
that night, the Mark showed him something he
had never even suspected.

There were two cupboards in Lavender's

409

bedroom. One she kept her clothes in and the other had this little chest of drawers in front of it. The Mark pulled the chest of drawers away and opened the cupboard that wasn't a cupboard. It was the entrance to another corridor that ran almost the length of the building and ended up at a locked door.

The Mark had the key to the door – 'Lavender gave it to me,' he said with a conspiratorial look, putting it in the lock and taking Golly through to another passage that led to more stairs. It came out into a large garage, off Rupert Street and a long way from the building where Lavender worked.

'There's not many people know about this place,' the Mark said. Very useful for parking, and more than useful for us.

The Mark had brought his car right up and close to the locked door and Golly helped get Manny Spellthorne's body through Lavender's bedroom, down the stairs. Along the passage and into the car.

'Nobody around. Quiet as the grave,' the Mark said, telling Golly to go back through the door so that he could lock him in. Golly, amazed, went back along the passage and closed the cupboard door, dragging the chest of drawers in front of the cupboard again.

It was four o'clock in the morning.

'Keep your mouth shut.' The Mark was nasty about it as well. He'd had another dust-up with Lavender before she left.

The next time Golly slept in Lavender's bedroom he heard the voice – only it was a man's voice to begin with. Said he had to get more wire. Told him where he'd find it. The week after that he killed a girl with the wire. Out near Ealing Common. Went there on the Tube. Saw her on the platform as she was getting off the train. Knew which one as soon as he saw her. It was night, and he followed her and killed her on the edge of the Common, because that was what the voice had told him to do.

He started to have the bad dreams after that, and then the creatures began to visit him. They were like huge crabs and great big spiders. The spiders had legs as thick as his little finger and, as they shuffled and scuttled over the lino in the bedroom they made drumming noises that got louder and then softer as they drew close. Golly wondered if these creatures were the ones that would do things bad to him if he didn't do as he was told.

Then the thing he called the Banshee came. Though he didn't know a Banshee from a speaking clock, this creature was like a big rat that walked on its hind legs and carried a banner. He couldn't see the Banshee properly, which was just as well because it would do harm if he saw the banner the Banshee carried. It frightened him, particularly when it started to whistle and shriek.

He was never told what the Mark had done with Manny Spellthorne's body, but the police came a couple of times asking questions. He didn't really know Manny Spellthorne, he told them. Saw him sometimes up Berwick Street Market, but never saw him at Lavender's place.

No, never, sir. Didn't know that Lavender knew him.

Anyway, the policemen didn't seem all that bothered really and Lavender told them he hadn't been to see her for a long time.

The police said that Manny Spellthorne had enemies.

You bet he did.

Suzie's mother filled up and had to fight back the tears when they met. 'Mummy, I don't know what to say. She was the best thing in my life, next to Daddy and you.' For a time they just clung to one another.

The Galloping Major came and gave her a hug. 'Suzie, I am so dreadfully sorry about Charlotte. What can I do to help?'

'Look after Mummy.'

Looking at her mother, she saw that Charlotte had been so like Helen. The image of Charlotte seemed to emerge and hang in the air between Suzie and her mother. She knew it was only her imagination, and that she was simply seeing her sister's image in her memory, but it was comforting.

'Susannah, are you sure you're up to it, going on with the investigation?' her mother asked.

'Yes,' she said. 'Absolutely certain,' she said. Then, 'It would be best.'

'Your chief superintendent seems a very good man.' The Galloping Major had talked with Tommy Livermore for some time. 'Seems a very good class of man. A well-educated sort of a person.'

Suzie told him, and he went away muttering, 'Lord Livermore? The Earl of Kingscote? Well I never. Thought he looked familiar. He'd be the younger brother to the Livermore who served with me and died in Flanders.'

She could hear Charlotte's voice singing, 'Bumpety-bumpety bumpety-bump, here comes the Galloping Major.' The old music hall song they used to warble to each other over the telephone.

Dandy Tom came in from seeing his 'spear carriers', with Molly Abelard sticking to him like a leech. Pete and Dave, the forensics boys, hovered in the background. Pete, Dave and Bert, the last being the best scenes-of-crime man they had. The other two, Laura Cotter and Ron Worrall, sat in one of the cars, didn't want to overcrowd the cottage.

'Peter and David will stay with the local boys. Albert as well. Everyone else back to London.'

Suzie talked with her mother for a while, after she'd brought down her case, glad they were leaving, didn't know how she'd have coped with staying in Falcon Cottage. As she'd brought her case down she had seen the copy of *For Whom the Bell Tolls* that she'd given to Charlotte that morning. It lay on a chair where she had left it. Before she wrapped it up Suzie had leafed through it and noticed one line, a girl in a love scene asking where the noses went, saying she had always wondered where the noses went. I know the feeling, she thought. Then she wondered what had happened to Ned? Brought me home for Christmas dinner

413

and found my sister dead. After that, not a word. Not a drum was heard, not a funeral note. Oh, well, easy come. She switched her attention back to her mother.

Yes of course, she'd be in touch as soon as possible. 'Of course I'll be coming for the funeral, Mummy. I'll come over to see the children now, before we leave.' Mummy had started to fuss which was a good sign, and Suzie had begun to see a side of the Galloping Major she hadn't known until now – the concern and care that he could give to her mother when she needed it. Had she been terribly mistaken when she thought he was treating her badly, even brutally? They did seem very close now in this time of family crisis.

As they prepared to go over to Rose Cottage she cornered the Chief Super.

'What's the gen, Guv?'

'He hid up in those trees behind the cottage. Peter thinks for quite a long time, but the light's been bad. Pray it doesn't rain tonight and wash away any evidence. They'll have another dig and delve at it tomorrow.'

Like the one outside Cambridge ... stock still for hours after he'd done it ... could smell the summer dust in the midst of those trees.

As they walked towards Rose Cottage she asked him if he had seen the children yet.

'Yes. The little girl's calm enough, but young Ben's a shade manic. It's frustrating.'

'What sir?'

'Well, it looks like he probably saw the bastard kill his mother. I can't ask him any

414

questions, it's frustrating as hell. If I could he wouldn't be able to reply, and in any case I've had difficulty getting him to even look at me. It's a bloody awful situation. Poor little chap.'

It wasn't unusual. Ben was canny. If he thought you were going to make him work hard at something he didn't want to do he'd studiously avoid looking at you. Whatever else he was, or was not, Ben wasn't a complete fool.

'And you think he saw the whole thing?'

'Lucy's confused but she talks about Ben going into the kitchen while she was playing with Mr Gherkin—'

'He's the teddy bear I gave to her.'

' "Ben went. I played with Mr Gherkin. Didn't go see Mummy with Ben, when she shouted. Went later and Mummy on the floor with Ben. Ben pointed at the door outside." That's basically what she's said. Looks to me as though she got into the kitchen after the event, while Ben was there when it happened.'

'So he's in a state?'

'You might say that. Frenzied would be the word I'd use.'

In his world of deep silence, Ben swam through the huge peaks and troughs of this strange day. Time was not a concept that Ben could under-stand, nor could he comprehend his own feelings that always blossomed or exploded in extremes. Ben was either placid and content, overactive and agitated, or angry and eruptive. There were no in betweens.

Something catastrophic had happened to

The One, and this had made him frightened and angry. He would never be able to describe any of those sensations, and he certainly couldn't begin to describe The One. For The One looked after him: fed him, cleaned him, dressed him, helped him in a thousand different ways, and something had happened to her. He'd seen it happen. The Odd Thing, unlike any he had ever seen, was doing something to The One, and now he was afraid. The One had gone to sleep and he wondered what would happen to him with no One to look after him.

There had been new things today as well. Pretty. Boxes with new things. New pictures for him to work on with the colour sticks. The pictures had faces. In his fear and anger, Ben tried to alter the faces. Tried to make them like the alarming Odd Thing who had done something terrible to The One.

He had no way of articulating the fear that filled him now. Oh where was The One? Oh-Oh-Oh-Oh. Ah-Ah-Ah-Ah. Where was The One?

In his anguish, Ben wept large tears like raindrops sliding down his pink cheeks.

After Tommy Livermore had given a statement to the journalists and sent them packing, they trooped over to Rose Cottage, eight of them. Suzie remembered looking at it this morning, seeing the scarlet hips among the haws in the hawthorne hedge that divided the two properties. It would look beautiful in the spring, she had thought, the wild roses mingling with the hawthorne. Her mother and the Galloping Major walked ahead with Mummy hanging on to his arm as though she might fall if he didn't hold her. Suzie walked with Tommy Livermore, Molly Abelard just behind and to their left. Then Pete, Dave and Bert followed up in the rear. The Guv'nor wanted the lads to see the children. Thought it was important.

Lucy remained passive, just as Tommy Livermore had perceived her earlier in the afternoon. Passive and playing with Mr Gherkin, but not overanxious to talk to people.

Helen went down on her knees to talk with her. She was very good with small children. 'Lucy, we're going to take you in the big car,' she said. 'You're going to stay with Grandma and Granddad in the house in Newbury – with the big garden. Do you remember the house?'

A silent, preoccupied nod. 'Can Mr Gherkin come as well?' She had to repeat it because Ben was making all kinds of loud noises nearby as he raked the crayons over picture after picture: soldiers, men-at-arms, beefeaters, peers of the realm, from that day when King George VI and Queen Elizabeth had been crowned in Westminster Abbey.

'Of course Mr Gherkin can come. And any more of your toys you'd like to bring.'

'Good.' The child looked up at her, then solemnly turned her eyes on to the Galloping Major. 'Mr Gherkin isn't very well.'

'I'm sorry, Lucy. What's wrong?'

'He's sad.'

Suzie just about controlled her emotions,

glanced at Dandy Tom, then kept looking at him. He had sidled over towards Ben and was now stooping forward absorbed in what the child was doing.

From the jumbled pile of drawings connected with the coronation in 1937, the child was pulling out picture after picture and placing them directly in front of him, on the floor. Each picture was swiftly chosen, all of them men – soldiers, clergy, peers, royal assistants. When the picture was placed exactly as Ben wanted it he would grab at a crayon, scribbling colour around the figure but not on it. Then he would pause, carefully take a crimson crayon holding it directly above the drawing's face, his arm in spasm, jerking and swaying, uncontrolled until he brought the tip of the crayon to a point just above the head. Then he slashed downwards carving out a lightning flash line from head to chin. The mark was the same every time no matter if the character was bareheaded or wore a cap, busby, cocked hat or special headdress. The red line divided the face with a small kink close to the nose, and the entire thing seldom deviated from an almost ritualistic enactment. Once the red lightning slash had been made, Ben would carefully toss the card into an untidy pile to his left.

As he performed, Ben appeared to be totally immersed in what he was doing, repeating the same motions again and again, noisily with wild aggression and the large tears still running from both eyes.

Helen and the Galloping Major continued to

talk quietly to Lucy, but the others now centred all their concentration on Tommy Livermore and Ben, whose actions appeared to be becoming more and more manic and violent.

In the crowded room, Suzie saw Miss Palmer and Miss Wren, cringing back from the child as though they feared him.

As they all watched, so Dandy Tom tried to make eye contact with Ben, but the boy wasn't inclined, wholly engrossed in what he was doing. In the end Tommy Livermore leaned over and picked up three of the colouring cards from the pile that Ben appeared to have placed to one side.

For a few seconds, the child was distracted by Tommy Livermore taking the cards. He stopped and looked accusingly at Tommy, then away, turning and looking at Suzie.

For a suspended moment the little boy confused Suzie with his mother. His face lit up and he smiled, putting out his arms in an obvious gesture of need. Suzie went down on her knees and could not stop her own tears. Ben fell sideways, as he often did when he had been engrossed in something on the floor, for altering or rearranging his position was always difficult. He recovered himself, began to crawl in his ungainly, irregular, unbalanced way towards Suzie, eventually flopping down and crowing with delight, the tears and anger forgotten for a few seconds.

Until Suzie put her arms around him and held him close.

It must be the smell, she reckoned through the emotional confusion. He knows I'm not Charlotte, because he knew Charlotte so well.

She was right. No sooner had Ben come close to her than he was sobbing and angry again, squirming and wriggling, pushing her away, then retreating back to the colouring cards.

For Suzie it was a rejection, a slap in the face, an added trauma. She bent double, like someone prostrating herself in a church or temple. Then all the passion she felt for Charlotte came roaring out of her in great sobs. She covered her face with her hands and, almost unbelievably, it was the Galloping Major who came to her, hugged and soothed her, coaxing her back to normality.

When she dared look around herself again, Dandy Tom had started to examine the colouring cards, glancing from time to time at the boy. The three he had taken were all soldiers in ceremonial dress, as they would have appeared in the coronation parade: a mounted drummer of the Life Guards; a drum major of the Royal Marines, and a tall Welsh Guardsman leading the exotic beast that was the regiment's mascot. The background of each was covered in a black, grey or brown vicious crayon scrawl, and all three faces had the thick, crimson line unevenly bisecting the face. Almost making the features separate left from right.

'Trying to tell us something.' Tommy Livermore scowled. 'And I feel I should know what he's saying.' He bent towards Ben, who, without warning, raised his head, looked the police-man in the face, put his hands above his head, waved them violently and let out a long almost mocking crow.

'Right,' said Livermore, raising his voice. 'Right, Ben. I understand and I'll get him for you. Good boy.' He gave the child a happy, two-handed thumbs-up sign.

Outside, as they got themselves into the cars, Dandy Tom asked Suzie if she had any idea of what Ben was trying to tell them, but she shook her head nonplussed. He turned to Molly Abelard, who seemed to be his oracle, but for once she had nothing to suggest except the obvious – he was trying to tell them who had killed his mother.

Molly sat beside their driver in the front of the Wolseley. Riding shotgun, Suzie thought, as she took her place in the back with the Chief Super. Laura Cotter and Ron Worrall went in the second car.

Ben's actions had obviously bitten into Tommy Livermore making him annoyed that he could not untangle what the boy was trying to tell them. 'It's almost as if he was turning someone into a monster with two faces,' he brooded.

'Chief?' Molly Abelard straightened in her seat. 'Two faced, Chief. Two-Faced Golly. When I was at Vine Street, Chief. That lad who sometimes works on Berwick Street Market. A bit simple. Cousin's a tom somewhere near Rupert Street. Poor bloke's hideous—'

'Yes, I know him. Wears a surgical mask and

a big-brimmed hat so people won't see his face?'

'Yes, Chief.'

'I know the one you mean. Well, yes. Could be I suppose.' Not convinced. Vine Street was the station that covered the West End, including Soho and the red light district. Every police patch in any big city has its share of odd characters and there were plenty in London's West End. They had unkempt women who lived on the street, one in particular, Greasy Joan, who they took in from time to time just to get her clean and deloused; shrewd children, slightly deranged who lived in derelict houses – a problem on the increase since the bombing started; and men like Long John Palmer who wouldn't hurt a fly, but was an oddity with a misshapen jaw that reached down to his chest. And of course there were people like Stuttering Bob, One-Eye Jacko, Splitty Williams, Nosey, or Two-Faced Golly. These were deformed folk, some of whom were disfigured mentally as well as physically. In their fear of abnormality, people sometimes treated these souls with a lack of respect bordering on cruelty, as they had treated the Elephant Man in the previous century.

'We'll check him out when we get back up the smoke.' Dandy Tom stretched out in his seat and closed his eyes, still puzzled at Ben and what he was trying to tell them. In his head he only vaguely recalled Two-Faced Golly, and then not clearly. 'God's comedians,' he muttered. 'Don't make that error: the one I like to call the Quasimodo Syndrome. It's the biggest cliché in the job, the one that suggests that ugliness and deformity signify evil within. Nothing scientific about that. Beware the bogeyman though. One time in a million it could turn out to be right – the monster within the monster, the so-called exception that proves the rule, though I've never really understood that.' So saying, he closed his eyes and grabbed forty winks.

They had the Home Guard out as well as the police. Golly plodded through the dark fields and meadows, moving in a great circle, avoiding the centre of Whitchurch and only coming close to habitation on the far side, almost at the hamlet of Laverstoke.

He came quite close to the road and could hear talking going on from a good mile away. Closer to the road he saw hooded lights and a big red lantern being waved around to bring the occasional car to a halt. He heard rifle butts on the macadam of the road, and the sounds of authority in the policemen's voices as they questioned drivers – not that there were many on the roads at this time Christmas night.

Nearer to the hedgerow he heard them grumbling. 'Whole family we got this year.' The crack of metal tips on boot heels hitting the road. 'Both boys got leave, and Janet came over from Basingstoke with her kids, and she'd had a surprise and all. Her Bill suddenly arrived home on leave. Bloody hell, they'll be heading back this evening, I reckon because they'll want a bit of hokey-cokey – "In out, in out, shake it all about." Eh?' Quiet, crude laughter.

'Well, she en't seen 'im since 'e come home after Dunkirk.'

'Poor bugger comes home and her dad's called out on active duty. We ought to get some extra time off for this.'

'But we won't, will we? They also bloody serve who only stand and piss, ennit?'

'Ey up, another car.'

'Advance, friend, and be recognized.'

'How d'you know it's a friend?'

' 'Cos that's Farmer Peter Hawkes's old car from over near Sutton Scotney. He'll be bringing his old mother home from his sister's at Oakley. Ask him if this is strictly farm business?'

'Yes, and ask him how much elderflower wine he's had with his puddin'.' More laughter. And as the Home Guard and police are busy dealing with Farmer Peter Hawkes from over near Sutton Scotney, so Golly squeezes through a gap in the hedge almost fifty yards from the roadblock, and is across the road silent as an owl striking a fieldmouse. Then through the hedge on the far side, along the meadow until he's opposite the cottages. Only then does he break cover and trot up to the porch.

Mum doesn't lock her door so he goes straight in this time. Knocked last night so as not to give her a shock.

'Oh, Golly, how wonderful. You're back before you expected to be. I got the turkey in the oven, so we can have a good old blowout. I got some crackers an' all.'

'Plum duff, Mum? You got plum duff as well?'

'Course I have. Got everything for my Golly: roast spuds, carrots and swedes all mashed together, sprouts, bread sauce, mince pies, rum butter, plum duff with custard.'

'Oh-my-oh-my-oh-my,' chuckles Golly, a child again, listening to the wireless as they did *Wind in the Willows*, and it's Ratty taking Mole on a picnic. 'Old Adolf en't stopping us enjoying our Christmas, then,' he giggles with glee.

'Take mor'n old Hitler to stop us enjoying Christmas. Come on in, Golly, it's right cold out there. Come in and make yourself comfy; I don't suppose you heard the King's broadcast, but the nine o'clock news just started on the BBC. You hear about the terrible goings in Overchurch?'

'What, the murder? I heard tell something about it. Someone mentioned it.'

'Get your coat off, young Golly. Sit in the warm. Listen to the news, it's Alvar Liddell reading it.'

So he sat and listened while the familiar scents of Christmas came wafting in from his mum's little kitchen. Then, towards the end of the news—

'In Hampshire tonight police are investigating the brutal murder of a housewife in the village of Overchurch, near Andover...'

You're on the news, Golly. You've made it. On the BBC.

'...The murdered woman, Mrs Vernon Fox,

was discovered dead by her two children, who raised the alarm. She was strangled with piano wire as she prepared the Christmas dinner. Detective Chief Superintendent the Honourable Thomas Livermore, who is investigating the case, said late this afternoon that it was too early to link this crime to the death of the BBC announcer Josephine Benton. Miss Benton was also strangled with piano wire in her home last week.

'Mr Livermore said, "There are similarities in the two cases, but that is all I'm prepared to say at this time." The murdered woman's husband has been given compassionate leave from the Royal Marines.'

Golly sat rigid with shock.

'What's up, Golly? You look like you seen a ghost. Golly, what's the matter?'

'I what? I what, Mum?'

'Look like you seen a ghost.'

'No ... No, Mum! They got it wrong! That was a lady policeman that got herself murdered. That's what I was told. Lady policeman. Her who was in the papers after that BBC woman was strangled. Choked. With the wire.'

'Oh, no, Golly, whoever told you that got it all wrong. It's just a girl whose husband's off fighting the war. Got two children, they said on BBC at lunchtime. One handicapped, can't walk, hear or talk, they said. Crippled deaf mute.'

'No, surely not, Mum. It was a lady policeman they said to me. Lady policeman. Got to be.'

She had gone back into her kitchen, quite used to Golly's fancies and obsessions, getting on with the Christmas dinner. Golly took a deep breath. She was right. He'd made a terrible mistake. In his head he saw the girl again, standing in her kitchen and it was the lady policeman he had seen before. It had to be.

But it wasn't.

'Put the crackers out, Golly. They got indoor fireworks in them it says on the box. They'll be good. They'll be good fun, fireworks.'

You must always do as you're told, Golly.

The Banshee would come. He'll come here, and if Golly didn't get it right—

Golly, you'll be put in a hole, that's what'll happen to you. Put in a hole.

Twenty-One

When he woke – on the way back to London, after his forty winks – Dandy Tom leaned back in his seat and quietly gave Suzie Mountford a little lecture on the art of interrogation. She had told him she was unhappy about the way she'd questioned Jo Benton's friends, so he felt it was his duty to provide her with a short course in technique. Tips of the trade, he called it. 'Time,' he said, 'is the most precious commodity in the interrogator's arsenal,' and he continued to go through the entire repertoire

427

of a skilled inquisitor.

He talked about the techniques that would put a subject at ease, and so lead him into the quicksands where he might miss his footing and stumble to destruction, giving her wisdom culled from barristers and policemen who'd made their names as interlocutors of great cunning.

'Lead them gently towards that trick question, the one that really matters, then watch their hands and their eyes. It's like that old Christmas game: hands behind the back with a coin; place the coin in one hand then bring both fists at arm's length in front of the body. You can always name the hand with the coin in it because everyone slightly favours the "hot" fist with his eyes.'

Sitting in the dark, in the back of the car, Dandy Tom, in his well-cut suit, handmade shirt, silk tie, splendidly tailored overcoat and the custom-made shoes, dispensed wisdom over a good ten miles. 'Here endeth the lesson,' he said finally and went quiet, closed down as the Wolseley ate up the road.

The Ghost of Christmas Past came into Suzie's mind. The fireproof imitation fir tree they had in the corner of what her mother liked to call the drawing room. Real candles burning on it when they had the presents and during afternoon tea. Some of the decorations that Daddy had bought years ago: a bird with a wonderful spun-glass tail, baubles that looked as though they were covered in frost, others with dimpled sides sparkling with colour. She thought of her sister, laughing and happy. Never again. What a way to be spending Christmas, she thought summoning up courage to ask him, 'You ready to give me the answers to those riddles yet, Guv?'

'Which riddles would those be, Suzie?'

'You told me to go away, and find the answers to two questions. Where would you hide a car? And what would you do with a poisonous spider kept in a bottle?'

He asked if she had any answers.

'I'm not sure, Guv. Unless you'd hide a car among other cars. Like hiding a tree in a forest.'

'Well done.' He was not patronizing. 'Terrific. Top of the class. And the bottled spider?'

'Use it to frighten people?'

'Or worse,' Molly from the front.

'That's about right, but so far it's only a theory based on some research. Molly knows some of it, but not all.' He raised his voice to the driver. 'Brian, stop your ears. This is none of your business. A terrible amount of work's been done in the last few days. Now it's time to open Pandora's box for you, Suzie.'

Brian grunted, and Dandy Tom continued without a pause. 'We've been looking through the records of other forces as well as the Met.' He had searched back a few years, checking on possible killings involving piano wire. 'It's a tedious business, getting other people to match files for you. We put a series of questions to the major forces in the United Kingdom; they've gone through their records and we've collated the results.'

The results, according to Tommy Livermore, were sobering. Since October 1938 they had turned up records of eleven unsolved murders in which piano wire had been the instrument. 'That amounts to either a large number of coincidences or one person: a single repeat offender.'

Suzie sensed him smiling in the darkness. It could not have been a simple job to gather these records. Everything had to be sorted manually, then telephoned, mailed or couriered up to DCS Livermore's murder room set up in Scotland Yard, among the offices of the Reserve Squad. Some people had burned much midnight oil to gather the statistics. 'The first thing that'll strike you is the distances involved in what appears to be a completely random business,' the Chief Superintendent said.

'The first recent killing was almost right under our noses. October 24th 1938, Ealing Common. Found on the morning of the twenty-fifth. Mary Elizabeth Tobin, aged sixteen, strangled with a piece of piano wire. Strangled and raped. She'd been out, up in the West End. She came home in a box.'

This is number one and the fun has just begun.

Pause as he reached into his memory. 'Not another until January 14th, 1939, and then it's a long way off. Geraldine Williams, aged twenty-seven, strangled with piano wire in her own kitchen at 25 Northumberland Avenue, Jesmond, Newcastle-upon-Tyne, Northumberland. In broad daylight. Strangled, raped and then abused with a kitchen knife.'

Pause to hold back the ghastly day. 'And there are added details: pan of water left simmering on the gas stove. Bedroom drawers rifled. Small amount of money stolen. That ring some bells?'

Suzie grunted, and Dandy Tom continued – 7 February 1939, Gillian Hunt, Birmingham, industrial Midlands. 'Happened in what passes for daylight around those dark satanic mills. In the victim's own kitchen, complete with pan simmering on the hob.' Are we dealing with a frustrated chef? Or someone who just likes kitchens. Kitchens become the favourite crime scenes.

20 April 1939, Dover, on the Kent coast, Pamela Lynne Harwood. Right under Dover Castle walls this time, and a different kind of wire. 'But the feel was for our chum. Deep cuts on the thighs and vagina. Unpleasant.' Dandy Tom spoke as though he was already entering into a close relationship with this shadowy killer.

24 May, Southampton, Brenda Bishop, again the victim's own kitchen. No pan of water, but there are stab wounds in the usual places. Vicious, deep gashes that were becoming par for the course. Very violent this one.

'Harrogate, Canterbury, York. June, July and August.' Tommy Livermore supplied names of victims but Suzie didn't retain them. Without photographs or further details they were mere shadows.

431

Types and shadows have their ending...
...For the newer rite is here

'Then a fallow period. Nothing at all for the rest of 1939, unless we've missed something, which is possible.' So, nothing until Patricia Cooke, in her own kitchen in the village of Snitterfield, Stratford-upon-Avon, Warwickshire, in May. She is followed in June by Marie Davidson, thirteen years old, in her dad's cottage near Trumpington, just outside Cambridge. 'With which we start to come up to date: December, Josephine Benton, Borough of Camford, London.'

'A busy little bee,' Molly Abelard muttered. Suzie thought there was something deeply unpleasant about Molly Abelard.

Tommy Livermore repeated all the crime sites as though he was ticking them off on his fingers, 'Ealing Common, London; then right up to the North East, Newcastle-upon-Tyne. Back to the Midlands, Birmingham. Down to the South Coast, Dover. Along the coast to Southampton. Then Harrogate in the North. Right down again to Canterbury in Kent. Back up to Yorkshire for York. Then down to the Midlands again with Stratford. Up to Cambridge, then London, Camford, for Jo Benton.'

Suzie tried to visualize the map, and in the darkness it seemed as random as scattershot.

'He's bouncing all over the place, like a ping-pong ball,' she thought, then realized she'd said it out aloud.

'And today,' Dandy Tom said quietly, 'the village of Overchurch, rural Hampshire. And only these last two seem to make any sense. What do you say, Suzie?'

'His job takes him all over the country.'

'Either that or he has a bike – I'm sorry, Suzie, not very sensitive of me. Give me the options.'

'Perhaps he's a lorry driver, delivery of goods. Or a representative, selling for his company. One whose work takes him all over the shop.'

'Yes, but it's a bit random isn't it? There's no obvious pattern. Reps who go around selling things for their firms prefer to work through areas. These are random journeys. Don't make sense. They're spotty, scattered.'

'Some kind of engineer who has to maintain a piece of equipment?' Suzie tried.

'The equipment would have to be quite minimal I would've thought; if that wasn't the case there'd be local maintenance. What were you thinking of?'

'Cinemas?' she suggested. 'Projection equipment?'

'That's good. But now we have the last two. Jo Benton and your sister. Let's presume they're connected – which they probably are. Why?'

'You already told me why, sir. He could've taken exception to a woman being in charge of the investigation.'

After a long pause. 'If that's the case he'll soon find out he's wrong and...?'

'Come after me again?'

'If it's important to him, yes. Possibly he's more interested in the killing. Got the flavour for it back in the autumn of 1938. Then, like Topsy, it just grow'd and grow'd. Which is where another of my theories comes in. If you want someone dead, what do you do?'

'Kill him...'

'Or?'

'Hire someone to do it for you.'

'Precisely.'

'Isn't that a bit melodramatic, sir?'

'Not if you're a melodramatic person who wants someone dead for melodramatic reasons. We live in a climate where death is commonplace. Has been in Europe for the past few years: the Spanish Civil War; Russia and Finland, now this.'

You've kept this pretty close to your chest, Tommy. Nothing in the press, no memos zipping between the Yard's Reserve Squad and other stations.

'We've been playing this close to the chest,' Livermore said, again as though reading her mind. 'I'm anxious not to alert anyone. Haven't even owned up to the connection between Camford and today's horror.'

There was silence for about a mile, then Dandy Tom spoke again. 'It's difficult to hold the entire picture in your head. Tomorrow we'll look at the map I've set up at the Yard. Give you the distances, the scattershot of deaths.'

'We need photographs as well, don't we?' Suzie asked. 'They're not real people unless we see them. Just names, apart from Jo Benton and my sister.' The sadness hurtled up into her throat and behind her eyes, so that she gave a small involuntary sob.

'Tomorrow,' he growled, quickly. 'Tomorrow we'll take a real look.'

'And a peep at your other theory, Guv. The bottled spider?'

'Yes, that as well. I'm a great fan of the Animated Bioscope, Suzie. Going to the pictures. I've been known to sneak in on a Saturday morning with the kids. They didn't have Saturday morning pictures when I was a lad, so I've been making up for lost time. At my local Picture Palace of a Saturday morning they've been showing two serials: *Custer's Last Stand* – which appears to have gone on for years – and a creepy thing called *The Clutching Hand*. In that little piece the villain has been quietly murdering jockeys with black widow spiders. Keeps them bottled up, then releases one into a gelatine capsule and seals it in just before the race, when he slips it down the back of his victim's shirt. The heat of the jockey's body melts the gelatine, out comes the black widow, which sinks its fangs into the jockey's naked flesh. Jockey then slides gracefully from his mount and ends up dead on the track. It's a load of extreme rubbish of course, but I wondered...'

'Yes, sir?'

'...wondered if it was feasible. Wondered if what we had here was a killer being manipulated by someone else, sent shooting all over the place to confuse people. Like some kind of bomb, or rocket, that could be guided to its target, or a deadly spider in a bottle, ready to be tipped down the victim's shirt. Maybe it's too fanciful.'

'I wouldn't say that, sir.' She wasn't totally convinced.

'Tomorrow,' Tommy Livermore stopped it there. 'Brian, put the wireless on. Let's have something cheerful.'

A woman sang with great gusto, 'There'll always be an England, and England will be free, if England means as much to you as England means to me.'

Suzie remembered singing patriotic songs like this at school. 'I vow to thee my country – all earthly things above.' It meant about as much as the words of 'There'll always be an England'. She felt absurdly guilty. She was much more concerned with there always being a Suzie than an England. Especially today. Already missing Charlotte like a lost limb. Needing to weep for her. But policewomen don't weep. Not in public.

They came into London through Hammersmith, then into disfigured Kensington High Street. It was dark and quiet on the road, not a soul stirring in the streets on this Christmas night. Nothing above them either. Nothing unloading bombs. London had been lucky, with relative peace over Christmas. Not so up north, where Manchester had taken a dreadful pounding starting on the Sunday night when folk were out at carol services and other church activities on that last grey, damp Sunday before Christmas. It began round about Evensong time and went on for thirty-six hours.

By Christmas Day a snow of charred paper was carried to the dormitory areas, while there was no gas or electricity to cook a Christmas dinner in the entire Greater Manchester area.

'You want to go straight to the Yard, Guv, or home?' Brian asked as they reached the Albert Hall. Across the road Prince Albert was huddled up against the bombs, though still not looking at the book he held.

'Upper St Martin's Lane, Brian. I'll direct you when we get there.' He turned his face towards Suzie. 'Is there an entrance at the back of your block of flats?'

'Yes, fire escapes from every flat at the back, Guv. Why?'

'I don't want to leave you on your own. Understand?'

'Of course, sir. Very good of you.'

'Not *good* of me at all. I'm not a *good* person, Suzie. I just don't want one of my people getting throttled with piano wire. You can never tell with a fellow like chummy. I think it's too soon for him to come looking, but who knows?'

When they got to Suzie's building the Guv'nor told her to stay in the car, then he got out and went to the other Wolseley which had pulled up just behind them. She turned right around to watch as he spoke to the people inside and was joined in the street by Ron Worrall. The pair of them walked back to the corner of St Martin's Lane and disappeared. Why didn't he take Molly? she wondered, and as if she'd heard Molly said, 'The Chief's good to his officers. He's the best chief super in the Met, and I don't care who knows it.' Her voice had an attractive throaty croak, like Jean Arthur's voice, Suzie thought.

'And I agree with you,' she said, sensing that Abelard was somehow criticizing her.

Tommy Livermore came back to the car about half-an-hour later, gave some instructions to Molly Abelard and nodded Suzie out of the back. 'Bring your case, I'm taking you home,' he told her, and together they went into the building and up to her floor.

In the flat he went from room to room, checking cupboards, looking behind curtains, his body tensed, electric, ready for violence. When he was satisfied he climbed out on to the fire escape and softly called down to Ron Worrall below. When he opened the window they could hear sounds of revelry coming from one of the flats below.

Finally contented, Dandy Tom came in and closed the window.

'There's nobody skulking around out there, and I've got a couple of traffic cars coming up, so you'll have two hairy great policemen at the front and two at the back. We'll wait until they arrive. Don't let anyone in unless you're sure you know them.'

'Don't worry, Guv, I'm not letting anyone in, even if I do know them.'

He nodded, and looked serious. 'I don't have to tell you again, but I want you to know how deeply sorry I am that this has happened to you. Try to sleep. Tomorrow we'll take a look at the photographs, put faces to names, okay? Nine o'clock'll be early enough. Billy Mulligan's in charge of the office. Fourth Floor.'

'Right, Guv, it'll be fine, Guv. We'll get him.'

He stretched out his arms and put a hand on each shoulder. Once more, she thought he was going to kiss her. Wanted him to kiss her. Wanted him dreadfully.

Where do the noses go?

But he just squeezed her shoulders, said, 'Sleep well. Lock the door after me,' and went.

She'd love to be given the opportunity to fall asleep to the sound of Dandy Tom giving her a lecture on the habits of the Greater London Cat Burglar.

Time is the most precious commodity.

Golly had drunk too much ginger wine. He always did at Christmas and he now felt content, safe and warm sitting in his mum's house with one of his mum's Christmas dinners inside of him. Good cook, Mum.

'Read out the motto in your cracker, Golly.'

'I 'ent no good at reading, Mum. You know that. I got me paper hat on.'

'Come on, Golly. You try. Read it out.'

'They're not mottoes this year, Mum. They're riddles.'

'Go on, Golly, read it out.'

He had the little slip of paper between his fingers and was able to focus on the words, trying to make sense of them – 'Qu-est ... Quest-ion. Question. Where do they ma-ake. Make. Where do they make. The mo-st mo-tor ho-rns. Where do they make the most motor horns, Mum?' Ah. He chuckled with glee. 'Give up? Give up, Mum?'

'Give up, right, Golly? I give up?'

'Hong Kong. Hong Kong, Mum. I don't understand it.'

'Honk-Honk, Golly. Like the noise a horn makes.'

'Oh, yes. Hah. Oh, yes. What's yours, Mum?' Golly had a selective sense of humour.

'Where do they make telephones? That's it, Golly. Where do they make telephones?'

'Dunno. Give up.'

'Tring.'

'What?'

'Tring, Golly. It's the name of a town: Tring. Telephones, tring-tring.'

'Oh.'

'Have some more nuts, Golly.'

'Yes, I will. That's what Mickey Mangle says – "Roll on Christmas and we'll all have some nuts." They have a laugh at that, but I don't understand it.' He took another swig of ginger wine, and his mum said hadn't he had enough? And Golly cheeked her, said he'd never had enough.

After a while she said: 'It's good having you here for Christmas, Golly.'

'Yeah, it is, isn't it? Got to go tomorrow, Mum.'

'Oh, not so soon. What'll I do with all this turkey?'

'You've got our Kath coming round tomorrow night, Mum. Coming round with Keith

Whatname, the boyfriend.' He giggled at the thought of Kath having a bloke.

'Well, it's be nice to have my whole family around me. All of you.'

'This Keith's not family.'

'No, but you are, Golly. You must know how much I care for you.'

You are the abomination of desolation, spoken of by Daniel the prophet.

'Yes, Mum, but I got to go back up the Smoke.'

'Going by train are you, Golly?' Resigned to it.

'No, I got a lift. Got to meet someone. Going tomorrow night.' I'll walk, he thought. I'll walk at night. Keep off the main roads. I'll find my way. Walk all through the nights. I'll be there by Saturday, easy. Saturday. When I get back to London I'll search for her: for the lady policeman. If I can get her before Emily Baccus comes to me again, I'll put it right.

'I'll make you some turkey sandwiches, then. Pack you a picnic. Turkey and tongue sandwiches I'll make for you.'

'Don't forget the mustard then, Mum. I likes a bit of mustard on a turkey sandwich.'

'Course you do, Golly.'

'And, Mum, I never been here, right? I never been here this Christmas. You never seen me, you don't know where I am. You don't even know my name, Mum, right?'

Suzie was done in. She looked in the mirror and felt like 'cheese at fourpence' – as her

441

mother would say. Who would have thought a bright, beautiful, happy day like this would end with such desolation?

She didn't have much to eat in the flat: the end of a loaf of bread she'd bought on Saturday; one egg; a couple of rashers of bacon in the cold cupboard, and a handful of potatoes. She didn't feel hungry but knew she must have something to eat as she'd had nothing since a very quick and snatched breakfast. In the end she had a long bath and did herself egg and bacon and a handful of chips.

Around ten her mother rang to say they had got home in good time and the children had settled in.

'We'll be eating turkey for weeks,' Helen Mountford said. 'Cold turkey.' They had just been sitting down to their Christmas meal when the telephone called them to Overchurch, and Suzie had insisted they take Charlotte's turkey and the ham back to Newbury with them. 'Don't care if I never see turkey again,' she said.

'Children are most adaptable,' Helen said now. 'Little Ben has settled down so well. He didn't seem to have a care in the world when I was bathing him tonight. Laughed away and gave me some wonderful smiles. Lucy's quiet, but she was as good as gold going to sleep. Did you say you bought her that bear?'

'She still likes it then?'

'Mr Gherkin's wonderful. He'll be a favourite for a long time.'

They had both said all they had to say to one

another, but Suzie stayed on the line for the sake of human contact.

'Vernon with you?' Suzie asked.

'Tomorrow. He's staying the night with a friend in Andover. The police won't let him stay in Falcon Cottage. Why is that, Suzie?'

'Still a crime scene, Mum. We have to be careful. Preserve everything just as it was. I don't want to talk about this. I never want to see the place again. Hope Vernon gets rid of it. Sells up and moves.'

Finally they said goodnight and Suzie made herself some cocoa. The milk had been delivered on Monday so it was fresh. She was carrying it through when the telephone rang again.

'Suzie, I'm so terribly sorry.' It was Shirley Cox and they went through a couple of minutes of polite conversation before she came to the real point of her call.

'Got something for you,' she lowered her voice. 'Pip Magnus.'

'Yes.'

'I was in yesterday morning. Clearing my desk.'

'Yes.'

'I think someone higher up should know this. Superintendent Sanders, or Chief Superintendent Livermore.'

'Well, you'll see Mr Livermore yourself, tomorrow. You're joining us aren't you?'

Tomorrow. Nine o'clock'll be early enough. Can't wait to see him. Dandy Tom.

'I think it's got to be someone with a bit of history, like yourself.'

443

'Well?'

'I was clearing up my desk, Christmas Eve. Pip Magnus was in and he took a call from Big Toe.'

'And?'

'He said to the caller, "Right, Guv. Yes, we've got them here. Don't worry. See you bright and early. They'll think it's Father Christmas come for his mince pies and glass of ginger wine".'

'He said this in front of you?'

'Didn't know I was there. He was lording it, sitting in Big Toe's office.'

'What else?'

'I've only just heard. The Balvak brothers. They were arrested just after seven o'clock this morning. Possession of firearms with no certificates. Receiving stolen goods. Seems as though Big Toe came back early with a search warrant. Went down into the Cut with Pip Magnus, Dougie Catermole and an army of uniforms, and brought the Balvaks out, charged them first thing this morning, but of course nobody's going to hear their side until tomorrow at the earliest. So—'

'Thanks, Shirley. I'll tell Mr Livermore in the morning. He already knows about the weapon—'

'It's weapons now, Skip. A damn great Colt and a German Luger.'

Suzie thanked her for the call and said she'd see her tomorrow. In her bedroom she drank her cocoa, then cried herself to sleep and entered the dark world of dreams she would never remember. The Balvaks really had no relevance now.

The telephone shrieked like a child in pain, then became the rattle of the bell. Suzie swam up from the black, dark depths of sleep, fumbled for the light switch, saw her alarm clock. It was half-past five and she could tell it was morning only by the feel of it. Then there was momentary relief. It isn't real, she imagined. Charlotte's not dead, they're ringing to tell me it's all a terrible mistake.

'You awake now? Suzie?' he said at the distant end. 'It's Tommy Livermore. I'm getting everyone in. We've got a break. At least I think it's a break. Need you here. The car in front of your place is ready to bring you in. Right?'

Twenty-Two

It was twenty-past two in the morning when Golly sat bolt upright on his mum's front-room couch and knew he had to leave. They'd only got to bed an hour ago but now he was wide-awake. He often had these sudden flashes of insight. They came, he was convinced, from a higher source. Higher even than Emily Baccus, who told him who to kill and where. And these sudden convictions were always right.

He got out of the made-up bed on the couch and went through to waken up his mum before he started to dress. His mum complained no end, but he couldn't help that. He had to go, and his mum had more sense than to argue with him. She knew Golly and his fancies of old, so she just got on with it and made him the turkey and tongue sandwiches, didn't forget the mustard, boiled him an egg as well, and put in a little screw of greaseproof with salt in it. Golly couldn't abide a hard-boiled egg without salt. In the end she did two eggs. She was lucky, out here in the country she could get eggs easily. In London they were as scarce as hen's teeth. Or as hen's eggs, come to that.

In all Mrs Ailsa (Beaky) Goldfinch – the Mrs was purely a courtesy title – had completed the food preparation within the half-hour and Golly was on his way out into the cold night. She came to the door, leaning on her stick, to see him off.

'And don't you forget, Mum. I never been near here. You never seen me for months. Never heard from me. I never write, because I can't. You don't know where I'm living at now. I'm a bad son, right?'

'I don't even know your name, Golly, if I ever knew it.'

'Well, don't you suddenly remember it, Mum. Don't you even dream of it. And make sure that our Kath keeps her lips buttoned up, and she's not to go blabbing to this bloke, what's *his* name?'

'Keith, and how would I know your name, Golly? Nobody ever calls you by your proper name, Adam.' She laughed loudly and Golly felt the anger fizz up in him like one of those damned silly indoor fireworks they had from the crackers last night. He saw red.

'Come on, son. Come on Adam, give your old mum a kiss goodbye.'

The car did the short trip to Scotland Yard in what could have been record time as there was nothing on the road. Usually at this hour of the morning the rubbish collection lorries and the street cleaners were about. A smattering of people would be going to work. But on Boxing Day morning London was deserted.

'The Chief Super said we had to bring you in at the speed of light,' the uniformed driver said. 'Told us we could use the gong if necessary.'

'We were sorry to hear about your trouble, miss,' the sergeant added a shade sanctimoniously.

'No need to call me miss,' she snapped. 'I'm a sergeant, just like you.'

'Not quite like me.' He didn't actually laugh but it was meant as a witty riposte – one-up against the WDS.

A skeleton staff worked at the Yard over Christmas but they were expecting her, which probably meant there was very little going on throughout the remainder of the building, apart from Dandy Tom's investigation.

Tommy Livermore had set up the murder office in the conference room behind his own private office as head of the Reserve Squad, on the fourth floor. In fact Dandy Tom's private army *was* the Reserve Squad, and for the first time Suzie realized what a large army it was. Later she would know all their functions: the smattering of uniformed men and women who contained people at crime scenes, or sometimes accompanied detectives as a kind of walking badge of office, the long arm of the law itself. Then there were the experts, the people trained by the book and by experience as detectives, each with his speciality from forensics to ballistics, from knowledge of confidence tricks to burglary methods. And of course there were the people who watched and waited, insinuated themselves into space close to a suspect and became part of the furniture, biding their time. Or watched over those at risk because of the sensitivity of some case or other, these people who lived like coiled springs, ready to unwind in a moment and leap into action, arrowing in at the speed of light, coming to the aid of those less fortunate.

The conference room had two long tables running down either side, with a shorter one across the far end – like a high table at a formal dinner. Half-a-dozen people were manning the telephones at the right hand table, while Dandy Tom sat like the guest of honour at the high table itself. He had two telephones in front of him and a blotter in a green and gold leather holder, notebooks, pencils and a couple of thick reference books. Sergeant Billy Mulligan sat on his right side and Molly Abelard on his left. They had managed to get the heating turned up and Abelard, being a cold-blooded creature, had stripped off her jacket. In shirtsleeves she proved to have a better figure than Suzie imagined. The uniform didn't do much for her. The removal of the jacket unveiled tight breasts like small Nazi helmets.

Directly against the back wall a tall map of the United Kingdom rose as high as the picture rail. Mounted on a larger board, the map had pink ribbons pinned to a number of place names, and the ribbons stretched out to photographs and cards lined with typed information. She spotted Ealing Common and Camford in the London area, and Newcastle-upon-Tyne in the North East. This had to be a detailed walk around the extent of the piano wire murders Dandy Tom had revealed to her on the way into London.

We've been playing this close to the chest.

He hasn't been to sleep, she thought. Doesn't show, because he's shaved and changed his shirt and suit, but he's been up all night and he's got a fire going in his belly. As she entered the room, Abelard looked up, saw Suzie and spoke to the Chief. In turn he caught her eye, smiled and told Abelard to take half-an-hour off or something similar because she got up and left the table.

On her way out, as she reached Suzie, Abelard said, 'You're to sit on the left hand of God, Sergeant Mountford. And the best of luck to you. He's in a filthy temper.' When she reached the chair vacated by Abelard, Dandy Tom was talking on the telephone, leaning back in his chair with his gold fountain pen hovering close to his mouth. He'd start tapping at his teeth any minute, she thought. Mulligan winked at her in a big-brotherly fashion and the Chief Super gave her a smile and raised a hand in greeting. Her hand came up automatically to tidy an imagined unruly strand of hair – *her* nervous habit, she thought.

'Yes,' Tommy Livermore said into the telephone. 'Yes, I understand all that but we do need people over there if you wouldn't mind. This is a man suspected of several appalling murders ... Yes ... At least eleven, possibly more. No, *probably* more ... Yes, sir, thank you very much.' He put down the handset and turned to Sergeant Mulligan. 'Billy, chief constables don't like being woken in the early hours of Boxing Day, even when it's as urgent as a graveyard. Hello, Suzie with a zed.'

She wasn't imagining it, there was that same electric spark between them even though he was talking to someone else. She had felt it the first time they had met in the foyer of that terrible block of service flats in Marylebone, and on every subsequent occasion she had been with him, or even spoken with him on the telephone. A girl can't be that wrong, surely? A girl knows, doesn't she? I can't have got the signals mixed that badly.

'They after doing it now, Guv?' Mulligan had a way of speaking out of the corner of his mouth, like an old lag, trained to converse in secret during the exercise periods observed by hawk-eyed screws who'd have you on report if you coughed.

'He says there've been people out watching the place front and back for the past hour. And it appears they've taken my advice. They're not going in until daybreak. Though I doubt if they're going to have the bodies there much before daybreak anyway. Everyone needs time to recover from a day off.'

'And Abelard's gone to Rupert Street?'

Dandy Tom gave him a nod. 'And Abelard's gone to Rupert Street, Billy.'

'I go and get a cuppa cha, then, Guv?'

'Bring one back for me, Bill, and one for Suzie here. How d'you take it, Sue?'

'Strong with sugar. Two please. Thanks.' Nobody ever called her Sue.

'You heard the lady, Billy. Walk on.' He could've been talking to a horse.

'What's up, Chief?' She had decided to adopt Abelard's mode of addressing him.

'We maybe know who the spider is. If it really *is* a spider.' He sounded deep and crisp, but certainly not even. 'The problem is that we don't seem to be able to put our hands on him.' He looked suddenly boyish. 'A temporary set-back, I'm sure.'

'Who?' She was equally crisp. He thinks he knows who killed my sister. I'd give a thousand pounds to know who killed her. If I had a thousand pounds.

'Well...' he began, then paused for an infuriating fifteen seconds or so. 'Well, there's a possibility that Molly was right. Two-Faced Golly Goldfinch. Myladdo she mentioned in the car.'

When they'd got back to the Yard, Molly had asked if she could take a look at Golly Goldfinch. 'She wanted to go on a paperchase. I saw no harm in it. Tell you the truth, I thought it'd eliminate Golly. You ever seen him, Golly, I mean?'

'Once, I think. I had a couple of weeks on nights from Vine Street, and a sergeant pointed him out to me. That was all of three years ago though, Chief, and I never saw his face.'

'He's a little simple. Two pence short of a bob. His mother was a short-timer in Soho and got caught out twice running, it seems. Mind you, things weren't all that sophisticated around the turn of the century. Some Holy Joes looked after her both times. Took her to some place for "bad girls" in the country. The daughter must be forty-one or two now, and Golly's forty. Forty with problems. We've got his whole record, and a photograph of him.'

He turned over a matt black and white that had been lying on the blotter in front of him, and pushed it towards her so that she got the full impact of the divided face, the kecked nose and slewed eye, the mouth askew showing long, sharp teeth protruding over his lip on the right side, in a kind of snarl. She had to remind herself that because he looks like a demon it doesn't necessarily follow that he *is* a demon. What had the Guv'nor said about that? Monster inside the monster. The exception that proved the rule.

'How'd you like to wake up to that peeping through your window?'

She gave an involuntary shudder.

'It's worse in colour,' Dandy Tom said, swiftly taking the photograph back, turning it over on

452

his blotter. 'I could never understand why the mother didn't get that face fixed. Plenty of surgeons would've done it for practice...'

You don't know what people get up to in them hospitals. You don't know what them doctors get up to when they've put you asleep.

He appeared to be lost in thought for a moment or two. 'So I let Molly go over to Vine Street. Nobody's very busy tonight, so they pulled everything they had on Golly Goldfinch. Turns out he's more interesting than I imagined. First off he's been associating with unpleasant company for a while now. Mickey Mangle? Know him?'

She shook her head.

'Likes you to think he's a bit of a tough guy. Talks a lot, plays the hard man; did a five on the Moor for receiving. He got the birch in there for coming the old soldier. Didn't like it. We've never collared him again. Very sneaky small-time crook who pretends to be a big man. Nasty. Spends a lot of time with a couple of other likely lads – Billy Joy-Joy—'

'I know *him*. Chink?'

London is a series of interlocking villages.

'Half chink.'

'Got him, and I think I know Mangle now. Who else, Chief?'

'Bruce the Bubble, another tasty little morsel. Handy with his fists. Same line of business; small con jobs; petty theft, stealing by finding, all that kind of rubbish. The occasional long firm fraud. A bit of protection. Toms and street traders mainly. But talk to them and they're a major crime syndicate, Al Capone and Spring Heel Jack rolled into one.'

'And Golly Goldfinch is part of that set-up?'

'Hung around them as a kid, they're a tiny bit older than him, and he's been hanging around with them since he came back to London.'

He filled in the background for her. 'Golly's mum used to work out of three rooms near to the John Snow public house. Up Broadwick Street. Fellow who owned the rooms looked after Ailsa – that was her name, Ailsa Goldfinch. This is all second hand, I'm not *that* old, but I know they called her Beaky. Had trunky trouble, as my old nanny liked to say; always sticking her nose into other people's business.'

Beaky Goldfinch had brought her kids up along the streets of Soho, but eventually she went to live with a relative, he thought it was her mother, out in the country somewhere, and took the children with her. But Golly didn't particularly enjoy the country. It could be that it had something to do with being sent to a reform school for truancy, threatening behaviour, theft, assaulting a teacher, malicious wounding. You name it. 'From there he went to an experimental mixed school – St Hilda's, near Whitchurch – there was a lot of speculative education at the time, completely buggered some people's lives.

'When he got out of there he left home and came back to look after his much younger cousin, Lavender, who was tomming it just off Rupert Street. Now here comes the first interesting bit.' Dandy Tom was edgy, and this was

454

a side of him she'd not yet seen. He kept fiddling with his tie and shirt cuffs, tapping his teeth with the gold pen. He jumped, turning his head sharply when one of the telephones rang. He was waiting for something dramatic – for news of Golly Goldfinch perhaps?

'You alright, Chief?' she asked as Billy Mulligan came back with the teas and a plate full of unappetizing-looking biscuits.

'I'll be okay directly. Too much milk in this tea, Billy. We've got several important things in the pipeline.' Then the dam broke and he gave her a slow, lovely, even ravishing smile that started at one corner of his mouth then spread right up his face. It was one of those hundred per cent smiles that lit up his eyes. He could have used that smile to do practically anything, she considered.

Go on, she challenged him in her head. Go on, try me.

He told her it was a little under a decade ago that Golly came back to look after the fair Lavender, but no sooner was he back than Vine Street was getting complaints – demanding with menaces, that kind of thing. And he got away with it for most of the time. 'People who get threatened when they're with a brass really don't want to advertise.'

It seemed that Golly had overstepped the mark on occasion. 'It's possible he didn't understand the rules,' Dandy Tom said. 'It was okay to demand with menaces while he was in the set of rooms which Lavender used to screw her clients, but once they were on the street they would, and did, bite back.'

Golly had developed other antisocial manners. He'd frighten people. Do a spot of petty larceny, that kind of thing. Got into a lot of trouble, but none of it desperate enough to send him to the Scrubs or Pentonville. People covered for him. He was a bad boy. 'A frighteningly bad boy. But he put on muscles humping boxes around Berwick Street Market. Got muscles on his muscles, and I suspect he had a few lessons from the likes of Mickey the Mangle and his pals. The next thing we've discovered is the kind of information that makes your thumbs prick.'

There were very few genuine freelance girls operating in Soho. Unless you had a good pimp you didn't get the street space. The other girls would ease you out sooner than look at you. To survive you had to be all pals together and jolly good company. If you tried to queue-jump, one of the girls' protectors – pimp isn't a word they like – would step in and give you a good spanking with his belt, like as not, and that was how things were.

Yet Lavender claimed to be freelance, and she never seemed to have any bother, but it wasn't Golly who kept order among the girls. Gradually it came to be known that Lavender had a ponce who made sure everything was neat, and allowed the streets to flow with cash. He was also heavy handed with any girl who crossed up Lavender, and the other ponces were scared of him as well. In general the girls tried to keep clear of him, and he gave one of them, Bridget, a right seeing to. The man who did all this was an unpleasant young spiv called Manny Spellthorne, and it was rumoured that he, like many after him, had friends in high places. Though nobody campaigned for him when the chips were down.

And the chips went down for Manny Spellthorne when his reign came to an abrupt end in late September, early October, 1938.

'He simply went missing.' Dandy Tom was playing with the gold pen as he spoke. 'Nobody would have known if it hadn't been for his wife. And certainly nobody knew about his wife, who came looking for him and found that the offices he had told her were his place of work turned out to be Lavender's business address, round the corner from Rupert Street.'

One night, Manny just dissolved into thin air, like the baseless fabric of Prospero's vision. And the only person who seemed in the least bit interested was Mrs Spellthorne, Clara Spellthorne, Crazy Clara as the police called her later. And she turned out to be insubstantial as well, because Manny's name wasn't Spellthorne after all but Collins. Pat Collins with a lust for the high life, and two other wives that he'd bigamously married at one time or another. Going missing laid waste the many secrets of Manny Spellthorne's life.

Among other people, the uniforms from Vine Street went round to see Lavender, who claimed to know nothing of any interest concerning Manny. No, she said, he wasn't my ponce. Yes, he occasionally helped out if there was a bit of bother. Yes, she knew he had given the girl Bridget a good hiding, but Bridget was a daft cat and had asked for it. Making trouble. 'No, Manny hadn't been round for a month or two. Well, six weeks, to be more precise.'

The uniforms from Vine Street had also been to see Golly. Golly didn't know Manny very well. Didn't really know him at all. To tell the truth scarcely knew him to talk to. Saw him up Berwick Street Market on occasion. 'Lavender? No, – Lavender wouldn't have nothing to do with someone like Manny Spellthorne. No, never seen him around Lavender.' That was Golly's line on 18 October 1938. The file on Spellthorne stayed open, but there were few entries after that.

Tommy Livermore smiled grimly. 'On the twenty-fourth we get sixteen-year-old Mary Elizabeth Tobin done to death with piano wire and raped on Ealing Common. In that order, choked and raped within a week of Golly talking about not knowing Manny Spellthorne.'

'Well—?' Suzie began.

'Well, indeed, Suzie with a zed. In that file there are several statements from people who say they saw Golly Goldfinch talking to this sprauncy young spiv called Manny Spellthorne. And there are three girls, none of whom I admit can be trusted, who state categorically that they've been warned off by Manny Spellthorne, threatened by Manny Spellthorne or, according to one girl, had Manny Spellthorne give her two stinging blows on her backside and told to keep out of

Lavender's way or he'd cut her. That's not including the girl who was given a good hiding: Bridget, who refused to sign a statement.

'It's also on record from another of the girls that Manny Spellthorne's main hobby appeared to be beating up Lavender. One of the interesting details from that account is that Golly, on several occasions, was heard to say such things as, "I'll swing for Manny Spellthorne". Or, "I'll do that bastard, Spellthorne", excuse the language lovely, Suzie.'

'It's still a big leap, Guv. From a repeat murderer to pinning it on Golly.'

His smile was almost sly. 'You know none of us are totally innocent,' he began and she sensed that he was going to make a confession to her. 'Narks never give you the full strength first time off. Experienced police officers are the same, they hold back information. And that's what I've done. It's pretty irresponsible, but I suppose we all want to look like Sherlock Holmes in the last reel. Showing off, my old nanny would've called it. Elementary, my dear Suzie.'

'You've got inside information?'

'I suppose you'd call it that. The day after they gave you the Jo Benton murder, I happened upon that creep Mickey the Mangle and it wasn't by accident. He was looking for me.'

He had gone out for a bit of solitude. Lunchtime the morning after Jo Benton was murdered and he was faced with talking young WDS Mountford through this hideously macabre killing. It was turning cold, so he walked rapidly, thinking and doing a circuit, Westminster Bridge up to Waterloo Bridge and back across the bridge and along Victoria Embankment. Mickey the Mangle was waiting for him on the Embankment.

'Bit worried, Mr Livermore, sir.'

'Talk to me then, Mick. Unless you want a tenner retainer. Turned grass, have you?'

'No, Guv'nor. Just worried about someone.'

He slowed down and the two men sauntered, side by side back towards the Yard. 'Who're you worried about?'

'Golly. Two-Faced Golly Goldfinch.'

Livermore nodded and waited.

'May be nothing, Guv. Just a kind of feeling I've got. The way he's been talking.'

'Well?'

'Been dropping hints. Like a kid. "I've got something *you* don't know" kind of thing.'

'Well, he *is* a big kid, Mickey. You know that.'

'Yes, but he talked to me a few days ago. Said he's got this lovely voice now. At night he hears the voice in his sleep. Tells him what to do.'

'Really?' Dandy Tom's ears pricked up.

'Yes, really, Guv. I don't like it. Says nobody else knows. Says nobody else can know. A woman, he says. A woman gives him instructions, orders. And he repeated a bit of the Bible to me. "There is a time to kill and a time to die." Is that the Bible, Guv'nor?'

'Sort of, Mick.' Dandy Tom was quite good at his Bible. Like Latin and Shakespeare they'd beaten it into him at his school. 'To every thing there is season,' he went on a bit and got the dying and killing in the right order.

'The point is, Guv,' Mickey continued, 'The point is, I *know* Golly and I'd stake my life on this being straight up – honest. I'd say someone really is talking to him.'

In the present he said to Suzie, 'I didn't think about it hard enough. The idea of someone being directed to do people to death was pretty much a wild idea. Viable, but – well, an idea. No more. Until it fused together when that poor little boy did his drawings, slashing the faces with his crayons.' He paused and looked up at her. 'I'm sorry, Suzie. I suppose I'm feeling a bit responsible for your sister's death. Should have taken more notice of Mickey the Mangle.'

'It's understandable,' she replied. 'Mangle sounds unpleasant – you had no reason to take him seriously.'

'Thank you.' He looked into her eyes steadily, then away.

'You never got to flog your peasants.' She opened her eyes wide.

'They'll forgive me. You okay?'

'Not really, but I will be. When we've got him. When we've got the...'

Nice girls don't swear, Susannah, Charlotte whispered, cheekily, in her ear.

He stretched out an arm and squeezed her left shoulder. It was a gesture of incredible intimacy, sending a delicious tingle from the nape of her neck to the junction of her thighs. 'Turns out that Golly's out of London at the moment.' He gave her a long look that said he

461

could quite easily drown in her eyes, and she invited him to try. Any time, Dandy Tom, she thought.

'He could have gone to his mother,' he led her on. 'Guess where his mother lives, Suzie?'

'Where?'

'Just outside Whitchurch. A hamlet called Laverstoke. Spit and a stride from Overchurch, and on the way to Basingstoke.'

She brought a fist down hard on the back of Golly's photograph. 'Got him.' She lit up, incandescent, and Dandy Tom gave her a smile that almost raised the roof.

She found it all hard to believe: things were moving faster than she could ever have imagined.

Over hill and over dale,
See we come together!

Golly marched through the night. It was only the early hours of Boxing Day, so it was all right to sing carols about the Three Wise Men who came to bring the gifts to Jesus, because they didn't get to the stable much before 'Pifany. That's what Mr Gregory called it. The Wise Men got to Bethlehem in 'Pifany, so he could sing 'Over hill and over dale'. Still, no bother, not that he was really singing it. Only doing it in his head as he blundered through the ice-cold night.

He knew he was going the right way. He had worked it out – bypass Basingstoke, then towards Reading. If he could get somewhere near

Basingstoke before dawn he'd be laughing. Find somewhere to lie up. Find an empty house perhaps. He was good at empty houses. That'd been an empty house where he'd done the first one ever. The dog who had growled at him. In the late afternoon when he was running away from the special school. Near Whitchurch that was, after they let him out of the Borstal Reform School and put him into St Hilda's. His plan had been to get to Andover, then steal money and get the train back to London. But it wasn't safe to move in the day-time – like now, he certainly could only move at night.

They were more careful nowadays because there was a war on. But, back then there wasn't any war. He had known the house was empty because of the bottles of milk on the doorstep and he went in, round the back. Nobody about and some fool had left the window open. Lavatory window. He squeezed in and then had the run of the house. Nobody around. Except the little girl who came into the garden, later.

There was this big cool hall – it had been a hot afternoon – paved with grey polished flagstones and windows that went right down to the floor.

He opened the windows, and that's when the dog, her dog – nasty little white thing with a long face – sniffed him out and barked at him, so he patted the dog and stroked it. He wasn't afraid of no dogs. Got a hand round the collar and twisted. It gave one little yelp then it died. Later he found out that he'd broken its neck.

463

That was the first time he knew it could be that quick, and that he was so strong.

'Whatcher done with my dog?' this little girl asked him. Standing there by the garden gate wearing a thin, long pink cotton dress. She had lovely hair: long, right down her back. He'd come outside, opened the back door. They'd left a key inside and he just turned the key and stepped out when the girl appeared.

'Done nothing with your dog. Here, you want to see something good?'

'What?'

'Never mind what. You come. En't half good,' and he went back into the house. She was like all little girls. Inquisitive, Beaky like his mum, so she came straight through the door and he took her from behind. Didn't mean it. Didn't mean to hurt her, but she went down like a sack of bricks and before he knew it she was dead and he had this lovely warm feeling. He put his arms round her and gave her a big squeeze and kissed her and she didn't try to get away from him like other girls did. He touched her all over and she didn't squirm or cry out or push him away. She let him do anything he wanted, and when he'd finished he went to the shed out the back of the house. Stayed there while people searched for her, calling out – 'Delphine... Delphine where are you? ... Delphine...?'

They didn't find her that night and he was away before dawn, well away. Knew enough to travel at night, and travel he did. Away from Andover, back the way he'd come. Four days of lying up and four nights travelling. He got nearly to London before they caught him and brought him back to Mr Gregory's school, St Hilda's School – called that because St Hilda had started a monastery for men and women, both, and that was what the school was: boys and girls, both. Delinquent boys and girls.

He expected to be beaten, but that didn't happen. The police asked him all kinds of questions. Where did he go first when he ran away? 'You went to Andover didn't you, lad?'

'No. Never been there. Went near to Newbury. Was going to London. That's where I wanted to be.'

'Boys get into trouble in London.'

'Yeah.' Delighted.

He stuck to his story. When they got cunning he was more sly; when they were full of guile he was foxy as hell.

'Golly, we know you didn't kill that girl—'

'What girl?'

'Come on, Golly, we know.'

'What you talking about? What girl?'

'She fell, Golly. We know she fell, caught her head on those stone slabs. Had what they call an eggshell skull. Broke easily. Nobody knew about her skull.'

'What you talking about? Eggshells?'

'But you killed the dog, Golly. We know that because someone strangled the dog. Very expert job that. You did well.'

'Don't know what you're talking about. I never did nothing to nobody, or a bloody dog.'

He knew he was safe. He had listened to plays

on the wireless, and he'd listened to the stories Mr Gregory and Miss Rae read to them. So he knew about fingerprints, upcoming science, and he had wiped the window ledge and cleaned off the doorknob, and the key in the back door. Saw his face in it, the doorknob, outside and in.

In the end it went away, and they didn't ask any more. Well, only about every six months, Mr Gregory would come out with it. Talking about something else he'd suddenly say, 'Golly, what was that girl wearing?' But he had become immune to that. It was a word that Mr Gregory had taught him. Immune. For Golly it meant counting to ten before ever answering any question. Twenty sometimes.

So he did another one almost straight away when he got back to London. Just happened and he was not even twenty. She was a kid, fourteen, fifteen maybe. Hackney it was, where they had begun to demolish some houses. He'd gone over to deliver a message from Mickey, and was going back towards the Tube. Met her and she said, 'You've got an 'orrible face. Ugh.'

The anger fizzed up inside him like it did. He wanted her because she was a nice bit, face like an educated monkey. That was what Bruce said when there was a picture of her in the papers a couple of days later – HACKNEY SCHOOL-GIRL MISSING FEARS. He saw red, and she didn't have time to scream and she was light as a feather. Lovely. Light as a feather and tight as a drum. They must have demolished the house the next day and accidentally buried her. Still there probably.

As he saw it he was doing them a wonderful favour. He believed in God, the Father Almighty and all that. When he choked a girl she went straight to God. The life everlasting, Amen.

Now, on this Boxing Day morning, in the bitter cold, he only got as far as the outskirts of Basingstoke before it got light. He found an old detached house with a For Sale notice outside, crept in, made sure there was nobody living there and broke in through some poorly secured French windows. Went through the entire place, all the furniture was covered with sheets, and dustcloths. But he gathered some bedding together, then tucked himself up near the front door and ate his sandwiches, turned on the water under the sink in the kitchen and had a drink. Then he slept.

Tonight he'd have to walk faster, move quicker. Sleep.

Miss Baccus didn't come to him with her orders. Maybe he could put it right in London. If he could get there in time.

'So when we got all this information from Abelard, about Golly and what a bad lad he was, we stooged over to Rupert Street, hoping to have a word with Golly, or maybe Lavender.' They had progressed to Dandy Tom's private office where he offered her breakfast.

The tea Billy Mulligan had brought from the canteen had been filthy. But now with the skill of a suave magician, Tommy Livermore

467

produced a coffeepot, a gas ring and a kettle, and he made toast on the gas fire at the end of the room. The toast was good and he had some great strawberry preserve that he had 'coaxed out of Fortnum's just before the festivities.' There was also rich, creamy butter, golden in a lordly dish.

'Home farm?' she asked him.

'Guilty.' He looked point nine of a shade sheepish and she said, 'No need to feel guilty. Home farms are very nice things to have in the family. Please go on. I want to have Two-Faced Golly on toast, just like this.'

'We went in mob-handed and found nobody at home, except a pair of dykey girls in the flat one floor up. I think we disturbed them. Anyway they had a touch of the vapours and I had to be kind and gentle, and tell them we needed a word with Golly.'

'We need to talk to Golly,' he said, and Dawn from the flat upstairs looked dropped on.

'He's usually here. Maybe he's gone home with Lavender,' she said, all of a'tremble.

Dandy Tom looked across at Suzie who was taking a bite of toast dripping with butter. 'Guess where Lavender lives, heart.'

'Tell.'

'Lavender has a house in Camford. Dyers Road. Number fourteen.'

Suzie's jaw dropped.

'So, heart, I rang your colleague, WDC Shirley Cox, and she went along to Dyers Road and chatted up Lavender. Golly has stayed there occasionally, but he's gone to spend Christmas with his old mum.'

The state of play at this hour was, two constables and Molly Abelard round the corner
from Rupert Street, just in case Golly returned. Out in darkest Hampshire there were four
constables and a Home Guard detachment
waiting in the dark, watching to see when they
were up and about in Ailsa Goldfinch's
cottage. 'She's an elderly lady and it'll be
alarming for her, so I've told them to hang on
'til dawn. There's a light on downstairs, but no
movement and it's silent as the grave.' He
wasn't worried about Golly. Golly was probably having a good sleep, and another four
uniforms and a car would be arriving at first
light. With any luck they'd have Golly in the net
soon after six thirty. In any case he wanted
them to wait for the car. Didn't want premature ejaculatory Home Guard people dragging
Golly Goldfinch along the road.

'And if he's not there?'

'Perish the thought. More coffee?'

'Please. But if he really isn't there?'

'We send the lads into the highways and
byways; compel him to come in. They'll find
him. We'll bracket him, then we'll move in and
nab him, feel his collar. Okay, heart?' That
smile again, the ravishing one that started at
the corner of his mouth then spread right
up his face. That, coupled with the 'heart'
seemed to do the trick. He had a special way of
saying that one word that shrunk everything
down to the two of you and nobody else.
Magic, she considered. Pure, unadulterated

white sparkling magic, heart.

And he didn't overuse it, or use it indiscriminately. He was careful and protective in its use.

Great heavens, Suzie sighs silkily. I want to explore him inside and out. Preferably outside first. Then, when I know every smooth, subtle inch of his skin, and when I've explored every fold in it, and after he's lit my fire about two million times, I'd like to check into his head. Mainly to see what he doesn't know, because I think he probably knows practically everything, so he'll make up for my deficiencies. Between us we could be one decent human being.

She asked him to kiss her, but he said certainly not. 'It's not that I don't want to, Suzie. It just wouldn't be right. This place is like a cathedral and you wouldn't steal a kiss in St Paul's, now would you?'

She supposed not, then the telephone on his desk started to ring and they both knew, by its shrillness, that it was bad news. It certainly broke the mood in more ways than one, because it was Bert speaking from darkest Hampshire. He carried news of Mrs Ailsa Goldfinch.

She looked at her watch. It was seven a.m. Didn't time fly when you were cruising off among the stars?

'Since the first moment I saw you,' she said to her Dandy Tom.

'Never happened to me before,' he said.

'Never ever happened to me.'

Twenty-Three

There were four Home Guard private soldiers with rifles round the back of the cottage, among the trees, and three at the front, standing well away from the hedge, with a pair of coppers at the back as well and two, including a sergeant, at the front.

'You sure those rifles work?' the police sergeant asked, very sarky, as they made their way towards the cottages.

'Course they work. We were all out on the range with them last month. This is a squad of picked men, Sergeant. Expert shots.'

'Picked bloody men, I should cocoa. Sooty Gibbs the sweep, Arthur Arbury from the outfitters, Fishy Whitcombe, Bill Badger from Ladies Fashions, Fanny Farmer from the Gasworks, and young Aubrey Kent who delivers groceries on a Saturday. I bet you're giving Hitler the heebie-jeebies.'

'Trained men,' replied Bill Cotterel who ran the toy shop with the two Miss Lewises and didn't have a girlfriend, which was the cause of a lot of talk. 'Trained men.'

'How come you got those rifles anyhow?' The sergeant pressed home his assault. 'I've heard tell there's a lot of Home Guard units armed only with pikes and old bayonets.'

471

'Well, we're lucky. The whole area's lucky because we've got them from the Grammar School Armoury, from the OTC, Officers Training Corps. Eight Lee-Enfield Mk IV .303s and plenty of ammo an' all.'

They stopped the chattering as they drew close to the cottages where they split up and waited, shivering with cold in the dark.

Around twenty past six, as the sky started to streak into a lighter shade of grey, and a rusty stain spread along the base of the clouds, a police car came rolling down the lane, free-wheeling, out of gear, its engine switched off. And with the car came a uniformed inspector full of importance, carrying a revolver and the latest technical marvel in the fight against crime – a megaphone that transformed your voice through its little microphone, magnifying and projecting your speech and, more often as not, distorting it out of all recognition.

There was a flurry of whispered instructions from the inspector – 'When I give the order, rush the door ... but *not* until I give the order...'

'When he gives the order...'

'Who?'

'...rush the door. Who d'you think? The Inspector...'

'*Not* until he gives the order...'

'Home Guard, if I tell you to shoot, you will fire over people's heads, unless I instruct you otherwise.'

'Won't make no difference, none of them is going to hit anything,' muttered the police sergeant, ' 'cept us, perhaps.'

There followed a lengthy wait while young Aubrey Kent was sent scuttling round the back to pass on the instructions.

Then – 'This is the pol...' The rest was lost in a screech of electronic scribble that finally disappeared. '...the police. This is the police.' More distortion. 'All occupants of Number One The Cottages come to the front door and leave the building with your hands on your heads. I repeat...' This, or variations of it, were repeated three times and the sergeant switched on the portable spotlight, aiming it at the porch, even though daylight was starting to lift the gloom.

Here comes a candle to light you to bed,
And here comes a chopper to chop off your head.

Children, bleary eyed, hung out of the up-stairs windows of the second cottage, wanting to see what all the fuss was about.

Not a sound from Ailsa Goldfinch's cottage, and the inspector was getting antsy. One last try with the megaphone, after which his options ran out.

'Armed Home Guard cover me. We're going in.' The inspector sounded very uncertain, so added in a lower voice, 'Sergeant, you and one constable go ahead. Smash the door down if you have to. I'll be right behind you.'

They clattered across the lane with the Home Guard lads flinging themselves down in the prone position on the iron-hard earth, rifles aimed at the door with their safety catches, sadly, in the *on* position. The sergeant and constable had their truncheons out, banging at the door.

Nothing.

'Break it down,' the inspector ordered and the sergeant leaned forward, turned the door-knob and pushed. The door opened inwards against a dead weight. The sergeant pushed harder and thought there was a bundle of old clothes in the way. Then he saw the blood and the pulverized face.

'Christ,' he said and threw up all over Ailsa Goldfinch's legs.

The face was a pulp, the bones broken and the flesh ruptured in a dozen places. Her dentures had fallen from her mouth, making it look as though they had been ripped out together with the gums, because a lot of blood had somehow found itself gushing out of the mouth. The head lay strange and crooked to one side, the result of the neck being broken by whoever threw the walking stick across her throat and then put their weight on it. The stick lay nearby as though cast truculently aside. It was covered in blood.

Golly's goodbye kiss.

They brought Abelard back for the conference, leaving the two DCs still on surveillance, covering Lavender's building. They had been there for some time now and had only seen Dawn – from the flat above – come out with her girl-friend. Dawn was really fed up with the police presence and hoped they would go away before she started working again tomorrow. Friday.

Golly's reappearance was unlikely as yet, the Detective Chief Superintendent said. 'It's not really on the cards that Golly's going to make it into London this quickly. Unless he's grown aerodynamically unsound wings on his ankles like Mercury, messenger of the gods.'

He had put down the telephone after talking to Bert in Hampshire, so Suzie was the first person to get the news. 'Golly's out of control, heart,' he said, and told her they'd found the battered body of Ailsa Goldfinch in her cottage.

A couple of hours later he held the conference for all his Spear Carriers except for Dave, Pete and Bert, who were still working the crime scene in Overchurch. Dandy Tom had spoken to the constabulary in Andover and arranged for his three lads to join whoever was taking a look at the Goldfinch cottage. 'No harm in having the lads there. They know what to look for.' He sounded distracted, as well he might. 'They'll see things the local helmets won't even think about.'

The sense of distraction had vanished by the time he rose to address the Spear Carriers. As ever, he was brisk and concise, telling them there was now a good case against Golly Goldfinch, who, it seemed, had done away with his mum sometime late on Christmas night or early Boxing Day morning.

'Means we have to pull out all the stops. Lightning fast. Full-scale manhunt to be called "Operation Bullring". Comb the ground

475

between Whitchurch and London: search woodland, barns, empty buildings, any possible hiding place. Deny the countryside to Golly Goldfinch. Cut him off and hunt him down before he gets into London and has another go, object of the exercise really.'

For the last hour and a half Tommy Livermore had been on the telephone arguing, wheedling and pleading with representatives from other constabularies: Hampshire; Dorset, in case he ran the other way; Berkshire, and right up through Surrey into Greater London.

'He'll try to get back into London because he's botched one killing.' He put his hand on Suzie's shoulder and filled in the blanks regarding Charlotte's death: outlining his theory that Golly would possibly be obsessed with vengeance, his heart set on killing the right person. 'Suzie's agreed to be our tethered goat,' he told them.

She had agreed no such thing, but it stood to reason that the obvious way forward was to have her staked out in some quiet place where Golly could get at her. In any case she was so besotted with Dandy Tom that if he had said, 'Stand on your head in the Dilly,' she'd have gone straight down, done it and hang the indignity.

'This is all Grade A blind, deaf and dumb stuff. The full three wise monkeys.' As he had already told them, he had spent the past hour and a half pleading his case to the top brass of various police forces – the prime movers being the Commander (Crime) at the Yard; the chief constables of assorted counties, and the Commissioner of the Metropolitan Police who wanted the whole business tied up yesterday, or quicker if they could manage it. Nobody was going to be happy until Golly was under lock and key.

Dandy Tom explained that he was more inclined to put a blanket over everything. There was a ninety per cent possibility that Golly was being manipulated. 'Trust me,' he said now, just as he'd already said to the top brass. It was almost impossible to get the powers that be to listen to him.

'Laid it all out, as one does. Response was we can argue about that later. Most important job is to get Golly into a dungeon in chains and surrounded by the Guards Armoured Division to keep him in.' They had done everything but suggest that the ' 'Orrible Murder by Disfigured Crazy Bloke' would help the war effort. 'Took me a terrible time to persuade them that two arrests are better than one, my view.'

In the end he had done the trick and they met him half-way. He had until Monday morning to nab Golly. If they hadn't got him by midnight on Sunday there'd be a statement to the press and the BBC, complete with photographs, not that pictures would do any good for the BBC, who'd closed down its meagre TV broadcasts at the beginning of the war.

'This is the man we're really searching for,' the press handout would say. 'Come forward anyone who has a clue and, Detective Chief Superintendent Tommy Livermore go back to directing traffic up the Mall and round Buck House now, no messing.'

First thing Monday there would be banner headlines saying that they were really searching for this unfortunately disfigured chap who's a nut case, and has been going round choking people with a bit of piano wire, and racking up quite a score. And please would everyone have a good look round, keep your eyes peeled and all that, eh?

'So, that's it. We've got three days, because you can't count today. Yes, Billy?'

Mulligan's hand shot up. 'What's to stop our comrades in arms from blowing the gaff to the press, Guv?'

'Absolutely nothing, except the brass've agreed not to spill the beans, even to their own people. I agree, Billy, rather trust a school of sharks but I've no option.'

Until midnight on Sunday the manhunt was to run under the cloak of being a military exercise in collaboration with some army units and the Home Guard, hence 'Bullring'. He had even scrounged a couple of Lysander aircraft, and they would be in play by first light tomorrow. To add further realism they were asking real estate agents to check empty properties.

'And good luck to them,' Tommy Livermore said. 'I gather they'll be warned that the exercise is to be realistic, and told to speak softly and carry a big stick.'

'Anything goes,' he told them. 'All options open. Golly's as cunning as a bag full of blue-based baboons and he'll probably travel only by night, but I wouldn't bank on it.'

This last raised a laugh.

The first combined police and Home Guard squads for 'Bullring' were to be marshalled by two experienced trackers who were being flown south from the commando school: Achnacarry in Scotland. These squads would be spread out in a line around a mile to a mile and a half long. 'They'll start as soon as possible from a point just the other side of Basingstoke,' he gave them a map reference, 'and they'll head in the general direction of Reading. Combing the ground and flushing Golly Goldfinch out.'

'And we're not going with them, Guv? That'll make a change,' from one of the lads.

'We'll stay here and prepare for trapping him when the manhunt fails.'

'That an option, Guv?' from Shirley Cox, who was making herself comfortable with Dandy Tom's unit.

'More than an option, Shirley. It's a definite possibility. Golly Goldfinch may not be a fully loaded gun, but he's sly and I wouldn't put it past him to evade them. The trick with a man like Golly is to lure him, like you do a trout. And I think we've got the perfect fly for him. Any more questions? No? Well, remember, this is a training exercise, and you've never even heard of Golly Goldfinch.'

At five-thirty Golly let himself out of the back door, sniffed the air and thought he could scent snow, then he slunk quietly away from

479

the buildings and made for the open countryside. He never travelled very far from the roads
and lanes that ran past Basingstoke, but by
seven he was close to Old Basing and could
make out the church with houses huddled in
its shelter. He was also aware of more traffic
than last evening: people he supposed were
going home after visiting friends over Christmas. For a lot of people it would be back to
work in the morning.

He noticed quite a few high-sided three-ton
military trucks, and motorcycles. He knew the
trucks because he had seen a lot of them in
London since the start of the war, and he knew
they were full of soldiers because as the trucks
went along the roads he could hear a raucous
singing; and some of the words were carried
back to him on the freezing air.

People like Golly, men and women who are
different, often have special talents. They can
sense things, and tonight Golly sensed danger
and difference. Somehow he knew he was
being hunted. He wondered how and why,
because he hadn't done anything since the
woman policeman – or the woman he thought
was the woman policeman. Why would they be
searching for him, then? He used primitive
logic and reasoned that it wasn't a personal
matter. They were simply searching for the
man who had killed the woman in Overchurch,
and they were taking it seriously, that's why
they had the Army in as well as the police. He
would have to be on his guard.

As he got to the other side of Old Basing,

480

looking out over the dark fields ahead he saw shapes moving and heard noises coming over a great distance, as they do at night. He'd have to hang back because he could just make out these men walking slowly in a long line, spanning a couple of fields at least.

A motorcycle roared up the road to his right, and he stood stock still, not moving, until it slowed down and stopped. Close to the hedge he realized there was a roadblock ahead, like the one he had seen last night. So he crawled gently up to the hedge and listened to the crack. There was always a bit of good crack when there were soldiers or policemen about.

The ditch ran along his side of the hedge, so he rolled into it making his way forward, crawling on his hands and knees until the roadblock was about five yards in front of him. Three or four men stamped their cold feet in the middle of the road trying to keep warm, talking among themselves.

'So we'd best put faces and personalities to the victims, Suzie with a zed.'

The Spear Carriers were back at work, Abelard had returned to her surveillance off Rupert Street and the lads manned the telephones. It was almost six o'clock. Tomorrow, he told her they would give her what he called 'A short course in survival, just in case.'

'Just in case of what?'

'Just in case Golly gets through and comes after you.'

Her stomach flipped and she couldn't work

out whether it was Dandy Tom's presence or fear of Golly coming for her with the wire.

He laid out folders and a large book, then escorted her up to the map of the UK. For the first time she appreciated the wide area the killer had covered. A lot of miles and a random list of victims.

'Why the blazes weren't all these linked to one man before this?'

'It's what I asked; and there's no simple answer, heart. The fellow's clever, for one. He may be unstable, obsessive, and short on one kind of intelligence. And it's possible that he's been manipulated. My point of view, just a gut feeling. That apart, he's never been seen – except for two glimpses near Stratford. If it is really Golly, then he has the ability of will-o'-the-wisp.' He was also cool and calm, Suzie thought. 'He worked very fast; even hung about at the scene of his atrocities, almost until the last minute.'

'And one of the obvious motivations is sex.'

She looked back at the map, made a little moue, wondered how much crime, how many murders, had sex as the prime mover.

'There is another side to it,' Tommy Livermore continued. 'Most of the people he's picked all have an easy suspect in their lives, close to them. The reason why so few of these cases have been linked to one another is because the investigating officers have suspected, chosen, and concentrated on one person. They've been isolated. Damn it, in the case of Debbie Howlet – Owlet, as she was known to her friends – there's a man actually doing time for her murder.'

Suzie frowned.

'See why I've been playing this close to my chest?'

'And you're sure this one – Owlet? – can be pinned on to Golly.'

'Make up your own mind, but there are going to be red faces in some county constabularies when we get him.'

'Tears before bedtime?'

He nodded. 'Bucketsful.' He touched the map, and pointed. 'Here we go,' he began, 'October 24th 1938. Mary Elizabeth Tobin. Aged sixteen. Ealing Common.' He opened the book and there was a cheeky looking girl staring back at them. Oval face, nice smile, slightly thick lips, dark hair cut in a bob. Tommy Livermore told her the background – father, Ambrose, was a storekeeper in a factory the other side of Ealing that dealt with fancy glassware. Mother, Peggy, housewife, had met her Ambrose in the 1920s at a dance. Live wires, settled down once they were married and Mary Elizabeth was on the way. On the way probably before they tied the knot. Mary Tobin was intelligent but didn't apply herself at school.

'Man mad,' her father said. She was in the second year of her first job, in a local cinema. Usherette. 'All them films turned her into a dreamer,' her mother told a newspaper. 24 October was a Monday, and Monday was Mary's day off. No cinema on Sundays and the two days following the weekend were slow days. Four usherettes, two of them got Mondays off and the other two got Tuesdays. 'Used the house like a hotel,' her father wailed, the eternal litany of parents.

'She'd gone up West for the day,' Tommy said, 'in her best Sunday clothes, a beige suit, her raincoat and a beret. What she actually did was meet a forbidden boyfriend.' Her dad had told her she was never to see him again because there was evidence they were 'going too far'. She had gone too far with him on 24 October as well, in a flat they'd borrowed from a friend of his in Harrow. They'd had a meal in Lyons Corner House, Marble Arch. Then they went to the pictures – *Rebecca* from the Daphne Du Maurier novel, starring Laurence Olivier, Joan Fontaine, George Sanders and Judith Anderson – then over to Harrow where they'd been at it like stoats, according to the pathology. But she *was* raped later on Ealing Common. Underclothes found several yards from the body and they'd done tests on what was left. Very difficult.

The DI in charge of the case had given a lot of time to Mary Tobin's prohibited boyfriend, Danny Taylor. Interrogated him with extreme hostility. Taken samples from him – forensics. Drew a blank. The DI, a man called Bligh – as in the mutiny – gave up hounding him with great reluctance. Tommy Livermore had spoken to him. 'Still thinks the lad was implicated in some way, even though all the evidence is against it.' Poor little bobbed Mary Tobin.

He showed her the pictures of the crime scene. Not the kind of thing you'd see in your local photographer's window, but she'd looked at worse. Tommy went into the minutiae of the murder, every tiny detail and then some. He made Mary Tobin live again, breathed life into her, described her laugh as Danny had so vividly described it – 'Like two sweet chiming bells, that was the sound of her laugh. You'd get a whole peal of them when she was really happy.' Great resurrectionist, Dandy Tom. As she listened to him, Suzie began to feel close to these murdered girls. After all she was one of this sisterhood by Charlotte's blood. She shivered, and wondered about the location of her own grave, and how ready it might be.

He moved on to Mrs Geraldine Williams, aged twenty seven, in her kitchen far away in the North East: in the nice little semi-detached house in Northumberland Avenue, Jesmond, that pleasant suburb of Newcastle-upon-Tyne with its beauty spot, Jesmond Dean, where people enjoyed the trees and the ornamental lake and the Repertory Theatre, where they put on a different play each week.

Dandy Tom filled in the particulars. Geraldine Harkness had been married for two years. No children, but there were rumours that things were not going well with the couple. There had been straws in the wind before the wedding, at St John's, Newcastle. Indeed, Geraldine had nearly backed out of things only a week before she was married.

Arthur Williams, the groom, was a fiery little

Welshman: short-tempered and self-opinionated, a clever electrical engineer who had landed himself an excellent job with the NES – the Newcastle Electricity Supply Company.

It had been a stormy romance, and the marriage was, after two years, if not stormy at least passing through troubled waters. On the morning of 14 January 1939, Geraldine had gone down to the shops at eleven o'clock, red hair bouncing against her shoulders, dressed very smartly. 'Always smart, Geraldine was,' said the woman who sold her the fish. 'You never saw her out without a hat and gloves. Very modish.' She had bought two plaice fillets, presumably for their evening meal, a small lamb chop and a packet of twenty Craven A cigarettes, with the black cat on the packet. She was killed while she was grilling the lamb chop and doing a few chips to go with it for her lunch.

When Arthur Williams came in, unexpectedly, at ten to one she was dead on the kitchen floor and whoever killed her had thoughtfully removed the chop from the grill and taken the chip pan off the hob, substituting a pan of water – already simmering when Arthur came in. It was quite clear that she had been raped, her skirt was up, underclothes were missing and there were four jagged cuts made near to the junction of her thighs.

When he showed her the photographs, Suzie said it was as though the killer was trying to cross out her sexual organs. Dandy Tom thought that was a most perceptive comment.

Of course, the local police said. And again, of course. Arthur Williams came home unexpectedly, killed his wife, raped her and rearranged the scenery. Then he went out once more and drove round the block. When he returned he was able to walk in and yell blue murder.

One of the reasons the murder didn't get much publicity down South was because the CID up in Newcastle believed they had a good case. No matter that they had nothing really firm to go on. Nobody had seen Arthur until he drove up to the house at ten minutes to one, when three people actually saw him arrive, looking calm and unruffled. There were twelve men and women who had either seen or served Geraldine when she went down to the shops. Nothing else: nobody saw a third person enter or leave the house; nobody heard anything untoward; and Arthur could account for all his movements from eight thirty that morning until twelve fifteen when he left a job to drive home, because he was working in the area. Yet the police spent nine and a half months trying to break Arthur Williams' alibi, or make the facts fit. They never did, and now Arthur was a sergeant pilot in the RAF and married to a girl he had met in Harwell, Oxfordshire, where there was an Operational Training Unit for Bomber Command.

Gillian Hunt, 7 February 1939, had a flat near the famous Birmingham Repertory Theatre where she worked as an assistant stage manager. Eighteen years old, learning her trade, being paid a pittance but the little flat was rent free, one of the perks. Again it was a lunch time. She had hurried back to the flat to grab a bowl of soup she'd made over the previous two days, out of a ham bone and vegetables.

They were rehearsing *Antigone* and had broken for ninety minutes at noon. Her closest female friend, Daphne Strong – another ASM – would never forgive herself. She usually shared lunch with Gill, but she had to go to the post office to deal with several small but urgent matters like cashing a postal order from her aunt and posting her laundry back to her mother. 'If I'd gone with Gill, as usual, I'm sure this would never have happened,' she told the *People*.

Again there was a man: older, married with the extra-marital relationship already on the blink. 'My fault,' the man, Percy Bankman, told the police. 'She was such a splendid girl. I shouldn't have led her on. We both knew it was wrong, but I never told her how wrong—' His wife was pregnant and he had behaved unforgivably, embarking on an affair that was totally one-sided. At the beginning Gill was very committed, prepared to wait for a divorce. Didn't realize that she was being used: a sexual stopgap. 'Divorces don't grow on trees,' Dandy Tom said apropos of nothing.

It was the Bankmans' third child, and the police had a field day, discovering he had found surrogates for sex during the closing stages of all his wife's pregnancies. During the first days of the investigation it became clear that Dianne Bankman, the wife, had known about his adultery for several weeks. Her sister was interviewed and told the police that Dianne had given Percy an ultimatum: either she goes or I do. Percy had a problem because that was roughly what Gill was also saying to him by this time and he didn't want to give up either of them.

It was from Gill's sister, Georgina Hunt, and her friend Daphne Strong that the police had built up a picture of the murdered girl: long legs, great figure, a bit of a gypsy to look at, pitch black hair and large dark eyes. She was demonstrative, tactile and very confident. 'Had a wonderful speaking voice, better than most actresses,' Daphne said. 'She was determined to learn all she could about the theatre.'

Daphne told the police, 'There are some lines in *Hamlet* that always make me think of Gill – "You would play upon me; you would seem to know my stops; you would pluck out the heart of my mystery; you would sound me from my lowest note to the top of my compass." That *was* Gill, absolutely. She was a great manipulator, but didn't realize it. In many ways an innocent, but warm and soft. Pliable if you like, while she, unknowingly, beguiled others.'

And Percy had nothing in the way of an alibi. He said he was on a train from London to Birmingham New Street at the time of the death, but nobody recognized him and he hadn't kept the ticket. Worse, he had stayed with a friend in London the night before but the friend, who was a bit of a toper, hadn't got

489

the dates right, so didn't give him the alibi he so desperately needed. Once more, a local police force thought they had him bang to rights, went for him with all guns blazing. Even now, to this day, like the Geraldine Williams case in Newcastle, there were CID officers who still believed Percy Bankman had killed the girl.

So, Dandy Tom leaped forward to 20 April and Pamela Lynne Harwood. Pam Harwood, thirty-one years of age, a barmaid by trade, stumbling half drunk that April evening, her short, straw-coloured hair dirty and in need of shampoo, too many boyfriends to be healthy. A mess, now dead under the walls of Dover Castle with few clues to unravel the puzzle. 'Not elementary, my dear Suzie.' Cause of death a piano wire ligature and a deranged volley of knife thrusts. If ever there was a case that should have been matched up it was the sad and sorry death of Pam Harwood.

The killings went on unconnected, as if the collators and criminal records people were blind. Brenda Bishop, a blowsy bottle blonde who used too much makeup and was closer to forty than she was to thirty. 'A loud girl, our Brenda,' said a local publican. A loud, vulgar, common piece. 'I think this was her destiny,' said a friend. 'I'm not being crude, but she seemed to fit the part – murder victim, know what I mean?' Southampton, 24 May 1939. This one was very violent: windpipe crushed in her throat, a fury of knife thrusts and cuts. She had fought and the killer had gone mad when she was dead as though killing her several times.

Sarah Tewksbury in Harrogate, nineteen, librarian, a bit of a prude, no sense of humour. 'Could be a bit shrill,' a friend told the police. 'Harsh,' said her immediate superior at the library. 'Never seemed to make the most of herself.' Dead in her kitchen by a wire ligature and stab wounds, 5 June 1939. Among the books in her little rented house were unexpected finds, some pieces by the Marquis de Sade – *Justine* and *Juliette* – in English, printed in Egypt, and a lurid book titled *The Kiss of the Whip* by nobody recognizable. In her wardrobe scandalously erotic and tarty underwear. They never uncovered what she got up to, or with whom. The investigation was still open. 'Not all of the local forces seem to agree with us as yet,' Dandy Tom said before passing on to:

Stephanie Cross, a Canterbury girl. Eighteen years old, a devout Christian, just left school and trying to make up her mind about her future. Helping in the cathedral bookshop, part-time and living at home. Father, mother and brother Donald were away on 20 July – going to see old friends in Margate. When they returned at seven that evening there was their lovely daughter, choked in the kitchen. The photographs of her before the murder showed a ravishing natural blonde, sun-tanned, bright, intelligent. Apart from the photograph there was not much to go on – the headmistress of her school, four or five friends. 'You get the feeling that she was still a child,' Tommy said, 'still a bit of a blank page waiting for a life to be written on it. And now that's not going to happen.'

The terrible waste weighed in on Suzie. All these girls robbed of their real time, some destroyed before they'd even lived. Like me, she thought. If he came after me and killed I would also die before I'd lived. She didn't count school, a secretary's job, working in a Knightsbridge store, and being a woman cop as living. Not in any real sense. There had to be more. Had she almost stumbled across the more with Dandy Tom Livermore?

In August '39, it was a case of too much detail. Debbie Howlet, known to her friends as Owlet, thirty-three, hotel receptionist. Lively. Put herself about. Before the present job in York she had been learning the hotel trade in Switzerland, but had come home quite suddenly after what was called 'a bit of a scandal' with one of the guests in Zurich. The Swiss were not amused, which is normal with a people who accept mistresses as long as they are kept at bay in the next town, and had one of the highest suicide rates in Europe. In this case it was obvious that the man had made the running while the lady got the blame. 'It's the same the whole world over, ain't it 'alf a bleedin' shame?' Tommy Livermore sang in a cracked and strained cockney.

Before Zurich, Debbie had tried her hand working at a hotel in Dublin, then a spell serving in Marks & Spencer in Bath, and latterly a few months managing a cinema in Leeds.

Finally she moved to York in the May of '39 and in between there were boatloads of boyfriends. 'Marched off the boat and straight into her bed,' a detective sergeant was supposed to have said. The officer in charge of the investigation caused an unpleasant rumpus after telling a reporter that, as far as he could see, 'her knickers could've understudied a yo-yo'. It was printed in the *News of the World* to the disgust and delight of many.

She didn't live on the premises of the Bishop's Parlour, where she was the receptionist, but round the corner in a tiny basement flat, where she was found dead of the usual method on 9 August – a Friday. The current boyfriend, Nicholas Booker, also thirty-three and prone to violence, was arrested and charged the next day. Booker was brought to trial, protesting innocence, but found guilty and sentenced to death, dragged from the dock shouting, 'I never done it!'

The appeal failed but the sentence was commuted to life imprisonment, because there was concern over the police holding back evidence that could have assisted the defence.

He was still in jail, in Dartmoor, and still saying he never done it.

By this time (it was nine o'clock in the evening) Suzie found it all too much, surrounded as she was by the ghosts of Golly's victims whom Dandy Tom had conjured from their graves. Indeed, Dandy Tom had become incredibly single-minded. He had made Suzie hear the voices of the dead, look into their sad eyes and smell the strawberry or melon scent of their hair. He had come so close to breathing life into them that she could almost explore their bodies. They thawed from their cold stone state into pulsing flesh and blood again under his lengthy erudite command of language.

'Now we know that these piano wire killings are down to one bloke, we can try and slot it all together. With things of this nature, investigation's often like peeling off the layers of an onion.'

Suzie had a mental picture of herself in some dreamlike kitchen peeling onions. 'Tommy, I've had enough,' she protested, quietly so as not to frighten the lads.

'We've only got Cooke at Snitterfield and Marie Davidson at Trumpington, then we're home and dry. Into Jo Benton and the rest. Let's get on with it, heart. Finish it. It'll only take a half-hour. Probably less.' Dandy Tom sounded positively ghoulish.

'I've got the message.' She looked at him imploringly, and he melted, telephoned a little place he knew, tucked away up near Covent Garden. 'They get the choicest titbits,' he said. And they also had introductions to the porters over at Smithfield, the city's principal meat market. 'Under control,' he told her. 'Make yourself comfy and I'll feed you, okay?'

She said it was more than okay, and nearly forgot herself, almost kissing his cheek in front of the lads. Then, just as they were leaving, Bert rang from Hampshire and they were delayed a further twenty minutes as Tommy listened to the scenes-of-crime man go on about what he'd found in Ailsa Goldfinch's cottage.

He got Brian, his favourite driver, to take them over to Covent Garden in his, Tommy's, private car, a lean and hungry looking maroon Daimler that smelled of polished leather. 'Brian, Sergeant Mountford and I are on urgent police business,' Dandy Tom said.

'So I see, sir, and I couldn't be more delighted.' Brian was smiling as they drew up a stone's throw from the restaurant, hidden away in a side street. Tommy took her hand, held on and led her along the dark street; long confident strides, his strength flowing through the firm grip. She almost had to run to keep up with him.

He was obviously known in the place, 'Mr Livermore, sir. I'm so delighted you could come.' A white-haired French *patron*, conducting them to their table in the long, narrow room, and his wife coming out from behind the tall cashier's desk. The room was half full, many of the men in strange uniforms, Poles, Suzie thought. Poles and Czechs. The prettiest girls were with French officers and the room smelled of wine, bread and pungent cigarettes. At the far end, in front of the cashier's desk was a large piece of white card with 'All Clear' written on it in heavy green crayon. No doubt the words 'Air Raid in Progress' could be found on the reverse, written in red.

'And how is His Grace?' the *patron* asked, signalling for the headwaiter to take over. 'And

Lady Eunice. They are well?'

'Excellent health and spirits, thank you.'

'And *madame*.' He bent low towards Suzie as she took her seat.

'On great form, thank you.'

She asked for a Dubonnet; Tommy ordered a gin and tonic and the instructions were passed down the chain-of-command, from the *patron* to the headwaiter to the bar waiter. 'And a bottle of your 72,' Tommy added. 'If you have any left.'

Finally settled in the restaurant, Suzie realized her appetite had returned. She hadn't really enjoyed a meal since Charlotte's death.

'They haven't given us a menu.'

'Bit of a surprise, heart,' Dandy Tom told her. 'Asked them to whip up a Christmas dinner,' he said, and there it was, a consommé to start, then the full moment of traditional turkey and all the trimmings as the headwaiter said, and Dandy Tom did a little imitation of Oliver Hardy fiddling with his tie and saying, 'Dinner is soived, from the soup to the nuts.'

'Home farm again?' she giggled.

'Only the turkey.' He grinned like a school-boy, and she knew for the first time, looking at his soft, polished and bronzed skin, and the wary reserve in the hazel-flecked eyes, that this was a man who needed to be loved.

So she sat back, enjoyed the dinner, listened to him as he told stories and kept off the matter at hand. Both matters in fact – death and where they were going. It was only when they were drinking a coffee that didn't taste of chicory that she brought them both back to earth.

'So,' she said softly, 'what have we really got here, sir?'

'The two of us?'

'Unless you've been giving me the wrong signals, or I've been reading them badly?' She made this last into a question.

'No, you've been translating me very precisely. As I think I've said before, I knew from the moment I walked into that block of service flats and saw you looking like Christmas Eve. Never happened to me before. Haven't got you out of my mind since. Off-putting, actually, heart.'

He wasn't an 'actually' kind of person, so she looked up sharply and saw he was smiling, making fun of himself.

'I'm glad. It's the same with me, as I know I've already told you.'

'Tell me more,' he asked, so she did, for about twenty minutes, and he listened attentively, and made the right noises at the right places – and meant it. 'Now,' she finally asked, 'what about the maniac we're dealing with? You still want me on the case?' She had been concerned about his manner while he had been going through the details of the killings. She thought maybe he had suddenly developed reservations about working on this case with a woman he suddenly felt strongly about.

He smiled: the slow burn. 'You're quick, heart. You pick up on things. I had some doubts earlier ... not about you, but about what

I may probably have to put you through. All
solved now. One's personal risk can sometimes
obscure the long view. And the long view's
difficult enough at this time in history, because
we're up against another maniac who's pouring
bombs on us and killing several hundred
people a week. Makes it tricky. My point of
view anyway.'

'Tommy – do you like being called Tommy?'

'Darling would be a mite better, heart.'

She was suddenly embarrassed, dropped her
eyes and reached over to cover the back of his
hand with hers. 'What did Bert want?'

'Quite good news. He's found a box full of
goodies at the cottage. It's marked "Golly" and
it was taped up. Inside there was a card addressed to his mum from Cambridge, with the
right date on the franking; a knife; and some of
the missing underwear.'

'Whose?'

'Not sure yet. Have to look through the
reports, but from his description and my
memory it's probably Geraldine Williams and
the Harwood girl. Souvenirs, I guess.'

'You really going to stake me out like a
tethered goat?'

He thought for a moment. 'No, like a sheep.'

They laughed, then she became nervous
again, embarrassed.

'What I think would be best—' he began.

'Can I just, perhaps, get on with the job, and
stay visible – visible to Goldfinch, I mean?'

'It was what I was going to suggest. It would
make it easier for us to keep tabs on you, dear

heart.' That smile would be her undoing. Then he said, 'You weren't happy about the interviews you'd already done. How about giving them a second shot?'

She didn't reply.

'I've forgotten who you've done. Tell me again.'

She went through her list, 'Jo Benton's agent, Webster; the fiancé, Fermin; Squadron Leader O'Dell; the actor, Gerald Vine; Barry Forbes, adviser to the PM; and Josh Dance, at the house agency.'

'You fancy any of them?'

She looked up sharply.

'I mean as possible manipulators?'

'Oh, yes. No. No, not really.'

'What does "not really" mean, darling heart?'

That stopped her dead in her tracks, and she swam in his eyes for a moment. Then, 'Well I've got to see Josh Dance again anyway.'

'Remind me.'

'To ask about Emily Baccus. See if she was connected to anyone else we're aware of. He'd know her history.'

That's who she looks like. Oh yes, of course. Now you see it, now you don't.

'Okay. Give him a ring. Take a look into her family tree. I should be peeping into yours as well.'

'Oh, I'm not nearly good enough for the likes of you, sir.'

'You'd better be.'

Another bit of drowning in each other's eyes.

'So you don't fancy any of the others?'

'I don't see Gerald Vine manipulating Golly Goldfinch. To do what? Deal with that little ASM in Birmingham because she gave him the wrong cue?'

'Barry Forbes?'

'I'd hardly think he'd be getting his own back on any of our victims. He's got enough to cope with advising Mr Churchill.'

'More than enough, because old Winnie's already got some brilliant financial advisers. Can't really see why he wants someone like Barry Forbes. You said he was a bit stroppy.'

'Thinks the sun shines out of his navel and places adjacent.'

'Flint?'

'Desperate Daniel Flint? Could be. Shifty. Small somehow. Small-minded, I mean.'

'Give him another whirl, heart. And this Dance character. You're edgy about him, aren't you?'

'He was wounded in France, before Dunkirk. Devastatingly good-looking, but there's something not quite right there.'

'Take Shirley Cox with you.'

She didn't reply and knew in the far corner of her mind that she wasn't going to do that. 'You are going to keep me covered, aren't you, Tommy?'

'Try and stop me.'

She studied his face for what seemed to be a long time. 'You going to take me home, sir?'

'Why not?'

When they got back to Upper St Martin's Lane he came up with her. Did all the usual

500

things. Checked the rooms, and the fire escape, looked behind the curtains. And in the cupboards, then kissed her in the hallway. Long, satisfying with plenty of sighing between the kisses.

'Will you stay?' she asked. 'I'd feel safer if you stayed.'

'If I asked you to marry me, what would you say, heart?'

'Yes, of course. Yes. I'd say yes. Yes, please.'

'Good. That's settled then. I'll tell my mother tomorrow.' He smiled at her, the smile as long as the last kiss.

'You got a spare room?' he asked.

'Yes.'

'Then I'll stay,' he said. 'No hanky-panky.'

'Oh, yes,' she said. And he kissed her again, and 'Oh,' she said, and 'Ah,' he said.

About an hour later, Suzie gave a little sigh, rolled over and groaned a bit and winced. 'Tommy darling, that means you've got to marry me.'

'Well, of course, heart. My intention, actually. Eh?'

She wondered if her eyes were as bright as his.

'More,' she said.

Golly was in trouble. Over all those years Golly had been in control. Since childhood it was his trick, seeing how long he could remain standing still, in command of his muscles. He was very, very good at it, standing still. In heat and freezing cold. Among trees or lying in bushes,

501

silent in the middle of a field.

And now, in this ditch, his muscles went out of control. He supposed he had overdone it, all night in those trees behind Falcon Cottage, followed by half of the day. That's what had done it. He'd got terribly cold and now, lying here listening, he had spun out of control.

He listened to the men on the roadblock, and couldn't understand half of what they said to one another. They were arguing – 'Bloody "Bullring",' one of them kept saying, kept repeating this one word, ' "Bullring". Bloody "Bullring". I don't believe it for a minute. This is for real. They're saying it's an exercise, but it's real and happening. Why the hell've we got live rounds? Tell me that, if it's an exercise why've they given us live rounds?'

'The officer who briefed us, he said they'd have aircraft up tomorrow. That doesn't sound like an exercise. Does it? What?'

'Yea, he's right,' said another. 'I heard that old Mr Tyler from up Marsh Cross, him that works at Armitage, Simmons & Faulds, estate agents, he's going round all their empty properties, and he's got a couple of policemen with him. They told him to take some protection with him, and he has done. Couple of big seething coppers.'

'This is really happening. They're after someone and don't want to tell us who they're after.'

'Or what?' said a fourth man sounding sinister.

'Yeah. "Operation Bullring". "Operation Bullshit" more like.'

Then the motorbike came up and the dispatch rider cut his engine, and Golly could hear what was said. 'They're about three-quarters of a mile away. Moving really slowly. Be here in about half-an-hour.'

'How much ground they covering?'

'About a mile either side of we here. Probably a little more.'

'And they're moving really slow?'

'About the speed you'd go if you was beating to put up birds on a shoot.'

'They're beating then?'

'Yes. Some've got sticks. But they haven't put anything up yet. 'Bout one in three've got sticks. The others've got rifles.'

'With live ammo?'

'Oh, yes. They got the order to put one up the spout before they set off. They're sort of dragging behind the first lot, the ones that went from the far side of Old Basing. Now, you'm got to dismantle this roadblock. Set it up again about a mile up the road. Mile, mile-and-a-half. That's what they told me.'

It was while they were packing their stuff into their fifteen hundredweight truck that Golly moved, just an inch or two and the cramp bit into him like some animal sinking its teeth into his leg. He was in terrible trouble, didn't know how to control himself. Almost gnawed through his lip with the agony that knotted up the muscles in his right leg.

How will I manage? How am I going to get out of this ditch? He was in real agony. The fifteen-hundredweight went off up the road, loaded with the equipment, full of the soldiers and police who had manned the roadblock, its engine noise dying as it got further away.

He rolled over and pulled himself out of the ditch, hauling himself up, clawing at the grass with his hands. In unbelievable pain he got on to his feet and hopped about, trying to undo the cramp. He jumped on one foot and then the other. Then his foot seized up, the left foot, bent down, arched down and locked so that you could almost hear the pain and couldn't move. He moaned and grunted. But slowly it drained away, leaving a kind of after-pain, so he could hobble about for ten, fifteen, minutes. Then he was exhausted, tired out, drooping.

It was while he was hobbling around that he heard the advancing second wave of beaters, searching as they went, so Golly forced himself to run up the side of the field, then across, to the left, further and further away from the road. A mile, perhaps two miles. In the end he stopped running, breathless, hands on his knees, gasping for breath.

Then he turned to face the noise that the lines of men made going through the fields. Even though he had run at least a mile to the side of them he was only about twenty or thirty yards from the left-hand end of the line.

They're going to have aircraft up tomorrow. Searching.

In the end there'd be nowhere for him to hide, so he stood still as a gravestone and waited until the second line of searchers had gone plodding up the field and into the next field, on and on to the horizon.

Slowly now, Golly made his way back towards the road. Had to have a road to know where he was going. He reached the hedgerow and the ditch he had sheltered in before, and decided to wait until morning. Wait in the ditch. Then, maybe, he'd see somewhere for him to hide up for the day. They've searched this bit, he reasoned. They're not going to search it again. He gathered some sticks and bracken together, thick with rime from the frost, then lay down on them in the ditch. Cold, dreadful cold, he felt, and for a while he drifted off into a lovely dream where Frost Maidens came out of the hedge and ministered to him. Golly didn't really know what that meant – ministered to him – but he had his own ideas, and even in the cold it seemed to work and warm him.

She was standing by the sink peeling a large onion. She held a sharp knife in her right hand and was using it to prise and scrape away the onion's outer skin. The scent of it filled her nostrils, rising up, making her eyes sting and water. Then, like a wind, Golly was suddenly in the kitchen. So fast that she cried out.

She saw his plundered face, rent in two, and the eyes slanted, one high above the other. She saw his sharp, glinting teeth bared, and heard the animal growl from deep in his throat.

He wore leather gloves and held a shining, thick silver loop of wire, and he was hurling himself towards her throat.

She screamed with the dread of it, then screamed again, loud and piercing. He had come to do the deed of darkness, so she screamed once more, shrieked in terror.

She was still screaming as she woke, and was thrashing about in the dream as Dandy Tom, her lovely man, put his arms around her, restraining her, holding her down, shushing her, calming her as she went on shouting hysterically.

'Suzie, darling. It's alright. It's okay. Shush, angel. Shush, heart. Shush – my darling, shush.'

Twenty-Four

Gypsy Petulengro was probably right, Golly thought, waking from a dull, uncertain sleep, lying in the ditch. Gypsy Petulengro was on *Children's Hour* and he talked about nature and the country. Golly liked *Children's Hour* with Uncle David and Uncle Mac. He was particularly fond of *Toytown* with Larry the Lamb and his friend Dennis the Dachshund. Last week, Gypsy Petulengro had said all the signs in the countryside pointed to it being a hard winter. Not quite as bad as last year, but still wretchedly cold. The signs were strong enough – the preponderance of berries and the amount of food animals were storing away. 'Going to be a cold winter,' Gypsy Petulengro said.

And that's how it's looking, Golly thought. For a few moments he imagined his own body had started to freeze. There were parts of him he could not feel, and in the icy darkness the cold burned into him. He sat up, could hardly move, then he managed to clamber out of the ditch again. He had no idea what time it was. 'Always darkest before the dawn,' he said to himself, that's what his mum would say. But it seemed to be getting light. He looked down and his duffel coat was rimed white with thick frost. Can't stay like this, Golly. Got to try and move. So he began trudging along the ditch. He didn't want to stay in the field in case he left footprints in the thick frost. His legs were hard to move, and his feet were locked freezing, so he couldn't feel them. But as he plodded on, so his feet seemed to return. Blood, he thought, flowing again. Under his breath he started to mutter, 'When icicles hang by the wall, and Dick the shepherd blows his nail.' He remembered the bus and the conductor singing, and the young girl in the house out in the countryside, near Stratford. How she screamed. 'When blood is nipped and ways be foul, then nightly sings the staring owl.' Good memory, Golly. 'Birds sit brooding in the snow, and Marion's nose looks red and raw. When blood is nipped and ways be foul.' If he set his mind to it he would be able to remember them all. All the pretty girls. Pretty maids all in a row, and he could see the bodies, lying side by side.

'Ways be foul.'

Golly pulled up the hood of his duffel coat,

pushed his head back and covered most of his face. He needed warmth more than anything in the world. More than the girls even: the lovely girls who did not fight back and were not repulsed by him.

He came to the top of the rise and saw the copse, trees running right up to the hedge, so he turned to the left, into the trees and barrelled on through them. He cut his hand on a trailing branch, barked his shin on a stump, but that didn't matter. Among the trees it was a bit warmer. He needed somewhere to curl up – and he found it. Just enough light to see. A little hide on the tree line, where hunters or birdwatchers could nestle down and wait for game to fly into their sights. There was a door on one side and there had been a padlock but it was broken off, leaving the door swinging. The beaters.

The two long lines of beaters, he decided. They'd gone through the copse like a dose of salts and looked inside to make sure Golly wasn't hiding in the hide. He giggled to himself, slid down and into the snugness of the place, got out the last of the sandwiches his mum had made for him. Ate them up, but left the crusts. Then he curled up. Warmer. Much warmer. Golly curled up and, out of the breeze and the frost hanging in the air, he became more comfortable in no time at all. Then he drifted off to sleep again, and dreamed of long grass and children laughing and their big sisters watching over them. He preferred the big sisters with their long legs and the softness, unprepared for him. Unprepared for death, which was the only way he'd have them.

He slept until the funny aeroplane turned up.

They woke very early, nuzzled each other's hair, then turned their attention to mouths and other interesting parts. Suzie was quite amazed at her unembarrassed lasciviousness. She had now dived deeply into the experience she had wondered and worried about since her early teens and found that, instead of uneasiness, there was a sense of amazement and comprehension.

Eventually they calmed down and she asked him about his theory – the bottled spider thing: the puppeteer pulling Golly Goldfinch's strings, lighting his touch paper, sending him, furious, towards a selected target.

Tommy said he still didn't know, but Jo Benton couldn't possibly be random: her murder had been thought out, the house watched and the deed done at a particular time. 'That one was picked,' he said softly. 'She was an undisputed target, and so were you, heart. I'm sorry.'

Suzie became upset and wept a little. She had yet to grieve fully, for the job got in the way of the anguish. But Dandy Tom was kind, careful, considerate, turning their conversation into a childlike game: about how they could dupe the Spear Carriers, not let them know how they'd spent the previous night.

He made all this into a kids' game, laughing and larking around, just as she used to do with Charlotte. It amazed her that this senior, revered police officer could act the fool and become immersed in plotting such a trivial thing as travelling together to work in a taxi and one of them bailing out in Whitehall as they approached the Yard.

'So which of us is going to jump clear, heart, eh?' He was like a little boy planning to avoid some disliked teacher at school. 'Which of us is going to ride in style and which walk?'

He devised a game whereby they dealt out two packs of cards to each other – 'First one to collect all the aces rides,' he told her bossily, then, she was pretty sure, he cheated to let her win.

When they actually did it, he made a great thing about watching for other colleagues on the pavement as they drove along Whitehall and he finally got the cabby to pull over so he could descend on to the cold streets.

Suzie turned around and watched him as he quickly disappeared into the trickle of hurrying civil servants all heading towards their boring government jobs. Not as many as usual because it was still the Christmas holiday period, but she saw him vanish, almost melt away, his breath hanging in the cold December air, there for a second, then gone. Dandy Tom, she thought, you're a wizard. Someone on the team – she thought it was Laura Cotter – had told her that Tommy was capable of turning into a brick wall when he put his mind to it. She hadn't taken her literally, thought she meant he was stubborn, until now.

Suzie walked into the Reserve Squad offices

with an outwardly severe frown and the smiling inner knowledge that she had achieved womanhood in the space of the last few hours.

Shirley was hanging around waiting for her. 'Skip, you had a chance to talk to the Guv'nor yet? About Big Toe and the Balvaks?'

'Not yet, Shirl, but he'll be in any minute, so why don't you talk with him yourself?' How do I know he'll be in shortly? Now she felt guilty and wondered if Shirley was looking at her in a suspicious way.

Molly Abelard was leaning against Tommy's door. 'We've got the gymnasium for the whole day. Set aside for our personal use. Billy's coming down later on, but I thought we should have a workout first. Eh, Sister Suzie?' The unpleasant edge was back in Molly's manner.

'Sure. Love to. I've just got to make a couple of telephone calls.'

'Well, be quick, then.' Abelard had a bit of a sneer in her lip that said, 'I want to take you apart.'

Suzie took out her notebook, found the number for Daniel Flint in Kensington, asked for it from the switchboard and heard it ring around fifteen times. If it's a business, the operator told her, it might not be opening again until next week. The New Year. She looked up Jewell, Baccus & Dance and asked the operator for GERrard 341, and when she was through – to a listless Miss Holroyd – she asked to speak to Mr Dance.

'Who's on the line, please?'

'WDS Mountford. Susannah Mountford

from Scotland Yard.'

'And what's it in relation to?' The clumsy sentence, the vowels mispronounced or over-stressed.

'I'd just like to speak to him, please.'

'One moment, caller.'

Then he was there. 'Josh Dance.' Pitched low, intense.

'Mr Dance.' She made it sound as though it was making her day just to hear him.

'Miss Mountford, what a nice surprise.'

'I hope you had a good Christmas, Mr Dance.'

'Quiet, you know. Very quiet. What can I do for you?'

'I was thinking of taking you up on that meal. You said any time.'

'Oh.' He sounded surprised, a little taken aback. 'Oh, how delightful. Yes indeed. That'd be lovely. Any particular day in mind?'

She said any time that would suit him, and he said how about Sunday? He was free Sunday night.

'Lovely. What time shall I come?'

'Let's say, five. I know it's early, but it'll give us a chance to have a drink. How would that suit?' A lot of people in London were eating much earlier in the evening because of the raids.

'Fine. I look forward to it.'

'So do I. I'll leave the business door open, so just ring and come in. I'll come down and meet you. Okay?'

'Right.'

512

'See you then.'

She was tempted to say she hoped he didn't think her too forward. No, bugger it, we live in a changing world. Keep him in relaxed expectancy, then hit him with a book full of innocent sounding questions.

Tommy had just come in. 'I've fixed Dance. Sunday evening, Guv. He's cooking dinner for me,' she told him with a sickly smile.

'What about Flint?' he replied, all business.

'Not answering, sir. May not be back at the treadmill until next week. He was going to stay with relatives in the West Country.'

Huge house, she remembered.

Tradition. Big tree in the drawing room. Carols, mince pies, Father Christmas arriving with the local hunt.

'Keep trying him.' She didn't like it that Tommy was being curt with her. Overreacting, she thought. Wouldn't hurt him to drop me a 'heart' now and again.

'Heart,' he called her back. 'Would you like me to do Flint?'

'As you please, sir.' She avoided temptation and didn't add, 'You're the boss.'

She went out being shadowed by Molly Abelard, who, as she left, told Dandy Tom that they'd give Suzie a good going over, which she thought was a bit cheeky.

They went down to the basement and drew standard issue PT kit and Abelard led her into the gym and over to the changing room. The Yard had yet to get around to having separate changing rooms, so there were never mixed workouts in the gym. It was the same in the nearest swimming baths.

Molly Abelard, Suzie noticed, wore sensible underwear with a leaning towards athleticism. On the other hand Suzie was embarrassed because she had dressed in full fig, mainly for Tommy's delight – the white parachute silk French pants Shirley had given her for Christmas, with the suspender belt and nice bra in ivory silk, a present from Charlotte.

'Tart's delight, eh?' Abelard sneered, needling her. What had Tommy said about her?

Have you on your back with a flick of the wrist.

She wondered what Molly Abelard's aggression was about, then thought it didn't matter because she was obviously bent on having some kind of set to. Abelard pulled four large exercise mats into the centre of the gym, making them into a square.

'How much d'you know about self-defence, Suzie?' Bouncing about on her toes like a tough little rubber ball. They both wore shorts and singlets, and Molly's muscles were obviously well toned.

'Oh, just the usual stuff,' she lied, because she had done the advanced course when she was on the beat in Piccadilly and Soho. She reckoned that would help but had no illusions about beating Abelard in a one to one.

Now Abelard had a nasty smirk on her face.

'Okay, just to test your reactions. A few defensive throws.' She moved to the right, then ducked the other way and came in low, hands going for Suzie's right wrist. Tough, I know that one. Suzie lifted her arms, locking her hands together to bring them down behind Abelard's neck. Be careful, you can break someone's neck, she heard an instructor from the past whisper in her ear, then the world turned upside down and she was low flying over the mats. When she shook the fuzz out of her brain she couldn't get up because Abelard was standing over her with a foot in the small of her back.

'Not a good idea to use that two-handed thing,' Abelard laughed. 'You leave yourself open and unprotected – as you've just discovered.'

Suzie turned over as Abelard stepped back, then rolled and made a grab for her foot, intent on twisting and flooring her opponent. But Molly was too fast for her, turning on one foot and catching Suzie as she tried to flip herself on to her feet again. Before she knew it, Suzie was face down with her arms held in a lock behind her back, causing her a nasty stab of pain that went right into her shoulders.

'You're here to learn, Mountford,' Molly snarled, 'not to try half-arsed tricks you haven't mastered properly. And you're too slow by half. Now listen to me and I'll teach you a couple of things.'

How easy it was to make an error, to misread a person or a map and take the wrong turning, make the inaccurate decision as she had done now. She had not seen Molly Abelard's needling for what it was: the spur for anger. She knew the rules, Suzie, and she'd strayed from them, and so been humbled. Now that was over they could start the real work.

First Molly taught her a number of throws and body moves that were not in any of the manuals. Soon she recognized the path they were taking: how not to be caught napping, or off guard.

She still didn't particularly like Abelard, but now met her halfway, acknowledged her superiority in matters of attack and defence, without any weapons except hands, feet, elbows, knees, or anything that came to hand, like the thin splintering wood of a Bryant & May match box. The outer sleeve of a wooden matchbox would break a person's nose if you hit them correctly, but so would a blow from the elbow, administered as you turned and struck sideways on. There was jubilation in it, hitting the right place, manipulating the attacker's body, felling the foe.

Concentrating on attacks from the rear, Abelard taught her how to use swivel techniques, to turn inwards on the aggressor and deal with him by using pressure points of vulnerable areas, like the carotid artery and the nose, then the chin, the eyes and throat. Later Billy Mulligan turned up and, together they went through mental exercises aimed at making her more alert, aware and more intuitive. 'You got to hone your intuition,' Billy kept saying.

Then Suzie learned the secret holds, the places where she could inflict maximum pain with minimum pressure: and so the lesson continued.

Should Golly not be caught, he would certainly come at Suzie from behind and out of the metaphorical sun one of these bright days.

They showered, changed and went up to the canteen for a light lunch. By now Suzie was talking amicably with Molly, learning a great deal about the girl's past. At sixteen she had worked as a waitress on one of Cunard's big liners. Travelled all over for a couple of years. One dark night in Hong Kong she'd been jumped by some foreign sailors, beaten, raped and left for dead. Cunard brought her home in the ship's hospital and when she was fully recovered she concentrated on getting fit and able to fight back. Come to that, able to fight anything. It became a reason for living, an obsession.

'That was quite a time ago,' she said, nibbling a sardine sandwich. 'I got fighting fit and joined the Met.'

'What she really means,' Billy Mulligan said, 'is that she's a Judo Master and a Karate Black Belt.'

Abelard waved a hand, laterally across her face, as if to say he was exaggerating.

'No, Molly, Suzie's working with you. She ought to know,' Billy continued. 'Molly is dangerous. She also did a weapons training course under the aegis of the Royal Marines, and I've heard all the stories. Bootnecks snickered at her when she arrived, but not for long. She beat every man jack of them with rifle and pistol. Got the highest score ever recorded on their range down in Devon.'

Suzie said nothing, but decided she'd rather have Abelard on her side, so they went back to the gym and worked solidly until just after five. 'That's about all I can teach you in the time,' Abelard told Suzie. 'Concentrate on watching your own back. That's the important thing. Look, over the next few days I'll try to sneak up behind you and touch your shoulder. Keep a look out.'

Billy Mulligan had also brought her a short baton, much shorter than the standard issue truncheon, and easier to carry hidden when in plainclothes. 'Very effective,' he said, and Molly showed her some nice moves with it. 'Keep it by you,' she advised.

'The Chief wants to see you, Skip,' one of the lads told her when she got back to the Reserve Squad office and she found Dandy Tom sitting at his desk looking reflective. He motioned for her to close the door.

'I haven't told anyone else yet, heart, but there are fears that we've lost Golly. For a man who's got a few of his pages stuck together he's proving ingenious. Thought we had him lunch-time, but he's gone again. I only hope, heart, that Abelard's managed to give you some of her physical wisdom. As from now she'll be hard on your tail, together with a couple of other people.' There was a bleakness in his eye that she could only read as fear.

She brushed a strand of hair from her forehead. 'Tommy,' she said softly, 'stop tapping your teeth with that blasted pen.'

★ ★ ★

Flight Lieutenant Casimir Szlapka, Royal Air Force, looked to left and right as he flew the Lysander directly over the church at Old Basing, then turned slightly to follow the secondary road south-east. Szlapka wasn't his real name, but an anglicized version. As was Casimir, for the RAF had put his real Christian name, Kazimierz, into their 'Too Difficult' file.

Casimir Szlapka had only recently done a conversion course on to the Westland Lysander. Until this morning he'd been cursing himself for being foolish enough to volunteer for what had been described as 'special duties'. So far he'd had a distinguished war, escaping from Poland last year, making his way to the West, joining the RAF, fighting with great credit through the Battle of Britain. Then, in a moment of anticlimax, going for what he thought would be a new thrill.

As soon as he volunteered he found himself taken off flying his beloved Hurricane and dropped into the long cockpit of the clumsy, slow Lysander. When he complained, the Wing Commander only laughed and said, 'Shouldn't have joined, old boy. They not teach you that in Poland?'

But this morning was different. 'Good experience for you, Cas, this one,' the wing co told him. They had told him, and the other pilot – 'Porky' Piecroft – that they were about to do an aerial search for a wanted criminal. It was real action again with a real target. 'A mad, vicious bloody killer,' they'd said.

The Lysander was an odd-looking kite: high-winged monoplane, long strange-shaped wings, with a fixed undercart, 'spats' on the wheels and a big radial air-cooled Bristol Mercury XX engine under the cowling. It could fly wonderfully slowly, while the pilot had an unprecedented view from the high 'greenhouse' cockpit.

Szlapka and Piecroft were in fact being trained to land in occupied France to drop or pick up agents operating in Nazi held Europe.

Cas Szlapka saw something now as he flew up the side of the secondary road a mile or two on from Old Basing. He had been aware of 'Porky' Piecroft's aircraft several miles away on his port side as he approached the road, then he glanced back to starboard, which was when he glimpsed the irregularity. He lifted the Lysander's nose because the ground sloped upwards towards a copse of pine and fir covering the top of the rise. Gaining a little height, he began a low sweeping turn to port, bringing the aircraft round a full 360 degrees.

Throttling back, he scanned the road and saw it was bordered by a tall thick hedge with a shallow ditch running along the field side of the road. The ground was deep white in a hard frost that even the sun had not begun to shift by this time of late morning. It was bitter and beautiful to see from the air, but something had walked purposefully up the ditch. Not an animal, but someone blundering along. Footprints on the pure white of the field and running up the ditch. Clear as day. At the top, they veered off – undoubtedly human footprints, tracking their way into the copse.

He turned the aircraft again – the slow circle – watching the sun glint harmlessly off the blinding carpet, taking a second look as he came level with the road.

Casimir Szlapka lazily buttoned the strap of his oxygen mask, and clicked down the radio switches. He repeated his call sign three times into the mask, 'Spartan One. Spartan One. Spartan One.' Waited, then heard a voice in his headphones from the ground around eight or nine miles distant. Casimir spoke a terse message, saying that Interloper – the code name for their quarry – was possibly in the copse below him, and repeating a map reference three times. The distant voice acknowledged, and Casimir put some pressure on his starboard rudder pedal, setting a course towards the point where the troops should, at this moment, be tumbling into a fifteen-hundredweight truck ready to drive back and clear the copse for a second time.

Golly heard the snarl in his head and woke, suddenly, didn't know where he was, couldn't place the sound. It came again, and this time he knew what it was, and where he was. He rolled off the bench inside the hide and flushed open the hinged slit that gaped wide, so that he could see out and look down the side of the hedge and the frosted ground sweeping below and away. He had come up along the hedge in the early hours; slept in the ditch; woke; came up here, he remembered, recalling the terrible cold, realizing that he was still numbed by it.

Now he saw the noise, coming as a huge bird hopping above the hedge and sweeping over the trees. He heard the rasp of its engine again and knew it was still close, so close that he crouched down, fearing that it would bring fire on him. Golly did not like fire: didn't know which was worse, the fire or the cold.

It went over again, the flying beast, and this time the sound of the engine began to decrease as it moved away. But it had shown interest: too much interest. Go, he heard the voice in his head. Go now. Get away.

He struggled from the hide, out into the copse, narrowing his eyes against the glare of the sun on the frost, pushing himself towards the hedge, then over and down the deep bank on to the road. On the road he looked around and waited.

Across the road there were more trees and a narrow lane with an archway of pine and fir above it. Golly made the decision and crossed to the lane and as he did so a figure stepped from the trees.

'Well done, Golly. I was just coming for you if you didn't come to me,' and he recognized the voice and the man in front of him, dressed in a smart beige coloured coat and with a flat cap cocked on his head at a jaunty angle.

It was the Mark. The Mark who had helped him with Manny Spellthorne. The Mark who knew his secrets. The Mark who'd been kind to him.

Maybe I'll get a pretty lady to come and whisper

in your ear.

'Come on, Golly, run. Trot. I've a car down the lane. Five minutes and we'll be out of here. It's all right; you're safe now. Safe for the time being.'

Twenty-Five

It was a black Riley saloon car that the Mark had tucked away, covered with branches. He'd slung a blanket over the bonnet together with a patent cover designed to keep the engine warm in a bad frost, such as this. 'Been watching you all the way, Golly,' he said as he got him into the back of the car. 'There's a blanket in there as well. Get down on the floor and cover yourself with the blanket. Get yourself warm.' He began to tear the boughs from the car.

'Cold,' Golly said, his whole body shivering, like an animal in shock.

'There's a heater in the car. Soon as I start her up you'll begin to get warm again.' The Mark climbed behind the wheel and started the engine. 'You keep down, Golly, just in case they're stopping cars again. They were stopping cars yesterday, last night. But don't worry, I'm here and I've always helped you, Golly. And I will again.'

The car moved, backed into the lane, then slowly began rolling forward, bumped a few times on the rough, rutted ground, then slowed and made a turn. In five minutes they were purring along the road, heading away from the searchers in the general direction of Basingstoke.

In the back Golly groaned.

'I'm going the long way round, to London,' the Mark said, but Golly, feeling the warmth, was drifting off to sleep in a euphoric state, almost hypothermic. In his head there was a blue sky, it wasn't cold any more, and yielding young women embraced him, sucking him into the quicksands of sleep.

He slept for four hours, only waking when the Mark shouted at him, clapping his hands, 'Golly! Wake up! Wakey-wakey!' Finally Golly grunted, startled, then asked if there was anything wrong.

'Nothing wrong, Goll. Nothing wrong, but I want to talk to you.'

They weren't driving any more, and Golly pulled himself up in the back of the car, looking out to find they were in some kind of parking place off the road, among trees with the light fading. 'Where?' he asked. 'Where are we, Mark?'

The Mark chuckled. 'We're between the dark and the daylight, Golly. Waiting for the night to lower, a few miles out of London. I don't want to drive in until it's really dark. Don't want to be stopped now we've come so far. The Law's after you, Golly. They're steamed up about you, searching for you.'

'Why?' he said, trying to get his brain around the events of the past days. 'What I done,

Mark?'

'Come on, Golly, you know what you've done.'

'Overchurch. That's it, isn't it? The lady policeman?'

'But it wasn't the lady policeman, Golly. You did the wrong one. I think the lovely lady of the night told you who you had to destroy.'

'Miss Baccus, yes. Told me. The lady policeman.'

'Well, they're looking for you because of that. And because of your mum, Golly.'

'What you mean, my mum? What you mean?' Disbelief.

'You know, Golly.'

'Mark, tell me what you mean. No, I don't know. My mum?'

'Golly, someone did her. Someone killed your mum. It must've been you. You starting to forget what you're up to, Goll?'

'I never. I never. I never did nothing to my mum, Mark. Not my mum. No I never.'

'We'll see, Golly, never mind. They *are* looking for you. The lady policeman's looking for you, and more besides. They've got people watching Lavender's flat. They're out the front, all day and all night. Lucky we found the other way in and out, when you did for Manny Spellthorne.'

Put him on the rubbish tip.

'I never did nothing to my mum. Give her a kiss before I went. Nothing else.'

'Maybe that was it, Golly. Maybe the kiss did it.'

'No ... no ... no...' Golly moaned and rocked in the back of the Riley.

'Come on, Golly. There are things you need to know.'

He continued his keening until the Mark shouted at him. 'Now listen!' He told Golly he'd been into Lavender's flat, had left everything clear so they could get Golly into her bedroom, up through the cupboard. He'd moved the little chest of drawers and everything.

'Isn't she there, then? Isn't Lavender there, Mark?'

'No, she's still on her Christmas holiday. Coming back in the New Year, Goll. It's all empty in her flat and we can get in.'

'Not my mum—'

'Shut up about your mum, Golly. Shut up and listen to me. You're going into Lavender's flat and you'll have to be quiet.'

'They'll see the lights if they're waiting.'

'No they won't. I put the blackouts up before I left. They didn't see me. You can switch the lights on and nobody'll be any the wiser. And listen, Golly, I've got food in there, in the little kitchen. There's tea, sugar, bread, cheese, milk and a chocolate cake. Plenty of cheese and a bottle of coffee. You'll like that.'

So the Mark turned around and drove into London right on into Piccadilly and round the Circus, then off to the back streets and almost into Rupert Street, turning into the entry for the garage that was their secret. The Mark got out and levered up the metal roller blind across the entrance and drove in. He had the key to the passageway as well and he took Golly all the way back into Lavender's bedroom.

'And look,' he said after he'd shown Golly the food, 'I bought these for you as well. Easier than getting out of bed and blundering around for the light switch.' The Mark had brought a box of nightlights, and a small box of Bryant & May matches. Golly put one nightlight by the bed. He agreed this was better than switching on the electric light.

The Mark told him he mustn't answer the telephone, or go out on the landing. The front door was locked. 'I've two keys to the door into the garage. If there's an air raid or anything you'll be able to get out, and I'll be able to get in.' Now, he said that he had to go back to his work, but he'd be up to see Golly tomorrow. Saturday.

Golly stretched out on Lavender's bed, had a rest then got himself some bread and cheese. The Mark had left a jar of home-made pickled onions as well, it said so on the label in ink – 'Mrs Harkness Quality Home Pickles, Monks Risborough, Bucks.' He ate six pickled onions and a big hunk of cheese with four slices of crusty bread. After that he belched and farted loudly, giggled, of course, told himself not to make so much noise and giggled again. Then he found the bottle of Camp Coffee and made himself a cup, drank it and curled up on Lavender's bed: for the first time since before Christmas, he felt safe. He could smell Lavender's scent, on the pillow. Nothing could touch him now.

Golly allowed sleep to creep in on him. He had meant to get undressed, properly, but – even after the four hours of rest – his state of exhaustion was complete. Both his mind and body were depleted and drained. So he fell deeply into a state of unknowing, and as he slept, so someone broke through the thin wall that divides consciousness and slumber.

When Dandy Tom came to Suzie's flat in Upper St Martin's Lane on that Friday evening he came on a little wave of irritation. She left the office just after six without seeing Tommy, because he had been called down to see the Commander (Crime), who was anxious to hear his report on the sequence of this morning's events, when they had lost Golly Goldfinch in Hampshire.

Suzie wanted to get back to St Martin's Lane because her mother was going to ring, as she usually did on a Friday evening, and because she intended to spill the beans about Tommy's proposal, and the fact that she loved him like nobody's business. So she could do without Tommy's physical presence in the flat, because he was distracting at the best of times and she wasn't certain how he would be while she broke the news to her mum.

To cover all eventualities she left a message with Shirley, who was still maundering on about Big Toe Harvey and the Balvak brothers being arrested on a trumped-up charge. Her message was straightforward. 'Tell the Guv'nor

I've had to go home. If he's got anything else for me he should ring because I'll be in all night. Got it Shirl?'

'Yes. No problem.'

'Just make sure he gets it – that I've gone home and he's to ring—'

'If he needs you, right?'

'If he has anything else for me to do. Right?'

As she left the Yard, Suzie was aware of the car. Then she looked at the two Spear Carriers, whom she recognized as watchdogs – one driving and one riding shotgun – in the car crawling after her bus. She usually walked, but tonight she felt like a rest. She'd had a shower after the long physical day with Molly Abelard, but she really needed a hot bath. Nothing she liked better than a long soak in a hot bath – well almost nothing. She thought to herself that she was preparing for a long physical night with Dandy Tom, and almost blushed as she sat there on the bus, surrounded by civil servants heading for Charing Cross, all of them looking shagged out after a day back at the salt mines of Whitehall. What a difference. She had nothing real to measure fantasies against until last night. Now – oh, wowee!

She felt the blush rising up her cheeks and her hand came up automatically to tidy away a strand of unruly hair that wasn't really there.

She had only just got into the flat when the telephone started to ring. And yes, it was her mum and, yes, this was the third time she'd tried Suzie already tonight. She often consumed entire Friday evenings ringing Suzie, who, since she had been posted to Camford, was seldom back before ten.

And yes, the children were fine. Ben seemed to have forgotten what had happened, but then Charlotte used to say he had little concept of time. 'Memory like a goldfish,' she'd remark, making light of it. Suzie had admired the way her sister made jokes about her beloved son's handicaps.

Lucy, her mum said, was gravely nonchalant: Mummy was with Jesus, so all was well.

Yes, she – Helen Gordon-Lowe – had started what she called 'the long business of coming to terms with it all'. She still had crying jags; came over her suddenly. Not surprising really; it hadn't been very long. But the Mountfords were made of sterner stuff with a tradition of getting on with life whatever happened: Suzie could only ever think of her mother as a Mountford, couldn't stand her being called Gordon-Lowe which was a phoney name anyway.

'Are you lot going full blast out to get the little bastard?' Suzie had rarely heard her mum swear.

'We're doing our best, Mum.'

'So, what news of you, Suzie? ... You're what?... What, you're...? ... What d'you mean, you're getting married? ... Suzie?'

So, first the Spanish Inquisition, then a great sunburst of delight, and a shriek when she heard it was Tommy Livermore. 'Ross'll be ecstatic. He was with his brother on the Somme.'

'No, Mum.' Suzie had the facts. The Livermore on the Somme was not a brother. An uncle maybe. Tommy had told her, an uncle, but only a hesitant uncle. Maybe.

This rather stopped her mum. Stopped her in her tracks, so what followed was the down side. You haven't known him five minutes, Susannah. Less. 'You certain he's serious?'

'Of course he's serious, Mum.' Yet underneath it all she was pushed into questioning. Does he really? Will he, won't he? Will he, won't he? Will he join the dance?

'Well, you know men, Susannah.'

'No, Mum, actually I don't know men, but Tommy's as serious as sin.'

'He'd better be, Susannah. I hope you haven't compromised yourself, dear.' And Suzie wanted to say we've been shagging like rattlesnakes, but she held her piece and they went on talking. And as they talked the usual happened: her mum went into this fantasy world of wedding dresses, bridesmaids, invitations, guests and perhaps they'd better hire a marquee for the lawn.

'You shouldn't even think about it, Mum.' A marquee was a non-essential and non-essentials were being discouraged. Don't you know there's a war on?

'However are we going to manage, Suzie?'

Perhaps she should simply have said that she was in love with him, and not mentioned marriage.

They went on for over twenty minutes.

The telephone rang again immediately.

531

'What happened, Suzie?' Dandy Tom sounding concerned and a bit frayed. 'You just left. I was looking for you.'

She was filled with that half delight of being wanted, and a pinch of worry that seemed to have arrived out of thin air.

'Did you get my message?'

'No. What message, heart?'

'I thought it was rather clever, actually. I told Shirley to say that I'd gone home, and if you had any more work for me I'd be in all evening and you could ring. It was meant to be cryptic.'

'Ah.'

'Tommy?'

'She did mutter something about you going home, but I think she missed out the second part. The part about you being home all night. If I'd got that bit it would've tipped me the wink. I was worried. Thought you were ill or something, heart. Shirley's been going on about your former boss and I thought this could be a bit of the same. We should really talk about that particular matter. Big Toe Harvey.'

'Can you come over here, then? We can talk as much as you like. Talk all night if you want. Do anything.' She knew exactly what she was up to. Rather revelled in it. 'Or d'you want me to come to you?'

'I'll be over. Half-an-hour.' Just a little too quick.

'Right.' So, why doesn't he want me over at his place? I've never seen his flat; he's never even talked about it.

Aloud she said, 'I don't know what we're

going to eat.'

'Don't worry, I've got food. What's wrong?'

'Nothing.'

'I can hear it in your voice. Something's up.'

'My mum rang. Made me a bit jumpy, that's all. Oh, and there are two of your lads hanging on to my skirt.'

'Yes, I should hope so. I've had their report. You just upped and walked out of the Yard. Shouldn't have done that, heart. There's been no sign of fellow-me-lad and there's a possibility that he's heading for London: which means heading for you. Did one of the lads see you in? Is the other one stationed at the back?'

'No, nobody saw me in. Were they supposed to?'

'My fault. You should've been properly briefed. The two lads are supposed to be close observers. Should've seen you in, had a look-see, spoken to you at regular intervals. They tried to ring you but the line's been engaged since you got in.'

'My mum, and then you, sweetheart.'

'Okay. Stay put. I'll be over. Less than twenty minutes. Right?'

'Tommy?' she shouted, not wanting him to hang up. 'Tommy. You say you've got food?'

'My mother was in town today. Always brings something up from the farm.' He took her silence as criticism.

'We're allowed,' Tommy said. 'It's not black market.' He chuckled. 'We're allowed, you know.'

'Oh.'

'See you soon, heart.'

His mother was in town today and Suzie hadn't been asked over to meet her. Also he was coming to her flat again. For the first time she thought it would've been better if he'd taken her over to his place. Dandy Tom's flat, the one she only saw in her imagination: the one with heavy curtains, bachelor stuff like they all had in the flicks. Leather-buttoned settees; straight-backed buttoned chairs; Hogarth prints and such, the odd Stubbs; leather-bound books; deep-pile carpets under foot. Oh nuts, and he hasn't let me set my nose inside it, let alone a foot. Big glass ashtrays, and heavy crystal drinking glasses.

She wanted a bath. Some deep soak treatment, but couldn't until Tommy arrived. She mooned around the flat alone, pacing from room to room, smoothing her hair automatically like someone who'd stooped to folly. Which, of course, she had.

Then Tommy Livermore was ringing the bell and she ran to open the door, sliding back the bolts and calling out.

He looked weighed down with worry, grimy from the day, yet still immaculate in his own way carrying two hefty brown-paper carrier bags and a Gladstone fat with files.

He was also annoyed.

'Suzie, heart, don't ever do that again.'

'Do what?' She closed the door, turned the key, slid the bolts home.

'You didn't check who was at the door.'

'I presumed it was you. You were on the way.'

534

'What if it had been Golly Goldfinch? What would you have done if it had been him with his bloody piano wire, heart? He's after you, Suzie, we're fairly certain of that.'

Then he told her about the Lysander and how the pilot had spotted footprints in the deep frost; and called up the beaters. 'Someone had been concealed in a birdwatcher's hide, on the edge of a copse outside Old Basing. It was right on the treeline, on top of a rise. Bits of food scattered around, crusts from sandwiches, and it wasn't like that when they went through in the morning.'

Then he told her that there was possibly another person involved. 'There's a chance Goldfinch's got an accomplice. Know what that means? It means he's twice as dangerous. It's my fault you weren't briefed, but – God in heaven – you could have used your common sense!'

He shouted the last part and Suzie felt about five years old, when Daddy got cross, and when he got cross ... Well!

'But it wasn't Golly,' she said in a little voice.

'Oh!' Tommy raged at himself as much as anyone. 'I thought you'd use your loaf.' He bent his knees and carefully put the bags on the floor, coming up again as if he was doing some physical training exercise.

She was not supposed to be left on her own outside the office. Not for a minute, he told her. He'd almost had a fit when Shirley told him she had gone; didn't know what she was thinking about. He went on for about three minutes, and Suzie felt somehow relieved that he was so obviously distressed.

'I'm sorry,' she said when he paused for breath. 'I'm terribly sorry, Tommy. What's in the bags?'

'Food.'

'Oh, yes, your mother's been in town, and I notice that I'm not asked to meet her.'

'You're not – what?'

'You said I had to meet your family. But you did nothing about it today.'

He didn't take her seriously; laughed, said, 'Please, heart.' Picked up one of the bags.

'Not joking, Tommy,' she raised her voice. 'And you've not let me anywhere near your flat, have you?'

He laughed again and she felt stupid. 'Listen, heart. My mother brings stuff up for me from the country, right? Today she was up for a meeting of some charity trustees. She's the chairwoman, right? Listen, I had no idea she was coming up today. She left these two bags and a scribbled note downstairs at the Yard. I didn't even hear her voice, let alone see her.'

'Oh. Never had—'

'No, and as for my flat, I've been in it once since last Sunday – just to collect some clothes that I've brought to the Yard. Last Sunday, when I was there it looked like a rubbish tip. It's much smaller than this, and twice as cluttered.' He waved a hand around, palm open and extended, signifying space and height – which actually he was exaggerating, heart. Then he went through the business of losing

Golly Goldfinch again: how they'd found broken boughs and signs that a car had been tucked away in the bushes. No tyre tracks because the ground was too hard. Golly might well have an accomplice, which he obviously found to be a worrying possibility.

'Remember that,' he said, a little harshly and all the aggression went out of her and she started to weep. 'Please God, heart, don't grizzle,' he snapped at her. So, Suzie, with her teenage experience in a nearly twenty-three-year-old body, thought it was all over. Finished.

'What's your mother been putting into your head, heart? I'm sorry, but it's been a difficult day and I can't stand tears, not tonight, angel,' he rumbled, putting his finger right on the real problem.

With a couple of debilitated sobs she told him that her mum had said they'd only known one another for five minutes, how could she be sure enough to think of marrying him? *And you know men, Susannah.*

Tommy groaned and called on God the Son for aid and strength. Then, calmly, told her that what he'd like best in all the world was a chance to speak to her mother, and in words of one syllable, explain to her how two people could set eyes on each other for the first time and know, immediately – without even the reflection of a shadow of doubt – that they loved one another. 'Because that's what's happened to me, and from my view as a trained observer, it's what seems to have happened to you, heart.'

Once more he told her how he felt about her. 'I've been searching for you all my life,' he said. 'And maybe for a lifetime before that.' Dead romantic. Not at all sentimental. Made her glow.

'I'd marry you tomorrow, heart, if I could. But, perhaps you're the one with doubts. Maybe you think I'm too old. I'm aware this has all been a bit quick.'

She told him that she didn't even know how old he was.

'Not forty yet, which I know is ancient to someone of seventeen, but—'

'I'm twenty-two.' She brightened. 'Almost twenty-three,' realizing she now knew what a tiny part of that wonderful attraction really was. As well as being whatever else she wanted in life, Dandy Tom was just a shade close to being a father figure.

These two – Susannah Mountford and Thomas Livermore – had spotted one another in that strange way in which one human seeks out another, knowing at a glance how it would be when they came together. It was, Suzie now knew, like that for her father and mother. Though she suspected her mother had lost sight of the fact.

She allowed herself to be enfolded in his arms, where she rocked to and fro in safety and, after a while, again asked what the brown paper carriers contained.

'There's cheese, made from my family's own recipe, and my family's own cows, two beef steaks, a cauliflower and a few other vegetables in short supply.'

'What's your fancy, sir?'

'Not food, but I suspect it would be prudent to eat. It's been a bitch of a day.'

'Steak and chips?'

'Wonderful.'

And while Suzie cooked and he assisted, he told her that he was totally frazzled, didn't like the business of having to saturate whole areas of England with police and military. People were worried enough by Hitler without having to deal with the ghostly ghoul that was Golly Goldfinch.

She also heard the subtext of what he said: that his own reputation was on the line, because if they had indeed missed him, God knew what Goldfinch was set to do if he were back in London: particularly if there was one person controlling his every move. Possibly someone who had brought him back to perform an act of an unscrupulously gross nature.

As he talked, Suzie saw the fatigue in his face and around his eyes; she heard the sagging lassitude in his voice and took note.

'The whole business is becoming so damned complex.' They sat having their dinner in her kitchen, with the oven still on and the door open to warm the room. The ancient heating, with the big cast-iron ribbed radiators – circa Crimean War – was on the blink again, so Suzie had taken special precautions, particularly in the bedroom: an Aladdin stove and three pairs of large earthenware flowerpots, a candle lit within a pot, the second pot upended. The result was a series of small heaters to supplement the paraffin stove. She knew that the ensuing scent would be with her always, reminding her of her first capitulation to Dandy Tom. Indeed, her first capitulation to any male.

'What with people still off work for Christmas–' he gave a frustrated sigh – 'I'm stalled out, Suzie. Been through all those other deaths with a currycomb. Want to get the Benton thing really sorted; what's the first thing you do in a murder inquiry?' Sudden changes of tack were pointers to Tommy Livermore's fatigue.

'After talking to scenes of crime and forensics?'

'Naturally.'

'You make a list of all family members and people known to the victim, then you sit down with them to see who had the opportunity. That gives you your shortlist to which you fit motive.'

That was roughly what you should do. They both knew it, just as they knew Suzie had started doing it in a desultory kind of way. 'You made a beginning,' he smiled across at her. 'I'm not criticizing, heart, but you didn't have the experience.' She had condemned herself, he pointed out. 'Said you didn't know the right questions; didn't have that sneaky way ancient inquisitors like me, Old Ginger Tom, have of pulling the truth out of a witness. This steak is damned good, heart. You got a secret recipe, some deft way with the spices?'

'Got it from my mother, Tommy. Listen, you've had one hell of a day. You're tired out. Why don't we take a hot bath – separately of course on account of there not being room for the two of us – then snuggle up and have a good long sleep. So tomorrow I can come to the Yard with you and we can go through every last name we find in Jo Benton's address books, her letters, notes, whatever's sitting in her file. Then you can plan a campaign. Decide who's going to interview who – or should that be whom?'

'Probably.'

He said that would be absolutely wonderful. He couldn't think of anything so perfect as not having to concentrate on these bloody murders any more today. If Suzie didn't know any better she would have thought him a trifle drunk, not three sheets in the wind drunk, but more your average tipsy drunk.

'I could kill for a banana,' he said as they were clearing the plates away. 'Go and get your bath, I'm going to lie down, then I can read you a bedtime story. What's your favourite?'

She made a face at him, pausing by the door. 'Oh, something by Agatha Christie probably.'

He groaned. 'Not that Belgian bugger with the little grey cells, please.'

Half-an-hour later, relaxed, with the after-glow of a scented hot bath, dressed in the sexiest nightdress she possessed – a pink diaphanous creation from Harvey Nicks, bought with her staff discount when she worked there before joining the Met. 'For my bottom drawer,' she said at the time.

'Lo, a wanton woman,' she said now entering the bedroom, posing by the door, à la Greek statuary, for the benefit of a comatose Tommy Livermore. With the help of her make-do heaters the room was moderately warm, and Tommy, having undressed, had got just as far as the bed where he now lay sprawled and naked, his manhood curled up with him like a small fossil on a beach.

'Ah,' she breathed, sensing that it was a privilege to be a woman with a lover so certain of her that he could doze off while waiting for her to come to him. She revived him half-an-hour later and he tottered off to the bathroom while she browsed through the latest copy of *Picture Post*.

An hour or so later, as they lay quietly together he said, 'I could spend the rest of my life labouring at the soft anvil between your thighs.'

'How lovely,' she breathed. 'Poetic.'

'Not original.' He propped himself on an elbow and looked down at her. 'Poetic, yes, but soft anvil is the work of, I think, John Wilmot, Earl of Rochester. Ask Molly, she'll know.'

'What's made Molly such an expert?'

'How much d'you know of her?'

'I know about the beating and rape in Hong Kong.'

'Then you know she set about learning to defend herself in both orthodox and unconventional ways?' He explained that, during the painful journey home from Hong Kong she had whiled away the days by examining all the dictionaries, encyclopaedias, and other research volumes in the ship's library. 'Soaked them up like a sponge. Now she knows what my old mum – forgive her, Suzie – refers to as the far end of a fart.'

She was consumed in a short burst of schoolgirl giggles.

'And your ma's a countess, isn't she?' As yet they hadn't touched on the title thing.

'More to the point my pa's the Earl of Kingscote. But don't get ideas above your station, heart. I'm almost certainly going to give up the title when it's hurled in my direction.'

'You are?'

'Don't hold with accidents of birth making you heir to titles and things. Actually, it's the titles I don't hold with. That's why I became a copper. That explain it, heart?'

'Yes, I suppose it does. But you can't escape the job can you? I mean the responsibility?'

He gave a little growl. 'No, and I wouldn't want to either. Happily I can see to it that the large areas of land and buildings of the family estate would be run properly, so there's no problem.'

'As long as you run me properly, Tommy.'

And after she said it, she realized how selfish she must have sounded, and apologized.

Later, on the cusp of sleep she wondered how the Earl and Countess of Kingscote would take the news of their engagement.

'Overjoyed, I should imagine.' He could smell the scent of melons again in her hair.

'They're sort of proud that I've come this far, but I know they've been waiting for a grand-child, so they'll be doubly happy.' He muttered on for a minute or so as they both dropped into what was happily a dreamless sleep.

Not so across London in another part of the forest of dreams and fantasy.

Golly heard the voice coming from a long way off, as though it was calling to him from beyond time and space. Only when it had fully penetrated his half-consciousness did he realize that the lovely voice had been preceded by the clatter of the great spiders. He could clearly hear the spiders still clicking away around his bed.

The voice began by simply calling, almost singing, his name: 'Go-lly. Go-lly. Listen Go-lly.' Then, when it had his attention, the voice became slightly harsher as she chided him for making such a bad mistake. 'Foolish. Foolish. Folly Golly. Killed the wrong girl, Golly. You must put that right. You *must* kill the lady policeman. You understand? Golly, kill.' Then she sang out the address where the lady police-man lived, and told him it was the only way.

He must watch closely. Watch where the lady policeman lived, then he must follow her when she went out. He must choose the right time. Choose when it was safe for her to die.

Then the voice went away for a while, but he knew she was still there in Lavender's room with him, just as he knew when the beast he thought of as the Banshee was also there.

544

And this was the most horrible thing so far when the voice, Miss Baccus, started to sing to him a second time.

'Go-lly. Go-lly. After you have killed the lady policeman there is one more great thing you have to do for me. It will be hard, Golly, but you must do it. Once you have done it you will be free of me for ever. Free to do whatever you desire.'

A tuneless singing now, followed by the clicking of the spiders. Then—

'Golly, my slave. You must do this last thing. Golly, you must kill Lavender. Kill Lavender with the wire.'

And Golly woke up, the sweat running off him and his hair on end as though a thousand swift creeping insects were playing on all the nerve ends at the back of his neck.

Kill Lavender with the wire.

He wondered if he had really heard that, and immediately knew he had.

He sat up, turned his head and screamed, for in the corner of the room, in the first hour of day as he lit the nightlight by his bed he saw the Banshee: the ratlike creature, standing on its hind legs, with the banner over its shoulder. Clear in all its lamentation, with the word in blood on the banner, as though rippling in a breeze that was not there. 'Death Rattle' it said, the blood dripping from the letters, and as he read the words so the spiders clicked their bony legs together in a haunting cacophonous clitter-clatter.

Kill Lavender, he knew.

Kill Lavender.

Kill with the wire.

How was he ever going to do that to Lavender?

Twenty-Six

They woke again a little after four in the morning, when they had another roll around. In turn this led to Tommy saying they really didn't need to be in the office until about eleven. Suzie reset the alarm for eight thirty. They got up at about nine thirty, but first Tommy telephoned Molly Abelard. Then he rang Billy Mulligan. As Suzie was tripping in and out of the bathroom she heard him say to Abelard, 'I'll arrange that with Billy. You just continue doing that job – what you do best ... Yes, Dance.'

And to Billy she heard him say, 'It's possible that we'll need to go in, so see one of your tame magistrates and get a warrant, okay?'

'Warrant for where?' she asked.

'Lavender's place. The girl supposed to be Goldfinch's cousin, the one he minds. Might be an idea to go in and take a look – her place just off Rupert Street, I mean. He used to sleep there most nights. My inclination is to find Lavender herself and bring her in, maybe to Camford or Vine Street.'

'For what?'

'The usual gentle chat. A few questions, a

546

couple of lies. Variations on a porkie or two. Sort out the sows from the hogs. Meet the hoggets. Take her down the Tombs, give her the third degree.' 'The Tombs' often figured in Hollywood cop films and was the New York City Prison, while the third degree was a very hostile form of American interrogation involving bright lights, harsh words and physical threats.

When she was dressed, Suzie went through to the kitchen. 'Your family keep pigs?' she called out.

'Why?'

'Your ma's sent you some bacon. Only just found it.'

'Treats and delights,' he shouted back. 'Let's have some for breakfast. Toast, grilled bacon and coffee. Best thing in the world for breakfast.'

There was a letter for her and she recognized the handwriting, but couldn't put a name to it.

'Oh lawks,' she said aloud when she opened it.

'Disappointed swain?' He was uncannily accurate.

'You're uncannily accurate,' she said. 'There was this uniformed chief super at Camford nick.'

'That twit Walter Sanders?' Tommy cocked an eyebrow at her.

She thought about her inexperience. Eventually – 'Tommy, I love you like anything, but how many girls have you had? You know, properly had?'

He frowned, looked at the ceiling, and began to make an exaggerated show of silently counting on his fingers.

'Don't be a clown.'

'That's bad news you know, heart?'

'What?'

'Talking to your true love about past lovers. Leads to perdition, privy conspiracy: come face to face with the old green-eyed monster, the one that gnaws at your soul.'

'I'm willing to risk that.'

'Well, not counting teenage crushes – and there was only one of those – the answer's five.'

'Tell me about them.'

'Tonight.'

'Now.' But already she was jealous of all the girls he'd kissed, and ... well ... in the past.

'Tonight, heart.' Suddenly he was very serious. 'Turning over the ground where you've walked with old lovers inevitably sets off traps and snares. There's really neither world enough nor time, or whatever Andrew Marvell said. Okay?'

She shrugged, capitulated and turned back to the letter from Sanders of the River.

My Dear Suzie

Today I've been officially told that you have left our little family in Camford, and have gone to work under the great Tommy Livermore. I can say truthfully that we shall all miss you here, but to work under Dandy Tom is a very great bonus. He's a wonderful officer, and you'll learn a great deal from

548

him.

I hope this does not mean that we will not meet again. Remember you have promised to have dinner with me soon. The flurry of changing jobs can be difficult, so I enclose my work and private numbers. Looking forward to hearing from you. As ever with much affection.

He signed himself, Wally Sanders, and she giggled out loud.

'What's funny?' Tommy slurped the last of his coffee.

'Mr Sanders says "to work under Dandy Tom" – that's you, sweetheart – "is a very great bonus". He doesn't know how great.'

'That's almost crude, heart. Very nearly ribald.'

'That's rich coming from someone who less than an hour ago...'

He flashed his ravishing smile, the one that consumed her alive, as he was putting on that spectacular overcoat, the double-breasted one, the military cut in a deep grey.

This time he ordered the taxi to drop them right in front of the Yard.

'I think a lot of people have already put two and two together. We can't stave off the inevitable, heart.'

She held his hand all the way there, and it took a great deal of personal discipline to let go and not walk into the Yard still with her hand clasped in his.

The Spear Carriers were already gathered

when they reached the conference room and Pete, Dave and Bert were back from darkest Hampshire. Abelard and Mulligan were, of course, conspicuous by their absence on the fourth floor.

The boys back from Hampshire had nothing really new. 'It wasn't quick for Ailsa Goldfinch,' Pete told them. 'I got the impression that Golly almost mucked it up.'

'Right enough,' Dave agreed. 'Nothing you could actually rely on. Just a sense that it wasn't as clean as his usual work. Unless you had our prior knowledge, I wouldn't even put Golly in the frame.'

Bert had the box with him – the one that included the card sent to Golly's mum from Cambridge. It was there, in a little cellophane bag – OLD COLLEDGES LOVLY. VERI BUTI-FUL; the other things also, in separate bags: the knife – a curved blade, very sharp and in a leather scabbard – and the black provocative underwear they had tied down to Geraldine Williams, choked with piano wire then raped and mutilated in her kitchen in Jesmond, New-castle-upon-Tyne.

Always smart. Geraldine was.

Suzie helped Tommy bring out the folders and separate file boxes that were usually kept in the big safe in his office. They contained all kinds of material, pieces of evidence, photographs, the detailed documents of the various killings linked by the use of the brutal piano wire.

'Right,' he began. 'This is what we're going to

550

do.' He chose to split the eight most experienced detectives into four pairs, allocating each team two or three of the murder investigations they now reckoned were tied into Golly Goldfinch.

'Nothing is better than the painstaking detail,' he told them. 'I want each of you to go over the investigation files again. Get in touch with officers who were originally on the cases – most of them're still around. Look at the evidence, see if there are any anomalies. If there are, go back to the prime sources, and keep your eyes out for anything that may link cases. I've been through them, and apart from the obvious errors of wasting too much time looking at husbands and boyfriends – even Nick Booker, now doing time for Owlet's murder – most of them have been investigated with great diligence, by first-class people. Door-to-door and every tiny piece of evidence are the things that usually lighten the darkness of crimes like these.' He also admitted there was a possibility that they'd eventually have to get out there and reopen cases on the ground. 'So try to look at things with new eyes.'

He told them that he would be dealing with the ongoing Jo Benton and Charlotte Fox – Charlotte Mountford – cases with the help of Sergeant Mountford, so together they settled in his office to sort through the pile of names pulled from Five Coram Cross Road, Camford. There were four more boxes than the ones Suzie remembered ordering to be brought to Camford Hill nick from the Coram Cross

Road house.

'When did these turn up?' she asked, puzzled.

'On the day you tootled off to Middle Wallop. The boys and girls thought we should take a dekko, so I trotted over to Camford, with a few of the lads. Had a picnic. Amazing what an inexperienced team misses. We found bills, letters, memos, even some contracts.'

'I could have sworn I went through all the desks.'

'The desks were cleared. It was cupboards and one or two other drawers that hadn't been done.'

They were just going through Suzie's original interview with Steven Fermin when Molly Abelard returned threading her way down through the conference room tables.

'We'll have to hear Molly out before we move on.' Suzie watched her warmly greeting Pete, Dave and Bert, looking like the cat who'd licked the cream.

'What's she been up to?' Molly seemed to be unusually chummy with Dave, the forensics officer.

'Doing an in-depth on the guy you're having dinner with tomorrow night. Didn't I tell you, heart?' he gave her a sly smile. 'Been at it ever since we got back actually. On the blower; traipsing the streets; policeman's lot not a happy one, she tells me.'

And Molly, as she put it a few moments later, had turned over a few interesting stones: uncovered the odd maggot.

The Mark came to see Golly in the morning. It was about half-past nine, and Golly was sitting on Lavender's bed looking nervous, unhappy, and very twitchy.

'What's up, Goll?' he asked.

'Nothing. Nothing's up, but I've got to get out of here. Can't stay with Lavender no more.'

'Come on, Golly. It's the only place you'll be safe.'

'I can look after myself, Mark. Take care of myself. Been doing it for years, so I can do it again now.'

The Mark tried to jolly him along. 'Well, just stay another night. I'll find you somewhere else after that. Why not?'

' 'Cos I've got something to do. Got to get out of here to do it.'

'I see. So you're going to do it today, whatever it is?'

'Tonight, prob'ly.'

'Well, come back here tonight, Golly. I haven't taken all these risks just to see you nicked on the streets. They *are* looking for you. Looking hard. They're everywhere.'

'I'll come back. Prob'ly. Prob'ly tonight.' He didn't believe a word, nor did the Mark who had brought some chocolate. 'Give you energy,' he said. There were two 2d bars of milk chocolate and a bar of Cadbury's Fruit and Nut. A big bar, so Golly ate some after the Mark left, then he began to make his plans.

Because of his face Golly had spent almost all of his life hiding. For years he'd known this

553

didn't mean simply staying inside, or covering up his deformities. Golly could be out in the open – in Piccadilly even – and still be hidden; just as he could walk along the Earl's Court Road and not attract a single glance. Also he could choose whether to be seen or not: at least that's what he imagined, and it appeared to work.

On days when he went out with his mask and his hat, heading to places where he was known he expected to be seen. People see what they're used to seeing. Change yourself and they don't immediately recognize you. He had discovered that relatively quickly. So when he really did not wish to be seen he had his own ways of hiding: like wearing his long mackintosh, the special dark glasses his mum had got made for him, and the flat cap he'd bought himself last year. Dolled up like this, nobody recognized him.

So he thought.

Now, in this fearsome time when he'd been told to kill the lady policeman and Lavender, it seemed as though he'd better wear his disguise. So today, Saturday, he put them on – the mac, glasses and the cap at a jaunty angle and took a walk – from near Rupert Street all the way to Upper St Martin's Lane.

He sang to himself, in his head, as he walked along the pavements—

> Over hill and over dale,
> See we come together.

The carol made him strong and happy. Put him in the right mood for what he was going to do; and when he got to the address in Upper St Martin's Lane – the one the nice voice had revealed to him – there were hardly any people about. Certainly there were no police looking for him. He knew how the police watched places. Golly even scanned nearby windows opposite the building where the lady policeman had her flat. He knew the signs, the spoor of policemen, and they definitely weren't watching her home. He reasoned, correctly, that if they weren't watching she was probably not at home.

Golly's as cunning as a bag full of blue-based baboons.

He sauntered across the road and walked up to the front door. How many people would be in on a day like this? On a Saturday? In this part of London? Not many, but he wasn't going to risk the old dodge of ringing a lot of bells in the hope that one would spring the automatic lock. Nor was he confident enough to hang around and wait to follow in the slipstream of another resident.

This was an old building, and it probably had a fire escape round the back, so he walked right around the block, noting the only alleyway that could take him to the rear of the flats, so he walked round a second time, ducked into the alley and, to his delight, found the zigzag of a solid fire escape running from top to bottom of the building. At each stage there was a grilled metal landing right below a high window. The steps to the landings were hinged, folded up out of reach because these were steps for coming down, not for going up. But the Civil Defence Volunteers and the Auxiliary Fire Service had been at work: brand new ropes hung from the hinged landings.

With one tug the first hinged section came dropping down. The hinges had even been nicely oiled so that the stretch of steps came down as smooth as the reaction to a dose of Eno's Fruit Salts.

The lady policeman lived on the fifth floor. Number fifty two. Kill, Golly said in his mind. He knew that was the only thing that mattered. He was only useful to other people if he killed when he was ordered. The wrong woman in Overchurch was just practice, he giggled and, counting cheerfully, he started to climb to the fifth floor. When he got there he was delighted to see how easy it was. The landing windows on each floor were like doors, wooden frameworks with a latch handle and a lock: windows in the top half shaped like small church windows.

The lock was easy. Mickey the Mangle had taught him all about locks, how to use a simple pick, and this lock wasn't simple, it was down-right wrong in the head: put up its hands and surrendered as soon as he got his little picks out. 'These'll come in useful one day,' Mickey the Mangle had said. 'Slide in the right pick; hold your breath, jiggle it a bit, like you would if it were your pego in a girl's diddley-pout.' Golly laughed now as he jiggled it about and turned it. With an easy click the bolt eased itself back, neat as a bee's toe, and he was in.

He took a step forward and knew it was the lady policeman's flat, it was where she lived, where she slept, had her life which he'd soon take from her. Golly grinned. Then he walked the flat, going from room to room, like a ghost who walked but was not seen. He even went to the bedroom, smelled the scent of her, opened the drawers in her dressing table and held her private things. It gave him a wonderful charge, like having sex with her.

He took several deep breaths and then began to look for things, and found them – or one at least. A little diary that had been left wide open on her bedside table. He could decipher the round neat writing, easy as pie. There was this note against Sunday 29th December 1940; and it said, Josh Dance, Dinner. 5 p.m. Then an address he could read because he knew where it was, near Albemarle Street. That was close by the Dilly. Knew it and knew Josh Dance as well. Lavender knew Josh Dance. Wouldn't let him come near her. 'Golly, don't ever let that man into the house. Throw him out, keep him away. He's rough stuff. Can do you damage. Give him the Sunday punch.'

And the lady policeman was going to see him at five o'clock tomorrow afternoon. Easy as mittens. Golly could set that up simple as kiss your arse. Maybe he wouldn't have to come here again, climb the fire escape as he'd planned.

He had thought of staying here in her flat now but that was a big risk. She might come home with someone else and that could be difficult, even dangerous. No, he slunk away, but left the door on to the fire escape closed, but unlocked. Just in case. Better be more safe than sorry, mum would say. If he did her near Josh Dance there would be a perfect suspect on hand. The filth *must* know about Josh Dance and how he gets his greens.

And off he went back to Lavender's.

Invisible.

Sitting in Dandy Tom's office, Suzie was developing an even deeper respect for Molly Abelard. She certainly knew her job. She sat there now telling them how she had pried open Josh Dance's secrets.

Some were in the files, but those had led her out and about, knocking on doors, talking to people who had known Josh Dance for a long time.

Josh Dance, as he now called himself, had a record. Two minor offences, one with a car and one as a kid, pinching stuff from Fortnum & Mason. Then there was his real 'trouble' in 1930. The 'trouble' was in connection with a common prostitute who had been so badly abused that it was thought she was going to die. And it was Josh Dance who had done the abusing. She was a girl called Moira. Moira Finisterre, if you could believe that. But she was a classy piece, Molly said. Very classy and used to be something in the rag trade, something to do with fashion. After that she had tried to be an actress, but that hadn't worked out, so by 1930 Moira was reduced to the most elderly of professions. By the end of July of that year she was doing well by the standards of the relatively undemanding frail sisterhood, offering herself as a specialist. She had a patch of pavement in Knightsbridge and had been known to advertise – 'Young lady willing to do anything on demand.' It was the kind of bait that would draw a man like Josh Dance, who was not Josh Dance then but David Slaughter – his true birth name.

His father was C. F. Slaughter, the artist. 'His works fetch a good price on the market these days...'

'And his son's got three in his flat. Good hedge against inflation, I'd think.' Suzie was glad to have this confirmed.

'Slaughter dated Moira Finisterre regularly – on a professional basis of course. I've talked to her and she says it was the lure of money. After the first time she couldn't pretend it was a surprise. He paid well and came back for more.' To start with it was just not unpleasant spankings, but it became more serious. 'He liked caning me on my bare bottom,' Moira had told her. It got worse, then on 10 August 1930, he almost beat her to death.

Moira Finisterre recovered because the police were called by a neighbour and David Slaughter was brought to trial. Claimed it was a sex game that got out of hand. The bench tut-tutted – you know how they can be – and Miss Finisterre was criticized and presented as a common prostitute. 'Mr Slaughter was let off with a slap on the wrist and advised not to get mixed up with women like Miss Finisterre ever again.' Molly smiled grimly.

It was C. F. Slaughter who threatened his son. Said he'd cut him off without the proverbial, so, David Slaughter changed his name to Josh Dance, cashed in some shares and became a partner of Jewell, Baccus & Dance. By 1932 he had begun to make his name in the business of estate agents. Very respectable.

'He also joined the Terriers' – the Terriers being the Territorial Army – 'but he didn't give up the ladies.' Molly laid a finger along the side of her nose and Tommy did the same as though it were a secret sign between the pair of them. 'I've talked to quite a few ladies of the night and he's *known*. Some girls went with him, some won't even think about it. Some only went once. Some ended up in hospital. But they all said he was up front. Always told them the truth.'

Josh Dance would approach girls, offer a lot of money and tell them exactly what he wanted. 'I like dominating women,' he would say, 'and I'm willing to pay.'

Molly said that some were quite interested because it was a bit of role reversal – 'It's usually the other way around. The gents want to have their bums whacked as a rule. But Josh Dance didn't stop at that. It got very hairy and I gather he has all the apparatus in that flat of his.'

'Really? That could be handy,' Tommy drawled.

'Ah, but there's been a recent change.' Molly raised a cautionary hand.

She had talked to one girl who went home with him on Christmas Eve. 'Yes, last week,' Abelard told them. 'She claimed he was honest with her. Gave her sexy underwear. Told her what to wear. Gave her a long spiel about what he'd like to do, then couldn't. Just lay there, cuddling her, stroking her, whispering to her. Couldn't seem to do anything else. Couldn't get it up. And another of the girls told me that he went on to her about having punished himself. Needed to. "I was worried about doing any real harm," he had said.'

'Does this help us at all?' Tommy Livermore asked.

'Well–' Abelard waggled her hand, unsure – 'there's a good side,' she continued. 'He showed great gallantry in France. He's now been invalided out of the Army. Badly wounded near Dunkirk. Got an MC for it.'

'Not really of interest to us, though, is it?' Dandy Tom remained unimpressed.

'Except the little matter of possible Baccus relatives,' Suzie reminded him.

'Want us to go in and put him to the question? The Tombs?' Tommy asked.

'Don't think so, Guv'nor. I can cope with dominant men,' Suzie remarked with the tiniest of smiles. Dandy Tom smiled back, frosty, and she wondered if she had gone too far, then his cockeyed look told her she hadn't.

When Abelard left they began to take a long and hard look at the list of people close to Jo

Benton, mapping out what order they should be interviewed.

Tommy maintained that this time they should do it together. 'To start with, I think we should walk in on the ones you've already interviewed, heart.'

'Some of them aren't really the kind of people you can walk in on, darling.'

'Let me teach you something, heart.' Tommy leaned back. 'The human being isn't born who can't be walked in on. Have the right kind of rank, and the correct motivation and you can even walk in on the King – unannounced and out of uniform.'

'Right, sir.'

'Right, heart.' Pause, count of five. 'I love you, heart. Don't ever forget it.'

'Right. That goes for me as well, sir. So we do the great Gerald Vine, Daniel Flint, Steven Fermin and Barry Forbes on Monday and Tuesday?'

'Mmmm.' He nodded. 'On second thoughts, I think we should arrange matters concerning Gerald Vine. Give him an appointment.'

'You know best, sir.'

On his way back to Soho – still invisible – Golly bought a copy of the *Evening News* from a vendor near Piccadilly. 'Hello, Golly, you been a naughty boy, haven't you?' the newspaper seller told him. 'They still looking for you then?' which made him scuttle off back to Lavender's place. In fact it so threw him that he almost went to the front of the building.

Then he remembered just in time and turned back, slipping through the garage.

Golly couldn't read well, but he could decipher things if he took it slowly, and on the front page he had spotted a photograph. It was a picture of Mr Churchill. The Prime Minister was walking towards his car, and by his side were two men one of whom was the Mark. Golly was quite taken aback. What was the Mark doing with a great man like Winston Churchill? Stuck up bugger, Mark. He should kill the sod.

Twenty-Seven

They had told her there was no need to worry – at least Dandy Tom had told her – and she knew they would be close at hand: Tommy Livermore, Molly Abelard and Shirley Cox. Brian at the wheel. They'd kept the circle of knowledge closed. The others were working on the old piano wire murder investigations, while Tommy had sent some of them back into the field – Camford and Hampshire – so what was there to be nervous about anyway? It wasn't as though she was going into a lion's den, or even anywhere she was certain of coming close to Golly Goldfinch, who hadn't even been caught yet though 'Operation Bullring' was still running: running quite fast at that.

On the Saturday night, after Dandy Tom had

been very attentive and Suzie really felt she was learning wonderful things, she had lain back in bed and thought about the horror of Golly Goldfinch.

His name had about it the ring of an end-of-the-pier comedian – 'Here he is, your own, your very own Golly Goldfinch.' 'Hello, hello, hello, I'm going to sing you a little song. Yes, I am. You may well laugh, missus, but I'm going to sing it: a little song – from the black book missus – entitled, "Ain't it grand to be blooming well dead". Take it away maestro.'

She had imagined what he sounded like and had that afternoon asked Tommy – 'He's like that geezer in the Bible,' Tom told her. 'Slow of speech, and of a slow tongue, but he's – pardon my French, heart – cunning as a shithouse rat – as they say.' Dandy Tom sometimes used shockingly coarse language, she considered.

Relentless. That was the word for Goldfinch, she decided. Relentless and now, possibly, unstoppable: a child of darkness. To her, Golly had assumed nightmare proportions: a marching figure who plodded on, never slowing down but killing anybody who got in his way. Killing them without even a thought; taking lives out of their bodies without any sane reason. He would kill anyone, and, if Tommy was right, he was being guided by someone who bore a dreadful grudge.

But now her sights were set on putting Josh Dance to the question, preferably without him realizing she was at it. She wore her heavy dark skirt, the one with the pockets because it was wide and she had been able to hide Billy Mulligan's eight-inch baton in the waistband: she'd sewn a deep pocket to steady it against her thigh. When she was dressing, Tommy came up behind her and slid a hand into one of the skirt's pockets. 'Oh, heart,' he had said. 'Would that I were small, dapper and neat. I could fit into this pocket of yours and touch the silk of your clothes, and the warmth of your lovely grommet.' And she had risen to his mood and told him, 'Unhand me, sir.'

Of course one thing had led to another, and she was out of skirt, pants, bra, the lot before they were done. But now, at this very moment, ten minutes to five on a bitter cold Sunday evening with few people about and a hint of mist in the air, she walked steadily up Piccadilly with her big coat over the dark wide skirt, a white blouse and a tight little bolero jacket of material matching the skirt. A friend had run them up last year with one or two other bits and pieces. She remembered saying to Charlotte that she'd be okay for clothes even if the war lasted seven years.

The thought of Charlotte made her feel low and depressed again. She'd been fighting it off all weekend, and here it was again just as she turned down Albemarle Street, crossing the road, as a car came blundering out into the Dilly. Through the murk she glimpsed an elderly woman in the back of the car, bending the driver's ear, yattering on and on at him.

She reached the familiar door with the discreet brass plate – 'Jewell, Baccus & Dance,

Estate & Lettings Agency'. Rang the bell, as she had been told, turned the doorknob and stepped inside.

Across the road, leaning against an area wall, having a quiet cigarette, his right shoulder on the stonework, Golly pushed himself up straight. He had at first seen only the outline of the woman. But this time he had no doubt, as the light from the interior fell across her, and as she turned to close the door that same light briefly lit her face and the gold hair above it, trapped in the scarf tied gypsy style around her head. I'll take the scarf, he decided. When she lies stone dead on the floor with her windpipe crushed and her tongue protruding, that's when I'll take the scarf: when I've done what I was instructed to do. Kill the lady policeman. Kill with the wire.

He began to walk up the street: not his usual plodding, unstoppable, unrelenting walk, his walk that was, in his head, like one of them German Panzer tanks he'd seen on the news-reels at the pictures. Instead, Golly straighten-ed up, squared his shoulders, walked with a certain air, and in his head he sang a song his mum used to sing in her little cracked voice—

> I know where I'm going,
> And I know who's going with me,
> I know who I love,
> But the dear knows who I'll marry.

Behind him he could hear footsteps and, coming nearer, a car. He marched on, not looking back, just walking, steady, knowing where he was going and what business he had there. The car had slowed, and was pulling up behind him. He heard the door slam and then the car pulled away again. The footsteps had ceased. So, he thought. A trap, he thought. No.

He turned left at the corner and the car, still moving very slowly, drove on.

'That someone alone and palely loitering?' Tommy asked.

'Someone walking their dog, I think, Guv'-nor. Too dark,' Molly Abelard said. 'You all right?' she asked Shirley who had got in again as instructed once Suzie was in the house.

'Not taking any chances,' Dandy Tom had said before they left. 'We'll do a slow circuit round the block, and keep it up until she comes out.' That's what they were doing now. Circling the block, right-hand turns, clockwise. He had told Suzie that should Dance become difficult she was to 'blow her police whistle until the pea came out or until hell freezes over – whichever is first, heart.'

Golly had stopped, listened, heard the car pulling away. He turned on his heel and began to run back silently from where he had come, across the road and up to the door. 'Jewell. Baccus & Dance.' In his head Golly was a fleet-footed Red Indian, like at the pictures. Soon another scalp would be dripping.

He pulled the knob towards him, holding it tight, always the best way to make a silent entry through an unlocked door. Turn the knob. Hold it, pull the door back against the jamb, then release and slowly open it. Golly was in. Two steps across the hall and into the cupboard under the stairs. Wait. Stay still. In his head, Golly sang again—

> Some say he's black,
> But I say he's bonny,
> The fairest of them all,
> My handsome, winsome Golly.

He smiled his odd smile and his sharp teeth touched his lower lip, almost piercing the skin.

Now, all I have to do is catch her on the turning of the stairs, or when she's coming down.

After that it will be terrible, because it'll be Lavender next. His right hand was in his pocket and the wire was ready, bound tightly at both ends. Ready for the lady policeman. He all but giggled. Had her name on it, he thought. Ha-ha.

'A glass of sherry?' Josh Dance still had his tan, his hair was shorter than the last time she'd seen him, but all in all he looked strikingly fit and smart in a double-breasted dark stripe. A military tailor, she thought. Maybe Gieves, maybe one of the others. He ushered her into the mellow light of his drawing room: two standard lamps switched on and the heavy dark green curtains drawn. The lamps were augmented by the picture lights above the Venetian, the Mall and the Champs-Élysées paintings, and the whole was set alight from a six-foot Christmas tree against the wall between the windows. The tree was decorated with expensive-looking baubles and miniature electric candles, something you didn't see much of. Christmas cards covered the false mantel and a pair of side tables. Suzie turned around to try and get a better impression of the whole room. Somehow, she thought, it reflected wealth. She couldn't have said why, but it was the first thing that came into her mind. Strange, she thought. The turmoil of war going on, yet in homes Christmas seemed untouched.

'I'd love a sherry.' She hoped it really was dry. The taste these days seemed to be angled towards sweet, which she couldn't bear. 'You have a good Christmas?' she asked. Gently, don't push him.

'Kw-Quiet you know. I had my sister and her two children over on C-Christmas night. That livened things up.' He came to her with the sherry – proper sherry glasses. She raised her glass to the light. Pale was all.

Suzie wanted to say things were livened up on her Christmas evening as well; her sister also had two children. Unfortunately she was killed cooking the Christmas dinner, but it was okay because her little boy couldn't speak anyway, and Lucy was dealing with it in her own way. Mummy's with Jesus.

She's gone for ever.

'Cheers,' she said. 'Happy New Year.'

'Ch-Cheers. Yes, and a Happy New Year to you.'

Suddenly she found it all intimidating. Where did you beat her up then, the girl you bought for Christmas Eve? she wanted to ask. Down here, was it, or up in the bedroom? And where's all the gear? Did Emily bring it over from Derbyshire Mansions?

'Strange,' she heard herself say. 'Something very strange.'

'Yes?'

'I remembered your bedroom when I was away. Over Christmas.'

'Oh.' He sounded concerned, worried.

'Up in your room, your bedroom, upstairs next to the dining room. You have a picture up there. A painting of a large country house and grounds, the land behind it slopes up to a skyline. Top of a church just visible at one end, and a little clump of trees at the other.'

'Yes. Overchurch Manor. You said you were going there for...' familiar hesitation, '...Christmas.'

'Not to the manor though. I went to a little cottage that doesn't show in that painting.'

'Yes. I had guessed. Oh my God, were you related to—?'

Not such a twit as she'd thought. 'Yes. My sister.'

'I'm so terribly sorry.'

For one horrible second she thought he was coming over to her. Arm round her shoulders, comforting. 'Whatever you do don't touch me,' she said, but not out loud.

'You're still on the c-case?'

She nodded. This was a very bad idea.

Shouldn't have come. 'Look—' she began.

'I understand.'

She doubted that.

'Is it the same man who ... Who ... Jo Benton?'

She nodded. 'Possibly.'

'And Emily?'

'We don't know about Emily Baccus. Not sure. I have some questions.'

He stood. 'I have to nip up to the k-kitchen. It's a very simple dinner, but I have to deal with something now.'

He went upstairs, hurrying, and Suzie was unnerved. She stood up, slid her hand into her waistband. Held the end of the truncheon. She took a look round, opened the door out to the office. One light burned overhead, but she saw the long mirror and the Breugel. She recognized the copy now, *Children's Games*, was it? She closed the door and walked over to the passage that led to the stairs.

It is an unconventional arrangement. Above here I have a dining room, kitchen and bedroom.

He came bustling down the stairs. 'There. All doing fine. A very simple meal.'

'What are we having?'

'Very simple. A ca-carrot soup. Some veal escalopes—'

'Where, in heaven did you—?'

'I have a friend. I thought I had told you. There are ways.' He shrugged, almost blushed. 'But you know that. You ca-catch them every day.' She said nothing, so he continued. 'Some duchesse potatoes; beans. I store them in salt.

571

In Ki-Kilner jars.'

'Mr Dance?'

'Mmm? Yes?'

'I want to ask you a couple of questions.' Get it out of the way, she thought, then she was saying he could sling her out if he liked, but someone else would come and ask. She thought this was the easier way. Did he mind if she smoked?

Not at all. He offered her one of his. Came over to light it for her. Just don't lay a hand on me. Stay back. She actively disliked him now she knew about what he did with – to – women.

'The picture? Overchurch Manor?'

'I've known the village since I was a ch-child.' He sat upright, spread his hands, palms inward, as though saying he had nothing to hide. 'My father did a large oil of the manor house. Knew the family – the Harricky family. Old Miss Harricky, as she is now, was a keen painter. My father gave her advice, lessons, and she painted that oil of the manor. There was something between my father and her, a long time ago. I don't know the full story but she gave him her painting and he couldn't bear to have it in the house. Passed it on to me. I've kept it because, well – because I like the manor. It's special for me.'

'You still go down there? Overchurch?'

'Sometimes.'

'When was the last time?'

He looked at her, a long time. Not properly with her for a minute or so. 'The last time?

572

Beginning of November. Second of November, near Guy Fawkes Night. I went down to—' He shook his head, said, 'No, you've no need to know all that.' Looked away, then said he'd been to see the vet. 'I needed to leave something with him.' Laugh. 'You had some serious questions?'

Suzie let it pass. Something had gone on with Josh Dance, but she didn't think it had anything to do with the killings. Probably had a lot to do with his past and, maybe the days just before Dunkirk. Serious questions?

'I'd like to talk to you about the Baccus family.'

'Oh, yes.' Guarded. Taking a step back.

She guessed that by now he'd realized that she knew something about his particular problems with women. Maybe he felt guilty. Regretted now – quickly – that she had not gone on with the plan to draw everything out of him in friendly conversation. Maybe she wasn't enough of an actress.

'How well did you know them?'

'Well enough. I knew the old man, of c-course. Quite a lad in his day.'

'Emily his only child?'

'Why d'you ask?'

'Mainly because we've noticed a similarity between Emily Baccus and a possible suspect. Also someone who claimed to know Emily well, then couldn't recognize her photograph.'

'Who? Well-known person, is it?'

'I can't tell you that.'

He remained silent for almost a minute. 'I

573

don't suppose there's any harm in telling you now. The old man rarely s-spread it around, didn't talk about it while he was alive. Fact is he had two other children. By two different women as well. Took responsibility for them. Paid for their upbringing, educations. Everything. S-Saw them as well, regularly while he was alive.'

'Emily knew? She see them as well?'

'Oh, yes. Like her father. Regularly.'

'And after his death?'

A short wait. 'Well, she saw her half-brother. I don't really know about the half-sister. She did speak to her, so I presume...'

'There was a boy and a girl?'

He nodded, said, 'Yes. Yes, he had the set.' Attractive smile.

'Names?'

'He gave them his name when they were born. The boy later changed his, retained the Christian name, but took on a new surname. The girl married. So...'

'And their names, now? At this moment?'

'I only know the girl because of hearing Emily telephoning her. She was Rosemary Baccus and her married name was, I think, Lattimer – bit of a dark horse, unsavoury character. Rosemary Lattimer. Husband killed '36 or '37. Bit infra dig actually, killed in some pub brawl by some lowlifes. Never pinned it on anybody, the police.'

'Got an address?'

'Afraid not. You'll probably find something among Emily's papers. There was some friction. Money of course. When Rosemary married, the old man cut back on the cash and left everything to Emily, with a discretionary clause about using her common sense regarding her half-sister.' He glanced down at his watch. 'We should go up. The soup's ready. I've only got to do the escalopes and the potatoes and beans will be right on time.'

'And the son?'

'Oh,' he sounded as though this was a trivial business. No need to waste time on it. 'Oh, Barry. Barry Baccus.'

'Changed his name to—?'

'Forbes. Barry Forbes. Old Paul Baccus had a cousin who married an eminent English doctor, called Forbes. He treated Barry like his own. Had another child a year or two later. They were like brothers.' And as he said it, the air-raid warning siren came rising up, growling, then wailing its horrible snarl across London. 'Damn,' he said. 'Have to go up. If that's a serious one I'll have to get out on the roof.' He led the way.

It was just after six o'clock, and it couldn't have been more serious. The aircraft came in, Heinkels and Dorniers from bases in northern France and Field Marshal Hugo Sperrle, commander of Luftflotte 3, had given tonight's raid a name. It was to be called 'the 29th Fire Blitz' and its object was to destroy the entire walled City of London by the saturation fire bombing of its one square mile.

Suzie followed Dance up the stairs, and remained close to him as he turned out the lights and opened the door to the roof. As he did so the sound of aircraft seemed to bump in on their ears – that strange noise of unsynchronized engines they would both remember all their lives. As she stepped out on to the roof, still close to him, she heard the sound of whistling in the air – not close, but eerie and followed by a clattering as though thousands of tin cans were falling in the streets to their east, close to the City.

It was much lighter out on the roof. Inside, with the lamps all turned off, it was pitch dark. Couldn't see a hand in front of you, as Golly found out when he emerged from the cupboard under the stairs. He had heard the noises and knew that something was going on upstairs. Wait, he told himself. Wait Golly. Your eyes'll get used to it.

Out on the roof, Suzie had followed Dance up to the corner, overlooking Piccadilly. She remembered that there was a good two and a half feet width between the pitch of the roof and the balustrade, an easy walk. From the corner they could see far off, over the buildings to the City of London. First, the great incendiary canisters had fallen, many short of their targets, carried on the stiffening wind. But others made it directly on to that history-soaked square mile, the canisters opening at one thousand feet and spewing out their smaller wicked incendiary bombs that came down in their hundreds, hitting the streets and buildings, bouncing vividly into being, spraying and showering the black streets and deserted buildings with phosphorus, igniting the fires that would rage through those same streets that Samuel Pepys wrote of during the Great Fire of London in 1666. Within a very short time those old streets were again ablaze and Suzie watched with horror from the roof of Josh Dance's building. Creed Lane, Ave Maria Lane, Amen Court and all the rest of them engulfed in fire: from Moorgate to Aldersgate, from Old Street to Cannon Street; up Ludgate Hill and around St Paul's Cathedral.

After some twenty minutes she knew that she would be there all night if she didn't move now. It was a terrible and beautiful sight, the sky becoming deep red with the flames, turning to a rose coloured reflection as clouds of smoke choked out the light.

She said nothing to Dance, just turned and picked her way back along the wide, flat gutter around the building. Above everything else she wanted her coat because the wind was getting colder, starting to cut through her as she had stood hypnotized by the flames.

She reached the outline of the doorway leading in to the upper quarters of Josh Dance's apartment. She stepped into the blackness and felt her way to the top of the stairs.

Resting her hand on the banister rail just inside the door, she paused, waiting in the hope that her eyes would adjust to the blackness. And as she did so, she felt another human hand cover her hand. A hand in a leather glove there in the dark.

Golly close beside her.

Twenty-Eight

She shrieked in terror. Screamed, turned, stumbled on the stairs, wanted to vomit then felt the piano wire brush across her hair. As she stumbled, Suzie grabbed for the waist of her skirt, missed the baton on the first grope, then held it, drew the weapon and slashed at the air like you'd slash at an angry wasp – to and fro, putting all her strength behind the blows.

She heard the animal growl in Golly's throat as he threw out his loop of piano wire a second time. He had flattened himself to one side against the wall waiting for her to go past, but in reaching out to steady himself he accidentally placed his hand over the back of her hand as she got to the top of the stairs. He knew that he could have failed again. Emily Baccus wouldn't like that and there would be some great punishment.

This had become a struggle at close quarters and Golly could only triumph from strength and surprise. His forte was attacking from ambush. Robbed of surprise and position he could only founder, incapable of fighting face to face.

Suzie lashed out, and again missed, then once more, and she felt the truncheon connect hard: heard the yelp of agony as Golly felt the bone-deep blow hard on his left shoulder. She was so close to him that she smelled his sour breath and the rancid sweat inside his shirt. In her head she thought this was the smell of death. Her final sensation in life. She flailed in his direction again and again, felt her wrist jar as she caught him on the top of his right arm. This time he cried out louder and she aimed her next blow downward at his head. But he was away, ducking under her raised arm, stumbling back, then finding his feet and charging down the stairs.

She heard the thudding of his boots as he broke clear and half-fell, half-ran from her. She gulped for air, then turned, pushed back, kicking at the open door leading on to the roof, closing it, then feeling for the light switch, relieved when the bulb flooded and brightened the corridor and stairs. Far away below in the entrance hall she heard the front door slam. Had he really gone?

Suzie was panting, scared half to death, her lungs straining as she drew in air, shoulders shaking as she began to cry: weeping with the relief of breaking free, for she was petrified, terrified of Golly and his dreadful presence. Dear God, if you let me live I'll never doubt you ever again. Sweet Jesus, help me. Holy Mary Mother of God, pray for us sinners, now and at the hour of our death.

She could still smell Golly and feel him close to her. Even though he had run from her Suzie could not accept it: she sensed him nearby, a powerful evil in the night and in this building, like a bright image burned on her retina, refusing to disappear.

She dragged her coat from where Dance had hung it in his office, slung it round her shoulders, then turned sideways on to the stairs and went down them fast, the truncheon raised against the beast that was Golly Goldfinch, ready should he still be waiting for her in the hallway or on the pavement outside.

The house trembled, shook as though it was built on subterranean tunnels through which huge shock waves were passing, attempting to rock and jolt its fabric. Under her feet she felt the ground sway and the stairs tip as she went down into the empty hallway, and straight out of the door. In the street the ground still tilted and rippled as the bombs exploded, far off on Ludgate Hill and around the great cathedral dome of St Paul's.

The air was fetid with the familiar singed stench that rose from the City and was carried west on the cold breeze. Even here, shielded by buildings, the sky was stained rust and crimson going to red, turning into a rosy glow as though the City of London was consumed by a hurricane of fire.

She had come out on to the street still with the truncheon raised, her body moving, from left to right, eyes everywhere, glancing behind her, then amidst the other noise she heard boots heavy on the pavement as Golly's footsteps winnowed away, deflected by other noises. Now, late and in terror she began to blow her police whistle.

Then she heard the car's engine as it bustled down the street towards her.

'In, heart,' Tommy called and Molly leaned out of the car to give her a hand and pull her into the back. Brian went smoothly through the gears, gathering speed towards Piccadilly.

'Did you see him?' she asked, still gulping for air.

'Who? Dance?'

'Goldfinch. Nearly had me.'

'Jesus! Which way? Which way did he go?'

'I don't know. I hit him a couple of times but he got away. I never want to...'

Tommy was shouting instructions and Brian performed some daredevil manoeuvre, turning the car round, spinning it on a sixpence.

'Go left first,' Tommy shouted. 'Slow down. Slower, Brian.' And for over half-an-hour they ploughed their way down every side street.

And saw nothing.

'We've got to go to the Yard,' Dandy Tom said, swivelling round, looking concerned, feeling her bruised flesh with his eyes. She opened her mouth to start telling him what had taken place, but he stopped her – 'Wait, don't talk about it yet, heart. Wait till we get to the Yard.' A pause. 'The City's in a dreadful state. On fire from end to end. I wouldn't be surprised if St Paul's has had it. Their bloody timing's immaculate. Couldn't be a better night for them to firebomb the City.'

Most of the City of London was empty on this, the last Sunday of the year. The churches were closed and warehouses and similar

581

buildings were locked and barred until Monday morning. In spite of the experience of the Manchester firebombing over Christmas, the City of London was woefully unprepared. Keyholders were absent, fire-watchers had not reported for duty – the following week fire-watching was made compulsory. Tonight there was not enough water to fight the fires, and the firemen couldn't even get it from the river because there was a neap tide that night. The river was so unnaturally low that when they did get a pump down, it quickly clogged with mud.

Then the wind aggravated matters; fire-storms spread through the narrow streets and lanes of the most historic area of London, great waves and walls of flame rising, devouring everything in their path. St Paul's Cathedral was hit by several incendiaries but no major fire caught hold, thanks to its Night Watch volunteers. In the end it stood, an icon of survival, ringed with fire. But the beautiful fifteenth-century Guildhall was not so lucky. The oldest building of its kind in England was consumed by waves of flame that raced down streets and lanes, sliding from windows, taking away almost everything it touched.

Streets became so hot that the asphalt caught fire, glass cracked and exploded from windows, iron girders twisted like seaside rock, blaze begat blaze as high explosive bombs followed the incendiaries and a senior fireman broke down saying they were like small boys peeing on a bonfire.

Twelve of the City's water mains were

fractured, so that the firemen eventually had to withdraw and let the fires burn themselves out. Over the entire area night became day and in the newspaper offices of Fleet Street, journalists and printers could read their copy without electric light.

At their worst the fires could be seen from some of the *Luftwaffe* bases in northern France. In railway stations glass and aluminium fittings melted and formed silver pools on the broken and shattered platforms.

It was said that Winston Churchill looked out on the fires that night and said, 'We'll get the bastards for this.' And the Deputy Chief of Air Staff, standing on the Air Ministry roof, muttered, 'Well, they are sowing the wind—'

It was not necessary for him to complete the saying about reaping the whirlwind.

And as the City burned, thousands of rats poured from the warehouses and cellars, escaping from the flames that enveloped the area, taking with it more than five hundred years of history.

Golly ran through the many side streets, trying to escape the anger he had felt when grappling with the lady policeman. Now he was frightened of what would happen to him. For a time he hid among some ornamental bushes fronting houses in a side street less than fifty yards from the offices of Jewell, Baccus & Dance. From this lair he watched as a car trawled the streets searching for him. When it passed for the third time he thought he could glimpse the lady policeman in the back, leaning forward to peer out, looking for him.

The ground still shook from the explosions, and a blizzard of burned paper swirled up from the firestorms around St Paul's, whirling as far west as Knightsbridge and Kensington. As he dodged from street to street, Golly actually thought it was real snow, until he saw the tiny white cobwebs of ash, and the glow of paper flakes still alight, like fireflies in the ice cold air.

He plodded on, and found doorways and darker places in which to hide. He made detours when he saw police, civil defence wardens, ambulances and firemen working ahead. His confidence returned and slowly he moved across the great capital city, heading towards his goal. What little reason he had told him that if the lady policeman was out searching for him, her home would be unguarded.

He knew how to get in.

He would wait for her there.

Dandy Tom called a meeting of his available people after he had spoken to Suzie Mountford in the privacy of his office. She told him what she had learned from Josh Dance. First the tenuous link he had with Overchurch, and his sinister refusal to go on talking about himself. 'There's some secret there,' she told him. 'But I'm not sure it has anything to do with crime.'

'Beating up toms is illegal if I catch him at it,' Tommy snapped.

Then she went on to talk about Paul Baccus and his family. 'Two other illegitimate children as well as Emily,' she told him, and then spoke of the way the son, Barry, had changed his name to Forbes, and that Rosemary had married a dodgy bloke called Lattimer who had died in some pub brawl. This, she considered, was probably the true reason for old Baccus cutting her out of his will. 'He seems to have gone out of his way to take care of them all until Rosemary's marriage. And it sounds as if he was a bit of an autocrat, even to the illegitimate children.'

Tommy said that it was no wonder she had spotted a similarity between Emily Baccus and Barry Forbes. 'Strange to think that Forbes could rise to such a position on the Prime Minister's staff, yet you know he would never have been allowed to rise in the Church, had he been that way inclined. Could never have been ordained a priest in the Church of England.'

Illegitimate males were still barred from the Anglican priesthood, as though the sin of fornication spilled over to stain them at birth. 'You can serve Mammon but not God.' Tommy laughed.

They had not gone down to the shelters. Work appeared to continue normally at the Yard where they were monitoring the situation in the City of London, receiving regular reports on how Ludgate Hill, at the bottom of Fleet Street, was ablaze, and many situation reports on the Tube and railway stations that were burning. Moorgate Station was engulfed in sheets of flame, and the Tube stations at Cannon Street and London Bridge were well ablaze. Then how London Bridge itself was on fire, and that the fleeing rats had run in droves into the West End to terrify those in the shelters and streets almost more than Hitler's bombs.

Tommy was up in the canteen with Suzie, getting their first food of the night when the All Clear finally sounded just after 11.40. Later they heard the great fire blitz would have gone on longer but for fog that had swept in over northern France, forcing the Germans to order aircraft back to their bases.

'I suppose we'd best get this show on the road then.' Tommy admitted that it went against the grain to be running after a simple-minded psychopath who killed indiscriminately and consorted with whores. As he said, he would rather have been down in the City, in the thick of the bombs and fires dealing with that German psychopath. 'Members of my family fought in the Crimea, at Waterloo and on the Western Front. What do I do? I become a Peeler and spend my time scrabbling around in the sewers chasing a half-witted strangler.'

'Yes, but you met me through your job, Tommy. Isn't that a bonus?' Suzie whispered.

'We'll see about that, heart,' he said cryptically, then smiled his splendid smile and began giving orders.

Billy Mulligan had a search warrant to hand. 'I want you to supervise it, Billy. Go through it like the proverbial dose of *Ipomoea purga*.'

'Education's a wonderful thing, Guv,' Billy grinned, 'but for the ignorant could you translate?'

'Jollop to you, Billy.'

The search warrant was for Lavender's business premises off Rupert Street. He wanted Billy to lead other officers in and, as he put it, 'Give it a search like God's revenge. I want every scrap of paper, everything that's not nailed down, every piece of furniture, clothes, even her spare knicker elastic. All of it, every last tic and flea. Put all of it in the forensics boys' hands and rake out every dust mote, give it the works.'

Next he singled out Molly Abelard to go and, as he put it, 'Lock up Forbes's house near Marble Arch. Don't let him out of your sight. Harass him. Stick to him like a piece of corn plaster. Get up his arse like a brown nose. I'm going to get a warrant so we can invite him in to assist with our enquiries as soon as possible in the morning.' He scratched his head elegantly – Suzie had decided there wasn't a thing he did not do elegantly – and mentioned setting up a trace on the Lattimer girl.

'So, we've also got to trace this Lattimer girl,' said Dandy Tom.

'Lattimer?' Shirley, who had been giving a good impression of a young woman nodding off to sleep, lifted her head.

'You got something to contribute, Shirley?'

'You mentioned a Lattimer, Guv.' Pulling herself together, dusting herself down, polishing her nails.

'So I did. For everybody's information, Rosemary Lattimer is the married name of the late

Emily Baccus's half-sister: the one born on the wrong side of the blanket. Anything to add, Shirl?'

'Yes, sir.' To give her her due, she had started to look sheepish. 'You remember when I went to have a look-see at Lavender the tom in her house in Camford?'

'I recall it clearly, Shirley. Fourteen Dyers Road, wasn't it?'

'I think it's her real name, Guv.'

'Whose real name?'

'Lavender's real name. I got a squint at some letters she had lying on a table in her front room. That's who they were addressed to – Mrs R. Lattimer, 14 Dyers Road, Camford.'

Almost before she had stopped talking, Tommy had a telephone to his ear, asking for Camford CID.

'No, sir,' Pip Magnus said. He answered Dandy Tom's call, and told him Detective Chief Inspector Anthony Harvey wasn't in. 'Only just back at work. He was badly injured in the Blitz, sir.' He would probably be back in the morning. Or if this was very urgent, sir, he was duty CID all through the night as the song had it. Detective Constable Philip Magnus, at your service, ready to do your bidding, kiss your arse and hope to die, Guv'nor.

'There's a tom in your area that we're very interested in,' Tommy almost drooled. 'Works out of a set of rooms quarter of an alley off Rupert Street, Soho. Has a respectable house in your manor, in Camford – fourteen Dyers Road. Goes by the name of Lavender, but is really Mrs Rosemary Lattimer. I'd be most grateful if you'd go along to her place at first light – or earlier if you could manage it. Ask her to wander in with you so that we can talk to her.' He stressed that Mr Magnus should not lose sight of this woman, and that they were exceptionally anxious to have words with her. 'Quite important, I'd say. I'll send someone over for her when you let my office know she's at your nick. Can you do that? Or shall I send over someone who can?' He omitted the 'heart' but would have used it had Magnus been a female of the species.

'I'll do it, Guv. It'll be a pleasure.' Pip Magnus hung up the earpiece of his telephone, got his overcoat and wandered upstairs, went through to the front of the police station, told the duty sergeant he was going to take a walk round the block and went out into the night.

He only got as far as the telephone box on the corner, outside the post office. Inside, he opened his notebook and struck a match to read off the number he required. In the distance the sky glowed a ferocious red and he muttered what passed for a prayer for the poor buggers who'd been caught in that lot. The operator told him to insert three pence into the coin box and press Button A when the party answered.

'Camford 649,' Lavender's bleary voice said, full of sleep.

'Lavender?'

'Yes.'

'It's Philip. You recognize my voice?'

589

'Yes, of course, Pip.'

'Big Toe would want me to do this, Lavender.'

'What?'

'Giving you a little warning, darlin'. I don't know what you've done, and I don't want to know. Sling your hook, right? Get on your bike, fast. The Yard want a word and their breath is already warming your ears.'

'Thanks, Pip. Thanks. Okay? Right?'

'Good luck, girl.'

Magnus walked slowly back to the nick, knowing that Big Toe would be delighted with his work that night.

Having set things in motion, Tommy decided that he was going to get a bit of rest until first light. 'You sound like an officer in the Great War getting ready to go over the top,' Suzie told him.

'That's exactly what I feel like, heart.' He shot her a tired smile and, in the back of the unmarked Wolseley she stretched like a dozy cat. They were being followed by another car holding two of the lads who would watch over them until early morning. Dandy Tom was still not taking any chances. He had set everything up by saying loudly that he felt it would be safer if 'I slept across your door, heart, and brought a couple of the lads with me'. Among his Spear Carriers knowing looks and raised eyebrows were exchanged.

They had to make a detour because Charing Cross Station was closed. An ugly great parachute mine hung precariously adjacent to the platforms. By the morning five railway stations and sixteen Underground stations were closed; nineteen churches destroyed; over 160 civilians killed and 500 injured.

When they finally arrived at Suzie Mount-ford's flat, Tommy got out of the Wolseley, walked back to the second car and gave some brief orders to the lads. 'Eyes back and front, In your arses and necks boys. Keep your ears open, your nasal passages clear and your sixth senses on the *qui vive.* You know the drill?'

'Don't worry, Guv. We'll keep you snug as a bug.'

'Snug as two bugs,' he corrected them.

And they went in. Up to the fifth floor and into Suzie's flat.

The telephone was ringing as they walked through the door and Suzie picked it up.

'I gather the Guv'nor's keeping his optics on your place, heart.' Molly Abelard did a pass-able imitation of Tommy at his most manner-ed.

She told her, yes, and Molly said she'd like a word.

'Cheeky cow,' Suzie mouthed towards Tom-my as he took the telephone. Then she mouth-ed that she was going for a pee and headed into the bathroom.

She switched the light on, slid the little bolt on the door, flicked her skirt up, hooked her fingers under her pants and turned to sit on the lavatory. And as she turned she saw Golly standing there grinning at her.

Twenty-Nine

For the second time in a matter of hours, Suzie faced the nightmare that had been with her since Charlotte's death. This time she was literally struck dumb: paralysed; wanted to cry out and couldn't, told her brain to kick the standing horror in the balls and couldn't. For what felt like minutes the only thing she seemed capable of doing was to let go of her skirt, then slowly she began to move, too late for the truncheon; too late for anything.

Her world alternated between slow action and slower reaction, like that silly funny doctored film of Hitler, speeded up and slowed down to make it appear as though he was dancing a strange and convoluted eighteenth-century jig.

Golly gave a low, grinning, breathy, almost lascivious laugh. His face was uncovered so that she looked clear into the awful features – the eyes set at different levels, red rimmed and glowering; the long, entrenched jagged scar, the lightning rune drawn deep down his face from hair line to jutted chin; the nose oddly split and the cockeyed mouth dragged askew. And from where she stood she was conscious of his dark breath: part dog, part decay.

I like to call it the Quasimodo syndrome, Dandy

Tom had said.

Golly was certainly a primitive. He was such a total evil. An unholy sacrament, the deformity being, in his case, an outward and all too visible sign of an inward, and unspiritual evil. He was the one in a million exception proving the rule.

Her hand seemed hardly to touch the truncheon before his sweating paws came up, banging hard on her shoulders knocking her almost off balance, then spinning her round so that her back was to him.

Now he could do it.

Now she was right.

His wrists crossed with the wire grasped tight, and he dropped it, quietly and accurately over her head and pulled.

> Over hill and over dale,
> See we come together.

She knew her breath was being wrenched out of her as he made the longer, stronger pull on the well-bound ends of the piano wire. She croaked out in a last desperate cry. Pushed back from her pelvis, felt his knee, painful in the small of her back and thought of the tiny poem that dear Dandy Tom had written and left on her pillow only a couple of nights ago—

> For the Chinese this year may be
> the Year of the Snake,
> But for me it will always be the
> Year of the Small of Your Back.

Then came the dreadful slicing agony as the wire bit. She had a vision of a grocer cutting a piece of cheese with wire and was aware that this was what was happening to her neck.

In a final hopeless attempt she did the standard shin- and foot-crushing move, the outside of her right shoe's sole smashing into his shin, grating down and hitting his foot jarringly hard. Golly must have felt the moment of pain, but he withstood the agony and increased the pressure in her neck. Jesus, she thought in prayer. Made an act of contrition, as she felt the anguish too much to bear. She knew she was sliding towards some green haven with water slowly trickling through it, an oasis where the pain and everything else would be left behind. Her neck was on fire but even that was bearable as the mist moved in and she felt herself going down, her knees buckling.

Then there was a change: a sudden drop and she was falling forever, escaping down and down a long tunnel, descending slowly, almost flying and crying out as she went – not a shout of fear but a cry of release.

And then snatches from another voice close to her. 'Stay down, you little bastard – Don't move, you abortion – You gimp! You mizzler! You junk! Stay where you are.'

She recognized the voice, felt the drilling torment in her neck, opened her eyes and realized she was on her bathroom floor. Trying to raise her head she saw Tommy Livermore's feet, and heard his voice again.

Later she was never certain if she had actually seen her rescue or simply imagined it, putting pictures in her head, illustrating the noises she could hear through the blurred and painful world around her. Dandy Tom smashing in the door with his shoulder, careering into the bathroom; the surprised look on Golly's face, thinking she had come into the house alone: not caring to believe what was happening. Then the way her darling Tommy launched himself at Golly, like a dreadful avenging angel, airborne for a second as he flung himself forward, stretched out towards Golly's loathsome face.

Tommy Livermore grabbed at one of Golly's wrists, lifted one arm behind his back bending him forward, and shouting in fury at the man who had taken too many souls already. Goldfinch's wrists were now manacled firmly behind his back, and Tommy had tipped him into the bath, screaming at him as if that was the only way he could be stopped from killing.

Certainly Suzie saw this last tableau because she remembered thinking that her Dandy Tom was frightened of Golly. Like someone who feared a deadly spider, he had his own brand of arachnophobia.

'Heart? Heart, can you hear me? Are you okay?' Then a terrible change of tone, 'Not you, you abomination. Not you. Still. Stay still, you ugly little bastard.'

She propped herself on one arm and saw feet protruding from the bath, heard ghastly cries as though from a ruptured voice box and finally perceived that the cries came from herself.

The voice belonging to the legs and feet hanging over the side of her bath was a different voice, the sound of a husky, slow and deformed voice – 'I dident mean – She told me to do it – She told me – Emily said I had to – I dident mean it—' and she saw the face, tearful and terrible in one mixture. The face of Golly Goldfinch, as her lover heaved him out of the bath by his handcuffed wrists and half threw him at the two uniformed lads whom he had somehow summoned.

And in the doorway stood a third figure – Molly Abelard – an arm outstretched with a pistol in her hand aimed squarely at Golly.

'I'll talk to him later,' Tommy snarled. 'Don't give the press a bloody thing. Just get him away from her. Don't give him an inch, Molly, hear me?'

Funny, Suzie wondered, is Molly allowed to do that? Is she allowed to carry a gun?

She had thought of Golly Goldfinch as relentless, she recalled. He was more. He was tenacious, resolute, inexorable, unshakeable until he came up against Dandy Tom Livermore, who was at this moment kneeling beside her and enfolding her, whispering endearments and giving her courage.

An ambulance was on the way, and a police doctor. In a little while she would be safe.

She felt the ragged traces of terror in her veins and could not control her limbs, didn't know if she'd ever use her voice again. Shivering there on the bathroom floor, wet and like a whipped puppy.

A pair of nurses and a doctor were suddenly there, as if Dandy Tom had waved a magic wand and brought them up out of a star trap. Was she in a pantomime? she wondered. Had Golly played the Demon King? Was Dandy Tom really Dandini?

As they carried her out, she croaked her thanks to Tommy, but she didn't know if he heard, or even understood.

But *she* heard. She heard a choir singing one of her favourite hymns. One her dad had liked as well and she knew he had somehow been very close to her in the past half-hour—

Immortal, invisible, God only wise,
In light inaccessible hid from our eyes
Most blessèd, most glorious, the Ancient of Days,
Almighty, victorious, Thy great name we praise.

And she really didn't know what that had to do with anything except, perhaps, that Golly was so warped and hazardous that he had been in danger of becoming the antithesis of all those sentiments.

In the ambulance the doctor gave her an injection and she slid quietly into sleep.

She woke a couple of times during what she thought was the night, to a feeling of great fear.

597

On both occasions she was aware of someone, or something, sitting near her bed. On the third occasion she burst through her fear and saw that it was a policewoman in uniform, though at the time she didn't believe it for a moment.

When she woke again it was Molly Abelard, in a twin-set and grey skirt. 'Shush, Suzie,' she soothed. So Suzie presumed that she had been talking in her sleep, or crying. She remembered the gun and how it seemed to have grown out of Molly's hand, and that frightened her.

It must have been the next day that she wakened properly, or maybe it was the day after that. A pair of nurses propped her up. Talked to her and listened as she tried to croak back. Propped up she found that it was difficult to move her head and there was a moment when she actually thought that if she moved it any further it would fall off. They gave her a pad of paper, like the ones she'd had at school, and several pencils so that she could communicate by writing. She didn't much feel like it though.

They fed her, painfully, with some kind of clear soup – a consommé with bits of spaghetti in it – and late at night Tommy Livermore visited her with the doctor.

The doctor asked a lot of questions. Could she feel this, or that, or the other thing? He looked down her throat with an unpleasant instrument, then got a nurse to take the bandages from her neck. His examination of the neck wasn't the most longed-for experience of her life.

'Want to have a look?' the doctor asked. She nodded and her head nearly fell off again. 'Shit!' she said, but not out loud. They held up a mirror and she couldn't bear to look for very long. Her neck was swollen and deformed, like a goitre, as if someone had forced a great raw misshapen red balloon under her skin, and through it there was a deep scarlet slice, a cavern disappearing into her flesh.

'It'll be back to normal in no time – well, a few weeks,' the doctor said. He wore an expensive suit, she noticed. Dark with chalk stripes, and he was very smoothly shaved. His skin glinted and he had presence. 'Everything will take time. You'll probably feel a bit strung out and generally dicey for a while, but you'll be fine when we've got you up and walking around.'

Oh certainly, she thought, if my head stays on and if I ever get my voice back, I'll feel over the moon. And if I manage to stop jumping at my reflection; or worrying in case that's Golly's soft footstep on the stair, coming closer to the door, on the landing.

Then Tommy stayed with her. He had brought flowers, a bottle of Lucozade and several cards – one each from Molly Abelard, Shirley Cox and Billy Mulligan, and a big one signed 'From the Lads and the Spear Carriers', with a row of Xs for kisses and Os for hugs. How did he know she liked Lucozade? When she had her tonsils out they gave her glasses of Lucozade with vanilla ice cream floating like icebergs in the fizzy liquid. That was when she was four years old.

Then there was the upsetting business of Ned Griffith. First, a long letter from him, full of sadness and what-ifs and buts and how he was sorry: a dull letter really except for his apology for his folly in Cambridge and for leaving Overchurch on Christmas afternoon. 'I did not see how I could help any more,' he wrote lamely about the latter event. The next week there was bad news. Ned Griffith was dead, bounced by Me109s over the Pas de Calais with another young pilot, Jamie Simnel; both wiped from the sky. Ned aged twenty-four; Simnel barely twenty. It was happening to all the best people in this washed-out, grey, tired and battered country where everything seemed to have been painted in insipid water-colours.

But, after the doctor left, on the night that Tommy brought her the cards and flowers she had a little cry and then asked – as best she could – if Golly was under lock and key. She was still terrified of him and would be for a long time to come. She reckoned Tommy was as well.

'Don't worry, heart, they're going to keep him locked up tight for the rest of his natural.' Golly was spending time with the trick cyclists, as Tommy called them. 'There's nothing remotely sophisticated about Golly. Just an efficient killing machine.' As for the trick cyclists, 'Funny people,' Dandy Tom said. 'Still, they did a lot for a pair of my uncles, and one almost cured my Aunt Annie.'

About Golly he said, 'Takes orders, then goes and does it. Totally cold-blooded. They say – the trick cyclists say – that he probably invented a voice in his head in the early stages. It's not uncommon, he'd believe it completely of course.' He reckoned that they could still uncover a lot of Golly's victims. 'Been at it since he was quite young. Then someone hit on a way of trying to use him. Quite clever. Sussed him out, crept up to him in the dark and whispered orders into his ear.'

'Other news?' Suzie wrote, wanting to get off the subject of Golly. But that was impossible.

They had arrested Barry Forbes. 'Good case against him: aiding and abetting Goldfinch; possibly two murder charges – we're almost certain he killed Emily Baccus and Golly's mother, Ailsa. He certainly had a solid personal motive to keep Golly a few steps ahead of the law.' Tommy told her they were piecing together the story of Manny Spellthorne's disappearance. 'Now Golly's starting to talk he's telling us all kinds of things.'

It looked as though Forbes had dogged Golly to Overchurch, then followed him afterwards. 'Haven't a clue about his motives, except that there was money in it somewhere along the way, and Lavender had him on a short leash as well. We're investigating the Benton/Baccus business, and that generated a lot of loot.' They were keeping that side of things a bit quiet though. 'The PM doesn't need that kind of scandal at the moment.' Forbes, he said, was ideally placed to provide certain introductions.

It was rather shocking really, Suzie thought, that there might be rotten apples in the government itself, particularly at this terrible time when the country seemed to be teetering on the brink of disaster. Unheard of, she imagined in her naivety.

After a while, Tommy told her he loved her, and that made her heart perform a few arias and took her mind off the worst excesses of this unpleasant business.

'Of course the other Baccus – Lavender – is *heavily* involved,' he said. 'It's really obvious now, couldn't have been anyone else – close to Golly for all that time. From what's been said, it was Lavender who involved Forbes, got him to dispose of Manny Spellthorne's body – so Golly says. If you can believe him.' A long pause and some tapping of the teeth with the gold pen. 'Incredibly odd relationship that – Lavender and Barry. Incestuous, I suppose.'

Certainly it was Lavender who had been the voice in the night, coming out of the dark to give Golly his instructions.

Kill with the wire.

They'd found two wigs in the Dyers Road house, and some photographs. Shirley Cox had been sent down to Middle Wallop to show a photograph to Fordham O'Dell. He had identified her, with her own hair, as the Emily Baccus he knew. Yet a photo of her in the dark wig made her almost a dead ringer for the real Emily. Shirley had come back thrilled to bits, having been dined in the officers' mess. 'Met some wizard chaps,' she had said. 'Got some pukkah gen. Piece of cake.'

'She's been going around using Raff slang ever since,' Tommy said, and they had a laugh about it, though Suzie couldn't laugh because it hurt and she found her face muscles impossible to move. She thought of the old joke about the soldier fighting the Zulus. Got a spear through his shoulder and dragged himself into the CO's office. 'Doesn't it hurt, Cogger?' asked the CO, to which Cogger replied, 'Only when I laugh, sir.' And that only made matters worse.

Eventually, Tommy turned back to the case. The one certain target, he reckoned, was Jo Benton. 'Worked together, played together, whored together and, I suspect, conned together and maybe blackmailed together as well. No doubt she enjoyed the games, but there was an even darker side. They were making a fortune one way or another – mainly the other.'

Benton's murder, he said, was hiding a tree in a forest: something they had discussed before. 'It was an idea I had. With murders that don't have an obvious suspect – particularly with repeats – you go through the whole spectrum. It was one possible, I thought; pretty far down the list, but there nevertheless.'

'Like the film you saw at Saturday pictures?' she wrote.

He laughed. '*The Clutching Hand?* Yes. Sure, heart.'

It was at this point that she mentioned Molly

Abelard to him: Molly Abelard and the pistol. Had she actually seen that, or was it an hallucination?

'Depends, heart, doesn't it?' With the cute smile and one eyebrow cocked upwards.

'Tommy don't be silly.' She was weary and almost ready to doze off again.

'With Molly, heart, you never know. She's given a lot of licence. People turn a blind eye.' Leaving her really none the wiser.

When Tommy came in on the following afternoon the news was not good. They had yet to trace Lavender. 'Didn't say anything last night. You were pretty harry flakers. Well, we toddled along, mob-handed, as they say, ready to batter her door down. Ended up looking like a posse of prats.'

'What's happened to her?'

He gave an immense Gallic shrug. 'Gone missing, heart.' Now he pulled a rueful face. 'Vamoosed, disappeared, evaporated. We're searching of course, and we'll eventually find her.' He tapped his teeth with the end of his gold fountain pen. 'Eventually.'

Between them, he told her, they'd run quite a service for our brave fighting men. Jo Benton, Emily Baccus, Lavender and probably the Wren, Monica Parker from HMS *Daedalus*, 'And who knows, what other girls. You saw the address books and diaries. Could've had another stable with a hundred beds. There was a great deal of money in it. We've found one set of books, and it's true what they say: where there's muck there's money.'

Everything pointed to an inevitable falling out between the various participants. Lavender, he claimed, turned out to be the most ruthless charmer of the lot. 'It was a bomb waiting to explode,' he said. Lavender also had a wonderful weapon in her bottled spider, Golly Goldfinch. 'Just pray she doesn't find another before we feel her collar.' A flicker of concern crossed his face before he quickly changed the subject, and Suzie knew he was somehow blaming himself for letting Lavender slip through his fingers; and he just couldn't leave it alone. 'I've no doubt that Lavender started the rot: that she's the prime cause for the killings. She manipulated Forbes and Golly – in different ways, but she was the one moving the pieces around.'

Then, of course, she'd had the cool nerve to order her own death. 'Cold calculating bitch that she is. Tells Goldfinch to kill her, cool as a corpse.'

'To mislead us?' She wrote the question on a blank page.

'Well, a couple of reasons, I guess,' he sighed. 'But she certainly expected to lead us astray, yes. Also I suspect she was trying to do away with him once and for all.'

Golly had already repeated the words he said Emily Baccus had used – 'It will be hard, Golly, but you must do it. Once you have done it you will be free of me for ever. Free to do whatever you desire. Kill Lavender.'

'For my money, heart, she was trying to corner him. First she told him to kill you, then herself, so when he came for her she'd be ripe and ready, scream blue murder, kill him probably. Self-defence, and we'd all say, "Ahhhhhhh. Never mind." She'd see to it that in the end it would be her, Lavender, who'd be Miss Right. With Golly dead, she'd figure we couldn't prove a damned thing.'

Finally he turned to her with one of his brilliant all consuming smiles. 'And how do *you* feel, heart?' He leaned over her bed and kissed her forehead. She made a sign with her hands that was clearly a message of thanks. He had undoubtedly saved her life, crashing into the bathroom, breaking down the door and fiercely restraining Golly. She also touched her left breast, then pointed to him, telling him she loved him.

'What of Josh Dance?' she asked.

'Ah, spent part of today with Mr Dance. Took him down the Tombs.' He grinned at the joke. 'Gave him the third degree, me and Molly. They let him out of the military not just because of his wound. He has other problems, our Mr Dance. The good side is that he's aware of them. Too aware. A normal bloke would think twice about doing what he's done. Had himself neutered by your local friendly vet in Overchurch. Got his balls lopped off. Afraid he'd end up killing someone. That's not altogether a normal reaction. Charming fellow but something's loose, heart. My view anyway.'

Suzie winced, cringed and again signified that she loved Tommy.

Tommy understood that all right. 'Naturally.' He beamed, and for a while she tried to work out exactly what that meant.

She also wanted to know if anything was happening about Big Toe Harvey and her suspicions concerning the corrupt ways of Camford CID. 'Yes, well,' he started, looking a mite sheepish. 'All very strange. The twins were up before Camford magistrates. No case to answer, it appears. Maybe that was the object of the exercise. In the fullness of time we'll know, I suppose. Harvey's asked for a transfer up West, I gather.'

In the here and now, she thought about her short time working in Camford and wondered what it would have been like if Tommy Livermore hadn't come along and saved her. Her knight in shining armour. Or maybe the Gibb's Dentifrice White Knight up against Golly's Demon Decay.

In fact, Suzie thought about a lot of things as she lay on her sick bed for several weeks. She remained nervous for much longer and pre-ferred to sleep with the light on for many months – years in fact.

When she could finally talk, when her mother and the Galloping Major were on their way to see her, she asked Tommy Livermore what the next move would be – when she was up and about.

'Oh, heart,' he replied. 'First we must deal with the important things.'

She was relieved at that.

'Yes, heart,' he said ambiguously. 'The sooner

we get you through the detective course and you're able to sit the sergeant's exam, the better it'll be for all of us.' He flashed his ravishing smile, the one that consumed her alive, and she realized it was going to be okay.

Probably.

DV.